"A man and woman find themselves in a complicated emotional web, a love/hate situation that will keep you reading the novel to its surprising conclusion. Linda Gale Vettel, a first time author, takes her characters from adventure to adventure in a story of intrigue complicated by human passions. Linda Gale Vettel's descriptive language and fertile imagination take flight in an extraordinary story of interpersonal struggle fraught with suspense and drama. You will want this new author to begin a sequel soon!"

Fran Armstrong, 1999 North Dakota Teacher of the Year;
Author of *My Heroes Have Always Been Cowboys*,
Sh-h-h! The Teacher's Coming! and *The Hills of Home*.

"The plan can be carried off without a hitch. I don't want any look of impropriety. We'll just make an official arrangement. I'll marry you on paper. You'll have a home and can see the baby. Of course, we'll have a prenuptial agreement. My daycare problem will be solved in an orderly fashion." He took a deep breath and added, "We don't have to speak to each other unless it has to do with her. Is this acceptable to you?"

"What else should I do? Stand on my head? You can't even call me by my name and now you make a business proposition? Is this some kind of joke? Are you proposing to get yourself out of a jam? I'm not an object for purchase." Tia, shocked at his brazen plan, felt like a pinball machine that had just registered tilt.

Ageless Tear

Linda Gale Vettel

SingleVision Publishing

Published in the United States by SingleVision Publishing, a division of SingleVision Printing & Publishing, Watford City, North Dakota.

www.singlevisionbooks.com
www.snglvsn.com

Library of Congress Catalog Card Number: 2004100907

ISBN 0-9716996-2-3

Cover illustration by:
Catherine Van Steenburgh

Cover and interior design by:
SingleVision Printing & Publishing

Edited by:
Robert Bousfield

Printed and Bound in the United States
1st Printing

Dedicated

To Wes

Whose hand is always ready to shake another

Whose handkerchief catches tears

Whose infectious smile breaks ice

Thank you for being my friend.

With love,

Your adventurous wife,

Linda

Acknowledgements

Special thanks:
To my editor and publishers, Robert and Cari Bousfield at SingleVision, for pouring their hearts into *Ageless Tear*. The miraculous birth of their daughter Faith occurred in the middle of book preparations. Faith adds a special touch of the joy of life to *Ageless Tear*.

Thank you:
To Fran Armstrong, ND teacher and author, for her awesome review and supportive words.

To Sister Thomas Welder, President of the University of Mary, for reading the manuscript and giving me insight.

To Catherine Van Steenburgh for her creative artwork and illustration of *Ageless Tear*.

To all the hunters and trapper friends, especially John Weinand, Arlen Kurtti, Myron Compton and Marty Heller.

To Neil Gallagher for his mini lesson in martial arts.

To all the precious Aglow friends in the United States, Canada and other nations, and many other friends who have stood by me with encouragement and prayer.

To my schoolteacher sister, Kathy, and my niece Jill, who encouraged me often.

To my sons and daughters-in-law, who told me *like it is* and told me to *go for it*.

To my Mom, Tillie Shipley, an avid reader and recorder of events, who set an excellent example.

To my Dad, Charles Shipley, a man of integrity, who I look up to with much respect.

To my husband, Wes, who has traveled the world of words with me and filled my mouth with laughter when I needed it most.

About the Illustrator

Catherine Van Steenburgh, the cover illustrator of *Ageless Tear*, has loved art from a very early age. Catherine, a 1979 graduate of High Point College with a BA in Art Education, resides in Winston-Salem, North Carolina with her husband Craig and her daughter Lisa. Her teaching career spans more than twenty years in North Carolina Public Schools. Upon special request, she has taught art in St. Petersburg and Moscow. She also teaches private lessons out of her home studio and plans to develop further as an illustrator.

Preface

The characters, names, places and personalities of *Ageless Tear* exist in my imagination. Any similarity to people, places or things is a coincidence.

I reveal myself through the art of picturesque writing by going deep into the epicenter of human emotion, reasoning and senses, developing each character from the depth of who I am, of who I want them to be. I trust readers of the novel to identify, to believe, to honor, to care, to see beyond the picture, to hear and, at times, feel their own guts wrenched out, crying for life.

Stimulating ideas, framed into *Ageless Tear*, paint the picture. The reader adds his own brush strokes, and hangs the design on the wall of his heart with his dreams.

Trusting that *Ageless Tear* will touch your life.

Respectfully,

Linda Gale Vettel

Ageless Tear

The Resolve of a Man

A silent cry mingled with the drizzling rain and the chill of what could have been. On Memorial Day, 1979, Fence Carpenter stood, like a lonely tree, over the gravesite of his wife and child, the only place he allowed tears to flood his eyes. Roses in his limp hand lowered their velveteen heads toward the earth in respect. The thorny briars stabbed his heart. Three long years had not lessened the memories or buried the pain. No one watched. Other mourners were wrapped up in their own sorrows. Patriotic flags remembering sons, fathers, brothers, the servant soldiers, were ineffective when it came to wiping tear-stricken faces.

Fence attempted to focus. He pictured Lily running into his arms, swinging her in circles, touching her rich black hair. She was like a leaf on the wings of the wind, one minute with him, the next gone. His warrior of freedom fought to the end. Now she was free. He wanted to recapture the past, to hold onto the lost dreams. Death stole them. He seemed to have no purpose without her. His arms hung loosely at his side. Numbness held him in place.

He listened. The twenty-one-gun salute rang in his ears. Looking upward, he pulled his coat collar close to his neck, hiding his distress. When the piercing echo died, Fence spoke to himself. "Once a year. Once a year I'll visit this place." His resolve stood firm. He had no plans to alter it. His feet moved in cold discomfort.

In the following weeks, Fence saturated himself in work to the point of addiction. With methodical, conditioned effort his logical brain dissected facts and figures in order to scourge grief. It took increased effort to exist. Like a chess game, Fence contemplated each move. But some things were just out of his control. He thought, *Losing never comes easy*. These words of his father haunted him.

Less than eight months later, his vow to visit cemeteries only once a year turned to dust. His childhood friend and classmate lay in the closed casket under the canopy. Fence stood motionless, shivering, performing his duty as an honorary pallbearer. One more gash on his heart, one more death to face. He grimaced, trying to clot the pain, wanting to reject bleeding, to stop the hemophiliac symptoms. His stomach churned. He felt sick inside. Hurt, loneliness and anger mixed together.

"There's much more here than meets the naked eye, volumes more," Fence muttered, clearing his throat and reeling in distress.

Authorities had prevented any disclosures, any viewing of Abe's body. The police report stated the cause of death as self-inflicted. Fence pondered, denying that Abe would resort to such violence. Suicide, a permanent escape to a temporary problem, was not a solution Abe would choose. Two and two did not add up to four. Fence held back a cough. He resented the job interview that had placed him at the wrong place at the wrong time, out of sync, in another state answering questions of another sort, unable to come to the rescue. He paid little heed to the reason he was there and wished he were not. *Funerals,* he thought.

The brisk January wind died with reluctance. As if in sequence, large snowflakes floated downward, laying out a white blanket. The minister rambled in monotone. The message of comfort, mixed with correction, irritated Fence. Impatience took over as he tuned out the man of the cloth.

Escape. The intense need overtook him. Death was too much, too close, too final. While heads were bowed in prayer, Fence broke away. Oblivious, he wandered, missing the last rights and avoiding the benediction. He knew the words by heart. *Ashes to ashes, dust to dust. He brought nothing into this world. He takes nothing o–u–t ... ... outtt!*

He told himself he did not care, that it did not matter, but it did. Tears rained down his cold, red face, freezing in place. Concentrating on the lie, his intellect battled with his wounded heart. Confusion swelled within his head. His crisp walk regressed with the added obstructions at his feet. He rammed into a standing grave marker, catching his foot in a misplaced shrub. Stumbling to his knees, he crawled on the frozen ground until his hand hit a stone. Of all the marble headstones, Fence had come face to face with his very own name, *CARPENTER.*

His elbows weakened like sponges being squeezed; his body fell prostrate. His aching head lay on the hard pillow with his arms sprawled out in front of him. A surge of resistance flowed through his veins. With his black-gloved fist, Fence beat the earth until his anger turned to powder and his strength to exasperation. *Why? Someone so young ... cheated ... robbed of life.*

How long he lay face down, he did not know, but when he arose, the funeral party had long gone. The canopy shelter was removed. All evidence of life had vanished. He had lain with death and now he must rise to live. Fence took a deep breath while his numb fingers fought off the clenched stiffness. He swung his empty arms around his body in crisscross fashion, shaking off the chill, holding himself. Swallowing, he managed to find his hoarse voice. He whispered, "Good bye my love ... my dove ... my long lost friend ... my child."

He paused. And then he ran. Heavy-laden evergreens cast long, looming shadows over him. Sundogs, rainbow pillars parenthesizing the sun's hazy, cold light with predictions of frigid air, gave the marked message. Winter had moved in. Fence put his hands over his ruby ears.

By the time he reached his charcoal vehicle he regained his composure. Inches of accumulated snow rested on it. Using his coat sleeve, Fence brushed off his buried car with his forearm. Its choked-up engine died twice, giving a stiff, grinding growl, before it fired to start. Fence shook his head. *Time to trade it in. Something white might be nice, something new, something without memories, something without stains.*

He rounded the graveyard, glancing in the rear view mirror, noticing the two-tire trail as he created it. His mental gears turned. From this day forward he was going someplace. He would leave the past behind, the darkness, the bitter roots; so he thought. He did not count on the bitterness being a tag-along, nor did he anticipate the challenge in front of him.

13

Leap Year

O N February 29, 1980, Fence arrived in Florida driving a snow-white station wagon. A new job, a new vehicle, a new place sparked a new drive within him. An infant carrier was strapped into the back passenger seat awaiting occupancy. Fence took a deep breath.

"Give a child life that you couldn't give your own," Abe said only a few days before his death. "The critical action will help a lineage live on. Do it for me friend, okay? You will be a changed man. Fence, it is time to quit mourning over Lily."

"It's a shot in the dark," Fence had replied, speculating. "But, why Florida?" He raised his head to listen to the blue-eyed friend with the dark, curly hair.

Abe went straight to the point, handing Fence the name of a contact. "I have a military connection in Florida. With a private adoption, you can skirt some complications." Abe exchanged a smile with Fence. "You know I'm adopted. I don't think I turned out too bad." The information spilled out of him.

Fence vaguely remembered overhearing his parents' conversation about Abe's mother remarrying and her adoption of Abe.

"See if you can get a job interview near the base." Abe had explained to Fence. "When I get finished with this current project, I'll be there with our next assignment."

The next assignment. Yes. That was eight weeks ago. Now there is no Abe, no Lily. Fence swallowed. *Abe's parents ... both had died in a car accident while Abe was in college.* Fence ran his fingers through his sandy-blond hair. *It's too late to bow out now.* He walked inside the building appearing quite confident.

The transition place, little more than a low office building, held no warmth until the tiny bundle was carried in. She was what he wanted and he fell in love with her at first sight. Fine angel hair rested around

14

her face, in front of her tiny ears, coal black and wavy. The perfect baby slept with peace wrapped around her—amazing after what she had been through, premature and all. As if in a momentary trance, Fence surveyed the situation, welcoming the warmth. He allowed himself to stand spellbound, a luxury he seldom indulged in. Her mother he presumed dead. He did not ask a lot of questions. An element of secrecy heightened the tension.

"Let's get on with it," he told the caseworker.

The woman in charge was not in the mood to be rushed by this impatient man. "What are you going to call her? We need a name for the birth certificate."

"Yes, Mrs. Stroup. You are right. I assumed all the papers were in order. I apologize for the inconvenience." He reached out to shake the middle-aged woman's taut hand.

"Never assume anything," she said. Her trained composure caught him off guard.

Fence worked up a sweat standing still. He tossed the fear of his improper qualifications around. Single men rarely received consideration to adopt a newborn. But, this was a rare situation. Abe's contact had done the groundwork, but necessity required following the proper channels to prevent legal problems later. Fence insisted that everything be above board.

A name? He thought she should have one. Fence looked at the tiny baby. A white homemade blanket rested on the foster lady's arm, the clandestine caregiver. He noted a beautiful rose on it, embroidered in soft pinks with a silver thread outline. "Her name will be Rose ... Marie, after my mother. Yes, Rose Marie Carpenter will be her name," he finalized, speaking with assurance.

All the papers were in order. Hastily, Fence signed his unreadable signature. Mrs. Stroup slid the document into a file folder marked confidential. A few moments later, Fence left the meeting place carrying a tiny Rose and her few items in his arms.

Fence had not thought of his own parents or communicated with them for months. He wanted to ignore their existence, at least for the time being. He was glad for the distance. Yet, even though they were twenty-five hundred miles away, a lifetime away, it was impossible to blot out the kindness his mother showed people, especially children, or how his dad would go out of his way to shake the hand of a little child. They were the lines and angles in his life that eventually pulled him into perspective. He pushed away their love. Too much complication stood between them, too much danger.

Fence strapped Rose's carrier in place, curious about the child's mother. She had not been married—died at childbirth. The baby needed him; or did he need her? Whatever the case, he would be her daddy. He would not reject this sweetness in his hands. Rose, proof of miraculous life, gave Fence renewed reason to live. He kissed her forehead, holding his lips on her face. *A father's love is what Rose needs.*

Focus

MORE than one voice cried for the child. How the mix-up happened was quite complicated.

A small-boned young woman, Tia, looked up and whispered, "She is my baby,"

"No, she is mine. I've waited all these months and now she is mine!" The tall blond stranger was full of facts and figures. His gray-green eyes were ready to make an argument. In her distraction Tia thought his eyes should be golden brown, to match the tanned olive skin. In her plight she tried to pull herself together. She spiraled downward, plummeting in loss. The man was so sure of himself. He was bound to win. An elaborate tangle of legal rights stood high between them. Shuffling through them would require keen legal eyes accompanied by intense investigation.

There was no moot point where a question could be argued. The decision, made first with the tongue and then with the pen, was legal and conclusive. However, the basis of the composition was a lie. Tia was not dead. She had not died as predicted. She had relinquished all rights in a comatose state. Now her child was in the hands of Fence Carpenter, an angry, grieving man who seemed to Tia a lost cause.

"The baby does not even look like you. She's probably not even yours!" Fence raged.

His words cut Tia to the heart. "I know," she said. Her humble answer came in tenderness.

"You have a lot of gall to think you can take my child back. You're not even supposed to be alive!" He spoke louder than he wanted to.

Not even, not even, not even. Tia's mind somersaulted. It was not even. It was not fair. The pretentious blond man was right. She could not hate him. His face looked so forlorn. Once again she stood on the threshold of pain, unable to bear the sight of someone suffering because of her. Her small-framed body fought for strength. Her stomach, still tender after the exploratory surgery the three military doctors performed, trembled in turmoil. A haze clouded her memory. Swallowed up in the past, she shuffled through the weather-beaten pages, trying to focus.

Chance

CHANCE Cumming's plane had vanished from sight while flying a solo mission over the Bermuda Triangle, or as some call it, the Devil's Triangle, somewhere off the West Indies. The authorities were conducting a thorough investigation into what took the multimillion-dollar plane and its pilot. Like the fifty-plus ships and aircraft that had strangely disappeared since 1854, no bodies, no evidence, no clues, no rational explanation existed. Scientists tried to blame the mysterious accidents on violent winds and swift-moving ocean currents. Chance had not radioed a message of distress. The plane had disappeared from the radar screen and he was presumed dead.

The wild sea and lightning sky were riled up, shaking the earth and the night. Tia set the fresh-cut Christmas tree into a stand. She dreamt of rocking the baby and holding it close to her. The thought kept her from feeling alone.

The landlord pounded on her door with persistence. "Open up." A robe of rudeness covered him. He started to unlock the door, mumbling. "That rotten Chance Cummings has a lot of nerve telling people that he can be reached using my phone. Too cheap to get his own! What is he up to now? Can't be anything good," he puffed, handing Tia a message scrawled on the back of an empty envelope.

Caught in an awkward defense, Tia answered holding emotion inside. "I'm sorry sir, I don't know where he is. He has been gone for some time."

"Well, do you think he's dead?" The little man stood watching her, wanting to see her reaction to the note. He grumbled, "Drinks too much. Doesn't even pick up his beer cans. Wonder who he bought off to get his pilot's wings."

Tia hid her discomfort. Holding the message near her heart, she made the alarming landlord wait, refusing to give him the satisfaction of

19

an answer.

Exasperated he exited, slamming the door. *So she's pregnant. I guessed as much. He used her too. Chance Cummings chews up women and spits them out. He pretends he is so chivalrous. That's a joke. He is rotten to the core.*

Report to headquarters ASAP. Plane lost.

The unusual message irritated Tia. Was the note for her or for Chance? Chance was in the air; or was he?

Tia squeezed her bulging body behind the steering wheel and had to stretch to see. Creepy, hostile trees lined the road, hiding secret enemies between mossy limbs. *Chance took too many uncalled-for risks*, she thought. Tia pushed the gas pedal down, catching her breath between teardrops. *Where is he?*

Heavy hurricane winds and horizontal rain blacked out the thin aisle of highway. Oncoming vehicle lights glared at her. Tia's old car hydroplaned out of control. A tall black form waved her to stop. She paid no heed. She did not see the yellow danger ribbons. A jackknifed eighteen-wheeler lay on its side spread across the road. Rounding the curve, Tia hit the brakes. It was too late.

She faded into unconsciousness. Her body, in a state of shock, shook. Her blood pressure plummeted. Emergency! Doctors left their Christmas gift opening to do the exploratory surgery. Tia was bleeding internally, no time to waste. No family had come to give permission for what had to be done.

"Can you hear me? My name is Dr. O'Leary. I need your signature."

Tia's arms lay motionless at her sides. The nurse on call stuffed a pen in her swollen right hand. Tia initialed, seeing nothing. Both mother and unborn child required immediate attention.

"We're losing her!" The short-staffed intensive care team scrambled. Somehow Tia summoned strength to look up. Reaching for the mound on her stomach, she found emptiness. "My child?"

"The baby is alive," a dark form spoke over her.

Tia drifted in and out of a comatose state. Tubes ran in and out of her. The crackling white paper crunched under her chin. Someone helped her hand move to sign the release papers. The documents were not hers; they were the baby's.

"You have no relatives, right? You weren't married to Chance

Cummings, right?"

She nodded.

"Will you release your organs, miss? Transplanters are crying for young kidneys, corneas and livers." They wanted her to sign again. Her hand fell limp, the paper left unsigned.

Six weeks passed. The coma had spared Tia both emotional and physical pain. Life support tubes ran in and out of her body. Outside her window rain poured down. A thunder crack and lightning strike awakened her out of deep sleep. Her blood pressure started to rise. Waking up brought with it the reality of all the senses. Warmth flowed through her veins. The stitches on her abdomen stung with shooting pain. Her parched lips and dry mouth longed for a chip of ice.

Tia lay two long hours before an aide checked on her. Filled with panic, the frightened candy striper ran out of the room. "Come quickly!" she yelled down the hospital corridor. In unbelief the head nurse shook her head, astonished. Plans were to remove the final lifegiving tubes that day to let Tia die peacefully.

Tia spoke softly, "Water? Please may I have something to drink?" Tia sensed their hurrying and scurrying, and the confusion of staff when the shock hit them. Tia, in her right mind, sent them into frenzy.

Two days later a curt charge nurse released her. "Sign here," she said.

Confused, Tia searched for her bearings. Another young aide rolled her to the driveway in a squeaky wheelchair. Tia looked up at the hospital, realizing the military base had transferred her out. She was not where she had thought she was.

The cabdriver opened the door, helping her in, like he would put luggage in a trunk. "Where to, miss?" He was half full of questions, half full of nosiness. "Do you have someone to take care of you? An orphan, you say? Well there must be someone. Have you tried the chapel on Chaffee Row? Maybe I should take you there."

"No sir, take me home, the little cottage house near Garden Street. I'll make it."

His Irish brogue revealed his birth country. This cabdriver of many years was one of the few who took time to offer a helping hand. He recognized trouble when he saw it. *Maybe my wife will bring the poor girl some soup,* he surmised, entering a wooded area on the outskirts of town. It was only a thought. He soon forgot it, remembering only his new story to tell.

The table was just as Tia left it on Christmas Eve. History, literature and accounting books lay closed in a mixed pile, as did the needles from the undecorated blue spruce tree, whose stock was bare. She stepped on the crinkled message the landlord had brought over that fretful night. Seeing her shoeprint on the paper, she reached to the dusty floor and stuck the note in her tattered coat pocket. Tia felt a cold chill fill the room. The electricity had been cut off. She opened the cellar door and found an old kerosene lantern, full of dusty cobwebs, hanging on a nail by the stairway. The house lacked warmth but supplied shelter.

A stock of wood stacked in the corner supplied fuel for the old stove. She was thankful. Lifting an ax-head by its three-foot handle would be too strenuous. The day Chance left, he had paid the lease in advance. Two more months remained. It was not an act of kindness or mercy, but of convenience. He had said he wanted the place when he returned.

Tia examined the few damp envelopes that were stuffed into the small, rusty mailbox. An official paper notified her that a gravesite had been established at a prestigious cemetery in memory of Chance. There was no body, only a cross to represent him. *It's final then.* Tia put the document in a dresser drawer and waited until daybreak to read the rest of the mail. "One step at a time," she said out loud.

With the letter opener, Tia slit the vanilla envelope containing her test results. The university offered congratulations on her outstanding achievement, accompanied by a scholarship grant. To Tia the good marks were a sign of hope. All the long hours of study had paid off factually, while tests of her physical and emotional stability were just beginning. No textbook existed to equip or prepare her.

The food pantry held a few items, canned berries, peaches and chicken. They stood in rows before her, lining the shelves, reflecting her creativity and industriousness. *It's enough,* she encouraged herself. Sitting back in the ragged, overstuffed chair, she pulled the blanket over her, desperate for warmth. Her energy spent, Tia longed for sleep. It was short lived. A sudden urge to search for anything that Chance might have left filled her with perplexing questions.

The rickety drawer in the old dresser rolled off the track. Tia attempted to adjust it, pulling it open. All evidence that he ever existed had vanished. *Strange,* she thought, realizing she had never opened his drawer before. An unexpired fishing license in her name was all that remained—that and a Latin cross on a chain. She placed the cross around her neck, not understanding what it meant. A feeling of kinship touched her, not with Chance, but with the cross.

She walked to the bank of the river in minutes. Quickly she cast her cane line in. No sun or even a hint of it could rescue her on the biting overcast morning. The fish took the bait without hesitation. She salted and fried the fish.

Chance had given her an engagement ring just before he had left— far from the usual manner of proposal. Of course, there was nothing usual about Chance Cummings. He had placed the ring in a Band-Aid box. "First-aid kits are always good to have on hand," he chided her. "If you skin your elbow or cut your finger, you have aid at your fingertips."

A few days later, Tia found the ring by accident when a neighbor boy tipped his bike coming down the hill, trying to make the corner. Tia soothed and comforted the boy, bandaging his wounds. There was no aid to bind her own. She had no intention of playing the game of deceit. She had placed the ring in a jar of nails in the antique Singer sewing machine drawer.

Chance had left no will. Tia knew he had not told his parents about her. She was a sideline for him. She loved him, even with this compromising position he had placed her in. No one would believe he had raped her. Under his nonchalant attitude lay abuse and neglect. He indulged himself in daily doses of alcohol, although he would never admit he had a drinking problem. He swore allegiance to himself, maintaining an air of respectability by covering up his illegitimate contacts under the guise of good management. Fancy maneuvering and incredible skills had enabled him to get his top-secret clearance and pilot's wings. Dogged by his own shadow, he was not the master man he pretended to be. Deception was part of the game. He presumed he knew how to play it well.

One night Chance took her to a flight party where Tia briefly met the base commander. He had been kind to her, aware of her situation and of Chance's charming, carefree personality. He also knew what a risk-taker Chance Cummings was. Tia had mixed feelings that night. Carefully retracing what had happened, she felt overcome with regret.

A civilian instructor pilot had approached her with threats of washing Chance out of the program if she did not succumb to his demands.

"Meet me tomorrow night at the alley lounge," the overconfident teacher persisted to blackmail her. His distasteful hands and lewd eyes hounded her to dance. Tia pushed him away, refusing him and the drink he had set in front of her. She desired protection. Slipping out the side door, she caught a ride on the shuttle back to town.

Chance had paid no heed, leaving Tia to fend for herself. No jealous bones existed in his body. "Let the punches fall where they will," he had said. She did not believe the off-the-cuff statement.

The car accident had occurred close to the base gates. Chance had given Tia a temporary pass with permission to enter. Otherwise, military medics would not have helped or been at the scene. Tia understood the reason the military had moved her to a community hospital by ambulance. They did not want to take responsibility for her. Having to call in emergency surgeons on Christmas Day placed her in the position of being a nuisance. They had not wanted to be bothered with a civilian, unmarried woman, nor with the child they had removed from her.

Recuperation remained a day-by-day struggle. Tia's fortitude was a bow in need of restringing. Concentrating on getting healthy, on running again, she chose to build up her courage, to see life in everything. Although the spring air breathed freshness into her, she could not empty her brain of penetrating memories. She lifted the cross to her lips. She longed to see the face of the unknown.

The Search

LATIN had flowed from Tia's mouth like it was her first language. Sisters at the orphanage school also planted seeds of Hebrew and Greek into the hungry student. They asked her to stay, to join them, to teach the orphans. At times Tia regretted her decision to leave the safe setting. She cherished the early learning years. Yet, destiny had drawn her out. Now the school of life continued to teach lessons with another pen, where mistakes could not be erased. Finding the answer to deep questions takes the whole person. She set her heart, mind and soul searching.

Urgently Tia delved into the dusty books shelved in the cottage backroom, seeking law that establishes law. She knew no lawyer with the art of persuasion and speaking. She knew no private investigator. Then, as if jerked awake, she remembered the nail jar.

The pawnshop, located a good two miles away, was situated in a rat-infested part of town. She hurried. Giving the impression of confidence, Tia walked inside. Yet, the underlining of fear cautioned her to be careful. She asked what they would give her for the twenty-four karat gold and solitaire. The shady man hemmed and hawed, telling her the ring was an imitation and of little value.

"I'll take it somewhere else. I know it's worth much more," Tia asserted herself. A customer entered behind her causing the miserly man to fidget.

"All right," he finally consented, wanting to get rid of her.

Tia exited. Paranoia increased, knowing she walked alone with money in her pocket. Her pace quickened. Her weakened condition required additional courage, let alone extraordinary strength and wisdom. Her steps progressed with surety and sensitivity to the dangerous surroundings.

The next item of business was to find out who adopted her child.

The puffy old lawyer sat in his office behind a mammoth mahogany desk stuffing tobacco into his pipe. The smell of cherries permeated the room. Tia liked the burly man immediately. "Yes," he would help her. "Yes," he was interested in getting to the bottom of it. "No," he would not leave her out on a limb. The man's word assured her. He agreed to do the search. Maturity of years had given the lawyer connections that went far beyond the walls of the city and state, to the nations afar. However, he divulged only as much as necessary. His grandfatherly stature appeared to calm the walls and tame the inanimate objects that surrounded him—the marble bookends, the elephant carvings, the graceful giraffe, the teakwood rhino. A huge picture of Theodore Roosevelt hunting African lions hung on the wall behind him.

Tia left the old brick office building the first of May, realizing she had barely tapped the surface of the eccentric lawyer. Sister Maria Thomas had given Tia his name. The wise woman exhibited confidence in the man, expressing past knowledge of Mr. Tuffty's abilities. Tia, reluctant to get her hopes too high, took the gravel trail home after that first appointment, kicking stumbling stones of defeat with her feet. She needed to trust the counsel.

The man's movements ground like wheels in ruts to Rome, none too hasty, but steadily. After an intricate, methodical search, Mr. Tuffty examined all the final pieces with some exasperation. He shook his head, thinking with his own masculine judgment. *The child is better off with the man.* To him, it was a matter of provision. His client needed to know the truth, or part of it. His fingers moved hastily, but with accuracy, on his old manual typewriter. He licked the ill-tasting envelope, sealing the official letter neatly inside. On his regular walk to the Post Office, he encountered a young woman helping a small child cross the street. His client, Miss Tia Bain, did not see him. Her eyes were on the child.

Mr. Tuffty meandered past the outside mail drop, muttering to himself while he rummaged through his pants pocket looking for his box key. "I don't know why we don't have combinations anymore." He had no trouble remembering that. He analyzed, *Too many other important things on my mind these days.*

Tia gripped the newly arrived envelope, fumbling with the letter opener. Anxiety ran through her veins. The letter, postmarked August 1st, 1980, took her breath out from under her. There was no friend with her, no mother, no father, no one with whom to share excitement or disappointment.

Dear Miss Bain,

A businessman in his late twenties, originally a resident of the North Central area of the country, adopted a baby girl born on December 25th. This appears to be the child you gave up on January 2nd. Six months have already passed. He has signed all the papers giving him full custody. He was told that the mother of the child had died. The baby is healthy and has settled in with him. The man has a good reputation. He is a hard worker, providing all her needs and much more. You should be thankful that she is in the hands of such an honorable man. If you wish to pursue this further, it will be an uphill battle that may not be worthwhile. You legally signed her away, all your rights, on your deathbed.

My sympathies and regrets,
Arnold D. Tuffty
Mr. Arnold D. Tuffty, Esq.
Attorney at Law

Tia read it over and over. She slunk down onto the front step in the fading sun. The letdown stole her joy, beating hopelessness down on her. A second letter from the landlord, nearly as traumatic as the first, was not unexpected.

Miss Bain,
I've done all I can do. Your lease is up, effective immediately. I have a renter who paid in advance.

Tia packed a few items of importance in a small bag, leaving the books behind. Nothing belonged to her in the furnished cottage. She walked away through the garden, wearing the cross. Tears filled her empty eyes while rejections tore at her heart. She clutched the only thing of love she ever had, an embroidered handkerchief. Shaking off depression, she dabbed her damp face dry.

Over the next few weeks Tia struggled with survival. The reality of life and death reactivated within her. Poignant paddles of fear bounced her emotions back and forth like aimless ping-pong balls. Danger loomed on every corner. She hid on the little traveled, yet treacherous trails, avoiding the shame of wine and theft that slunk around. She would not allow her spirit to be pistol-whipped or beaten. She went to the homeless shelter to shower, cooked over a barrel by the river and found clothing at the thrift shop. Tia's chapped, but caring hands offered help to hurting children. They needed her. She needed them. The job only reminded her of her empty arms. She repressed the invasion of unworthiness.

What are my options? Tia continued to reason. *If this is a reasonable man, maybe I could meet him, see for myself. Maybe he will let me see my baby. Maybe Mr. Tuffty will agree to set it up. Why wasn't anything said about a mother?*

Tia was not a quitter. She was not dead. She was alive. The injustice of life overwhelmed her.

Although her persistence annoyed Mr. Tuffty, he secretly admired the fortitude of the young blond woman. He marveled at her resilience in spite of her circumstances. The woman was determined to see her baby. He could see no end to it. *I will get no rest with her constant pestering.* She reminded him of someone he knew long ago. He scratched his chin, reluctant to put the finger of remembrance on it. Finally, enough time passed. He agreed to set up a meeting, after a reluctant acceptance by a Mr. Fence Carpenter. Tia's perseverance and last penny with Mr. Tuffty hung on the edge of success.

And then the long-awaited day came. Tia shuddered in anticipation. She closed her eyes, longing to touch the unknown.

The man, Mr. Carpenter, stood six feet from her with his hands on his hips and his head leaning forward. "I said she does not look like you! She is my child," he repeated.

No, the baby did not look like she expected. *Maybe she isn't mine.*

The stranger, locked in his own world, would not allow her entrance. Intimidation, a tool of offence, warded her off. The precarious self-protective façade reminded Tia of a thick high wall, impervious to penetration. She looked downward, watching his heels as he walked out.

Pulling herself together, Tia hesitated before taking her next step. The fresh air greeted her nostrils. *I can't give up. I won't give up.* Lifting her hand she hailed a somewhat familiar yellow cab. The driver drained her pocket of its last few dollars.

Although the chapel at the orphanage offered a standing invitation to Tia, shame had kept her from its doors. She did not want mercy. There was no place else to go. She clung to the only security she had ever known. Closing her eyes, a vision of her parents swimming in a river passed before her. *It's all in my imagination. I've never seen them. I was the baby left on the doorstep with no name, wrapped in a towel with some man's handkerchief stuck under my head.* She knew the story of her abandonment very well.

"They left you to die!" The brash remarks she overheard in her later years wanted to resurface. Tia had pushed them aside. Sister Hummel, the kind woman who held her close, had comforted her. "Someone placed you in the precise spot where you could be found. We saw you and knew you were a gift to us," she had told Tia.

Tia entered the empty sanctuary and surrendered herself to the communion rail. It had padded her heart with hope before. She craved encouragement, no different from any other child or adult. One thought helped her resist depression. One impression helped her think in the positive. Her baby was alive and beautiful. "She has a home. She has a name," Tia whispered. In the darkness Tia was filled with an unusual peace. *I survived if only to give that little life to the tall stranger.* It anesthetized the pain for the moment.

Decision Time

FENCE arrived home exhausted. He wrapped little Rose in his empty arms, collapsing into his deep wine rocker-recliner. Holding the delicate innocence against his brawny, bare chest, the troubled man read *Green Eggs and Ham*. Rose's head lay in the blanket of hair against his muscles, resting in sweet sleep. She picked up the smell of his cologne. He admired the wee one against his skin, closing the book that was beyond the baby's age. Fence read to himself as much as to Rose. The words did not soothe the new father.

Wrapped up in his thoughts, he remembered the encounter with the woman with the blond hair. He stroked Rose's forehead. "You don't look like me either Little One, but you are mine." The statement did not reassure him. The fact that he had been cruel and overpowering to the woman claiming to be the baby's mother seared Fence's conscience. Yes, he had legal rights. *I could have been decent.* He churned inside.

She wasn't much to look at, wearing those shabby clothes. She doesn't have the means to take care of a child. He reasoned with fruitless excuses, *What could she offer my baby? Why does she have to keep staring at me with those empty eyes?* He could not turn off the desperate picture, that look of longing a mother has for an infant. He laid Rose in the white crib he bought, caressing her little face. He loved her so much. She responded to him with a cooing sound, closing her eyes. Fence left the room and the peaceful thoughts.

The way he had treated the blond woman tormented him. He paced until his anger brewed. He turned toward the recliner and slammed the back of his fist against the headrest. "Why didn't she blow up at me?" Then he would have felt better; then he could have justified his brutal comments.

He sat in the chair, holding his aching head in his hands. *I can't handle this. How much can a man take? I got my way and now I'm unhappy. It's only Rose that keeps me going. That woman could understand. I've gone on with my life. Why can't she go on with hers?* The whole situation was spinning out of control. He ran his fingers through his hair, troubled.

He fell asleep in the chair trying to change the subject by reading the newspaper. He did not remember anything he read. *The news, what did it say about a missing heir, about a mysterious case twenty some years ago?*

Fence rarely dreamed but this night he did. The little woman rocked Rose in his chair. His baby was very sick and he didn't know what to do. He jerked himself awake. He wrestled with the fear that the dream would come true. *What is this, prophetic or something? I've got to get some perspective here.* To shake it off was impossible. What was happening to him? He had to think this thing through. He had no time for this. *Why did she have to look so pathetic?*

The next days passed with the empty eyes haunting him. They followed him continually. His work became all muddled, and then his good sitter resigned, leaving him with a deplorable daycare situation. The aloof area of the large city made it difficult to find a reliable woman. Fence had to come up with a plan, one that would double as cover for his latest assignment, one that would release him from guilt. How could he come out a winner? How could he avoid a legal battle?

Abe, where are you now with all your advice? What would you do? You got me into this mess.

Fence tossed the pros and cons of the new idea around, checking out flaws, weighing the danger. With renewed determination, Fence decided to implement the plan. This time he chose to set up the meeting, not expecting any problems. He was wrong.

Mr. Tuffty, the woman's lawyer, was having trouble locating his client. Being forced to wait made Fence's patience register on the low end. The virtue eluded him as the burden grew. *I could take the baby and run.* He toyed with the thought, knowing escape would not solve his problem. He had tried that before.

"Nothing like diving in head first," Abe had said more times than Fence could count. His longtime friend thrived on head-on confrontation. Fence usually waited for green lights. *Breaking out of the mold,* he reasoned, *will not be easy.*

No one deserves abusive treatment, no matter what they have done. Now his mother's words surfaced, adding to guilt. Fence's innate

31

character was always honorable, not abrupt or rude. He had to get it off his chest. It was not his nature to be unkind.

Fence arrived early, expecting the woman to be there. He saw her as he entered the outer room. She stood looking out the window with her back toward him, tall for a small woman. Her golden hair looked natural. He wanted to believe that she rang true. His brain denied it. His heart did not. He needed to apologize to her. How could he do it without looking like a fool? Humility was not one of his strong suits.

He approached her with his togetherness mask on. "Ma'am?" He did not want to startle her. Was she aware of his presence? Would she throw anger at him? He watched her turn slowly and look up at his face. Her appealing eyes unnerved him, especially when he needed to make a confession. "Ma'am?" He hesitated. "I guess I was kind of hard on you."

"My name is Tia," she said softly.

Fence tried again, still leaving out her name. "I was wrong to say what I did. I'm not like that. I don't know what has gotten into me lately. We started out on the wrong foot, ma'am."

"Please, I am Tia. My name is the only thing I have. Please, sir."

He looked away and then noticed she was still appealing to him. She looked better than the last time he saw her. He must speak. Before he knew it, words poured out of his mouth presenting his plan of restitution. "I have an idea that may satisfy us both. I figure it this way. I need someone to care for Rose when I'm gone. I know you don't have a place to live. I've put a lot of thought into this. You can have the guest bedroom next to Rose. This is a quick arrangement I know, but I don't have time for a bunch of legal hassle and I don't want to have to deal with this so-called mediator your lawyer set up. Besides, it's costing you money you don't have."

He continued. "The plan can be carried off without a hitch. I don't want any look of impropriety. We'll just make an official arrangement. I'll marry you on paper. You'll have a home and can see the baby. Of course, we'll have a prenuptial agreement. My daycare problem will be solved in an orderly fashion." He took a deep breath and added, "We don't have to speak to each other unless it has to do with her. Is this acceptable to you?"

"What else should I do? Stand on my head? You can't even call me by my name and now you make a business proposition? Is this some kind of joke? Are you proposing to get yourself out of a jam? I'm not an object for purchase." Tia, shocked at his brazen plan, felt like a pinball machine that had just registered tilt.

Fence had an answer ready. "I look at it this way. Most marriages are merely signed documents for the betterment of those involved. In many other countries this is done all the time, so the arrangement shouldn't be so foreign to you. Of course it involves a commitment, but not a romance. It will be a legal contract."

Tia's eyes widened. *This man is incredible! He's acting like a purchasing agent and I'm the merchandise.*

Fence knew little about her, except her lawyer said she recently became homeless. Mr. Tuffty highly respected her and affirmed to him, "The child's mother is not a tramp or a street urchin. She is clean, street wise and quite educated. The least you can do is let her see the child. You owe her that much. After all, she gave the baby life."

Fence rationalized, trying to accept that fact. He wanted blind commitment. It did not matter that she knew nothing about him. He had set his mind on carrying out the novice plan.

"Do I have time to consider the matter?" She replied with as much strength as she could muster.

"Not really." They both looked up as a tart, gaudy woman came in carrying baby Rose. "Mrs. Kroomclee is filling in for the day care gal," Fence said.

The woman was not only rough looking but unkempt and impatient. Her chin was in the air. She gave a huff and left, carrying her superiority. Tia noticed Fence take a breath of relief at the abrasive woman's abrupt departure.

The moment Tia had noticed the severe disposition of the caustic woman her stomach started quivering. Anxious thoughts raced through her head. *My baby with this abominable woman! I can't bear the thought.*

"She only watches her in case of an emergency," Fence interjected. He uncovered Rose and put his finger in her little hand.

Tia, overwhelmed with the need to care for her daughter, was relieved to see Fence Carpenter's gentleness with her. She watched him with longing. He embraced the baby. She stuttered, "Please, may I, may I hold her?"

Fence had figured that would be the first question. He nodded, lay Rose in the young woman's arms, then turned away. The act sapped more strength from him than he anticipated. *What am I doing giving her this plan? What if she refuses me? What if she accepts? Are we going to have to consummate the marriage? My God, I must be out of my mind!*

A lullaby filled Tia's head. She shifted Rose to her breast and held her, smelling her little head. She reeled with the presence, the closeness, the miracle. Discovering her baby's breath took hers away. She told herself to breathe. *I must keep my composure.* The tall man looked out the window, watching the mediator walk up the driveway.

Tia kissed Rose's cheek. *What is this marriage proposal compared to what I've been through? I don't have a better option. He's not giving me a ring in a Band-Aid box. I have nowhere else to go.*

With Rose in her arms, she took a step toward the sandy-blond-haired man, trying to catch his eye. He looked down into her wide, open eyes. They held his. She whispered, "Mr. Carpenter, I will accept your offer."

He said with kindness, "My name is Fence."

The Caretaker

THE Justice of the Peace on the 16th floor passed off the ceremony as an everyday occurrence. The twenty-fifth of August was just another day of duty marked by a quick marriage. He hardly noticed the eight-month-old baby.

Tia Rose Bain was now Tia Rose Carpenter in name only. No rings exchanged hands—no celebration, no wedding cake—only words repeated in agreement. She told herself, *This is for Rose.* In spite of the circumstances, every word spoken tattooed itself to Tia's heart.

Fence felt it too, although his admittance to the fact was rooted in his own motivation. It just seemed right to him. Conditions beyond his control pressed him into the hasty plan. One precious baby girl named Rose became the main connection. She lay in her carrier playing with the toys suspended in front of her, swinging them back and forth. *She's a good baby,* Tia decided, not wanting to take her eyes off her.

Transfixed in an aura of unbelief, Tia stretched her chin up and head back, looking at the fluorescent lamp overhead, assessing, *This is a strange man.* Her eyes closed in the light. She whispered, "Thank you."

Tia was not a bride or a mother, but the caretaker for her own baby. She served as the immediate solution to Fence's childcare problem. Rose no longer needed to be shifted around, or be in the care of Mrs. Kroomclee—a relief to them both.

Tia, the new occupant in Fence's house, cherished the privacy of her own room. She felt like an inanimate object in the traditional white structure, like a piece of furniture stuck in a corner. Seeing no other alternative, she reasoned with herself, *All that matters is my daughter. We have a roof over our heads.* Most items that would make it a home were missing, except for those who lived there. Tia made herself scarce when Fence was around. Few things were in the right order.

Awkwardness prevailed.

The feminine presence seemed awkward, but the sight of Rose made Fence smile. He liked the conveniences of coming home to his baby and not having to take her out every day. He did not worry about her care.

The two unsettled people floundered in each other's presence, stuck like strangers passing time without words. Fence kept silent, avoiding her. He asked no questions. Absorbing himself in work, he chose to shun all conversation and contact with the woman in his house. He did not expect her to cook. He did not eat meals with her. He gave his daughter's caretaker the least of attention. However, he noticed more than he let on. Her gratefulness did not escape him. The obvious bond between his child and the woman continually tugged at the shirttail of his heart, a fact he could not deny.

Tia, full of thanksgiving for every moment with Rose, sang to her by the hour and soothed her to sleep. The baby took to her immediately. She seemed to remember Tia's voice from the womb. Tia slept peacefully, comforted by Fence's kindness to her child.

Two nights before Thanksgiving, Fence came home with a plane ticket. "I have business in New York. I'll be gone for a week. You can handle things while I'm gone."

His approach left Tia bewildered. He existed, not lived. Groping to understand, she shoved down the ill-tasting instructions.

Fence turned to say goodbye to Rose. Her baby hair rested on Tia's neck. The innocent child stared at him. A lonesome, big tear rolled down her soft, pink cheek. She wanted to go with him. Before Tia knew what she was saying, the words burst out of her mouth. "Give a kiss to daddy."

Fence, caught off guard, reached for his daughter, accepting her, unable to resist. She squeezed his neck, clinging to him. Opening her mouth, she pressed a childlike kiss onto his cheek. The sudden act sent warmth through him. He could not help himself. He could not stop the tear in his own eye.

Tia's acknowledgment of him as Rose's father took him off guard; or was it Rose's love? Something was happening to him. Tia's words struck like arrows in his heart, a factor he wanted to avoid. She broke through his wall of resistance. He had not counted on his own sternness appealing to her. He shuddered inside. Her kindness pushed him to break his vow of being right, of being in control. The tear rolled down his face. He turned away, brushing the moment off.

Different Eyes

FENCE gave the cabdriver a generous tip. Hurrying, he leapt up the steps with his carry-on to catch the early flight. His shirt pocket hid a strange message. He pulled it out, trying to read between the lines.

LaGuardia Airport. I will meet you.

The possibility of discovering clues to Abe's death hung foremost on the list in Fence's mind. Abe's family life did not appear to be unusual. He never thought about it before. He deliberated, remembering Abe's older stepbrother, Merdone. Fence had only seen an old picture years ago, once when he stayed at Abe's. To his knowledge, the unknown Merdone had not shown up at Abe's funeral.

Closing his eyes, Fence feigned sleep. The overbooked Thanksgiving eve flight churned with overactive, restless people, who were too anxious to sleep.

Busy people rushed from terminal to terminal in the famous airport. Not knowing where, who or what the assignment might be, Fence loitered by the gate searching for his contact. No one came. His shoulders rose, inhaling the heavy air. He hesitated momentarily before proceeding to the International Baggage Claim.

Stopping short, he turned, colliding with an older man. The well-dressed Jamaican stood eye to eye with him. His ebony face shone. *Rather angelic,* Fence thought. The man's immense handshake impressed Fence. "How did you find me?" Fence said. "There must be some urgency."

The brilliant black man responded with cautiousness in his bass voice. "Certainly sir, but we must not linger. Did you locate a place of obscurity for our business?"

Fence's suspicion rose with his curiosity. "I'll be staying at the Gramercy Hotel. There's a park across the street. Tonight at dark, when the lights come out," Fence said and then added, "The gate will be locked, but I'll have a key."

"It is set then, my friend." The tall tree departed without a claim.

Fence's involvement with undercover operations had begun in college. Multicultural connections led him across borders to other nations, to the islands, to no man's land. He belonged to the International Club by proxy. He encountered numerous contacts—many in disguise. Clues appeared fastened to the legs of carrier pigeons in England, seeing-eye dogs directed him in the dark on Native reservations and conch shells gave him more than the sound of the sea. Well aware of dangerous situations and the elements of risk, second thoughts surfaced. Today he had more to lose than yesterday.

The wood-smelling walls of the 1920's elevator spoke to him of history. He lifted to the 6th floor. Each room held an interesting element for prestigious guests. The bed welcomed him with warmth. Fence rested on its springs. He dosed. While he slept he dreamt about Tia.

The fair blond-haired angel asked the children to kiss him. She tormented him with kindness. He had no weapons to fight with. She brought him fresh homemade bread, the offering of peace.

Fence tried to lift his head. Weariness overcame him. *Too many nights up with Rose.* He fell into the dream again.

The Jamaican carried Tia to safety while darkness hovered over her. Danger signs gave warnings. Someone wanted her dead. Someone wanted her out of the picture.

Fence wrenched himself up. *I need a hot shower to move into reality.* He tried to dismiss the thoughts. He rubbed the soapy shampoo on his head. It would not wash out. Alert signals continued to flash into his brain.

The black rod iron fence, with its spokes pointing upward, surrounded the quaint park. Fence waited in the shadows thinking he was alone.

"I'm behind you." The deep sound murmured, "Don't move. I'll talk." Fence froze in place, resembling a statue. Silence surrounded them.

"The girl you married, she was smuggled to America. Someone saved her from death early on," the blackness spoke.

Perplexed, Fence asked, "How do you know this?"

"I carried her. Her parents gave her to me," the Jamaican said, telling a partial truth.

Appalled, Fence's mouth dropped open. "And you gave her away!"

"No." He continued, "You misunderstand. A black man raising a white baby, even in America eyebrows rise, questions are asked." The Jamaican waited. "The murderers still look for her. Twists of fate have kept her alive. I left her at the orphanage to protect her." He paused again. "It is by accident that you have become involved, but maybe not, because of Abe."

"What about Abe? He was murdered, wasn't he? Who are you anyway?" Fence's eagerness showed.

"Other matters come first. Listen carefully. The accident where the young woman nearly died, it was a setup to kill her. Somebody knows who she is." He pulled back into the shadows. "Her family is heir to a massive fortune. It's all under the sea, so they say, and only she holds the access key."

"Do you believe all that?" Fence grappled with the incredulous news.

"One never knows. Swiss accounts hold more than Jewish fortunes. A death threat has been on her since birth. Your assignment is to intervene and expose them, but I warn you, they are greedy, full of revenge and their connections with darkness are powerful. They identify with men in high places. Beware of evil."

"What proof do I have that it isn't you?" Fence probed.

"I risked my life many times for the girl, even to contact you. She saw me when I tried to flag her down to prevent the crash. I called the base control tower to bring the rescue team." The Jamaican looked around. "Keep your guard up, but carry on as normal. You will cover for her." Fence could barely hear him.

The wind carried the sounds of dignity away as quickly as they had come. Fence expected to find clues to Abe's death, his close friend, not get into the middle of a complicated situation with the caretaker of his child. The urgency to get home weighed on him while the strange drama with the Jamaican replayed. He completed the prearranged engineering business with his mind miles away.

The lighting of the huge Christmas tree in Rockefeller Plaza held little interest for Fence. He had no choice. Another night in the crowded city faced him. Stirring inside was the ironic situation he found himself in. Preoccupied with his need to care for Rose, he recognized his neglect of the caretaker. It never crossed his mind that divine destiny had brought them together.

Miles away, Tia's hands crossed her heart in an "X." What was happening to it? Rose, the connecting factor, linked her to Fence. She did not know if she liked it. Yet, all she ever wanted was to be a family. The whole situation was anything but normal. She rocked Rose, looking out the sliding glass door into Fence's backyard, seeing the neglect. It reminded her of a piercing television ad when a tear streamed down a man's dark face. The Native American looked over the land, saddened by the pollution of mankind, devastated, like his ancestors, when thousands of buffalo, their sustenance, lay dead and skinless on the prairie. *The voice of the tear speaks louder than words.* Tia weighed the thoughts. *It calls out to the masses to recall, restore, reclaim.*

Tia identified with grief, with the lonely tear. It watered her heart. *The green briar has attached itself to the tea rose.* She trembled. Was it something she read? Tia did not know. All she knew was that Fence's tear changed her. She began to look at him with different eyes, eyes of respect, of compassion. In spite of the change, she still did not understand the complex man.

A New Perspective

MIDNIGHT *mass can't hurt,* Fence reasoned, trying to downplay his duty of protector. *Get her out of the house. She hasn't gone anywhere since she arrived.* He said, "Take the station wagon."

Fence's quick consent took Tia by surprise. She wanted to be in church on Christmas Eve. She felt reluctant to ask him for anything. He had no clue that she needed to overcome fear. They had never discussed Rose's birth. He did not ask for details.

She backed out of the driveway, needing to readjust the mirrors. The vehicle controls were foreign to her. She kept her composure, not letting the sight or loud sound of a passing eighteen-wheeler take control. Flashbacks of the year before pressured her to take her time. She mused, *Do all people who survive a tragic accident go through this?* Thankful for the short drive, she hastened inside the archway, observant of candles reflecting against the stained glass windows. "My Rose, thank God for you, and for life."

Meanwhile Fence paced through the house, looking at the bare tree in the living room. Rose slept on her comfy blanket on the floor. *A child needs Christmas.*

He missed the snow and the northern winter, contrary to his previous opinion. Getting the decorations out of the attic took every muscle in his body. Even with the move, the dust of four years covered the big box, but more seemed to cover Fence's heart.

Looking around, he could see the need for a lot of cleanup. He did not know if he would ever be up to it. Maybe in time he would face the mess. He dared not think too much. He had to concentrate on Rose and her mother Tia.

Maybe I shouldn't have let her out of my sight, he deliberated, remembering what the black man had said. An alarming sense had invaded the house. It was not just the attic. *Is he spying on us? How*

41

come he's always in the right place at the right time? If there is a plot to kill her, she doesn't have a clue. The merry-go-round moved his thoughts up and down, round and round.

Fence found some miniature colored lights to put on the tree. He positioned red holly berries with their deep green sprigs in between before he ran a silver garland through the branches. Then he covered all the empty spots with white eagle feathers. It was enough. He carried Rose to his bed and covered her. Tucking the blanket around her little body, he whispered, "Hey Little One. Tomorrow is your birthday. You will be one year old."

Since Thanksgiving, he had found himself placed more formally in the role of protector. He was unable to brush off the Jamaican's words. Realizing the seriousness of the responsibility, he operated with discretion. All of his other activities subsided, except electrical engineering projects, which remained a secure place to function. *I have to be on guard more than ever.*

Something else troubled Fence. *What does the Jamaican know about Abe's death? Why did he say that other matters come first? Is there a connection between Abe and Tia, the caretaker of Rose?*

Reviewing the dangers, Fence started in the logical place, the kitchen, hoping he had enough time. He now hoped she would stay away until he finished. His stomach rocked back and forth with uneasiness. He checked the phones for wiretaps. His brown leather jacket hung from the wooden coat tree. Grabbing it, he took the twelve-foot ladder from the garage outside. He examined the roofline, looking for hidden cameras. No new tracks were in the yard. He searched his property, confident of his thoroughness. Taking all the precautionary measures, he connected an invisible security system, engineering his own project. He hurried, getting everything in place, not wanting Tia to walk in on him.

When the garage door opener buzzed, Fence raced to his bedroom and listened to make certain she was safe. He heard her lock the doors with the double bolt. At least she followed his safety instructions. She had never questioned why.

Tia sat for a long time admiring the interesting fir. Although it was covered with feathers, its top was bare. The tree needed a crown. Tia tiptoed to the kitchen where she fashioned a silver star from foil, recalling a Christmas when she was young. At the orphanage the children filled the simple trees with creative art. Each orphan was thankful and full of joy. "You touch the Master's Hand through your gifts of love," Sister

Maria Thomas had told them. Climbing the rungs to the top of the six-foot stepladder, Tia put the creation in place. Satisfied, she stood back in admiration, grateful for the picture that was so opposite from the year before.

Tia found the small quilt she had made for Rose hidden in her room. She placed it unwrapped under the unusual tree. Beside it she positioned a simple, homemade Christmas card for Fence. A piece of white lace covered it, along with three very old buttons she had found in the nail jar, and a small olive branch. It said one word, *PEACE*.

What is she doing? Fence suppressed his desire to interfere. Knowing she was in the kitchen and wandering around the house made him apprehensive. *Did I remember to put all my tools away?* He could not help himself; his ear had been trained to work overtime. He spied through the crack, aggravated but somewhat curious as to why she had invaded his territory. He disdained the scratchy, repelling noise she was making. Time stretched to 3:00 a.m. An unexplainable magnetic pull drew him toward her.

Fence peered into the living room. "Finally, peace and quiet," he whispered to himself. With hushed movement he moved to the tree and stuck the red envelope in a low branch, repressing the urge to put it in Tia's hand. The woman slept, curled up in a ball, still in her clothes like a package waiting to be opened. Her angelic hair lay like a golden gift at the foot of the tree, reminding Fence of a summer day. He looked up, noticing the star. Intrigue covered him when he saw what she had done. *Definitely, she is an innocent one.* He shook his head. *Naïve people fall into trouble without a clue.* He crept to bed.

Tia had rested her head on Rose's gift. The mother's desire to see Rose Christmas morning waxed strong in her. Unable to leave the tree, slumber had taken control.

Orange sunlight blazed through the upper window, waking her. Deep in the tree, stuck between the feathers, she saw a reflection of red, like a bird with a morning song. The card displayed her name, *Tia*.

She reached through the prickly, green needles, securing the unsealed envelope. The reality that Fence had stood over her in the night embarrassed her. Her soft hands trembled as she fumbled with the lip. Tia's eyes opened like faucets running. Mixed tears of joy and sadness flowed. She could not shut them off. The note was more than she could fathom.

Tia,
Thanks for giving Rose life.
Sincerely,
FENCE

Tangled in wrinkles of discomfort, Tia let the card fall. Fence had entered the room, holding Rose. Tia had no place to hide except in the knowledge that Fence admitted she was Rose's mother. *There is so much this man does not know.*

Rose squealed with delight, seeing the lit-up tree. Fence set her down by the couch, fixing his eyes on his daughter. "It's time for your birthday party, Rose."

Tia straightened herself out, her composure regained. Filled with an overpowering sense that she had made the right decision, Tia hugged the baby quilt to her face. Then, bravely, she stretched out the folded blanket. "For you Rose." She laid the gift equidistant between Fence and Rose.

"I think she wants to walk," Tia said, speaking with renewed strength. Her mind was focused away from herself. "Look, she's going for the tree."

Fence stationed himself between the pine and Rose, holding his arms out. Rose's head twisted toward Tia. "Mama?" she said, her eyes questioning.

"Go to daddy," Tia encouraged. Three baby steps pressed forward.

"Rose Marie Carpenter! You outshine all the lights on your first birthday," Fence exclaimed. A wide grin wrapped across the pleased father's face.

"She's the best gift this Christmas," Tia said, thinking of the card. Fence smiled at her understanding the message. She penetrated his being again.

Together they shared the moment of joy. Fence did not mention the star. She did not mention his card. The stillness lasted a brief moment. They were each in different worlds, yet the same. Fence turned the stereo on. Christmas carols set the tone. Fence spent the day absorbed with Rose. Tia watched from a distance.

The tree remained up until the end of January. Fence took it down at midnight.

Fever

O N February 1, 1981, a bedraggled Fence shook with chills. Shoving the kitchen door open, he leaned forward. Profuse sweat dripped from his temples. He prevented himself from collapsing, grabbing hold of the corners of the crock-colored kitchen countertop. He did not call out. Struggling, he dragged himself to his bed and sat precariously on its end.

Tia heard the unusual sounds. Standing outside his door, she disregarded self and questioned, "Are you okay?"

Fence tried to look up. "I don't know. I have to lie down." His pillow seemed miles away. He fell backwards across the bed. His knees and feet hung down the side. He was sick, very sick.

Tia rushed in, dispelling her fears. She knelt at his feet, loosening his shoes. Using all her strength to lift his legs, she pulled them sideways to position him fully on his bed. She pulled the homemade quilt bedcover halfway up from the opposite side, wrapping him in the hours of needlework, the squares that had been on a quilt frame. Tia recognized the piece as a work of art, unlike anything she had ever touched. *A masterpiece,* she thought.

Fence seemed to be comforted. Tia heard him make a soft sound, a murmur of satisfaction that a child makes with a mother's touch. *He must have been loved.* She tried to get the pillow under his head. She loosened his tie and pulled it out, then opened the buttons on the top of his shirt, wishing he had a cotton tee shirt underneath, something to absorb the sweat. He was drenched. She wiped his forehead with a washcloth, sponging his face. The man, held captive by the fever, lay exhausted. The situation demanded sick leave. *He pushes himself nonstop. I don't know what he does with his time. Even Rose isn't melting the stress built up inside of him.*

Rose, now thirteen months old, called for Fence from her crib, "Da-

da-da."

Give her a bottle. No. Put her in the highchair. No. Move her to the bedroom where Fence is, move the play crib in. Tia organized her care-taking responsibilities in her head, imagining what a mother would do. The actions came with no second thoughts, as natural as getting up in the morning.

All evening, all night she attended Fence, like she would care for any human being. Tia remained attentive and alert, serving him. She pulled his head up in her hand and whispered, "Fence, you have to have liquids. Drink this. Take little sips."

He did not speak, just assented. He did not keep it down. Tia insisted he swallow cold drinks of water, pitcher after pitcher. She slept half sitting on an armchair with her head wrapped in her arms on the side of the bed. She waited patiently for him to show signs of recovery. Until now, she had never crossed the threshold of his bedroom. They had never passed in the dark.

Fence kept his workplace number on the counter, prepared for emergencies. At 6:00 a.m. Tia picked up the phone and dialed. "May I speak with Mr. Browning?"

"Who's calling?" the faceless voice said.

"Tia Carpenter." She said her new last name out loud for the first time. Tia contemplated, listening to the hold music, wanting to guard Fence's reputation with her words. *I must think before I speak.*

"Mr. Browning, Fence will not be able to come in today. I'm calling for permission for him to have the day off. Thank you, sir." She hung up the phone.

Fence jarred out of his position, not realizing where he was. He saw the clock. 10:00 a.m. His weak body slunk on the bed. Soft white dishtowels stuck on him, inside his shirt on his chest and on his back. Thirsty, he reached for the water glass on the bed stand. It fell to the floor and broke. The premature effort failed. He tried to remember how he got into the bed. His pants were still on; his belt and tie were off. *Where's Rose?* Worry crowded him. "Rose?" he called out.

Tia heard the glass crash. Fence saw her in the hallway and tried to sit up. She struggled with an overflowing laundry basket. "Please wait a minute until I can help you," Tia said, setting it down. Determined, he struggled but felt woozy. She stuck the pillows behind his back and left him, remembering the best medicine, Rose.

The warm baby wanted to crawl into bed with Fence. He let her.

Tia saw his eyes enlarge with the realization it was Friday, not Saturday. Before he could speak, Tia explained, "You have the day off. I called in early to ask for you. I didn't tell him about the fever. I'm sorry if I overstepped my bounds."

He looked with amazement at Tia. "Thanks" was all he said. He expressed kindness, not anger toward her. On Monday he must get a checkup.

Diagnosis

POISON. "Poisoning is the only explanation. It went to your liver through your blood. Are you on any drugs or drinking alcohol?" Doc Bridger questioned.

"No. I think you've known me long enough to know that. Even if it has been cross country." Fence wanted to examine the blood test results himself. Doc kept them undercover.

"Well, maybe it's food poisoning." Doc looked at him seriously, knowing his original diagnosis was right. "You never know these days. Watch your back. Something is foul here."

"Doc, you've been around here for a long time. You know Christ Child's Orphanage? Have you ever been there?"

"Well, not as an orphan." He laughed. "I can tell you one thing, they aren't the ones trying to poison you!"

"Seriously, I'm talking about life and death here. I need some information in all confidentiality. It won't break your code of ethics. I promise." Fence grinned at the man with the white whiskers.

"Well, son, you always were one of my favorites. Your grandfather and I were fraters in the same hall together. Built a few parade floats together too. You remind me of him. He was quite amiable, heaped full of integrity, but he wasn't afraid to pull a prank once in a while." Doc's eyes twinkled. "What can I help you with?"

Fence sobered. "Did you ever hear about an orphan girl left on their steps? I'd say twenty-three years ago or so." He guessed at Tia's age. The two plastic bags she came with had revealed nothing.

Doc Bridger pulled out his pocket-watch, holding it in his palm, clicking it open. "It's already six o'clock. Everyone has left the clinic. Come to my office." Fence followed him while looking over Doc's bald spot, leery of ears hiding in corners.

"Have a seat." Doc poured out the rotten coffee and offered Fence

48

ice water before he sat down behind a camouflaged desk cascading with papers. "First of all, do you have a need to know?"

Fence smiled and shook his head in unbelief. "Yeah, I guess so. She's my wife."

"Man to man, what I am about to tell you stays within these walls. I don't want the innocent placed in danger." Fence could tell the serious wheels were turning in Doc's brain. His grandfather's friend removed his glasses and started cleaning them with his over-scrubbed hands.

Doc Bridger carefully continued. "Indeed, how could I forget? It was a task keeping it hidden from the newspapers. Sister Maria Thomas called me in to give the tiny child an exam and help with the birth certificate. They named her on the spot. I remember it well, Tia, short for Tiara, like a crown of roses or jewels, because of her thick blond curls. We estimated she was between three and four months old." Doc scratched his chin. "A good baby she was." He emptied his glass to the bottom before continuing. "A beauty, yes? ... So you remarried?"

"We have a baby girl, thirteen months old now. Her name is Rose."

"Congratulations young man. That girl, I mean the orphan, Tia, is a special one. I've had an interest in her through the years, but lost track of her when she left the orphanage. I'm glad you found her."

"To be honest, she found me," Fence added, disclosing only a small parcel of the story.

Doc Bridger resumed speaking. "The only thing of identification we found was an embroidered handkerchief. It was under her head, totally unfamiliar to me." The doctor stood up. "So why are you asking me all these questions? Why don't you ask her?"

"I... well, sir. That's a good question," Fence, uncomfortable, answered in a professional manner. "I have reason to believe her life is in danger."

"Looks like yours is, too. It's not everyday I have a patient who comes in poisoned. I'll keep this under my hat. My operating eyes are on alert. I'll be considering what procedure will work to remedy your unusual case." He grinned at Fence with his medical look.

"There's more than meets the eye in this case, Doc."

"Indeed, I can see that. So, it needs to be examined with a stethoscope and tongue depressor?" The white-haired doctor put his glasses on.

Fence opened his mouth with a smile. "I'll take all the support and examination I can get."

Doc Bridger's hand reached out.

Fence's gripped it in agreement. "Thanks, I owe you," he said.

Doc handed him an orange sucker. "For your little daughter, Rose," he said, returning the smile.

Fence left feeling better. All it took was Doc's dose of wisdom. His humor did not hurt either.

Twice Refined Treasure

FENCE said her name for the first time since the fever. "Tia?" he repeated. He had not bothered her, not made any requests nor given sharp orders. He had restrained himself from making quick judgments. The woman who took care of Rose avoided him. He called her name again, peeking in through three inches of openness. Her door was ajar. She stared out the sliding glass doors of her bedroom into the bare garden. "Tia!" His voice sounded louder than he wanted. Fence waited.

Weeks had passed with only brief words between them, although Fence took stock of her actions. She went nowhere. She absorbed herself in endless reading in his library. Starting college correspondence courses kept her nights busy. *At least she wants to make something of herself.* Often he overheard her teaching Rose, counting with her in Spanish. He wondered where she had learned it, but did not ask. They didn't seem to have anything in common except Rose.

At night he traveled different roads home, mixing up his schedule, staying out of routines. Tia's routine varied little from day to day. Between Rose and her studies, she was too preoccupied to dwell much on the past. She pushed back prior struggles to make ends meet, the harsh treatment, the close call with death. Laughter lifted the veil of tears, but never in front of Fence. She cherished every minute, every giggle, every bit of Rose's growth.

At times bewilderment invaded her privacy. *How did I ever get involved with Chance Cummings?* The memory of him making fun of her tormented her. His lies still tied her up in knots. How could she love and hate him at the same time? His subtle control lived on. Tia shook off heaviness. *Oh, Rose. You help me forget.* Tia watched her, not realizing that Rose was also the reason she could never forget.

Fence had not had a day off since Tia asked for it. Relaxation, now a foreign word, had left him months before. Memorial Day closed in on him. Compelled to keep his yearly appointment at Lily's grave, he drove home from work making another hasty decision. Not that he wanted to; he needed to. Hesitant to leave Tia alone, he considered his next move as he pulled into the bank's drive-through.

He did not charge into his house. His precise steps were to find her. Quietly he knocked, shoving the door open with a gentle nudge. "Tia?" He stood in the doorway, his hand secure on the doorknob. "My vacation starts today. Will you pack your things?"

Tia's insides jolted. She had just completed exams. The pressure still hovered over her. She remained motionless, listening to interrupting thoughts. *He wants me to leave. I don't want to be separated from Rose. I can't do this.* She felt worn out.

Fence kept talking. She tried to divide her thoughts and the words the man spoke. Rejection wanted to overtake her. *Pack your things?* Her subconscious avoided the question. She missed the little cottage, the wood fire, the smoky smell, the majestic trees. Potential pulled her, but until Fence opened the door, she would not ask for permission. Her mind searched the backyard. "I'd like to work in the garden," she said out loud.

He stopped his mouth and repeated himself, inserting an extra line. "The garden? You're free to do whatever you like. Now back to vacation. We have an hour to get ready. We're going to the Rocky Mountains. It's a long drive." He leaned his other hand against the doorframe, more for lack of knowing where to put it than balance. "We'll buy some camping food at the store and some things for Rose."

Tia jerked her head up, out of her daydream. Fence's words registered. Did he want her to go with him? She tossed it around in her distressed mind. To comprehend that he included her required effort. After nine months caring for his daughter, he finally spoke to her. She could go no further than when he said her name, when he gave permission to touch the neglected flowerbed. Her thought pattern stymied. Cognizance attempted to adjust itself in her.

"Will you go?" He saw her frozen state and reached his hand up to his forehead. *Why do I have to be so blunt? Why do I treat her like merchandise?* He turned to walk away, while he beat himself up on the inside.

Seventeen-month-old Rose heard her daddy's voice even as Fence heard her. "Dad-ee, Dad-ee." Shaking off the punches at himself, he grabbed her up into his arms and said, "We're going for a ride." She snuggled into his shoulder on his arm, feeling content.

Tia remembered Mother's Day the year before—the emptiness. Allowing herself time to adjust, she decided, *Yes, this is an appropriate time.* She swallowed hard. Tia needed a vacation as much as Fence. No wedding ring graced her finger. She could not bear the thought of losing Rose now that she had found her. Gathering her meager belongings, she placed them in a plastic bag, and nearly ran into Fence. He handed her a black suitcase.

"We'll get some things to fill it," he said, noticing her simplicity, her selflessness, her humility. For a second, her character reminded Fence of Abe.

"Thank you. I'll put Rose's things in here," Tia responded without feeling. The mechanical function surrounded her in safety.

Fence packed the cooler and baggage into the station wagon with efficiency. He turned. Tia stood, watching him. Ignoring her, he strapped Rose into the child seat. Tia crawled into the seat behind him, not even thinking she belonged anywhere else.

"You're a happy baby. You know we're going on an adventure, little girl?" Tia spoke to her like a much older child. Rose nodded her little head up and down.

Fence turned around awkwardly and handed Tia an envelope. It held a one hundred dollar bill and five twenties. "Thought you might need some money." He spoke in a loud voice, "I want you to have it. It's yours."

After they drove for couple of miles Tia noticed a sign, *GARAGE SALE.*

"Fence, I don't want to bother you. Please, could we stop for a few minutes?"

He waited, watching with reluctance, granting Tia her request. *She has never asked me to do anything before today and now she wants to stop for rummage. She must have been homeless. I should've taken her shopping.*

Ten minutes later, Tia returned with two plastic bags filled with items. Fence shook his head. *Not more plastic bags!* He turned the other way trying not to stare and contemplated. *I've been worrying about her safety. Guess I've forgotten other needs.*

"Fence, there's a floatation device for a small child on the driveway. Could you...?" she said with a burst of courage.

He interrupted, "Well, I'm not interested." The need to get moving pushed at him, not to mention his reticence to buy other people's junk.

Tia looked away, fearing she had said too much.

Feeling guilty, he relented, lifting the door handle without saying a word. Tia waited with Rose, bewildered by Fence.

Fence quickly returned from the homemade sale at a half run. Inwardly, he felt a bit proud of himself. He had found more than he imagined. His mouth unclamped long enough to loose his lips in an unusual smile. "You were right. It wasn't so bad."

Tia acknowledged him with a slight nod of the head, glad for the man's moment of enjoyment, for his discovery of twice refined treasure. Laying her head back, she closed her eyes, gratified that Fence had the chance to experience worth in what someone else had valued.

Fence unlocked the wagon hatch, dropping it down. He threw the floater inside, along with a couple of plastic sacks of his own. *Acting like nothing is wrong is quite a job!*

To the Rockies

TIA read the rummaged, dog-eared book out loud, more to herself than to Rose, marveling at how the power of a child's love gave life to the velveteen rabbit. She related to the stuffed animal. Unobserved, Fence listened. He perceived more than he let on.

The station wagon made the long climb toward the northwest bucking a headwind. Sunset settled upon them. Rose finally fell into dreamland. Out of the blue, Fence asked Tia, "Do you want to drive for a while?"

She shoved her fears down her throat. "If you like," she answered from the back seat.

At the next rest area Tia took the wheel. She sat forward, seeking a closer, fuller view. Her petite body sunk. She stretched to see over the steering wheel.

Out of the corner of his eye, Fence noticed her dilemma. Without speaking, he reached to the back seat, grabbed her pillow and gave it to her to sit on. She made the necessary adjustments. Almost immediately, he fell asleep in the passenger seat. The marked map lay under his palm, stretched over his left leg.

The fact that Fence could sleep with her driving seemed unimaginable to Tia. To think that he trusted her was a foreign concept. He always seemed so much in charge. She laid aside her lack of understanding to concentrate. For the first time in a year and a half she actually enjoyed the freedom of driving. The release soothed her.

Needing to see which turn to take, she reached to pull out the map. Her hand trembled. She lifted Fence's heavy arm to the side without waking him. *He must be totally exhausted.* She squinted, studying the marked yellow lines that stretched northwest across the United States. She tried to understand the intricate twine. *Is he planning to travel across the whole country?* The man's head rested her way. She did not disturb him, remaining perplexed.

After several hours she pulled off the road at an interstate truck stop. The gas gauge showed red. Hopping down with a giant step, her foot reached the ground. She twisted the gas cap off with care, only to find Fence by her side getting the nozzle out of the pump. He spoke softly. "Thanks for driving."

Tia answered as if he were still resting, "Thank you for letting me drive. I didn't want to wake you."

He affirmed her. "You did a good job. Took a big load off me. Where are we?"

She swallowed hard, not quite certain where they were. He seemed cognizant of her distress. "That's okay, I recognize this place. After you check Rose, you can sit up in front. The passenger seat reclines so you can catch a nap."

Tia's tenseness broke. The first exposure to the passenger side melted her strength. She relaxed on the mammoth bench seat. Dark clouds released their full force of rain. Fence squared his shoulders, eyeing the rear view mirror. Someone followed. Alert to the dangerous air, his concern heightened. The barometric pressure plummeted. Hidden in the downpour of the cloud, they lost the lights behind them.

A couple of tedious hours passed before the station wagon halted, jarring Tia out of her dream. Leaving Tia and Rose, Fence ran inside the motel lobby. Rose stirred. Tia opened the back door to unbuckle her daughter. Rose's little arms reached out. "Ma, Ma," she cried.

"I'll carry her," the voice spoke behind her.

Taken back, Tia stepped out of the way. Fence lifted Rose with his muscular arms. Tia sheltered her head from the rainfall. Submissiveness took over.

Fence explained, "We got the last room. I'm sorry. Rose will have to sleep in the middle. I couldn't get two beds. It's a king size." Tia followed, covered from the rain.

The room welcomed them. Energized, Rose played with her soft doll.

Rummage sacks landed on the bed in spread array. Tia dried off her face and climbed onto the heavy-laden mattress. She sat cross-legged with her elbows on her knees and hands on her chin. Her blond hair fell on her shoulders in giant waves. She held up a tiny swimsuit and several outfits. "Rose, see what I got for you?" Color invaded the room.

Fence did not miss her movement, aware, but not looking. Realness showed for the first time since the day Rose first walked. He remembered the "peace" card in his dresser drawer. He glanced at Tia and said to his wandering child, "If I'd have known that stopping at a rummage sale would make your mother this happy, Rose, I would have taken her before." For the first time, he verbally acknowledged Tia as Rose's mother. It took him by surprise. Fortunately, the unexpected words seemed to go over Tia's head as well as the child's. Fence walked to the door and picked up two plastic bags. "For you and Rose," he said, quickly dropping them unopened on the bed.

Tia stared down, feeling her breath being swept away. "I, I wasn't, ahhh. Thank you," she finally said, pulling out a nighty for Rose along with a hooded swim towel.

"Will it fit her?" He reached out and touched the clothes like they might break.

The fragile moment struck Tia with bewilderment. She remained silent. They looked a little large. It seemed that Fence was not really looking for a reply.

"This is for you." He handed the black leather jacket to Tia. "It may be a little too big for you. I noticed you didn't bring a jacket. It gets cool in the mountains at night."

Not knowing what to say, Tia remained lost in thought. *So that's why he smiled when he returned to the car from the garage sale.* Instinctively she stood up on the bed, put the jacket on and looked in the mirror. "It's beautiful. I love it." In a sporadic, uncustomary move she jumped off the bed, took a twirl, and swung her arms around Fence. "Thank you so much." The overwhelming impulse caught them both off guard. She reached for her stomach. Ignoring the pain, she turned the other way to pull herself together.

Fence remained curious. *I wonder if she'll wear it all night.* He adjusted his thinking before adding, "I have something else."

She turned around, trying to hide her shaking hands and the pain, in order to receive the gift. A coral terry robe and a nightgown were balled inside. She had seen them herself, but had left them behind. Tia admired what she held, taking time to draw them to her heart, oversensitive to Fence's closeness.

"What's this?" he asked, seeing her embarrassment. He reached for the remaining plastic bag on the floor. Pulling out a denim shirt and picture album, Fence realized it was for him.

"For Rose's pictures," Tia said, watching.

Taken back by Tia's generosity, Fence opened his dry mouth. The young woman perplexed him. The strange relationship entailed more than he expected. *I must be careful not to get attached. Duty has to stay free of emotions.* The responsibility for caring for Tia was growing.

Rose moved her hands in the excitement. It was 2:30 a.m. and sleep was vacant from her mind. Tia suggested a bath. Fence did not hesitate. He scooped Rose into the air, bathing her in warm, sudsy water. Energetically he folded her into a snuggly, warm towel.

Wearing her new nighty, Rose proudly took her daddy's hand and paraded to the bed. Tia had pulled back the giant spread.

Apprehensive, Tia sought privacy. The past few hours were anything but real. She knelt on the bathmat with tears running, touching the nightclothes.

Fence lay with his arm around Rose. *He is a good father,* she admitted, thankful she was not alone in the dark room. She quietly sat on the edge of the bed, reluctant to accept the strange circumstances. Finally, she gave in to the situation, adjusting to the oversized pillow, and reached her head over to kiss Rose. "I love you," she whispered. Her lips touched Rose's forehead. She rolled on her back, reaching her hand out for Rose's little one.

Fence's arm lifted over Rose. His large hand landed on top of the two smaller hands. They fell asleep—the three hands together—with Rose nestled in between.

Infected

THE night stretched long past daybreak. A bright sunray addressed Tia through the blue drapes. She slipped out to start the coffeemaker. Listening to the dripping sound, she brushed her hair, thinking about Fence's acts of kindness. She had known much rejection and abandonment in her life. Fence did not make her feel that way. The night of realness had entered through the unexpected. She exhaled, peeking out the window between the curtain cracks.

The tender scar on Tia's stomach ached. Since the accident and surgery months before, it continued to trouble her. The wound was red and inflamed. At the bathroom mirror she lifted her new nightgown to check on it, wondering if she needed to get her prescription refilled. She had battled infection nearly a year before. She turned to find Fence staring at her.

"That looks infected. Why didn't you tell me? We need to get you to a doctor." Tia grabbed her robe, wrapping it tightly around her. She looked somberly at the floor, wishing to melt into it.

Fence's genuine concern helped cover up her obvious discomfort. Diagnostic deductions registered in his mind. *Maybe I've been expecting too much from her. What if she developed a hernia from carrying Rose around? Why didn't I notice before?* He shook his head, recalling the vacuum marks on the carpet that she obviously had made.

"I have a prescription." She went to her handbag and gave it to him.

Fence noted the date. Tia had gotten it from a critical care clinic. *It must have been when she was homeless. My God, it's amazing the girl is alive.*

Fence came out of the drugstore with rubbing alcohol, hydrogen peroxide and antibiotic cream. A bundle of red roses with stems in water pockets were cradled in his left arm. He drove back to the motel to find Rose and Tia ready to go. The pressures of his job had finally stripped away from him. More important things occupied his mind. Tia was different from anyone he had ever known. *She never complains.*

"Lay down, Tia. I'm going to help you." He dabbed the salve onto the eight-inch vertical scar. "What happened to you?" he said with compassion. Tia fought off the shame of exposure.

"It will be okay." She avoided the question. "Rose is healthy and alive; that's what matters." His gentle words and soft manner had a healing effect that no medicine on a flesh wound had. As she yielded to his care, Fence seemed to touch her heart with renewed strength.

Protector qualities rose up in Fence. He was becoming more and more Tia's bodyguard. She did not suspect. The roundabout route he had taken early on, when leaving the city, had lost the car that had been tailing them. "Think I'll stop at a car dealership," he said out loud to himself. "Lock the doors will you?" He hesitated and then exited, leaving them waiting.

This man is getting harder and harder to understand. I'm starting to feel smothered. If only he would treat me like an adult instead of a child. She tried to straighten out the confusion. *Fast and furious. He walks like he's on a mission.*

"These are for you. Catch." He threw her a new set of keys. Driving around the lot, he stopped by a burgundy van.

"Ride with me up front," Fence requested. He loaded the new vehicle with their belongings.

Three days of driving weighed heavily on them all. Double beds met them after the first night, so the awkwardness waned. Each time Fence placed Rose beside Tia. On the road Tia seemed consumed, reading the three classics she had bought at the rummage sale. At other times she read out loud to Rose—mountains of children's books—fascinating the little child with precious words.

Miles and mountain ranges later they entered a cemetery. The stark silence had not been broken for hours. Tia rolled her window down. Her mind was lost in the ocean of headstones. The giant panorama of emptiness spread out before her, filled with untold stories.

Purple and white lilacs greeted her senses with an intoxicating smell, penetrating Tia. *Lilacs ... where love begins.* Someone had written that, but she could not remember where she had read it. Old churchyards and praying grandmothers wore the fragrance, breathing life into stones.

To Tia, that kind of affection existed only in fairy tales. She wrapped her fingers in Rose's black curls. They reminded her of Chance Cummings.

Fence left with a bouquet of wilted roses. The flowers in his hand emitted little fragrance, overpowered by blooming lilacs. He knelt by Lily's grave, reflecting, not wanting to ever let her go. His fingerprints flatly touched his mouth. Taking a kiss from his lips, he pressed one on her name and then on baby Ann's. "My loved ones." A quiet moment passed. Fence sighed, exhaling. "Oh Lily, I miss you." He could see her plain as day, his woman of purity.

Tia watched him through the window opening, off in the distance. Amazement washed over her. A barrage of questions bombarded her mind. *Whose headstone is he touching*? Answers ran wild in her imagination. Time passed slowly while she waited. The spacious van was comfortable. Why was she feeling as if she were in a coffin?

When Fence finally stood, he inhaled, taking in the clean smell of the pines. Their peaked points spoke in sign language … *Look up, not down. Look beyond* … as if to say the future held more than an empty glare, more than a stare into outer space. Abe had told him to quit mourning Lily. He did not think he could do that yet.

Fence stopped to talk to his old friend whose grave was nearby. "Abe, you were right. I took your advice and adopted the baby. Got a little more than I expected with her. I miss our adventures. Haven't forgotten you. I intend to find out what really happened. It's just that I've been a little preoccupied. You might call it sidetracked. Still don't know if I did the right thing. Maybe I plunged in headfirst. I keep telling myself I did it for you. Don't know if that's the whole truth or not. I only have a couple pieces to your puzzle right now, but I'll find the rest. And the assignment? Well, I'm still not totally certain what that is. I'm wrapped up in another problem for the moment. Until next year, my friend."

Fence turned away from the stones. He temporarily unloaded his burden. In some ways he felt lighter. The smell of death no longer rested on him.

Without a word Fence resumed driving. Tia did not press him. More rested in the unspoken than he could ever say. She needed wisdom. She desperately tried to understand the confusing man. His only words were to Rose. At the next stop, Tia climbed in back. She sang a Latin song to Rose. Then she told her about flowers.

Fence was off in another world, another time, when things were different, when he laughed a lot and fed on adventure, when he was free. He suffered from more than the loss of Lily. He had lost the childhood songs, the early morning adventures in the woods, the elk hunts with his dad. He no longer whistled, imitating birds, tracking the wild. Seriousness muted him. He looked back at Rose. She keyed memories of the wind blowing through his mouth. It made him think of what his mother had always said, "Ears of corn perk up and listen to the sound of a song. Tobacco waves its peace pipe. Birds become a symphony." In her native tongue, Fence's mother had sung her own poetry. "Buttercup squash, fill with orange."

But now, Fence was still, his windpipe dry, his tongue swollen and stiff. No word formation took place. His lungs held no vibrations. Fence had stood still in grief. He had absorbed himself in work, the real and the undercover. His bow collected dust in a corner. *It's time to get a new hunting coat and throw the old one. It doesn't fit anymore.* It carried a double meaning. Fence knew it.

Glancing over his right shoulder, he marveled at Rose. She tried to sing with Tia. The baby was as good as gold, or better. She drank apple juice from her cup, holding it with dexterous little fingers. No one would guess that she was premature, except for her fine-boned, petite body. Even that was not a clue. Her hair glistened.

The innocence of children is irreplaceable. Fence's mother's words pushed through again. Rose's hands tangled into Tia's hair. Fence froze in reality. Rose resembled Tia in more ways than he wanted to admit, the fine features, the strength within, the tone of voice.

Winding and weaving on narrow, often breathtaking roads, they climbed higher. Fence's concentration zeroed in on the road. He tried to pull himself together on the hairpin curves. *I have to get a grip.*

Then there's the issue of Tia. He had pulled her into a situation of danger when it did not matter, but now things had gotten out of hand. Someone was after her. *Maybe it was fate that I adopted her child.* He let his integrity guide him, pioneering his own trail. Finally he broke the sound barrier. "Not much longer. We'll be there soon." They turned off the pavement onto a rough, steep-graded gravel road.

Tia had no idea where "there" was. Ten minutes later her question was answered. The lonely rustic log cabin was sheltered in the darkness of lodgepole pines. Fence went to the hidden breaker box and turned on the porch light. The key hid, nestled above the shutters of the front window frame.

Heading straight to the wood stove, Tia turned the crank. The chill in the room vanished with warmth of the soon-made fire. Fence looked distant, but somehow pleased that she did not fear. She handled the situation with ease. For some reason it did not surprise him, probably because she had been homeless. He considered, *I can't let her know I've been investigating her.*

Tia sensed that his eyes were following her. She tried to avert them. The fire started to crackle. The warm air made them all sleepy. "I feel like I've come home," she said, speaking to the logs. Home to Tia was a place of physical warmth, of not being cold.

"Hot, hot. The fire is hot," she explained to Rose, the whole time wondering what the sleeping conditions would be. The entire trip was getting more and more entangled. How could she be comfortable and uncomfortable at the same time? She examined the kitchen, deciding that toast and hot chocolate would satisfy the evening hunger. Together they dunked and ate the toast without a word between them.

Near the door a silver shoehorn rested next to three pairs of weary-looking shoes. Tia awaited instructions. Fence refrained from his usual order giving. He had spent all his energy driving and visiting the cemetery. Rejuvenating from the trauma usually required more than a day. He pulled Rose close, holding her near to him as both fell asleep in the old, padded wicker rocker.

Tia found a bed and crawled in, clothes and all. A minute later Fence whispered, "Are you asleep?" He laid Rose next to her before coming around to her side. Leaning close, he asked quietly, "Did you clean your incision?"

"No, I guess I didn't," Tia answered half-asleep, feeling warmer because Rose was now near her.

Fence lit the small lantern on the wooden crate. "I'm a trained EMT, not very active now, but I know infection when I see it. I know I haven't been very good company. But that doesn't mean I can't help you." His voice was getting a little louder; Rose stirred. He softened up a bit, "Tia, please let me help you. We have to get that healed up or you'll end up in the hospital."

He carefully redressed the incision, cleansing the wound and placing clean gauze over it. "Do you want your nightclothes? They would be less binding than jeans." He found them in Rose's suitcase and brought them to her. Then he left the room contemplating the whole situation.

He found her attractive. *I can't even carry on an intelligent conversation with her and she can't with me. Guess I haven't let her. Why didn't she tell me about the infected wound?* He was having a hard time understanding. For that matter, he had not told her his past. She did not have any reason to share hers. He found himself caring for the little woman with the thick blond hair. The marital business arrangement was becoming more awkward by the minute. Contracts do not involve feelings; or do they?

Fence decided against sleeping alone in the loft, drawn to the gentle presence of Tia and his need to guard her. He worried about her. For the first time, he tried to understand her. He pulled on his gym trunks and quietly crawled under the giant quilt.

Mountain night air invaded. The stove fire died. He moved closer to Rose. He was almost face to face with Tia. "Are you cold?" he quietly said to her.

"A little," she answered.

Before he could take it back, he spoke. "I'll hold you. Tuck Rose on the other side of you and we'll keep each other warm." His arm surrounded them in a cup. Tia was trembling again, either from the cold or Fence breathing on her neck. She thought it was both. She never had anyone hold her like that. She had always been alone. The situation was not forced. She felt Fence's respect for her. In spite of his bluntness and past rudeness, he had a gentle heart. He comforted her after the trying day as much as she comforted him. She did not read more into it than that. She did not allow herself to dream beyond that. Fence fell asleep immediately with a peace he had not known in years. Her weakness imparted strength to him in an unpredictable way. He kept her warm all night without effort.

Arising early, Fence brewed coffee. The aroma filled the cabin. Rose played with Tia's hair. "Come on Rose. Let's see what's happening in the kitchen. I know you're hungry." Their stomachs attempted to adjust to the two-hour time gain.

Fence wore the new denim shirt. His sleeves were rolled up to mid-forearm. His blue jean pocket bulged with his billfold. "How did you sleep?" he asked.

"Better than I have for a long time. Thank you. I like it here," she said.

Fence turned the eggs before turning around to hoist Rose into the wooden highchair. He tied a square dishtowel around her waist to hold her in place. "How about a walk after breakfast?" he asked, watching

Tia pull the kitchen curtains back to let more of the sun in. She opened the window to remove the stifling haze of smoke. Fence scratched his unshaven face and looked at her. "I like being with you," he commented, and then wondered why he said it.

Was she hearing him right? She tried to eat. "Is there a chapel nearby?" she asked, laying her fork down, not waiting for Fence to answer. "Could we talk?" she began cautiously. "Here we are. We really don't know anything about each other. We can't even say we're friends. I don't know how long you want me to stay around as a daycare person. I just need a friend. I know I shouldn't be lonely, but I don't have an adult to respond back to me. I don't mean to offend you. It seems that we're still on the wrong foot. We've both been closed books," she rattled on. It seemed to him that she had her head in enough books in the past couple days. He was not ready for her to read him in any way, shape or form.

"Rose?" he said, placing some midget pancake rounds near the child's miniature fingers.

Tia continued, "I want to tell you how Rose was born. I want you to tell me about your childhood." She took a breath after the mouthful and changed course. "Thank you for taking me on vacation with you. I don't mean to sound ungrateful," she said, sniffing the pine breeze that softly blew the curtain.

Fence looked down, apprehensive about looking her in the eye. "There's a country chapel near the ridge. I guess it is Sunday," he confessed.

Collapse

THE 1920 inscription faded into the rustic country church, marking its maturity. The cornerstone, strategically stationed, resembled a big toe at the foot of the aged foundation. The building's body bulged with muscles of hand-peeled, handpicked logs. Physically, it blended with the tall stature of the ponderosa forest. The fortification, looking larger than life, was graced with heavy double doors, which were blocked open with a granite rock. The greeter, not as stiff as the structure, asked their names and ushered them to a small space.

Fence's long legs assumed an awkward position on the short-seated pews with the uncomfortable backs. He sat arm to arm with Tia while Rose hugged his neck. The closeness comforted and unnerved them like opposite twins. From the outside, the building had appeared lifeless, but once inside, the crowd breathed more life than Tia was used to. Amidst the tightness, Fence leaned toward her ear in a deliberate move. "All makes and models come here. I guess the differences add depth."

The Memorial Day Service was unlike any other that they had ever attended. An American flag draped the altar communion table, resembling a covered coffin. A list of "Missing-in-Action" lay scrolled on top of the blue. Names of soldiers who died fighting for peace rested on the white stripe, while the list of war prisoners lay wrapped in red. The minister compared it with the need to remember Christ as the One who died for freedom.

"Freedom is never free," he reiterated. "Someone paid the price."

Fence's head touched hers with a short statement of explanation. "How a person dies reflects what he treasures."

"So does how he lives," Tia whispered back in irritation. She was thinking of Chance Cummings and the Latin cross encircling her neck, trying desperately to remember the best qualities of her daughter's father. She lifted her forefinger to Fence's shoulder, placing it under Rose's palm, letting her grip it tightly. Rose turned her head to Tia.

Does everyone have to bear a cross? Tia questioned herself. She turned the thoughts over before drifting back to the core of the message.

"Let's all join hands in silent prayer." The tall, stately, middle-aged minister spoke with assurance. "In closing, we'll unite in the Lord's prayer." Fence took Tia's hand in his like it belonged there. Something was happening on a deeper level. Neither of them could put their finger on it.

The organist played the closing song rigorously. All stood registering patriotic respect. "God Bless America. Land that I love." The song triggered thoughts in Fence. What had his father said? *Some memories last forever.* A memory was in progress, a good one, one that lived. He smelled Rose's head resting below his chin. He caught Tia's eye, winking an affirmation. "Sleeping?" he questioned. During the benediction, he continued to hold her hand like a safety pin. She did not pull away, nor did she look Fence's way.

"THE LORD BLESS YOU AND KEEP YOU, THE LORD MAKE HIS FACE SHINE UPON YOU AND BE GRACIOUS TO YOU, THE LORD TURN HIS FACE TOWARD YOU AND GIVE YOU PEACE," the minister pronounced. He held his right hand up and out, blessing the congregation.

Fence lifted her hand to his lips and kissed the top of it before releasing it. "Peace?" he whispered. Tia flushed, not knowing what to say.

"I have something to show you," he said. He drove in the opposite direction of the cabin. The old silver mining town sat tucked in the canyon, like a piece of jewelry. "There's a little shop down the street. It's over a hundred years old," Fence said.

Once inside, the historic items fascinated Tia. She held Rose's hand, trying to keep her from reaching the items. Fence busied himself visiting with someone he seemed to know. A native man had a long scar running down the side of his neck. Fence lifted his chin, motioning to her to come to him.

"I want you to meet Claude Walking Elk. We've been like brothers since we were very young. He's a silversmith and not bad if I do say so myself."

Tia wanted to say, *You don't look like brothers!* She held her tongue. She immediately liked the tall, brown-skinned man with the long, coal-black braid hanging down his back. Claude moved with a proud carriage, yet unpretentious and humble as he walked behind the glass case.

Fence addressed her by name, pulling her out of the observance of the quaint surrounding. "Tia, what do you think of these?" Rows of Montana silver rings were displayed next to rings made of gold from the Black Hills.

The awkward question took her by surprise. Struggling with what to think, her mouth would not open. She did not know whether her opinion counted. "They're nice," she answered cautiously.

Claude placed the tray of rings on the counter, questioning Fence with his eye. "You two need wedding rings? As your long time friend, I pick these. They are matching silver, braided with gold. Diamonds are embedded in the silver centers. Try them on?" He handed one to Fence. It was for a woman. "You two are married right? These handmade rings are my gift to you."

Fence and Tia stood before him. Rose hugged a leg of each of them. Their thoughts were jumbled. Tia's mouth dropped, half-open. The matching bands were crafted with incredible skill. "What do you think?" Fence repeated.

"You do not think. You receive." Claude put them both in Fence's hand.

Knowing it was rude to refuse a native gift of love, Fence's chin went down and up in a short acknowledging movement. "My brother, thank you."

Fence looked at Tia, scratching his head with a smile, "Looks like we have wedding rings. Will you let me put yours on you?" She lifted her hand to him, looking at her feet. Tears filled her eyes. Fence felt her softness, hoping she would not get emotional on him. Not that she ever had.

Claude tapped her on the shoulder. "Lady, put my brother's band on him."

Fence lifted his hand. Tia pushed it slowly on. His gray-green eyes misted over. *I must be nuts. This is only a façade of a marriage.* He reeled inside at the whole cover up.

Claude, out from behind the counter, stepped softly to the piles of Pendleton wool blankets, picking out a beautifully marked one. He approached Fence and Tia from behind, draping the blanket around their shoulders, wrapping them together. "It's the Indian way," he said. "You are one. One together under the shelter."

Tia felt her strength giving way. "I think I'm going to faint," she told Fence. She collapsed. He caught her in his arms before she hit the wood floor.

"Is she in a family way?" Tamsen Walking Elk called out, running to the rescue.

"No, she isn't." Fence answered a little too firmly, sounding crude.

Scooping Rose into her arms, Tamsen pressed her cheek to the little child. "It's okay baby."

"We need an emergency room. Are there any doctors around?" Fence asked with authority. Tia, wrapped in the blanket, heard nothing.

"Yesterday I saw that doctor fellow. He's a big surgeon in Minnesota now ... vacations here every year," Claude inserted with a calmness transcending knowledge.

I Don't Want to Lose You

DOCTOR Tello came to the mountains to get away from medical work. One look at Tia changed his mind. "She's bleeding internally. Lost a lot of blood. What's her blood type?"

"I don't know. I can give her blood if it's O-positive," Fence said.

The urgency set the doctor into motion, reopening, cleaning, cauterizing. An inflamed hernia had formed beneath the surface, along with a tearing of the uterine wall. The small clinic had only a couple of beds. Intravenous feeding was set up. Antibiotics were administered. Tia lay motionless.

"All right Mr. Carpenter. Your wife needs you. Her blood type is the same as yours." The doctor stepped toward Fence. "Are you all right?"

"No. I mean, yes. I need to make one phone call. I'll be right back." In automatic reflex Fence ran to the lobby pay phone. "Dad, will you come to the cabin? I'm at the old mountain clinic. I need your help. I have something to tell you. Bring my old handgun and shoulder holster. Thanks."

Two hours later, Mack and Marie Carpenter knocked on the clinic door, moments before midnight. "You're white as a ghost. What is it, son?" Alarm rang out in Mack Carpenter's expression.

Fence lowered his head, not to add color to his face, but intending to have a grip on his speech. "Thanks for coming. Would you be willing to take care of our baby Rose? Tamsen would take her but she had to work." Fence looked away and then down, agonizing in pain. He did not want it to show. "I can't go into detail. I'm sorry." He moved his feet back and forth. "I know I haven't been a very good son. I've made a lot of mistakes." He swallowed hard, trying to remain tough. With his parents, he realized that was futile. He had to be as honest as possible. He straightened his back. "I don't know what I'll do if anything else

70

happens. I was wrong not to confide in you, not to call. I've been a jerk. I'm not good at apologies." His emotions jolted out of control; or was it the fact that he had just given blood?

The thick frame of Mack Carpenter embraced Fence's belly to himself. He had not seen Fence since Lily's death. His broken son needed fixing, although ordinarily Fence was not one to admit it. The thought of denying love never occurred to Mack. "You're forgiven, son. Sure have missed you." He grinned. "Let me look you over. Still got guts I see."

Marie's mother-heart beat out of her chest. Fence was home again. "Our family is strong. It's a good place to heal and," she added, "to have a meal," Marie smiled at Fence, encouraging her son. Her instinct sill flagged trouble.

Mack and Marie Carpenter left later that night carrying a new bundle of joy and even greater love for their only blood-born son. Although questions lingered in the air, they chose not to dwell on them. More urgent matters concerned them, like caring for a granddaughter for the first time. The day proved to be more than memorable.

Tia came to, trembling. Her whole body shook. Feeling desperate, she tried to get her thought pattern back in order. Everything was in disarray. She heard a familiar voice by her bedside. Fence spoke with urgency to the nurse. "Would you get some hot blankets to lay over her and warm her up?" Tia felt him tucking them in around her with gentle, firm hands. Her body would not stop shaking. On the chair beside the bed was the Nez Percé wedding gift, the woolen blanket. Fence shook it out, and wrapped it around her. The warmth of the heavy wool settled Tia into sleep.

An hour later she called out, grasping at breaths, trying not to panic. "Where is my baby? Rose? Rose? Where is she?" she demanded with a voice of breaths.

"She's with my folks," Fence answered, grasping for a calming effect to quiet her.

Tia's face looked troubled. "Your folks? I don't know them."

"Just get well, Tia. Rose is fine. I'm staying with you." Fence had not forgotten how she had cared for him when he was sick, how kind she had been to him the day someone had tried to poison him. The sedative took hold. Tia faded.

"I want to be with her," he told the doctor repeatedly until he was released to be by her side. He took her cold hand and talked half to Tia, half to himself, dosing off and on. "Fight, Tia. We need you. Rose needs you. There are so many things you don't know about yourself." And then before he could retract his words he admitted, "I don't want to lose you."

Fence assisted Doctor Tello, not missing a step. Tia had never had anyone take personal care of her. From a little child, she had been alone at the orphanage. God was her friend. Now a man, who was bonded to her in word and in name only, leaned over her, watching her vital signs with surreal attention.

Fence encountered a different kind of pain, his own infirmity. Flashbacks of Lily flooded his brain. Panic made his heart beat spasmodically. Although Lily was dead, her memory penetrated him. He had never released Lily. He had not released himself. Fence tried to shake the fear of death off. It loomed over him. He struggled to stay alert, pulling his chair as close as possible. He cupped Tia's shoulder, holding it securely. His eyelids drooped. He slept with his head on the hospital bed.

Immediately he was in another world. No nightmares had plagued him since he had become "daddy" to little Rose. In his exhaustion and fear, he was pulled into the past. He spoke out loud. "Lily, you can't die. I love you Lily. There's a whole ocean to sail. Don't let your ship sink."

Lily whispered to him in his dream. "If I go to the bottom of the sea, God is there. If I climb to the mountain peak, He is there."

Then the nightmare resumed. *"I can't save you Lily. I can't even rescue you. I can't reach you. You're slipping away. Lily." He cried her name. He could do nothing on his own. He could not help her. He could not give her life. He was not in control. "God where are You?" The echo reverberated over and over again. There was no panacea, no strength, no remedy for ills, for problems, for death. Nothing and no one could help. The hurt went deep.*

"I love you more than life itself." He spoke out loud, condemning himself for not doing more, for not being more, for being so desperate, for failing.

A loud thunder crack, sending its strike, jolted him out of the horror. "That was close!" He looked out the window into the wooded area, keenly aware of the danger of fire. He had to keep better watch.

The blond-haired woman named Tia with the azure blue eyes awoke. Her hand lifted up, but she did not speak. Her body was warm.

I married her. What have I gotten myself into? How can I tell her? Will she understand? I think I'll always love Lily. Urgency faced him from all directions. *If it weren't for Rose... I had better take better care of them.* Fence put his holster harness on under his shirt. He secured it into position before getting a cup of coffee.

Not Here by Accident

THE intelligent doctor stipulated, "No risk-taking … okay? Just make sure she doesn't do any lifting. I'm putting her into your care. She's not out of the woods yet. No intimacy for a while."

Fence hoped Tia missed that remark. He signed the release papers with a quick scrawl and then reached to shake the doctor's hand. "I appreciate you taking time from your vacation."

"Certainly Mr. Carpenter. By the way, thanks for donating the blood for the transfusion. That saved me some trouble."

Tia took it all in, not understanding the last comment. *What was Doctor Tello saying? Did Fence give blood?* The idea of someone helping her without a self-centered motive rocked her thinking.

Fence bit his lower lip, touching his teeth with his tongue, anxious to change the subject. "Doctor? Claude and Tamsen Walking Elk have asked us to stop by their ranch. Do we have your permission?"

The youthful surgeon's eyes fell on the beautiful wife of Fence Carpenter, nodding. "As long as you don't get me out of bed. I'm meeting my fiancée tonight and we would prefer no interruptions. Besides, this small infirmary is not equipped to handle major operations."

"The blanket?" Tia remembered. "It's on the chair." Fence turned back, checking the room while Tia waited at the discharge door. He returned on the run. Relief swept over her. She was not alone. Fence lapped the blanket over her shoulders and began to push the well-oiled wheelchair to the burgundy van. Fresh air greeted Tia's nostrils, liberating her from sterile smells and white sheets. Fence stayed close by her side.

"You're going to be alright," Fence said, seeing the healthy color in her face. "Claude and Tam say that the best medicine is to hear the wind whistle by their open campfire."

The Walking Elk Ranch extended an openhearted welcome. A dog, half wolf, half German shepherd, ran to them. Fence bent down on his haunches to greet Gray Wolf with a friendly neck rub. The animal took ownership of him by licking his cheeks and hands, then by walking at his side. Fence and the dog guided Tia into the home. Tamsen came from the background, drying her hands with her apron. The tall hostess greeted them simply. "Come," she said. Her voice was filled with warmth.

Walking Elk hospitality permeated the room. Fragrant crabapple blossoms overflowed the clay vase in the center of a huge rough oak table, surrounded by an abundance of food. Fence bowed down to Tia's ear, speaking secretly. "They'll want you to try it all. Take little portions each time." Tia's stomach growled in anticipation, relieved to be free of intravenous feeding.

Claude tended fresh salmon on the grill behind the house. The aroma filled the air until the fish melted into their watering mouths. "This tastes …" Tia said, swallowing a mouthful.

Fence finished her sentence. "Out of this world." His rescue gave her a chance to drink the cherry juice. At the first private moment, he whispered, "It's improper to resist native kindness."

"But I … Fence, I wasn't." Tia said, starting to defend herself. "Where are the children? I miss Ro—" Claude's entrance interrupted her sentence.

"Follow me," Claude said, leading them outside to a teardrop fire-pit. It sunk into the earth a foot deep and was lined with rock. Claude built a teepee with kindling sticks over dry leaves. "The howling wind can't make up its mind tonight. The smoke blows every direction," he explained. They sat on stumps, watching the orange tongues lick the logs until they settled down, sleepy after the big meal.

When the wind died, Claude resumed speaking. "There is something about a fire that takes one back to the primitive roots of existence… to where all that matters is the warmth of family and shelter and where the next meal comes from." Rising up with his words, he motioned to Fence. "Come and see my new silver shop."

Tia tried not to feel abandoned when the men left. She did not want to be alone. Tamsen's keen senses picked up on Tia's uneasiness. She spoke out of instinct, moving closer to Fence's new wife. "Your little Rose was good for me. She sings all the time. You taught her well. There is no need to worry." Her statement of confidence possessed no doubt. She continued respectfully. "Fence has wonderful parents. They are full of kindness. They'll take good care of your little one. Rose went to them with no fear."

Tia listened, anxious to leave. The wearing of surgery depleted her strength. She felt empty, longing to hold her child. Her body stayed stationary. Her mind moved in and out. She stared straight ahead, trying to figure out the configuration of burning logs crumbling before her. Like looking at the clouds, she had no control of how they would shift together or dwindle.

"Trust ... takes the whole heart," Tamsen said. "Creation moves at the hand of the Creator." She stirred the coals. "We expect a child also ... after the harvest ... after Thanksgiving ... with the first snow." The coals flamed up again. "You and Fence must want a son too?"

A son! All I want is Rose. Tia held her tongue. The fact that Fence had hidden the truth of the marriage arrangement increased the awkwardness. Adjustment was proving more difficult by the minute. She summoned all the courage she could find. Interestingly, it came to her through the Indian woman.

"I will play the flute for you," Tamsen said. "Music brings health to the heart." Pressing the wooden instrument to her lips, she played the healing notes that flowed with the smooth tone of a dove.

Soothed by the cooing sound, Tia whispered, "That was beautiful. Thank you for all your kindness to me."

Tamsen laid the flute on Tia's lap. The woman who had just checked out of the hospital needed encouragement, needed a sister. Tamsen chose not to address the empty eyes. Instead she focused on the glowing coals.

Tia caressed the instrument, moving her finger in a circle ... touching the round openings. She blew out a deep breath, overcome with an unexplainable passion. It drew her fingers to another circle, the ring that represented an unusual marriage. A chill went through her. She moved closer to the pit to gather warmth.

Tamsen lifted her head to breathe the campfire smell, noticing Tia's despondence. "The wind whistles a song through the holes of the tree branch."

"This is my first time to the mountains," Tia said. She gave the limited information, changing the subject.

"You are not here by accident. You are a sign of peace. I'll tell you a true story about a woman who carried peace, who kept men from war," Tamsen began. "Long ago white men and an Indian woman came to our village to secure horses. The woman, Sacajawea, spoke our tongue. She carried her young son on her back. As a young girl, she had been stolen from us during a raid ... adopted by another tribe. When she returned to the land, she recognized the leader of our tribe, her blood brother who did not know her. She took her blanket, wrapped it around her brother, kissed him and revealed her identity. They wept. Much rejoicing took place. She loved our people, who were also her people."

Although Tamsen's historic tales were fascinating, Tia's mind continued to wander. Another Indian blanket cloaked her thoughts ... the one Claude Walking Elk wrapped around her and Fence the day she collapsed.

She struggled to sort out the present, trying to digest the whole evening. A whirlwind of events had transpired in a mere week. Watching the red coals, she remembered the strange name Fence called her in the recovery room. "Tamsen, who is Lily?"

"It is not my place to tell," she answered. Her loyalty spoke louder than her words. Tamsen's memories of Lily emerged out of the darkness, as if she were alive and present. Fence's first wife's influence had reached beyond the area, to the nations, across oceans. How well Tamsen remembered. Lily was not native, but she was. It haunted Tamsen. *Oh Lily. Your white moccasin feet dance on golden wings of wind in another land, free from bondage, free to be.* The mountain rose higher at the thought. "Her words still speak," Tamsen spoke out of the cloud. "Yesterday's wind is gone. Face today's wind with yesterday's wisdom."

"What did you say?" Tia asked.

"It was just the wind," Tamsen answered, cautious to speak more. Her black eyes turned away. She touched Tia's golden hair, understanding the state of confusion that she must be in. Seeing Fence's new wife in turmoil bothered Tamsen. She stuck a stick in the fire, stirring the coals. A wave of love swelled in Tamsen's heart for the woman who must have suffered much, who did not know about Lily. Tamsen had seen emptiness in Tia's ocean eyes. Yet, somehow, the blond-haired woman represented courage. Tia and Little Rose had brought Fence Carpenter out of his shell, to the country of the big sky, home to the mountains. Hope welled up in Tamsen. "Tia, we are your people now," she said with native authority.

Tia smiled and surprised Tamsen with a rare kind of humor. "Guess

I blew in with the wind."

Tamsen laughed. "I must go check my brothers," she said, leaving Tia on the stump alone. *Why are the men taking so long? What kind of trouble is Fence in?*

The Meaning of Silver

FENCE'S conversations with Claude Walking Elk had remained *still in time* since Abe's death. Fence had lost one close friend, Abe, and he was not going to jeopardize another. At least, not while he did undercover work investigating the mysterious incident. But being with Claude, face to face, stimulated nerve endings that had gone numb. He had closed Claude out, the man who called him brother.

"Silver, my brother," the artisan explained, showing Fence his work area, "is a very old metal, much harder than gold." Grunting, Claude lifted the strapped metal box to the chest-high workbench. "It weighs much." He made an affirmative gesture, opening the treasure. Layered on top of each other were a collection of books, not ordinary books, but those of a collector. The heavy-laden pages stuck together. Claude opened the first book, revealing rare silver dollars displayed in round impressions. Block printing identified the mint year beneath the circles of coin. "Ninety percent silver, ten percent copper." Claude mused. "Most came from the Butte mine ... made before 1965."

It was not the silver that captivated Fence, but the letters, AMP, etched on the interior of the box. "Are they yours?" Fence asked.

"As you see, they are not. They were left in my keeping until a certain date. His strict instructions came prior to his death. He said that right timing eventually releases truth."

Fence whistled. "I'm not sure what is going on, but this box should be in some kind of safe. Who knows about this?"

"Just the three of us."

The initials AMP did, in fact, stand for Abraham Maxwell Pearl, their mutual friend. "Claude? His death was ... ?" Fence asked.

Claude deliberately shook his head back and forth one time. "Not a suicide." Claude lifted the 1864 Liberty Head coin, the series of silver dollars first printed with *In God We Trust*. He flipped the coin over with a silversmith tool, revealing the symbol of freedom … the eagle. "Abe is free from pain. He would want justice." Claude replaced the lid, leaving Fence in wonderment. Fence continued to sort out factors in his head, lining up his thoughts.

Claude turned and pulled out little drawers of silver settings, the stock prepared for gem placement. From the bottom drawer his fingertips slipped out a silver ring, size fourteen, already set with an elk ivory. "This is for a man with big hands, for Mack Carpenter. The ivory tooth is from a big bull he shot with a bow. We hunted together last October." The skilled man placed the ring in Fence's hand. "Your father Mack is a great chief to our people. I don't say that lightly, for only one with greatness receives the title. He is like a father to me. Fence, give him the ring … a gift from me."

Fence had missed the hunting expedition. Mack had filled the gap. That was like his dad, friend and brother to the native people. Mack was the white man who Native Americans nicknamed *Half Breed*. The complimentary title expressed the awesome humor Fence grew up with. Mack's chest and arms suntanned, but his swimming legs remained white, half tanned. With the thought, Fence laughed inside like he had as a child. "You honor the Half Breed, crafting with great skill." Fence carefully examined the ring. He grinned while he listened with his head tilted to one side.

Claude laid out a thread of silver as fine as hair. "See the silver luster? The silver strand stands for wisdom of the old ones. Silver-haired elders speak little, but say much."

Fence picked up the strand. Claude always said more than what was in the line. Fence was not offended by Claude's example; yet, a flashback of Lily being at a campfire, a different place, a different time invaded his thoughts. Fence, sorting out the past and the present, consciously placed Lily's memory in the background, worrying that Tia was getting wind weary. Time ticked away. He did not want her left alone.

Claude's right middle finger touched the top of Fence's left hand. "Silver bands connect you and Tia." He pressed gently. "White men came to America with a silver tongue, not keeping covenants. Very persuasive, but not pure. Wise men hold to their word. They ring true like the clear musical sound of the silver tone. It is wise to ring true. A brave warrior wins the heart of a maiden's father."

"Claude, I tell you this in confidence. Tia is an orphan," Fence clarified. "There was no father or mother to talk to, if that's what you're getting at."

"I only say, silver medicine heals the heart. Laughter is good." Claude embedded the nuggets into Fence.

Meanwhile, Tia sat alone watching the dying embers, trying to put reoccurring memories of Chance Cummings out of her mind. Chance's relentless force still hovered over her. Clammy feelings swept in with the fog, chilling the night air, carrying haunting ghosts from the past. *Why couldn't he have loved me? It's almost like he comes alive and catches me unaware. Why am I afraid of a dead man?* She repressed the unpleasant thoughts. Pulling the Latin cross to her lips, she put her brain on hold, transfixed by the whitened coals.

Fence approached her from behind, seeing her silhouette with the firelight surrounding her. Unaware of his presence, she sat motionless, absorbed into the night. They were alone, guarding their hearts. "Are you all right?" Fence said. "Beautiful night, isn't it?" He wanted to put his hands on her shoulders. His feet stuck in old tracks until he nudged his legs to move near. He pulled a stump beside her, watching the fire burn low, hearing only the sound of stillness. He savored the moment, daring not to disturb the delicate peace that rested in their presence. So close, yet so far away, she absorbed in her own world and he in his. The new testing ground, like a thin ice crust, could not be walked on yet. The heavy weight of yesterday would sink today.

Tia pulled the blanket around her. The chill of the night fogged them in. Haze surrounded them. Creaking of the trees was the only sound. "It's time to go," Fence said. He reached his right hand out and pulled her up. When his fingers touched her ring, Claude's stark words surfaced, reminding Fence of the deception. He had stepped into a trap of his own making. He had pulled Tia into it with him. He caught the blanket and wrapped it tightly about her, putting his arm around her back with Tia's long blond hair caught beneath it.

Fence helped her into the van. Her downcast stare alarmed him. He took the back of his right thumb and impulsively ran it down her jaw line, lifting her chin until her eyes met his. "I like you," he said.

She was crying. He did not want to hurt her. She had been hurt enough.

Legal Consultation

MR. Tuffty walked back and forth on the well-worn Oriental rug that adorned the wood floors of his Florida law office. He pressed out each problem at a measured pace, unaware that Miss Tia Bain sat beside a fire pit twenty-five hundred miles away, or that she was now Mrs. Fence Carpenter. The methodical lawyer had packed his pipe the same way for fifty-five of his seventy years. He was not about to change. However, he had learned the hard way that change is sometimes necessary. Few will pay the cost of the will. He shut the heavy walnut door behind him, glancing at the spectacle rims of his partner in law. "So, what would you advise, Mr. President? I know. You would send her to the Badlands to recuperate, to escape this complicated situation. You always did have big dreams. Do I have to hire an investigator to find her?"

Theodore Roosevelt's picture focused on the pursuit. There was no doubt that Old Four Eyes had keen insight as well as foresight. Otherwise the roughrider would not have hunted lions in Africa. Arnold Tuffty admired his courageous law partner, consulting with him on every case for years and of course, Teddy's rebuttal most always agreed with his. Arnold and the President met eye to eye. Counsel Tuffty directed the discussion. The picture had become his most trusted confidant. "You think we have trouble, don't you?"

Mr. Tuffty continued speaking to the air, sorting the mail into the pigeonholes of the other desk. "All documents must have a home," he interjected. "Back to the case, my friend." Arnold's head popped up. "Sister Maria Thomas recently brought Miss Bain to my attention, as did an old crony, a pillar of the bar, a trusted protégé who has stood time's test. Still living of course." For a moment his mind was in another place until he caught the eyes on the picture.

"Your frame is crooked, Theodore. I'll have to straighten you out.

Guess I must have bumped you." Mr. Tuffty took great pleasure in adjusting the cockeyed picture. "So, my friend, champion of justice that you are, mighty warrior of conservation." He addressed the President once again. "Were you aware of the young woman's plight? I didn't think so. She's in grave danger. Sir, I do believe you and I have been in the dark on this one." The noble painting stared at him in agreement.

Laying Low

PITCH black surrounded Fence and Tia. The cabin light was not on. "Wait in the van," he ordered her. "Lock the doors and get down on the floor boards. Please do as I say. Don't panic. Somebody has been watching us."

Incredulous, Tia obeyed, thinking she really was in the dark.

"You have to trust me. Tia, do you hear me?" he reiterated with authoritative eyes.

"Yes." She pushed down a gasp. "I know how to use a gun. Chance taught me."

"Who is Chance?" Fence questioned with his analytic curiosity.

"Rose's birth father." Tia was shaking, not from fear, but from the thought of Rose's conception.

"Oh," Fence spoke with a letdown in his voice. He was mystified by her disclosure. He lifted her chin again. "We have to talk—later."

Approaching the cabin from the side, Fence looked for tracks or anything unusual. His thoughts scrambled. *Where is Rose? Where are my folks? This is not like them,* he deliberated, stepping into every crevice he remembered from childhood. The detective words of his eccentric grandfather surfaced. *Shadows are not always gray.*

The lifeless cabin blended into the woods. Tracks showed that his parents' pickup had been there. Inside he found Tia's meager clothing strewn around, the bedding torn apart. Grabbing what he could, Fence looked up at the skylights. *Now this is not like Dad. He would leave a sign or signal.*

The dusty ash pail sat on top of granite stones near the wood stove. A small paper bag, pancaked beneath, poked its pointed tip out—not the usual method his dad used for messages. Dust flew as Fence pulled it out. The note was scribbled in red crayon. Fence did a quick read and pocketed it. The need to hurry crowded him.

Fence would report the break-in later. Vandalism of unused cabins happened occasionally. Local authorities prioritized offences as to their seriousness. Nothing appeared to be missing or damaged, except the front door lock. *I can't afford to get into a long explanation. The implications will only confuse them if there's no other evidence for me to give, and too much is at stake.* Rose and her mother were foremost on his mind.

Fence secured the door with two old padlocks that he had found hidden in a cowhide boot inside the cabin. Quickly, he sealed the place up. Sneaking back to the van with light-footed steps, his vigilance heightened.

Tia's heart pounded in her throat, hammering an unwelcome fear into the pit of her stomach. She feared for him, not herself. He seemed to know what he was doing. Yet, there was a strangeness about him.

She tried to put two and two together. *Is he really an engineer? I called his workplace. How did I get mixed up with such a character?* Tia reflected, trying to get comfortable in the cramped position. She held her head in her hands. *Someone followed us for a long time when I was driving. Is that why he cautioned me at the cemetery? And why did he trade in the station wagon and purchase the van? I've been so preoccupied with Rose these past months. Rose!*

Tia jerked at a sudden knock on the window. Her feet collided with the Florida license plates lying discarded on the van floor, the ones Fence had removed from the station wagon.

"Open up, it's me Fence."

Tia told her body to obey.

"We're not staying here tonight," he said. She unlocked the door. "Someone has ransacked the cabin. Tia, did you have anything important in those plastic bags?" He threw the retrieved items in the back seat.

"I only have one thing of importance. That's in my pocket," she said boldly.

Fence did not pry any more. Circling around, he jumped into the driver seat of the van, locking the door behind him. His mind was on survival.

She grasped his arm, unable to hide her alarm. "Rose?"

Starting the engine, he handed her the sign language note. "It's from my Dad. She's safe. See the wild prairie rose with a smile. Those points must be mountains. Dad would never leave a post unless he was getting someone to safety."

Tia's hands shook. She tried to focus on the code.

"Are you okay?" he asked with his protective voice.

She nodded.

"Let's get out of here. There's no way we can reach my parents' ranch tonight. I have an idea."

Fence took a rough back trail to the highway, hoping the van's high center of gravity wouldn't be a problem on the uneven road. "You have to get some rest or I'll be in big trouble with Doctor Tello. I gave my word. Guess I haven't been very sensitive dragging you around the country."

Tia was too tired to speak or bombard him with questions.

Fence pulled onto an approach to fix the van's back cushions into a temporary bed. "Rest here," he instructed. Tia curled up in fetal position. Her eyes, heavy with the day, closed in exhaustion. Fence shook his head. *What am I going to do with her?*

Truth Revealed

FENCE beat on a large wooden door. "Charlie. It's Fence Carpenter. I need a bed." The bed-and-breakfast lacked winter customers— too late in the season. The white gold had melted off the slopes. Only sparse snow remained. Summer visitors would wait another week into June for the chill to die off.

The bed-and-breakfast tender growled like a grizzly, slapping Fence on the back. His French Canadian brogue graveled out a greeting. "That's what I'm here for." He stood back with his belly bulging out his white undershirt. "See you finally remembered an old friend."

"Charlie, I'm here on business, similar to the kind I've had before. I need my van to vanish from sight for a couple days. Got a spot?" Fence raised an eyebrow with an inquisitive trust in the burley man with the big heart.

"What's goin' on? It can't be that bad." The man chuckled in jolly humor with a comforting undertone.

"I'm not here if anyone inquires. And," he added, "There will be two of us for breakfast tomorrow." Fence made an intriguing expression with his face. "I think."

Charlie had looked out for him before. He scratched the mixed multitude of whiskers. His gray-blue eyes squinted with a knowing look. "I'll be closed for business until you leave. How's that for hospitality?"

"Great. Where to?" Fence asked. Charlie pointed upward with his head.

Fence carried Tia, wrapped in the native blanket, to the highest bedroom in the old log building. He dropped himself on top of the spread beside her with uneasiness. His brain worked overtime.

Impatience ruled. He slipped down to the large kitchen. Charlie had left a note in the coffee filter.

I'll be on watch.
Loft over garage.
Make yourself at home.
From the Eagle's Nest,
Big C

Fence clattered and clanged around, making more noise than he intended. Tia stood in the doorway behind him with her hair pulled around to one side and tied together, watching his back. Before she could speak, he sensed a presence in the room. He drew his handgun in a flash. He jumped three feet to the side in a crouched position. He gasped. "Tia! Do you want to get yourself killed?" Harshness shot out of his mouth.

Tia hit the floor. "Fence!" Her hands went to her mouth blocking a shriek.

In a second he flew to her, helping her up. "Don't ever come up on me like that, please. I could have killed you. Do you know how close I came to firing the pistol?" Fence fired the words instead.

His immediate anger pierced Tia like a knife. Tears ran down her cheeks in windfalls. Her attempt to hold them back failed. Catching a breath between the sobs, she defended herself. "I'm sorry. I woke up alone. I had no clue where I was. I followed the noise down here."

"It's okay Tia. Don't cry, please." He took the side of his arm and tried to wipe her face.

"I have a handkerchief." She pushed him away, pulling it out from under her buttoned top. She carried it near her heart.

Fence watched her, noticing the affection she had for the inanimate object. He pulled out a wooden chair for her. "Are you hungry?" he asked, trying to take the edge off.

Tia bit her lower lip. Taking a deep breath, she laid the handkerchief on the table. She had a large lump in her throat. "No, just confused."

Fence set the coffee on the table, making small talk. "Needs real cream and sugar," he hedged.

Tia cleared her throat, staring at him with large eyes. "Fence, what's going on? Where is Rose? Why are you whisking me away? Why are you carrying a gun?" Questions fell out of her mouth like a waterfall. She spoke adamantly, determined to understand the man in front of her.

"Wait a minute," Fence interrupted. "Only one at a time." He picked up the hanky and held it up with care. "What can you tell me about this? I think this is what they were looking for at the cabin. Tia, your life is in danger. I've known it for some time now." He studied the hanky, not looking at her.

"But why? I have nothing, nothing but Rose. Right now I don't even have her." She was bewildered. "Fence, orphans don't have anything but each other."

Fence wanted to break it to her gently, but was having little success. "Tiara," Fence stopped short, noticing a weaving on the hanky, not realizing that he called her by her real name. "Take a look at this!"

"I have it memorized." She burst inside at his audacity. He totally ignored her question. *Do I trust him or not? He is totally confusing.* Redirecting the conversation, she was unyielding. "Where did you get the name Tiara?" she demanded.

Fence fidgeted with the mug, not intending to give her any more information than necessary. "I have a confession to make. Well, I guess I have more than one confession to make. I'll probably be trying to explain this for the rest of my life." He pushed his hair back with his hand. "I'm involved in more than just medical or engineering operations. That's one of the reasons why I didn't want to get into a legal battle over Rose. It involves security and information."

"Are you telling me you're a spy? Well, what are you doing with me?" she demanded, thinking of the mysteries in his library, stuck in between CS Lewis and Robert Louis Stevenson. She was beginning to feel like a character in one of the novels.

"I don't know. I'm not sure why I came up with such a crazy idea. I got involved with you by accident. That's a pun if I have to say so myself." Fence tried to insert a semi-smile, but thought better of it. "I had no clue who you were or that you were the heir to a fortune."

"You don't know? What? What are you talking about? Answer my question. Why did you call me Tiara?" she persisted.

"Because that's what Doc Bridger told me. Now that is confidential, between him and us, okay?" Fence's voice was stiff.

"I think my head is spinning. I suppose you know my middle name is Rose too." There was fight in her and Fence liked it.

"No, you're one up on me there." He paused with a sparkle in his eyes. "It's Tia Rose, is it? Nice name," he gently teased her.

She tried to read his eyes. "Well, Mr. Fence Carpenter, is that your real name or did I marry a man with a fictitious name? How do I fit into the picture anyway? Is Rose's adoption on the up and up?" Her mind was a racetrack. *I think I've been reading too many books or maybe*

I shouldn't be reading any. My life seems to be writing a book of its own.

"Are you telling the truth or making up a story?" Tia asked with resolve.

"I like it when you smile, and yes, that is my given name, by my folks that is." He got up and started opening cupboard doors. "I'm hungry for popcorn."

"That's one way to change the subject," Tia said. Fence's glint of humor had caught her off guard. She did not know this man. Ironically, his altered disposition drew her closer to him, like a magnet, into his protection. All five feet of her stood. "I'm going to bed," she declared.

Fence picked up the handkerchief. "I'd like to keep this until morning."

She gave him a look with reluctance written all over it.

He relinquished with a half smile. "All right. It's the only thing you have." He placed it in her hand.

It was 5:00 a.m. before Fence climbed the steps to the top loft. The hanky lay on his pillow with a brief note.

MAKING PEACE. Until tomorrow, Tia Rose.

It reminded him of the one word Christmas card she had given him. He still did not understand it. *So her middle name is Rose.* He removed his gun belt, laying it on the bed stand. Impulsively he pulled the white treasured cloth to his nose, smelling its age and feminine ownership. His deep thinking attempted to decipher the situation with little success. He flatly placed the square on top of the old brandished weapon, along with her miniature message. He stopped, observing her sound sleep, sorting out his crowded thoughts.

For a little woman, you sure have dogged determination—more spunk than I expected. Her long eyelashes curled naturally, like her waved hair. Whether out of mischief or sheer impulse, he leaned over and lightly kissed her on the lips, breathing softness. "Peace to you too, Tia Rose."

Searching His Pockets

TIA, determined to investigate on her own, awakened early. Fence was zonked, totally oblivious to her. The hanky covered the pistol in an ark-like fashion giving her comfort. She read the bed-and-breakfast brochure, studying the maps and exploring the place in a discreet manner, considering details piece by piece.

Hatred causes one to see every flaw. From the time she was a small girl she knew the importance of love, of seeing the best in people, of trust. The choice, though difficult, gave her reason to live. And yet, the times of broken sticks of trust were many. *Fence, what is with you? You're dangerous.*

She searched his pockets, but knew what he was hiding was not on the outside. The dark, deep interior of his heart held an element of intrigue for experts at secrets. *Is this what it's like to explore a forest's unending mysteries?* she questioned.

The bed-and-breakfast provided heavy bathrobes. Spare swimsuits lined the hall closet complete with hot tub instructions. She had never been in one. No one was around. She stretched downward, tenaciously trying to take the cover off in the hazardous surroundings. The doctor's lifting instructions weighed heavily on her shoulders.

The heavy-duty planked deck surrounded by towering evergreens gave an open-armed invitation. The boards muffled the sound of Fence's approach. "I'll do that."

Tia dropped the board, backing up, embarrassed by his intrusion. His rugged and hard-muscled limbs lifted the cover with ease in a crane-like maneuver. She waited for him to scold her.

He acted like nothing was wrong, commenting with care. "The hot water should help heal your incision. Did you have trouble getting that suit on?"

"A little," she said with modest shyness, wanting to sink beneath her feet. "Why do you follow me around? You're smothering me."

"It's my job watching you." Fence followed her into the water.

"Your job! What other excuses do you have?" she retorted.

"Well, I'm married to you, right? I keep my commitments. Besides, that tall black man told me not to let you out of my sight," he answered from the opposite side.

"What black man?"

"Barabbas … Barbados … I don't know his name; made that one up. The one who tried to stop you from running into the jackknifed semi." He watched her mouth drop open. "He said the so-called accident was a setup to get you out of the way. I'm not the one trapping you." Her scrapping mood had activated Fence. "Sometimes you can be a little spitfire."

She added, goading his curiosity, "Good thing, or I wouldn't be alive!" Tia tried to relax, but Fence did not make it easy. She thought out loud. "I could only see the whites of his eyes. He wore a white hat. I was going too fast." She looked at Fence. The vivid sight of the fearful black face and the waving long arms flashed before her. Her body shook; her blue eyes rounded. "How did you find him anyway?" she asked.

"He found me! Like you found me. I don't know. You brought a lot of baggage with you that you don't know about. He said he was the one who left you at the orphanage." Fence disclosed the news, waiting for a reaction. The rose on her cheeks showed. She plunged into deep thinking.

"I don't think they like me either," he said. Fence dunked his blond head under the bubbling water, popping back out. "I never had someone try to poison me before."

Tia's face gave him a puzzled look. Fence had decided in advance to solve the riddle. "When I was so sick in January? Doc Bridger checked me out. That was the only explanation he could come up with. So your doctoring saved my life." Fence flicked water on her.

Ignoring the gesture, she laid her head back, looking at the pine branches. "This can't be real."

Observant of her discomfort, Fence mellowed. "They smell good don't they?" Nodding, Tia relaxed. She did not want to talk anymore. Her mind needed to process what she had heard. She kept her distance.

"We're going to the ranch. There's been a change of plans." Fence told her two days later.

Will I ever become accustomed to his constant changes? She questioned, "What ranch?"

Meeting the Carpenters

MARIE Carpenter, looking younger than her years, sat in the old-fashioned wooden rocker. Her dark skin and high cheekbones enhanced her beauty. Rose slept cradled in her lap. She said softly, "We left the cabin just in time. Do you think Fence found the clue?"

"No doubt in my mind. He's a Carpenter. He has that trained eye. He'll be on the lookout. He probably stopped at Charlie's." He pulled back the lace curtain over the sink. "A van is coming up the trail. It's them." Mack opened the door displaying a warmhearted smile.

"Thanks Dad," Fence said, appreciating the receptivity of the man he greatly admired. Tia's whole body felt the welcome. "Tia, please meet my mother and father, Marie Deer Path and Mackabee Carpenter."

The muscled hand stretched out to Tia, shaking hers with the strength of a lion and gentleness of a lamb. "Call me Mack." In a loving gesture he helped remove her jacket, throwing it three feet to catch the wooden hook. Reaching out with his hardy arms, he placed both his hands on her shoulders, looked her straight in the eyes and said, "Welcome Tia. Welcome to our family." He winked at Fence with a mischievous look and added, "She's a beauty, Fence."

Fence thought his dad was going overboard, examining her like one of his prize livestock. Tia blushed, unable to resist Mack's acceptance. Marie rose up, graceful as a doe, moving toward Tia. Embracing her with great expression and sincerity, she whispered in Tia's ear, "Thank you for bringing Fence home and for giving us such a perfect granddaughter. We be friends." Her native blood slipped out in her speech.

No, Fence does not look like his mother. Marie's wholesomeness reminded Tia of a tall tree. *She's unusual to say the least. I must be dreaming.* She smiled as the thought crossed her mind. *She is someone out of time, out of history.*

Anxious to see Rose, Tia knelt to the floor, meeting Fence face to face. She whispered to him, "I need to hold Rose." Grasping her child, she pulled her close. "Rose, I missed you so much. Mommy loves you."

"So, you found your way home," Mack addressed Fence as he stood up. "Figured you would eventually know that the two mountains meant the M / M Ranch. Marie and I had a strange sensation at the cabin. Decided to get out of there. I brought the rifles home and the archery equipment. I know it's none of my business, but we're blood, and I'll back you all the way." Mack chewed on a piece of buffalo jerky, swallowing before continuing. "What's the scoop? What do you want me to do?" He held up the jerky. "Want one?"

"Help us relax for one night," Fence said. "We've had an incredible week." He pulled his dad to the side. "What do you think of this?" Fence handed him the linen handkerchief. Seeing the seriousness of the situation, Mack entered the great room, flipping the light on.

"This is quite unusual. It definitely represents a family, maybe in a different country. Let me think about it tonight. Any prints?"

"If there were, they're long gone." Fence gave Mack little information, returning the folded handkerchief to his back pocket.

True to form, Mack grilled buffalo burgers. The outdoor brick fireplace steamed with heat. Rose hung on to Tia and Fence, going back and forth. Fence's parents were as different as night and day. Mack had an attractive sparkle in his eye; Marie had an appealing inner laughter.

Tia, drained of energy, leaned against the house. It did not escape Fence's attention. He went to her, putting his hand on the wall over her. "Tia, it's time for bed."

"See you in the morning," Mack chimed in. With a fatherly knowing, he patted Fence on the side of his arm.

"Say, Dad." Fence pulled the ring out of his pocket and handed it over. "Claude said you would know what this is all about. You know him; he has a little silver for everyone. Said it's from the hunt last fall."

Mack slipped it on, grinning. "Perfect fit. Memories," Mack said, examining the elk tooth bud. "Those at the edge of the wilderness I never forget."

Fence bent down, kissing his mom on the cheek. "Nite Mom and thanks."

Tia's clothes, washed and clean, were stacked on a hand-carved pine dresser in the guestroom. "Your parents are kind. I've never met anyone like them." Tia laid her hand on the folded clothes, watching. Fence laid Rose in the middle of the opened bed. Soft cream sheets smelled like fresh air.

"Tia, sit on the bed with me please. I have something to tell you." He hesitated. "Mom and Dad think Rose is mine."

"She is yours," Tia replied.

His face was hot. "They think I'm Rose's father," he continued.

"You are her father," Tia answered.

"No Tia, they think we had Rose together. And I didn't try to change their minds."

"Oh," she said in final awareness. "Is that why you married me, for impression? Or was it to inherit a fortune?" She felt cold, knowing she sounded sarcastic.

"I was wrong, Tia. I didn't mean to hurt you." A desire to take her in his arms came over him. Whether out of a need to be right or a desire to be kind, he sensed Tia's reserve and resisted his impulse. He handed her the clean nightgown, contemplating, *Things will be better in the morning. They have to be. I need some perspective.* He walked to the door. "When you're ready I'll dress the wound. I need to check it." The emergency medical training in him was almost more than either of them could handle. He left the room. How could he be investigating and protecting her at the same time? Conviction pierced him. They balanced on different wavelengths.

Tia regretted her sharp words. She had pierced Fence with bitter rejection. After all, he had been kind to her. The tables turned, melting her. She ached for him, for herself. *Whose grave did he visit? Is he just being protective again? Why his strange disposition? Who is Lily? What sort of situation have I put him in?* Her mind reeled with questions.

Thunder rumbled. Rose tugged on the Latin cross. "Mine?" she asked.

"Yours, sweetheart," Tia said, placing it in Rose's hand.

Another storm stirred. Fence returned heavy of heart. He disarmed himself, laying the handgun on the guest dresser near the clean clothes. He sank into bed, miles from them. Tia punished herself for not listening, for not hearing him out, for her shortness. She reached across Rose's little form and touched his bare shoulder, whispering softly, "Fence, I reacted. Please forgive me."

He said as a broken man, "I deserved it."

She shivered. "Will you hold me?" She started to weep a silent cry. Her face, her hair, her pillow were wet with tears. They kept coming like soft rain, the tension letting down. With extreme gentleness, Fence held her close to him. He kissed her hair. She lay limp in his arms. "I like you Fence," she struggled to say, drifting off to sleep.

He thought he heard her.

Assessment

A T dawn Mack and Marie walked together, watching the early birds, taking in the cedar smells after the fresh rain. The aroma revitalized them. Bold morning sunrays warmed their faces. They stepped with care on the rocks, avoiding the slippery clay places. "The eagle mates for life," Marie commented.

"It's up there." Mack said, pointing toward the cliff. "Fence wouldn't leave Tia's side. I don't understand what's going on. Whatever it is, I'm glad he's home." Mack's mind raced a mile a minute. Aspens brushed shoulders with him.

"A long four years. Hard on a mother's heart," Marie said.

"Fence called in time of need. He's been through more than we know. I think Abe's death took a bigger toll on him than we thought. I'm surprised he has a wife and child. I think he loves her, Marie. Maybe she's not like Lily. He's trying to come to terms with it. I don't think he's locked talons with her. He will, sure as the eagle." Mack took a deep breath.

"Maybe he hasn't. It is not our problem. Mack, he's like you and your father Reed. More so than you like to admit. He won't quit until he has every last puzzle piece in place, a complete composite." She leaned against a lodgepole pine.

Mack surveyed her. "What are you thinking?"

"Something is not right. I dreamt there was a fight over Prairie Rose Flower," Marie relayed her dream. "There's turbulence in the air."

Mack took Marie's hand. "Lady Deer Path, we trusted him this far. It won't do to stop now."

"I wonder what your dad would advise," Marie said, lost in thought.

"No doubt, he would give us white-haired wisdom, he and old Doc Bridger. Probably more than we want." Mack smiled. "He probably knows more than we do already. That wouldn't surprise me."

The couple headed home, stopping to check the ravine for June berries, finding them too green to pick.

"Gam, Gam." Rose slid off the bedside, waddling to the door. She heard them coming.

Marie smiled at Fence. "I'll take her. When have you gotten a good night sleep?"

"It's been a while," he answered, noticing the plaque on the mantle.

Home is where the heart is.

Fence thought it hung in a fitting place, above the fireplace. He popped a kiss on Rose's cheek, placing her into her grandmother's arms.

Reluctant, Fence crawled in beside Tia. He leaned on his elbow with his hand under his chin. Out of convenience and grief, he had chosen her. She fit in with the assignment. Now she was the assignment. Out of duty he stayed committed. But now he cared, really cared. Her face shone with peace. She slept, exhausted after the week's ordeal. *Perhaps Dad is right.* He closed his eyes. *What had she been through?* His medical training kept him alert. He guarded her in his sleep.

Less than two hours away, Fence's grandfather, Reed Carpenter, rested his elbow against the wingback chair, dialing the old phone. "Hello Clem, returning your call. I suppose you think I need an examination." His smile lines creased inward and upward with the thought of playful mischief.

Holding the phone with his chin, Dr. Clem Bridger removed his white medical jacket as he spoke. "Of course I do. Pretty hard to do that over the phone."

"All right, all right Clem. Don't keep me in suspense! What's the diagnosis?"

"Well, for an old friend, you're not too bad. I'm coming your way. Met your grandson Fence not long ago. We had quite an interesting conversation. Trouble is on his heels. Came in to see me with a bad case of poisoning. He's a Carpenter all right. Reed, I think he's following in your tracks."

"You think so, huh? He'll have to grow a couple inches." Reed's curiosity was getting the best of him. "All right. Come on out. Fly to the capitol. Better connections."

Doc sorted through the mountain of paper on his desk with his thoughts caught in the middle of the heap. *I need to get to the bottom of this!*

Stolen Information

A red half-ton pickup approached the cabin with road dust kicking up from its mud-flapping wheels. The man in it was on a mission. The files clenched in his hand were stolen from the hospital records department. His false ID sat on the black dashboard. His heavy foot lavished in the no-speed-limit state.

He felt good about his risky detective tactics and his ingenuity. He had taken a chance that there could only be one T.R. Bain. By a stroke of luck, he had overheard a call requesting info on Miss Bain for emergency reasons. The foolish nurse left a trail a mile wide. He had stood out of sight, not wanting anyone to know he was lurking. "The blond wig and mustache fooled them. Didn't think I'd remember how to walk stooped like that." It had taken all his effort to make his legs not reveal their true colors. "I was in the right place at the right time." He stroked his upper lip.

I'll shock her. Shouldn't be too big of a problem. He strutted beside the vehicle, flaunting his arrogance. *I pulled off a good one this time.*

Thoughts flew around in his head with precision. *I'll have to remember to thank Major Merdone for helping me get back into the country, although he is a wretch of a man. Even with his prestigious connections I have to be leery of him. He oversteps his bounds whenever he gets an open door. Someday his own mouth will swallow him alive, although I've got enough dirt to pull his buttons off. He'd be in the brig faster than a jet takes off.*

He puffed himself up in the forbidden knowledge as he swallowed two "no dose" tablets. *When the dust settles, I'll have a beer.* His obsessive thirst spoke. Glancing at the empty gas gauge, he grumbled, "Never thought I'd have to drive twenty-five hundred miles when I could be flying my own plane."

Rebellion was a hidden nature he masked in disguise. Suppressing it had become a method of survival. He liked doing things alone without hovering shadows, resenting anyone who looked over his shoulder. He submitted partially to conditions, of course. He would never let on. He was good at playing the game.

He refueled. He pursued T.R. with a distorted passion, like a hound after a downed pheasant. His secret schemes brewed. He sped on. The highway glared before him like a mirage. Socked in his pride, he exaggerated the power and prestige of his newest mission. The fact that he was merely a pawn being moved by evil did not cross his mind. The cash token was only a taste of what they offered. He gloated in the thought, basking in vacation promises of island sun. *Montego Bay, I can see it now.*

His hair, the color of midnight, was shaggier than his former clean-cut military look. He did not miss the head shaves. In a little over a week his black beard grew itchy, but developed nicely. The wig was balled up on the floor beneath the stick gearshift, too hot to wear, and now he may not need it. He had ripped off the mustache early on. His nose was set to sniff out T.R. Bain.

The girl had been a naïve pigeon, an easy mark. This would be no different. *It was in the cards.* He pictured himself trumping an ace of hearts with the deuce of spades.

Unbelievable that she didn't die the first time around. He pushed on, kicking any thought of failure out of his troubled mind. The top dog said the scraggly girl and her child were invaluable.

The miserly mountain town gave him no information. "A little research will remedy that." Detours did not shake him. He scouted local shops, eavesdropping wherever he entered. By a slim chance, he overheard a man talking to an Indian about taking a patient to the Carpenter cabin to recuperate. He would just ask directions from that overzealous teenager working at the gas station at the end of town. He learned more than he intended from the liberal kid. *He'd never make it in the military.*

There was no one at the cabin. He searched it from head to toe. "Nothing here of any value." He scoffed at the deserted building. "Oh well, I have another lead."

The Fight

MACK heard an engine barrel around the curve heading straight toward the M / M Ranch. A tall, raven-haired man jumped down from the new red pickup, staring around. No detail seemed to escape the shrewd hawk eyes. The man moved forward with proud shoulders taking turns pushing each other. Mack's keen insight to the character of people sent red alert signals into the air. Observing the man's demeanor, he motioned to Marie, remembering her warning dream. Carpenter men were protectors.

Rose sat quietly eating strawberries in her highchair. A painting of a robin singing in a snowstorm hung on the wall behind her.

The insightful stranger stalked toward the doorway with authority. Sky, Mack's furry Norwegian elkhound, stood her ground like a sentry. She guarded the entry post, growling with a deep bass sound as the intruder approached. Mack opened the big ranch door, harnessing its frame around his square shoulders. He spoke to the watchdog. "Sky, be still." Before the stranger could speak, Mack Carpenter threw out the first words. "Howdy. What can I do for you?"

The confident man came to an abrupt halt, taken back by the authoritative figure. No welcoming hand greeted him. He answered carefully, trying to be tactful, testing the waters. It was obvious the dog was not his friend. "Is this the Carpenter Ranch? I'm looking for a Miss T.R. Bain, my fiancée. I heard I could find her here." He lied for leverage. His eyes nosed around, catching a glimpse of the highchair with the singing baby. It was an obvious move. His uncanny luck had brought him this far. He was in a pushing mode. He quickly threw caution to the wind. His jaw was down. "Where is she?"

"We don't know a T.R. Bain. Our son and daughter-in-law are the only ones here." Mack laid out the facts.

"Whose baby?" The strange man pressed.

"She's mine." Fence came out of the back room with his blue jeans on and his chest bare. "Dad, I'll handle this."

Jarred out of her sleep by the commotion, Tia pulled herself to a sitting position. The hair on her arms stood on end. The stranger's voice sounded familiar. *Is my mind playing tricks on me?* She tried to kill her fears with darts of courage. *He can't be— He can't be alive!* She tied her robe at the waist. Impulse took over. She slipped Fence's pistol into her pocket. Stepping into the family room, she stopped short.

Mack stood with his hands on his hips and leg cocked to the side. He had no intention of missing anything. Marie laid down her dishtowel by the kitchen sink. Sky's ears lay back. The dog awaited Mack's command. Nearby Fence Carpenter stood in an unprecedented stance. The two Carpenter pillars formed a hedge in front of Tia. She moved so she could see. Her shaking hands crossed over her heart. A stunned look covered her face, trapping her in acknowledgment. She tried to speak. "I— I— thought..." She stopped mid-sentence, staring at the man halted in the doorway.

The stranger saw her and said through them all, "You thought I was dead. Well, I'm not. I'm alive and well. Now, get your things T.R." He issued the ultimatum. "You're coming with me. Orders from headquarters." He lied with ease, advancing toward her. Confusion and fear gripped her throat.

Fence quickly stepped in front of the crazed man, intending to terminate the militant march. "I don't know who you are, mister, but rank or no rank, this is my wife and you have no authority over her. I say get your hide out of here or I'll tan it!"

The man coolly sidestepped toward Rose, pointing. "That baby goes with me!" The invader's eyes blazed with fire. "She's mine! My heir! My daughter!" he threatened, heading straight for the child.

"Keep your filthy hands off her!" Fence hollered. He had no intention of letting the stranger invade his daughter's life. No way would Fence let him touch her. Moving between Rose and the stranger, Fence shoved the man's shoulders with both hands. "Get out of here." The man's brakes stopped him from stumbling backwards.

It was Tia's turn. She stepped ahead, in front of Fence, taking charge of the situation before anyone could move or speak. "She is not yours! This is my husband," she declared, grasping Fence's arm, releasing it quickly and placing her hand on Rose. "This is my daughter through marriage. I will not have her torn apart. You have no right!" Tia's thoughts ran wild. *This can't be happening!*

She held her own ground and Fence noticed. Tia blasted the intruder with her directness. "Why now? We don't belong to you! You don't own us! You go around raping women and then claiming their children. You command them to get rid of their babies. You take life into your own hands! You let everyone believe you're dead and suddenly you show up alive. And now, you want to claim my baby?" She stopped abruptly in her tracks and bit her tongue, holding it between her teeth. She had cut him below the belt.

The man glared at Tia in a full armor of anger. He should have known she'd be full of fight. *She always was a feisty one.* He would try a different tactic. "Where's the box?" he drilled. Tia gave him a puzzled look.

His finger pointed to his head out of a clenched fist, emphasizing that she was a ludicrous fool. "You know, the first-aid kit?" His hands opened empty, flat out and palm up. "The Band-Aid box, the diamond, my mother's diamond? Let me see your hands. Turn them over." Tia reluctantly obeyed. "The gold band and karat, where are they?" His face turned mean. "I am speaking to you!"

Tia answered with as much reserve as she could muster. "In the wreck—my car was totaled—" She hesitated. "It went to the dumps. The first-aid kit was in it. It's gone. There was a truck jackknifed around a curve. I didn't see it. They tried to stop me. I didn't know." Her body trembled, remembering. She looked at the miserable man with overwhelming pity, wanting to cry. "Chance, I thought you were dead." Her heart ached like it had been run over with a car. Torn between the two men, she longed for peace. There was none.

"Well, I'm alive! Get the baby and let's get out of here." Chance had no intention of backing off. Unaware that he had met his match in Fence Carpenter, he stood staunch, issuing challenges, certain of his ability to persuade her. "I went to a lot of trouble to find you! You know you belong to me."

Fence champed at the bit. He'd had it. "Tia move out of the way! NOW!" Fence shoved her to the side in the knick of time. He had no intention of ducking his head beneath his wings. A blaring, angry yell came out of him as he got in Chance's face. "GET OUT OF HERE!"

Chance wasted no time. His right fist shot out like lightning to land a blow on Fence's jaw. He had an arrogant pride of superiority in his golden glove training, knowing it would come in handy at the drop of a dime and now was the time. It was not going to be a civil thing. Fence dodged. The punch slipped over his shoulder.

Chance glared momentarily at Fence with venomous eyes. *So, the defender didn't take the rabbit punch. Well, the real thing is about to come.* He was not one to follow rules in a fight. Using his full body strength, Chance hauled out a left uppercut to Fence's jugular. Immediately, he followed it, shooting a gloveless right punch. The canon blow hit Fence in the gut.

Mack Carpenter burst into action, grabbing the highchair, rescuing Rose from the fight's path. *No one is going to steal my grandchild.* He placed her in Marie's care.

Quickly Marie unfastened Rose's seatbelt. She held the screaming child close to her as she exited out the back door onto the patio. The warning dream from the night before replayed. Nothing she could do would stop it.

The room was fast becoming an action-packed ring. Reluctant to call authorities, Mack circled the room. He regretted not getting more information from Fence. His rifles and the shotgun were locked up in the basement where he had been cleaning them. It certainly would not come to that, would it? Why had he started that project now? Mack, on his way, rumbled down the steps to the Carpenter shop.

Grasping for air and trying to pull his head out of the spin, Fence pulled back. When he stood up, Chance head-butted him.

Again, Chance bared his teeth, holding his pointed chin against his neck. The crazed man assumed the traditional boxing stance, firing his bare-knuckled blows like ramrods. Then he rammed his sharp elbow against Fence's jaw. The destructive man had lots of power behind his punch and lots of practice hitting the target.

A sharp, stinging head blow threw Fence off balance. He staggered back, speechless, creating an opening for a second cutting jab. Blood was running from the gash on Fence's head. Chance's arm traveled in a straight line to take out Fence. The punishing vengeance had the history of ancient Iraqi brutality. It was in Chance's blood. The more he fought the more vicious he became. He was no longer calm and collected; he was charged with madness.

Fence deflected some of the blows, but had underestimated the raging man's strength. Although his boxing skills were meager, grappling was as natural as breathing. Indian wrestling, inbred from childhood, magnified his warrior sense of courage and determination. The prehistoric skills, passed down from generation to generation, required topnotch physical shape and grueling endurance.

Claude Walking Elk, Abraham Pearl and Fence had spent many childhood hours practicing new moves. They ran the distance up and down the mountains, increasing their lung capacity. Fence had been in better shape, but never had he had more reason to fight.

Fence knew wrestling was mostly above the neck and to execute skills with a boxer would take all his imagination, speed and strength. He dove at Chance's midsection with the force of a bull, knocking the cocky man across the room into the round table, shattering the glass stand.

Fence was ready again with a cross-ankle-pick-up that sent Chance to the wooden floor. They grappled in hand to hand combat, throwing each other with violent force. With brute strength, Fence wrenched his elbow into Chance's nose. He heard the crunch of cartilage. Grabbing the intruder's leg, Fence applied relentless pressure as he pushed it to the breaking point, but his good-heartedness caused him to release too soon. Letting up on the guy meant trouble.

Tia retreated to the back wall, traumatized. Shocked in disbelief, she watched the two fighters shift back and forth tackling, twisting and turning over and over. She struggled to focus. Feelings of loss and betrayal were replacing feelings of love for Chance Cummings.

With his wind back, Chance roared like a furious lion. Greediness consumed him. He was determined to punch out Fence's lights. With his rabid strength he baited Fence, running at the mouth with sarcasm, taunting, mocking, ridiculing. The air turned blue with vulgarity. He spit with killer vengeance. His arms locked around Fence's neck whose bruised eye was already swelled shut. Blood streamed down both faces.

Somehow Chance slipped on the floor. His heel hooked onto an ice cube from a spilled drink, causing his leg to shoot straight out in front of him. The fall broke his hold on Fence.

Wasting no time, Fence put a stranglehold on the downed man. He was not letting up this time. Fence increased the pressure. Chance gagged in repulsiveness, desperate to make a last ditch effort through the drooling blood. The choking man turned blue.

Then, the tables turned. Chance bellowed like a roped calf. Jerking abruptly with phantom power, he threw an elbow into the center of Fence's ribcage, wrenching himself out and into position to reach for his knife. The switchblade shot out; he held it to Fence's neck. "Now who's in charge?" Chance spat out in a muffled underworld brogue. The blade edge cut into Fence's throat. Blood streamed down his neck and chest. Chance's hammering kneecap pounded the middle of Fence's back. He twisted Fence's arm out of its socket with his vulgar vice-grip strength.

Darkness consumed Fence.

"T.R. move. Get that baby." Orders belched from Chance's chest as he yelled.

Blood curdling sounds of screams and guns rang out. Then, only heavy breathing could be heard. Two men lay on the bloodstained floor, licking the dust. The brutal physical match was over.

Fierceness had turned the neat room inside out. Marie and little Rose were outside listening through the back door. *Where is Mack?* She stood tall like the warrior woman she was. Her first concern was to quiet the fretting child. The gunshots sent shivers through them both.

Marie hummed and swayed to settle her granddaughter. Suddenly, the calm came. Peace rested on the child. Rose started to sing—softly, innocently, in her baby language. The childlike song went beyond understanding, soothing the turbulent air.

The petite blond woman loomed over the situation with gigantic courage. Both men, stopped in their tracks, lay motionless. She dropped the pistol, running to them. Blood was shooting from Chance's mouth, appearing to drown Fence in it. Fence struggled to throw the vile man off, but his own strength had been completely expelled.

Mack laid his rifle down on the table beside the remains of Chance's switchblade. He proceeded to lift the collapsed man off Fence. He was not dead.

Tia, still in her nightclothes, bent down between them. She spoke in a trance-like manner. "Fence, I need to talk to him." She knelt by the broken man's head, grabbing a dishtowel to clean his face.

Fence was not sure whose blood was whose. In spite of the confusion, jealousy arose in him. He wanted, needed Tia's attention.

Mack's perception was keen. He wrapped his son's neck in his own shirt.

In dogged determination, Fence dragged his half-dressed, bruised body behind Tia, whispering, "I'm not leaving your side." His stomach was still fighting. *So she was raped.* The fact ate at him, more than taking the man's punches. *The man is an utter fool.* Fence stewed. *How can Tia forgive him? What if she goes with him? What if she still loves him? She nearly died because of the man who makes a habit of rape? What if he lives?* The dying man rattled Fence.

Violence, strangely connected to love, had left its mark. Fence's thoughts chased each other. He wanted them to run away. Engrained in him were his Dad's words. *The madder you get the more hopeless you become.* The old statement hit him where he lived.

Tia talked to Chance with unfathomable kindness. Her tear dropped on his chest. "I didn't mean to hurt you." Her voice aroused him.

"Doesn't matter, does it? Guess what comes around goes around. I never should have showed you how to use a gun." Chance's eyes were glossy, half from extreme anger, half from the uncanny effect she was having on him. "Do you love him?" Chance asked mockingly, referring to the man behind her.

"I don't know. I know I don't love you and think I never did. I was pregnant and alone. I wanted you to care, to marry me. I would have forgotten the pressure if you had only loved me. Chance, you have no room to love anyone cause you're too filled with yourself. Don't you see? There's no future in living that way. That's why I couldn't have an abortion. I knew the baby was meant to be, just like you were meant to be." Tia talked faster than normal, sensing the urgency of the moment.

"You always called me Chancey, now it's Chance. Does he treat you better than I?"

She held her peace and nodded slightly, looking down.

"He does, doesn't he? I thought so." He gagged. Thinking of the inheritance, he said bitterly, "I saw the silver wedding ring on your hand." It was a sneer. Greed had a bitter grip on him. Chance struggled. His mouth contorted with a second thought. "The baby … sheeeee looks like … my … my mother." He gulped.

Tia reached out in a consoling way, touching his hand for a moment. "Your mother is a good woman. You are her son and you must be very special to her." She hesitated, hoping. "Chance? You will find someone when you come to the end of yourself." Tia, the woman who did not give up on people, still believed beyond belief that a man could change.

Chance spoke listlessly with a slow, wry smile. "My mother? She thinks I'm dead and buried. She'd never forgive me. She always wanted a grandchild. Fools die young you know." He had no more strength to fight. It was the luck of the draw. He had other irons in the fire. Deep inside he realized T.R. was a stranger. He never really knew her. Money was the bottom line. The dollar spoke louder than feelings. Yet Tia was digging deep into his pockets. He shrugged it off and said, scrambling his words, "It doesn't matter."

Tia turned, looking to Marie. "Please, bring Rose."

Tenderly, Tia wiped Chance's bloodied hand with the bottom of her robe. She gently lifted it to Rose's little cheek. "Chance, meet Miss Rose Marie Carpenter." Chance looked at the baby, gasping for air. A slight smile crossed his broken face.

"Yours." Rose laid the Latin cross on Chance's hand and ran back to her grandmother. Marie waited, crouching at a distance, with outstretched arms to embrace her grandchild.

Tia lifted the broken man's head into her lap. Chance turned his eyes away. "It's my heart, it's bursting. You never knew. I sold out—sold ou—t on you."

A moment of silence passed. Tia wiped his face. Chance managed to twist and cast his eyes toward the woman above him. Then, with his meager remaining strength, he raised his hand to his forehead, thumb to palm. The sides of his fingers pressed together, straight out. "My regards Mrs. Carpenter," he said, saluting the woman by his side, the one cradling his head. He held his last cough in. There was no mocking, no disgust left. With his last breath, Chance Cummings gave honor where honor was due. Then, his fingers dropped. His head fell back in finality. Tia laid him down. She closed his eyelids, thinking of Rose. The cross lay still by Chance's side. His light had gone out.

"Tia," Fence spoke softly, awkwardly touching her soft back. "I have big shoulders."

She turned to him, like a fragile flower leaning against an oak tree with sap running down. She grieved at what the fight had done to him, to her, to Rose. She laid her head on his heart, feeling the wetness of his sweaty chest. She could hear his heart beating, like an African djembe, the drum played by an unseen hand, pounding with strength. He had poured out his salt for her. In submission she let his perspiration absorb her.

Fence laid his beat-up knuckled hand on the back of her hair and held her with one arm. The remarkable woman had shown a rare sense of courage—courage crowned with wisdom. Few women he knew possessed the fearless nature, the inbred stamina that is in the blood of the brave. Bizarrely, it was her kindness to the unworthy man that impressed him.

The gold in the strands of her hair glistened like it did the night she had slept under the Christmas tree. There was more to her than Fence had thought. The sun shone through the big bay window, the spot where Marie's African violets flourished. The peaceful light followed the storm.

Tia, numb to her toes, refrained from moving, overcome with the magnitude of the situation. For the first time in her life she knew. She knew who she was, *Mrs. Fence Carpenter.* What would she do with it?

Block the Blood Out

WHEN realization struck, Tia gasped. Rose's birth father, Chance Cummings, lay dead and mangled beneath her. Her chest started to heave, up and down, in and out. She began to hyperventilate. Her face flushed red with overcoming heat. *I've got to get out of here.* The compulsion to escape consumed her.

She pulled away from the body of warmth holding her. At that moment Fence Carpenter could have been anyone. She had no feeling for him. He had fought for her and that she could not comprehend. She would not think about that now even if she could understand. She needed air … cool air. Grasping her queasy stomach, she ran outside, fleeing the scene. She had to throw up. She grabbed her abdomen, resisting the sting of recent stitches. She groaned. *God, help me.*

She ran aimlessly. Pines pointing at the sun lined up in front of her. One with a bold trunk met her head on. She held on to it. She turned abruptly. The western hemlock quickly held the small of her back. She slid down it. The smell of death hung in the air. Nearby, buzzards with ugly red beaks circled over a near-dead animal. The smell of death repulsed her. She gagged. Again, the taste of vomit spoiled her mouth. She lurched. Dry heaves forced their way out. Her throat cried for water.

Urgency took over. She moved along the edge of the natural grove, trying to lose herself in a staggered run. Her tousled hair, flying, wild on the windless day, followed a step behind, with her half-open robe.

Block them out. Block the blood out. Block Rose's screams out! The resonance only grew. She covered her ears. There was no other choice. Chance lay dead by her hand. Her hands! There was blood on them. Murder was never in her heart. She had killed by impulse. She had done what she thought was right. No way existed to change the past, to redeem the life of the man who had fathered her child.

She climbed progressively, until a running creek met up with her. For a second she halted to listen and catch her breath. Detesting the uncleanness, Tia knelt to wash her stained hands and face. She longed to cover her bareness, to eradicate the naked reality. *Chance was dead.* It was not a dream. The clear water cleansed her hands. It did not have the power or the capability to remove the stains soiling her heart.

Carefully stepping on the smoother exposed rocks, she crossed the fast-moving stream. Her bare feet winced. *Is there a safe place to walk?* Sharpness pressed into her. She settled her chilled body under some shrub, leaving her back exposed to the sun's rays. *I have to rest, rest and think.* She curled into a crouched position, holding her throbbing head.

It seemed her eyes were going to fall out. She wished to hold them in her hands and comfort them. The shadow of death still hung over her, a dark cloud in bright daylight. Deep within, she mourned. She could not stop the groans, the regrets, the rejections. Guilt weighed her down like a heavy, ragged, old coat, stained with blood and condemnation. Trembling, Tia scooped up a handful of earth, wondering if it longed for life that much. *Dust to dust.* She let the rich loamy dirt, filled with ancient bones, run between her fingers.

I killed him. I didn't want to. She had pulled the trigger without anger. Deliberation gave her no consolation. It was done. She had meddled with trouble. It had taken the best from her and the worst. The scene could not be erased. She could not relive the day, or her life. She was who she was. She longed to change history, but there was no way. She did not want to learn anymore. *No more lessons.* She exhaled.

Her life seemed so shallow right now. Searching for purpose, she took a dead branch, a mere stick. She guided the point of the stick, digging a path on the ground. She started to draw the symbol for infinity, but it turned into a fish, a fish with a small cross for an eye. For a second she stopped to listen. *Freedom isn't free.* The fisheye stared at her.

It was the Memorial Day message. What had the minister said about the cost of peace—about the irony of the cross—about Christ? The old but new speech pressed into Tia like a soothing balm, like the warmth of summer sun. It was then that she saw the oval agate, no bigger than a dime.

Her fingers set the small stone in place—below the eye—an oval agate for an ageless tear ... a heavy tear ... a beautiful tear ... dropping from the corner of the eye. The teardrop gave the eye a new dimension, one that Tia identified with. Suddenly the cross went deep, taking her pain, her guilt and the detestable shame. A peace she could not explain wrapped around her like a blanket.

She examined the palms of her hands. All she could see was the lifeline. She pressed her finger to her neck, locating her pulse. Her heart still beat. She was alive. She had survived.

Then Tia folded her hands together and brought them to her lips, one inside the other. *Who am I?* For a moment after the fight she thought she knew, but not now. The diamond on top of the wedding ring flickered. *Who is Fence Carpenter anyway?*

Tia's eyelids drooped in exhaustion. She laid her hands under her forehead, trying to process what had happened since she left the orphanage. Her thoughts veered to the night Fence laid his hand on top of hers and Rose's. With that, Tia rested in the unsafe place, secure for the time being.

Wake Up Daddy

THE fight had left Fence in bewilderment, disoriented from the loss of blood. Tia had pushed him away. He had no way to keep her there. He tilted his numbed head back. For a moment he closed his eyes. He needed to put things into perspective. Fence struggled to stand. He placed his hand on a nearby wall for balance. A stranger named Chance Cummings lay beneath him, no longer alive. Groping to get his wits, Fence stepped over the dead man and wove his way out of the room. Tensely he maneuvered his wrenched body to a bathroom, staggering like a drunk. His father's flannel shirt, twisted about his neck, was soaked with blood and sweat. The plaid cloth dropped to the floor.

The showerhead pulsed cold water over Fence's aching body ... over his head, his shoulders ... over his thoughts. His hands pressed the shower wall attempting to push away the blur and the pain. He lifted his head, letting the water beat his face. He was not thinking straight. *What happened to Tia?* He dabbed his face and body dry.

Awkwardly, Fence tied a thin rag of a towel, ripped lengthwise, around his throat. His muscled fingers operated with sluggish agility. Blood wept through the cloth. He stopped and stooped over the bath counter to get air. Orientation took longer than usual. The fight had taken more out of Fence than he wanted to admit.

He re-envisioned Chance's militant eyes crushing Tia, forcing her to meet selfish, deceptive demands. The man never loved her, only used her, stealing her dignity, her honor. The invasive man had done all he could to ruin her. But, no way existed for Chance Cummings to destroy the dauntless courage Tia had exhibited. Fence reran the reel. He had met challenges before, but never against a brutal man who excelled with such deception, who intended to kill to get what he wanted. Fence exhaled, still amazed.

He wanted to rub his aching back, but could not reach it. Was it his imagination, or was Chance's knee still pressing into the core of his being? *The man! How could he have fathered Rose?* Fence felt the saliva build up in his mouth. He spit blood into the porcelain sink.

I must have hated him all along ... long before I knew his name. The thought rattled Fence. He was keenly aware of anger's ability to promote itself to justification and then to vengeance. It was not an attribute he desired. "Hatred impairs rational judgment," he said out loud, fighting to ignore the pain in his body.

Staring into the mirror did not make him feel better. He searched the hairline curves through the blur, seeing dark shadows of reality. His left eye, swollen to a slit, fought to focus. The brass surrounding the looking glass gave a distorted reflection, but the color was true. The truth was not pretty.

Words surfaced. *Dutybound men do what they have to.* He had never applied it to a woman before. *Tia clearly understands that concept.*

Thirsty, Fence set a cup under the faucet. Swirling pictures ran out. *No one wins a fight by death.* He was weak. He rubbed a missed smudge off his cheek, letting his mind wash back and forth. His head ached. He ran his fingers through his wet hair, thinking of Rose. His battered body tottered to the side. His balance shifted. *Lie on my back. Shut the brain off. Quit trying to think.* He knelt to the floor, functioning on remote.

The comfort of the rag rug beneath his cranial nerve soothed him. His strength dwindled like an inner tube with all the air let out. The burns on his neck, next to the cut, were hot. He was hot. His abused muscles, sore and swollen, seemed useless. He had to lie still, to rest for a moment—no more thinking. His head swept into oblivion, lapsing into slow motion. He wanted to run, but his legs, his body would not move. He became the main character in the dream's drama.

He picked up an old weapon that hung on a wooden peg in the shed. He restrung the bow and waxed its linen string smooth. Stalwartly, he hiked the deer path along the rippling water with the quiver over his shoulder. A few more steps pushed him to his grandfather Reed's old spot where Fence had learned more than fishing. The stream waited with a thirst of its own. Squatting, like a watchman with one knee to the ground and the other holding his arm, he scanned the ravine. Nothing.

Making a handmade cup, he dipped into the clear water,

scooping up the cold stones. He placed them in the center of his handkerchief. No. It was Tia's, or was it his? He dreamt he was dreaming. He made a cold pack for his eye. With the other eye he watched the ripples.

Pulling an arrow from his quiver, he tied a line near the flight feather, notching the arrow into the bowstring. He waited. Instinctively he calculated the distance, aiming to outwit the fish. The brown trout did not have a chance. Fence pulled the line in. But, it was not the catch that was on his mind. It was Rose's mother. Tia had saved his life, or was it Lily? His past tangled into the present. Loose ends hung all around him, behind and in front.

The hallucination held him captive in its quickening realism. *What am I doing anyway? Who can't I give up?* He floated in and out, attempting to place all stray thinking into the now, where his body lay. He looked at his stiff fists and large fingers, bending them, thinking of the fight and Tia. *Had she laid her head on his heart like she belonged?*

She is innocent. She is no more guilty of murder than I am. The feel of Tia leaning against his chest, her closeness, aroused a sense of urgency. Peace eluded him. *Where is she? Where did she go? They want to kill her. NO! I have to stop them.*

"Dad...dee, Dad...dee! Up pah, ake up...pah." Rose pulled at his fingers, calling out, "Gam, Dad...dee ... boke. Bix Dad...dee." She cried. Her sad eyes looked to her grandmother to fix her daddy.

Marie had followed Rose. Bending down to Fence, she lifted his swollen eyelids. "Fence, are you okay?"

The voice in his ear, like a blue jay screech, pulled Fence out of the trance—that, and thoughts of his baby. He murmured, "Where am I?" He struggled to rise. "I have to find her." His attempt to move collapsed. He fought to speak. "Rose?" he asked. Confusion crowded him.

"Rose is fine," Fence's mother replied, "I've kept her away from the commotion. The fight is over. She is safe."

Marie Carpenter looked at her grown son with urgent intensity. "Stay still," she commanded. "You took a blow to the head."

He shrugged in obedience, passing out. There was nowhere he could go. He faded into another dimension.

Rose laid her little body over him, resting her head on Fence's chest. She whispered in the love language of a child, "Wuv...you, Dad—dee."

Coronary

MACK Carpenter watched Tia run out without a word. Then Fence staggered to a back room, leaving him to deal with the details. Confident that Marie had already escorted Little Prairie Rose away from the tragedy, Mack began to survey the situation before him. The kitchen and dining room were swirled about, turned into a mangled mess by the dead man's depravity, as if a tornado had struck. Picking up the telephone, Mack dialed the number he knew by heart. He cleared his throat and calmed his voice. "Hello Pop, we could use a little professional help down here. Fence is home."

"Be there by noon or before. Hold tight," Reed Carpenter said with assurance. The distinguished man held his imagination in check. Like Fence, he was accustomed to processing facts, not ideas. However, the urgency in Mack's voice summoned him to action. Reed Carpenter, Mack's highly respected father, was not one to waste time, especially when it came to Fence, his only grandson.

Meanwhile Mack covered Chance Cummings' body with a small tarp. He worried about Fence's wife, Tia. Apparently, she had a lot to process and rightfully so. Marie was right. The turbulent fight changed the ranch's peacefulness into erratic wildness. For the moment, stillness prevailed. Mack spent the next hour picking up broken pieces of glass and gathering information, waiting for his father.

After the call from Mack, Reed Carpenter's piercing blue eyes searched the phone book while his fingers turned back the pages. He looked and acted young for his seventy-five years. His fair hair, camouflaged with gray, gave him a look of authority. The Capitol Hotel was underlined. "Clem Bridger, there you are."

Reed dialed the phone, anxious to pass on the round robin of information. "Yeah, Clem. Good thing you flew in yesterday. We have

118

ourselves an assignment. It involves my grandson, Fence. You were right. Trouble has shown up. I just got a call from Mack."

Doctor Clem Bridger, lugging a mountain of crumpled papers shoved inside an overstuffed black leather bag, arrived with the distinguished Reed Carpenter in record time. The two older men entered the main door of the M / M Ranch.

Having wandered out of his stupor, Fence, who was eager to get out of the house to search for Tia, met his grandfather and the doctor face to face. The men wanted to talk, to get explanations, to get to the straight skinny. But, upon seeing the condition of Fence's body, they just stared at him wide-eyed, head to foot, silently asking questions.

"Let me see that," Doc said with his medical tongue, referring to Fence's neck. He pulled Fence to the side and pushed him into an armchair, giving him a wry smile. "I examine the living before the dead. Now sit here," Doc insisted. "It's for your own good." He unwrapped the rag. Fence lifted his chin. Before he could take a deep breath, Doc Bridger started stitching the three-inch cut.

Fence had already lost over an hour with his head in a daze, passed out on the bathroom floor. Having no other recourse, Fence submitted to the brief delay, but not to explanations or giving a report. His mind was moving in another direction, rushing out the door, ahead of his body. He needed to find Tia.

His grandfather Reed probed. "Fence, where's the girl? I mean your wife? You can't leave her alone in unfamiliar country. This isn't Florida."

"I'm well aware of that, Gramp," Fence said between the stitches.

Doc pushed his glasses up with the side of his arm, glancing at Fence's wounded eye. "Good thing Marie put eggshell skins over the cuts. Your mother always did have her moccasins full of ideas." Doc pulled the under layer of skin together. "Indeed! Those new finagled interns, with all their new tricks, could get an education from her native remedies." Doc cut the thread with a brisk snip.

Fence winced. "Take it easy." He wished Doc Bridger would quit talking and watch what he was doing. Fence blew out a deep breath. In spite of the holdup, Fence could not get angry with the two older men even if he wanted to. He had too much love and respect for them. He asked, "How do you and Gramp always manage to show up with trouble?"

Doc ignored the comment and focused on the examination. "Now, look me in the eye." He stretched each one open. "Looks like you have a slight concussion. Nothing that staying up for a while won't fix." He gave Fence his medical examination look and then grinned. "You're all pulled together, just like new. Now go hunting."

Fence attempted a wink as he downed a quart of water. "That makes the second time you've worked at fixing me up. I owe ya Doc," he said, hurrying. "Thanks, both of you." Fence let the screen door slam behind him.

Busy outside, Mack carefully checked Chance Cummings' vehicle. He wished he were skinning buffalo, or doing anything else. Having a son that took after his father Reed had proved challenging in more ways than one. He stepped onto the porch, meeting Fence eye to eye as he rushed out of the house. "She headed toward the ridge," Mack offered.

Fence nodded a hasty confirmation. The moves made his head ache. "Thanks," he said, skirting around his father.

While Fence was gone, the two older men examined the corpse, the ram, the wig and then the file. The investigators left no stone unturned. They questioned Mack inside and out until they sensed his frustration with them.

Meticulously Doc's coroner skills went to work. "Well, I have news for you. Chance Cummings didn't die of a gunshot wound. Look here. See this? The bullet went clear through his right shoulder."

"What then?" Reed raised a questioning eyebrow to Doc.

"All signs point to a massive heart attack. See this? I need to do an autopsy."

Reed's head raced with more questions, questions he had no answers for. He reassembled what was left of the knife and placed it on the table under a magnifying glass. The handle was wholly detached. "Whew. It looks like Mack's shot sharpened this steel blue. He cut the handle right off. He always could hit the nail on the head." Reed set the evidence down in a neat row. "Guess that explains those burns on Fence's neck."

Doc listened as he worked. "And the ones on Chance Cummings hands. Talk about cutting things close!" Doc Bridger inserted. "Between the knife, the bullet and the stitches, I would say your grandson is one lucky young man."

Reed shook his head, surmising the situation. "It's not him I'm worried about. It's the girl! From what you've told me, he may have bitten off more than he can chew. Good thing we showed up."

Doc scratched his chin through his whiskers, remembering the feminine infant left at an orphanage twenty years before. "I'm still perplexed how the two of them got hooked up."

"Knowing Fence, he chased her until she caught him." Reed grinned. He liked his grandson, not just because he was who he was, but also because he had adventure in his spirit.

"Actually, Fence said she was the one who found him. But I think there's more to it than that." Doctor Clem Bridger plunged into the leather recliner, wondering how he always got his nose into other people's business.

Reed bent over the body, taking fingerprints. He spoke while he worked. "Wish Abe Pearl was around to help us. He was a prime investigator if I ever saw one. Fence has been off track ever since his death. I don't think he believes Abe committed suicide. Do you?"

"Can't say that I ever knew Abe. All I know is that someone is out to knock your grandson off, and maybe his wife too."

Mack re-entered the room. Immediately he noticed the stranger's wallet stuck under the toe-kick of the kitchen cabinets. He retrieved it. "Here's the identification. Pop, I don't think this is his real name … Carson Collins?"

Nonchalantly, Mack tossed the stranger's false ID to his investigator father. "It would be wise to bury him by it. His initials are still C.C. He already died once under the name Cummings. Anyway that's what she, I mean Tia, indicated. A man shouldn't die twice under the same name."

Examining the ID, Reed asked Mack, "What has Fence got himself into now?" Reed tilted forward, smelling the money inside the stranger's wallet. "Doc told me someone tried to poison Fence and that he married an orphan."

Mack circled the room, avoiding the comment. The new nugget of truth did not surprise him. Pop always knew more than he did, caulking more into the frame of his factual brain than most seventy-five-year-old men. "All I know is that Fence put his life on the line. He fought for her."

Reed Carpenter shuffled through the stiff twenty-dollar bills. "From the looks of it, she seems to have no problem holding her own. Anyway, the girl can shoot." Reed gave his opinion. He snapped the identification closed. His logistical brain operated in high gear. He picked up the pistol, smelling it for the third time, counting how many bullets were left unused. "No wonder this gun looks familiar. It was mine before Fence begged it off me. He must have been twelve then."

"Eleven," Mack corrected. "He's always treasured it. First thing he asked me to bring him before Tia's surgery on Memorial Day."

Wheels turned in Mack's head, grinding away thoughts regarding Fence's new wife. *Orphan or not, there's chemistry between Fence and Tia.* He had that figured out. *Anyone in his right mind can feel the undercurrent.*

Snakes In the Grass

FOUR hours had passed since the fight. The search for Tia took longer than Fence expected. He paused, relieved but troubled at the sight he saw. Tia, hunched down in her nightgown and robe, had been drawing in the dirt. She was unaware of his presence. Anyone or anything could have snuck up on her.

"Too many snakes in the grass to be out here alone," Fence said. He startled her.

Instantly Tia snapped back, firing ammunition with her mouth. "Right now I don't care. I like the space."

"It wasn't your fault you know," he said kindly.

"I don't need a lecture. I just need—" She stopped abruptly before revealing any more.

"A hand?" He finished her sentence, stretching out his arm in front of him.

"Right." She mellowed. "I'm a..." Again she stopped short.

"A mess, like me?" He grinned. "We make quite a sight." She reached upward awkwardly. He pulled her up, immediately dropping her hand so she could brush off. "It gets a bit dangerous around here when the sun creeps over the hill. Besides, I think we have a little girl who needs us."

Her lips pursed together with a nod of affirmation. She pulled her robe around her tightly. Fence ran his fingers through his sandy-blond hair. He let his mouth blow out relief.

"Do you want me to carry you?" he said, noticing her shoeless feet. "This isn't barefoot country. Plenty of Blackfeet nearby though. You'll probably fit right in if they don't look at your hair." He spoke in a lighthearted tone.

Her tough reply was no surprise. "I've been in worse places. Thanks."

123

"Not much. One cactus needle is worse than Doc Bridger's surgical stitches and that's pretty bad." He lifted his chin to the side showing her his neck.

He was right. He looked terrible. She gasped. "Ah, are you all right? I haven't been able to think straight."

He gave her a mischievous grin. "Me either. I seem to have been knocked in the head." Fence wasted no more time. He whispered, "If we don't get back before dark, Mack and Marie will send out a search party. That's not to mention my Grandfather Reed and Doc Bridger." He scooped her up from behind. She did not resist. Tia felt weak and more vulnerable than she wanted.

Not Guilty

THE ranch sat hushed in the valley with only caved evidence that it had been disturbed. Fence climbed over the rocks out of the creek draw located down from the ridge covered with pines. Tia slept heavily on his shoulder. Ordinarily, she would have been light as a feather. Now her weight agitated his bruises and his brain. Brilliant orange sun filtered through dusty particles on the indigo horizon. He adjusted his eyes, placing the view into his memory album. Who could have predicted the past twenty-four hours?

Yesterday he and Tia had come to his childhood home anticipating safety and security, hungry for rest and reprieve from pursuers. He had tried to shield her. Ironically, she had saved his life. His skull tipped forward until his chin touched the top of her head. He needed to talk to her, not that he wanted to. He wanted to say something that was not just a bunch of words. Cookie-cutter explanations would not cut it. Only with predictable circumstances is the normal mold valid. This did not come close.

We hardly know each other and there is so much water under our bridge. Fence took a giant step off a low boulder, jolting Tia out of her slumber. Wide eyed, her lips cracked open.

"I can walk." Her independence peaked. She pushed out of his hold. He set her to the ground, shaking his head. She charged off with unusual endurance.

"You have big dreams, but your feet will soon disagree!" He hollered after her. She ignored him.

Off in the distance, the eager elkhound wagged her curled tail, waiting for Fence. Tia darted into the big house, bypassing the dog, without another word.

Mack caught Fence by the arm before he walked inside. "Fence, I need to talk to you a minute. One of those father to son talks?"

125

"Yeah, Dad, I could use a little advice, but not right now," he answered bluntly.

"I know you're in over your head Fence. Slow down. Give her some room." Mack caught his eye and held his hand on his arm.

"You're right Dad. I'm sorry about the vague explanation. I'm not at liberty to give out information."

"I know." Mack swung his arm over his son's back. "I'm glad to have you home. I have something to show you." They walked together to the M / M tack house where Mack kept all the saddle gear. He waited for Fence to open up and say something, but his son remained tightlipped. Disturbing the silence, Mack began, "There's something weird about this whole thing. We don't think Chance Cummings was acting alone. And, by the way, Tia didn't kill him. The man had a bad heart."

"In more ways than one," Fence said, more than a bit relieved at the news. "Dad, trouble has only just begun. I want you to set up security around this place, besides Sky. Dogs can't keep out hired killers. I know it's your nature to trust most people, but this is one time we need to be careful."

By the time Fence opened the big door of the ranch house it was dark. He had a lot on his mind. Old issues had been ignored too long. A mysterious fact troubled him. Someone had told Mack that Abe's stepbrother had been seen recently at the courthouse in town.

Tia sat on the floor with socks on her feet next to Rose's crib in the newly restored nursery. She cradled her head in her hands while Rose turned in circles, experiencing dizziness for the first time. When she fell, the little girl laughed and rose up to do it all over again, oblivious to the tragedy of the day. Rose stopped still, looking like a mannequin when Fence stepped into the darkened room. She ran to him with unconditional arms spread like a butterfly. "Dad-dee."

Fence crouched down and held his child's comforting body close to him, lifting her up. "I love you." He swung her in a circle, stopping abruptly to turn on the lamp. Gently he set her down in front of him. He placed a small box in her eager hand. "Take this to Tia." He hesitated. "Your mommy, please? Go ahead."

Tia wore Fence's new denim shirt and her jeans. Her arms were wrapped around her knees. She was deep in thought. *Another world. She doesn't know she's innocent,* Fence thought.

Rose handed Tia the gold box. Printed on the outside was the Walking Elk silver logo. Tia looked up, giving Fence a puzzled glance. "I missed Mother's Day. Pretty insensitive of me, huh?" he confessed.

"I'm not your mother!" she rebutted in a feisty tone.

Plunging into an instinctive explanation, Fence attempted to cover the blunder. Tension filled the room. "It's from Rose! I got one for my mom from me. Claude made them."

Taking her glare off him, Tia reached out to the precious child, like a little girl herself, mellowed at the sight of innocence, the purity of her little child. "Thank you. Rose, will you help me open it?" The Black Hills gold heart locket had a silver rose set into it. Inside was a miniature baby picture of Rose. Tia resisted tears, trying to get up.

Fence knelt down next to her. "I'll give you another hand." He pulled her up. Slowly, she turned her back to him, avoiding his face.

"Would you mind latching it please?" she asked. His unnatural touch on the delicate chain took him longer than he wanted.

Mellowed, she whispered. "Thank you." Her head still hung over. "It means a lot to me."

Impulsively, he set his hands on her shoulders, moving next to her. "Tia, I— I— uh—you— you mean a lot to me." He stuttered the words out, altering what his heart held imprisoned. Her hair smelled clean. "I have something to tell you." He waited a moment. "I have to go away for a few days. I'll be back. I promise to be back soon. I have something very important to take care of. You must stay here for now. My folks will take care of you."

Mack and Marie came through the door, disturbing the moment of communication. Fence's Grandfather Reed followed. The whole Carpenter clan filled the small room. Fence released her shoulders. Quickly he grabbed his keys, his change, his wallet and an old shirt from the closet. Urgency moved his bruised body. Impulsively he dropped the second box in Marie's apron pocket. "Happy Mother's Day. A little late." He embraced her and then turned to his dad.

"Will you and Gramp do me a favor? Take care of things for me? You know what I mean?" He gestured toward the three pair of feminine eyes in the room.

"Mom, help Tia dress her incision, will you please? I have some business I have to attend to. I can't tell you why now. I'll be back as soon as I can."

"You can count on us." The trio spoke almost in unison. Bewildered,

Tia watched the peculiar episode.

Fence advanced to the door, knowing he would lose his resolve if he did not move promptly. He was not acting impulsively, but with purpose. EMTs were taught to be responders first. He had fallen far short. He reached the screen door and turned back to Tia who stood, following him with sky-wide eyes. She looked down when he approached her.

"Tia, look at me." He cupped her chin upward with his stiff fingers. "You're a very brave woman. I'll miss you." His words seeped into her soul, sounding more final than he intended. "I'm telling you the truth. Chance is dead, but not by your hand. Mack will tell you about it. Understand?" He bent his head to her soft face and kissed her on the forehead. "It's going to be okay. Keep Rose close to you."

Perplexed, she stood motionless. Everything was happening too fast. Fence Carpenter vanished out the door. Rose clung to her leg.

Cleaning Out the Cobwebs

FENCE lay back against the headrest, thankful for a friend like Claude Walking Elk, who had driven him to the airport to catch the late flight out of Montana. He hated to leave his daughter and Tia behind. He struggled, realizing he needed to face the buried bitterness alone. Dealing with the memories of Lily had been ignored too long.

Two airline connections and a flight delay added to Fence's discontentment. Irritation plagued him. His thoughts turned to Abe. He felt a little disgruntled with the concoction of the so-called assignment. Not that he was wrong, but Abe was not alive to help carry it through or explain the details.

Fence pushed himself to keep going. His aching body, especially his head, had started to turn black and blue. He could not hide the fact that he had been in a fight. At this point he did not care. He was tired.

The Florida house stood lonely and in need of attention, in more ways than one. The yard needed to be mowed. The lawn service, a block away, moved his way noisily. The minor detail frustrated him. Sweat beads formed, like tears, on his face in the muggy air.

He pulled down the creaky hideaway steps, watching bits of blown-in insulation descend. Steadily he climbed. The antique wood and alligator-skin trunk hid in the east corner of the attic. A triangular window near the attic apex emitted little light. Fence seemed to notice it for the first time. He pulled the drawstring. The lone bulb lit up. With much effort Fence worked the awkward chest out of the cobwebs. *History hidden away. Life hidden away in the interior of a box.*

Opening the latch, he lifted the arched lid, revealing the set-in yellowed box shelf. Gagged by the heavy odor of mothballs, Fence sat back. Waxed lilies lay on top, along with a small white cloth-covered Bible. Fence opened the silver-bound pages looking for clues to Lily's past, looking for his heart, digging for understanding. Deep inside he found the water-stained journal. It no longer carried evidence of her smell. Four years had already drained it of whiteness. But the timeless treasure of her recorded words stepped off the page, alive.

Everyone is looking for love. They just don't know what it is.

Fence revered love. It kept him alive. Whether he knew what it was, he was not certain.

I see where I've been. Do I see where I'm going?

Lily's pen pulled Fence into mysterious nostalgia. He leaned his back against the chest.

When Fence saw Lily Mansfield for the first time she was with Marena Luttwig, a blond German girl from the Black Forest who wore biker leathers. The two European girls took backpacks from Swiss Alp adventures across the outback in Australia, through Kenyan jungles, to Tibetan mosques, then spelunking in Missouri caves and cross-country skiing in Canada. Tracking her had been like taking a world tour. Lily carried little evidence of where she had been, except in her heart. "Elusive" was the right word for her.

Fence had been determined. He had managed to encounter her hiking on Trail Ridge Road. Lily was all her father had said and she was much more—romantic, secretive, imaginative, full of spirit. The slight-of-build Scottish girl moved with grace, a rare breed, taking after her French mother. When she walked into a room the whole atmosphere changed. Native Americans loved her. She was one of them in her own way. True to her word, no pretence or deception controlled her. Like natives, Lily did not know how to be neutral. Respectfully, she did not look them in the eye but honored their reverence. She conveyed her emotions with gestures and drama, glowing as she danced, pantomiming and telling stories with her hands.

Smitten, Fence Carpenter had sought her attention. Lily had been too free to be interested. Marena's influence had helped win Lily. The whirlwind wedding day had brought sunshine and music to them. In an outdoor summer ceremony Lily and Fence had exchanged vows on a mountaintop. Mack and Marie Carpenter had come, along with Claude, his best man who was engaged to Tamsen at the time. Like a knight in shining armor, Fence had basked in the dream.

Lily, with her irresistible smile, her effervescence, always radiated joy wherever she went. Why was Fence being forced to remember her? Why couldn't he lay the joy of his life to rest? They had been so much in love. She had wanted children so badly. She had insisted and Fence could not deny her.

"But the doctor said the tumor in your brain might become active. Why, Lily, do you persist?" The tumor from birth had remained dormant until Lily had turned eighteen. Severe headaches had begun early in high school and had escalated to excruciating pain. Just before her twenty-fourth birthday she endured a thirteen-hour emergency brain surgery in Baltimore with the best doctors in the world, the best treatment. The wee baby was stillborn, but medical specialists had given Lily hope. She had improved, never giving an ounce of complaint. On the fourth day she looked at Fence, speaking the same words that Fence now read.

I'm on a road that turns to gold.

Baby Ann had been laid in Lily's arms. An ascending white dove carrying two lilies was etched in a mural on the outside of the golden coffin. Arthur Mansfield had stood next to Fence in a rare somber mood. Once again he had released his daughter. He had told Fence, "She flew away a long time ago on the wings of an angel. She never was mine."

But Fence held to Lily and to her dreams, embracing loss. He played the drama out, the drama with bitterroot and no song. It had stolen the moisture from his hopes and purposes, crowding them out, squeezing them to emptiness. The crushing changed his pursuit. He saw it clearly now. He had never stopped punishing himself for her death. He had taken revenge on himself, lingering in a mournful state of mind, not so much for Lily, but for himself. He had married Tia for convenience. He had been anything but fair to her. *No wonder she feels trapped.*

Where has life gone? Fence weighed what he was before and what he had become. Closing Lily's journal, her last words stuck to him.

It costs to love.

He mulled it over, taking himself beyond the point of assessment to reassessment. Backing up, he bumped the box of Christmas decorations. Tia's homemade star fell onto the attic floor. Fence blew the dust off and closed the trunk, no longer in the freeze frame of the past.

Moments later, Fence descended with the star. He glanced around the house. It had never been a home. The garden and flowerbed were still undone. The rooms were cold, except for the memories of Rose and Tia. *Yes, Tia.* He laid the silver star on his bed. He had decisions to make. He foresaw weeks ahead of investigative work, not to mention getting the house on the market, job closure and the fact that he needed to heal up. His pillow was too close, too appealing. He fell asleep.

Feeling revived, Fence made preparations. The week passed quickly. Walking into the garage, he noticed the overflowing newspaper box in need of recycling. He moved the box away from the wall. Somehow, his tired eyes caught the date of an issue that had been cramped between the wall and the box. It was the day he had met Tia, that first day he had feared losing his baby Rose to the unknown woman.

Fence put the rest of the paper in a recycling container. He pressed the keepsake, the crumpled issue, into the side pocket of his leather travel bag for further review, sometime downstream. He needed to talk to the businesswoman, the realtor, who had sold him the house.

One last check revealed that the locks on the front door had been tampered with. Nothing was missing. Recovering the surveillance film from his observation camera, Fence eagerly evaluated it. The back of an unidentifiable redheaded woman had stood twice at the door. Fence sensed urgency. "Time to make a call," he said out loud.

"Reed Carpenter, please." Fence spoke quickly. "Gramp, I'm going to Europe. Have to. Don't let up on the surveillance. Do me a favor and run a check on Abe's stepbrother. Thanks." He thought it better not to mention Lily's father. Fence set the pay phone into its cradle, weighing his decision.

Business Abroad

TURBULENCE rocked the plane as it crossed the Atlantic. Fence tilted his head to see over the sleeping woman next to him. Addressing unfinished business was not always first on his list, but this time necessity bit him.

A wind shear left the jet circling the runway. Finally, London met Fence Carpenter with a reticent landing. Mid-June held the chill of fall. He pulled his jacket on, resisting the cool dampness. He wasted no time renting a German car. The steering wheel on the left side had lost its appeal of four years prior. Fence paced himself, searching through old documents, then stopping at the shipyards and waiting. He found himself caught in a flashback of rain.

He had gained and lost when he had gone to the ivy-league school, led by scholarships in track and field. The field house with its climbing vines, where rivalry rode high, had allowed Fence to soar into a world of knowledge. Fence, a bull's-eye shot with a rifle, had practiced his favorite elective in the soundproofed bomb shelter below the gymnasium. He had received the expert marksmanship award. It landed on the wayside, caught in the middle of electrical engineering and architectural courses for the season.

Fence had left the sounds of trees, the taste of the berries, the wild plums, the chokecherries at home, along with his nightly runs with Claude. He had left the elk hunt and the rainbow trout to get educated. And then there was Abe, whom he missed most. They had remained connected only through undercover investigations initiated by Fence's grandfather.

Fence had graduated summa cum laude; the honorable golden braid circled his neck. His intense work ethic always drove him to excel. Mack and Marie Carpenter had sat in the reserved parent row, absorbing the honors with their handsome son, as if all their dreams for themselves were coming true in him. His grandfather Reed had sat with Doc Bridger scrutinizing the ceremony, yet secretly proud of the young accomplished man.

Everyone had said that the sabbatical to Scotland for a year was an engineering opportunity of a lifetime. Fence agreed. The trip had encompassed much more than met the eye.

Windswept moors and misty highlands beckoned the adventurer to experience a land seasoned with history. The three-hundred-year-old stone house, amidst lush green fields, stretched Fence's horizons beyond the border of the American dream. Traditional Scottish dishes and dances intrigued him. The indigenous native Shoshone, the Nez Percé and the Crow, next to the Celts of Britain, were not that much different.

He had met Arthur Mansfield on a field trip to Stonehenge. The jovial man with the vivid imagination was full of wit and seriousness mixed together. *The man could laugh, by George.* He slapped his knee with delight whenever he "pulled Fence's leg" in jest. Fence could not help but like the native Britain with his receding hair and mischievous wit. Arthur had often served him scalding hot tea with cream in wedge wood pottery while his young seven-year-old son ran wild on the rocks. The lad, Edin, could count sheep in old Celtic numbers.

Arthur's place usually blazed with flowers that edified the old mossy walls. The live painting had left a lasting impression on Fence. The sharp contrast of bright colors on intense green had left an imprint on the canvas of his heart. Fence had complimented Arthur on the cheerful beauty. The man had replied poetically, "I have one beauty that outshines them all, a live lily, a daughter with wings of a dove."

That's how the search for Arthur's daughter Lily, had begun. Fence had been in love with her before he had ever laid eyes on her. That had occurred a year later, across the sea, in Fence's homeland.

Those days had come and gone. Fence retrieved his thoughts, parking the car at the end of the lane.

Arthur shook his head in disbelief when he saw the blond American walking through the flowers. "By George, just the man I needed to see." His garden-gloved hands dropped little clogs of dirt as Arthur beat Fence on the back. "Son, I've been waiting for you," he said with a glint in his eye. Fence felt no condemnation from the warmhearted man.

The serious conversation began after tea with cream. "He's been stealing, running wild with the wolf-pack." Arthur expressed his genuine concern for his teenage son. "He no longer cares about the flowers or the sheep. He thinks the world owes him a living. His moods slip from raging out of control to bottling himself up. He likes the rum. I think he tries to drown himself in it."

Edin, who had idolized his sister, was angry—angry to lose her, bitter to lose her to death. The fact that an American had stolen her away magnified Edin's hatred. Their mother had died when Edin was three from a rare health problem closely related to Lily's. She represented the only female figure in his early years. Now his life was not worth living. At least not like his father wanted. "Trouble follows the boy." Arthur poured out his heart. Fence listened, regretting having waited so long to return.

"Last week Edin took off his belt and whipped the dog. Lad is soaking up the sun trying to heal. He's on the ground over by the porch." Fence's grieved eyes turned toward the old sheepdog. "No matter how much you kick him around, that dog seems to come back," Arthur added.

"I have a room at the inn," Fence said, declining the man's invitation to stay in the ancient house. "I don't fit here anymore," he told the captivating man. "I remarried."

That night, resolutions spun around in Fence's head. He was unable to sleep in the dingy inn room—too much burned in his brain. He remembered an old coffee and tobacco shop that had stood the test of time. A blue smoke filled the rich-smelling room. Fence sat alone at a dark table in the corner, wishing for company, hoping his father was keeping Tia and Rose safe, wondering what kind of investigating his grandfather was up to. Then his mind returned to Scotland.

Suspicions of Edin's involvement with the underground plagued Fence. Contorted implications compelled him to resolve lingering questions, to find Lily's brother. And how did this relate to Tia and precious Rose, if it did? *There are no coincidences*, Abe had often stated.

Fence was unaware that the youth trudged the streets and alleys like a lost dog, kicking the cobblestones in front of him. The night crowd had dissipated. The atmosphere remained moody. Hate had grown thick in Edin. His mischievous associates were hard-pressed to find anything suitable about him. Meanness ruled his life.

Having grown sleepy, Fence retired from the coffee shop. Exiting, he nearly stumbled over a snarling teen, not recognizing him. "Sorry. Didn't mean to run into you. How about…ah?"

The kid was on some wild trip and could not sort out reality. Rudely, he had bumped against Fence in an awkward crash, and then vanished from sight.

Brushing himself off, Fence noticed that his jacket felt empty. No wallet, no journal, no money, no driver's license. The kid had stolen the whole works. "I should have known better than to get taken," he murmured, regretting his uncustomary carelessness. He trudged to the police station to no avail, knowing he would end up doing his own private investigation. Besides, there was more at stake.

"Tia's hanky!" He reached under his shirt, making certain he still had it. The cotton tee shirt underneath had a pocket for his true valuables. Relieved, he returned to his room. He could not shake the idea that the kid seemed familiar.

Empty and disillusioned, Fence searched his black leather bag, looking for the news page. Tia was on his mind. He weighed the pros and cons of telling her the truth. Chance Cummings had fed her enough lies to last a lifetime. He hated feeding her more. Fence rolled up his shirtsleeves. He was hot.

Off in the distance Edin raced to a scummy hideout. He peeled out the American bills, emptying the wallet dry. With a side throw, he discarded the container. He clasped the book, opening it for hidden treasure—a jewel, or key to a safety deposit box, something to gamble with. What met his hungry eyes was not what he expected. The handwritten lines formed a progression. The script drew Edin inward.

Some things need to die, like anger that burns in the heart, the furnace where greed wants to blaze, stealing, robbing the things that give perpetual warmth. No prosperous function happens when a body burns with rage. It only depletes a man, leaving him hollow.

Edin put the book into better light, devouring the words. *Might be valuable.*

Forgiveness won't live unless anger dies.

Edin slammed the journal shut, speaking to himself. "It might fill up the boring times. Sounds like Sir Walter Scott or someone I've read before." His sister Lily never entered his mind. A drug deal was too close at hand. He had international aspirations. Fence's identity hid in his pocket.

Fence could have used a song about now, one that lifted his spirit. His search for Edin had not gone well. Arthur Mansfield had no recent photograph and no recent contact with his wandering son. Irish and English ballads filled most of the pubs, but no Edin.

The bruises on Fence gradually began to fade away on the exterior. Inside, he longed for little Rose, especially when he observed the Scottish children playing a game in the streets, jumping over sticks and letting out a loud holler every once in a while. The clogging movement of their feet, with hands hanging at their sides, had a rhythm that reminded him of Rose's twirling the day he left. *I wonder if Tia dances.*

The next night the investigation went to a higher level, or lower, depending how integrity is defined. His grandfather Reed had wired him the name of the Englishman. Fence memorized it and then destroyed the paper. Another week passed before Fence was able to arrange a meeting.

"Fence Carpenter." Fence gave his name, stretching his hand forward to meet the man with a white goatee who had just returned from a safari hunt in Kenya.

"Ivan Burns," the man answered. "So, we meet again."

"Oh?" Fence questioned.

"We English have a way of knowing." His reserved answer was typical.

"How long will this investigation take?" Fence asked.

"A month or more," the Englishman replied.

Fence's pulse rate was on the rise. "I don't know if I have that much time."

"You can't afford not to." Ivan Burns checked his watch for Zulu time.

"Maybe not. Is this connected to T.R. Bain?"

The man looked Fence in the eyes, riveting him to truth. "Indeed, it is. You see, Abraham Pearl contacted me just before he died, wanting to rescue her baby."

"Yes?" Fence prodded. "Please continue."

Before answering, the Englishman briefly lifted his chin so the point of his goatee stuck straight out. "It seems he was made aware of a plot to expose her real identity. The baby got caught in the middle."

Fence's mouth dropped open. His eyes widened. His head nodded with two little jerks. *So that's why Abe was so adamant I adopt the baby and lay Lily to rest.* He cocked his head to the side to ask Ivan Burns the next question. "What made him think I would go through with it?"

"He knows you well."

"But why didn't he give me the information?" Fence probed.

"When things happen naturally, suspicions get squelched."

"Abe must have known the Jamaican too," Fence half-asked, remembering the meeting at Gramercy Park.

"Possibly," the man answered.

"Probably," Fence reinforced.

"This is bigger than you think, Fence Carpenter."

"Apparently." Somewhat reassured, Fence began to carefully explain the loss of his identification and the search for Edin Mansfield.

"That's only one of our problems," Ivan specified. "A fine possibility exists that your lack of identity may help expose an international crime ring. You will operate undercover. It will come naturally. In due time you will return to the United States." Ivan Burns gave no smile.

The Warm Cocoon

CHANCE Cummings was gone. The autopsy showed he had died of heart malfunction from undue stress. The pressure had been immense, the fight grueling. Tia knew Chance drank heavily before military physicals, much more than usual. "I need to thin out my blood," he had told her. Chance walked a shade below the truth and that was how he died.

Authorities shipped his body in a sealed casket to a private cemetery near Shreveport under his assumed name. His mother would never know his death was not heroic over the Devil's Triangle, the place where bones and curses lie together. Chance paid the untold price with his life. He sold out to the enemy. The profitless endeavor left him empty. One too many risks took the toll. Living on the edge reduced him to nothing.

"He died with only his secrets," Tia said to Mack one day. After that, she never mentioned Chance Cummings or anything about him, closing the subject to everyone but herself.

The M / M Ranch moved with activity. It was a strange and different world, one to which Tia Rose Carpenter was unaccustomed. The trees moved with a different sound than those of Florida. Aspen leaves chattered busy songs in the ravines. They reminded her of another tree with a message, the Christmas tree—the one Fence had covered with white feathers. She pondered her strange relationship with Fence Carpenter—the man whose name she bore—the one who left her nested in an unknown tree of life. *I don't know him. I don't know his family.*

In all her years as an orphan, Tia had only imagined what a family would be like. She had spent hours longing for parents, daydreaming. Her face flushed when Mack referred to her as his daughter, endearing her to himself. *Strange,* Tia thought. *Sometimes I feel like the ragged velveteen rabbit.* She stretched the collar of the leather jacket close to her neck, clinging to Fence's father's expression of love.

Tia found Rose helping Marie tend the garden. Marie's heart seemed to touch the soil. She sang to the young plants, hovering over them. With each note the tenderlings seemed to blossom, opening to life. Tia reached for the hand creased with earth. "Marie, how do you know what is right?"

Drawn to the woman her son had married, the woman with a well of wisdom spoke with ease. "Loving does not come easy, it takes much courage. One must learn how, one must choose. Growth..." Marie pruned the tomato plant, "can be painful."

Rose wiggled her little body in between them, joining the moment with grown up words. "Dad-dee come home. Want Dad-dee."

Off in the distance Mack's buffalo herd grazed. The goodhearted man gave away all the hides and most of the meat to the tribes on the reservation nearby. His lavishness did not go unnoticed by Tia. "Generosity breaks greed's back," he had told her.

The giving hearts of Mack and Marie carried rewards that went far beyond fences, breaking off centuries of curses. Nations, tongues and tribes melted together in their presence. "Peace is written in the same color of blood," he said.

Natives respected the man of gentle strength. They honored him. Tia understood why. Freedom covered the Carpenter land. The ranch provided safety. Mack indulged Tia in stories of Indians making summer camp in the front yard, how they were welcomed when he was a child, how his father and mother never turned anyone away.

Only a year before, Tia had been homeless. She could not help but wish she had known someone like Mack Carpenter, noting his integrity, especially his ability to teach responsibility. In a unique way, Mack Carpenter, the man who kept his word, smoked a pipe of peace.

Like an endangered species, Mack wanted to protect Tia and preserve her until Fence returned. That is, if he returned. *What had he gotten himself into anyway? What was he thinking, leaving a delicate child and her mother, abandoning them at the doorstep?*

Clouds gathered above the mountains. Mack put his hat on. Few memories of Fence's first wife remained, but the contrast was great. Lily was so sure of herself, never needing a father. But this girl, Tia— although undoubtedly courageous and very private—needed to belong. Mack's love for her grew. She was the daughter he never had, emanating fresh beauty. She laughed at his jokes and absorbed what he said like a dry sponge receives water, slowly at first, but surely. Mack had seen her grimace in pain, but the girl never complained. He had seen her fight like a warrior to survive and admired her ability to face obstacles head on, to persevere humbly. In adverse situations, Tia made wise choices. "After all, she married our son," Mack told Marie.

But Mack could see that Tia was lonely. The interior cover-up troubled him. *Is she protecting Fence?* He could not read her. The aggravation gnawed at Mack. *She must be eaten away with questions, but she does not ask.* Restless, he braved a question. "Are you in love with my son?" Mack pried, reluctant to dig too deep. The last thing he wanted to do was to raise a barrier between Tia and Fence.

"Mack, I am his wife and he has given me a home and Rose. I'll be forever grateful," Tia answered with kindness, avoiding any mention of love. Tia had no intention of being cornered. She left the conversation broken. Fence had left her in an odd predicament without explanation. She had no way to explain the situation to Mack.

Mack and Marie looked at each other like newlyweds, fascinated in young love, full of youth, dreaming and talking. Tia never imagined that there could be such love between two people. Mack honored his native wife. Tia did not take them for granted. She had never taken anyone for granted. She was first beginning to understand what she never had. That she had been deprived had never occurred to her.

The home circled Tia. She thrived in the warm cocoon, in the freedom of belonging. There was something about the generations of Carpenter men—some truth of protection, of provision, of honor, of purpose, of what a family should be. *Are women empty without men like these?* Yet Tia could not bring herself to be dependent on them. She contemplated whether she was overextending her stay on the M / M Ranch, longing to find her place.

"Tell me about your ring?" Tia asked Mack one morning at breakfast. A tooth filled the cavity in the size-fourteen silver ring braided with gold. It hung tightly around the fourth finger of the man's huge right hand, simultaneously exhibiting beauty and hardiness of hours of work.

"It's an elk ivory." In a fatherly fashion, Mack explained from beginning to end the process of the elk hunt. "It's not like hunting prairie dogs in the Dakotas, nor is it like kayaking down the big white water in Alaska with bells on leather loops to keep the bears away." He laughed and Marie laughed with him.

It was more than Tia could fathom, that is, the love of a father.

141

Immersed in the immense revelation, she knew Fence had to come home soon, for Rose's sake, and maybe for hers.

Strange Safety Net

DECISIVE and straight to the point, Reed said without hesitation, "Mack! Get a handle on Fence's activities. He's in the middle of an investigation. We're certain of it." Beating around the bush was not Reed's method. "This place is a danger zone."

"You two are about as discreet as wall pegs. Tia has been holed up here and it seems to be as safe as anywhere." Mack poured the coffee.

"Just don't want your head in the sand. You've been so preoccupied with taking care of the girl. Have you forgotten how international underground rings operate?" Reed admonished.

"Pop, I gave my word. I don't plan to break a promise to my son," Mack defended. The answer had a slight edge to it. The undercut was not like him. He immediately regretted it. Attempting to rectify, he smiled, a bit coarser than before. "Doc and you are more trouble than a pile of renegades."

Mack genuinely trusted people until proven wrong. Unlike Fence or his father Reed, he nested somewhere in-between, content with peacemaking. Although he was the most skilled with a weapon, a phantom could easily enter and he knew it. Mack wanted to be without error. His mercy-heart won out more than not. Yet, he was not naïve enough to believe he was right all the time.

In the interim Tia was safe, but trapped. The cocoon was getting too hot for comfort. Days turned into weeks. Rose cried for her daddy. She seemed lost without him. Mack filled in by loving his granddaughter with increased enthusiasm. Although he tried with all his ability, "Papa" could not fill the gap.

Caught in the tightly woven net, Tia sensed underlying deception amidst the stability. She struggled to sort out the complexity, wanting to break out and stay at the same time. An undercurrent of contradictions plagued her. Little remarks, secrets, strange stops of conversation occurred when she entered the room. Adding to the apprehension, Fence's grandfather and the mysterious Doctor Bridger had taken up residence at the M / M Ranch.

Doc coughed and spat out the dry dust in his throat, disdaining the ruggedness of the area, wishing for a more sterile environment. He stood, wiping his glasses for the third time. "Looks like that security system has some flaws. Good thing for the humped grizzlies and the pointed snouts of the black bears. Keeps the riff-raff out." The unorthodox protection followed the fence line, crossing miles of rugged terrain and thick brush.

"Since when did you become a mountain man?" Reed chided. "Bears sleep in the winter."

Each man had developed his own idiosyncrasies. Fifty-five years only sharpened their differences—differences that kept them friends. Reed saw footprints as types of shoes and sizes of intruders. His eyes were in the back of his head as well as the front. However, he was not beyond a good laugh or a joke. Neither was Doc, whose unorganized precision made investigation all the more intriguing. It kept them both on the cutting edge.

Tia bit her tongue, overhearing the two old men. *Walls patrolled against invaders? What kind of a statement was that?* The isolation chilled her. She wanted to escape from the assuming family, who, on one hand, smothered her and Rose with affection. On the other, they kept her on a leash, delicately twisting what she said. Fence Carpenter's vanishing act did not help matters. She clawed at the wall of the guestroom near the open window. There was no place to go. Suddenly, she resented the assumptions of the Carpenter family.

She wrapped her hair up to the crown of her head in a quick knot, restraining it. She had more to think about than herself. There was Rose holding her in place. Wisdom told her not to react. Once again, the requirement for peace of mind linked with patience.

Flowers

CLAUDE Walking Elk extended the twenty-inch cedar instrument to Tia. She stepped back. A carved bird perched on the end of the flute. "This one is for Fence. It's a gift from me. My brother will come home soon," he encouraged.

Soon? Does he know something I don't? Her unspoken question held a hint of disgust.

"Take no chances," Claude counseled.

One Chance was enough. Tia, feeling a bit bitter, did not respond. She remained curious whether Fence had confided in Claude, wishing Tamsen had come instead. The unexpected visit carried an element of mystery.

"I will tell you the story of how the flute came to be," Claude continued. For the second time Tia listened to the tale of the mighty warrior who had nothing to give the Indian maiden but the strength of a song. The masculine version gripped Tia. She focused on the cedar bird.

Fence's friend was too close for comfort; or was it the message? Tia had no reason to fear Claude. However, her trust level, lower than it had been, raised her guard. She spoke nothing with her mouth. A nod of the head was enough to thank the Indian man who left as quickly as he had arrived.

Moments later Mack made an offer. "She's yours." He held the reins of one of his broke-for-a-woman horses, trained to come at the snap of a finger. Tia had ridden the palomino several times, and now Fence's father was giving her the horse! Mack had a way of smoothing out awkward situations. Most of the time, he managed to get away with his methodology, pulling smiles out of nowhere. Tia shook her head at him. Satisfaction settled into Mack. Her eyes sparkled.

A brown delivery truck bounced over the dirt trail into the yard, jerking to a stop. "Go over and check what Dennis has for us," Mack said with a grin. Tia dismounted, dropping the reins into Mack's big hands.

"Flowers! For who?" she inquired.

"Mrs. Carpenter." The slim deliveryman, wearing knee-length shorts, puffed in the heat. "Like an armed prison to get in here."

Ignoring his remark, Tia carried the bundle to the porch, thinking it must be Marie's birthday. Mack hollered. "Open it up. Who they for?" Her heart leaped when she saw the private card with an olive branch drawn in the corner.

"I don't know for sure," she yelled.

Mack haltered the horses and walked to her. She stood over the bouquet breathing the perfume with longing. Mack spoke with a smile, resembling Fence. "They must be for you, 'cause I'm the only one who ever gets flowers for Marie, and I didn't order any. Besides, she likes wild ones."

Tia tore off the outer wrap. The dozen coral roses, mixed with white baby breath, took her breath away. She clutched the card to her breast seeking the strength to open it. Mack, sensitive to her need for privacy, looked away, quenching his desire to know.

Tia
I did not forget our first anniversary.
Until tomorrow, peace to you.
Fence

Tia closed her eyes. Her heart throbbed, beating double time. No one had ever sent her flowers. "They're from Fence," she whispered. In the quiet moment she confided in her father-in-law.

"I thought so." Mack grinned. "Marie's in the garden. Go share the news."

Marie reached to a high shelf, lowering the homemade pottery vase. "It's made from various colors of clay," she said. "Why don't you move into Fence's old room, closer to Rose?"

The ivory teardrop on the dark crock transfixed Tia. One by one she placed the roses in the rainwater.

Fence's room was filled with artifacts collected after fresh rains, each holding a hidden story. The pine dresser-top left little space for more of the outdoors. Tia made room in front of the mirror, placing the roses so she could see their reflection, near the flute. The floral arrangement compelled her to come close.

Tia released her hair. Easing the knot on top out, she let it fall down her back. Overwhelmed, she sank into Fence's queen-size bed near the window. She had to reassure herself. *Fence is not a figment of my imagination. I know he's real, but I feel like I'm in a dream.* She held the little card in her left hand next to the silver wedding ring, rehearsing the note. *When is tomorrow?* Tia questioned. She rolled onto her side, hugging the pillow until sleep settled her.

Less than a mile away, the smell of home greeted Fence's nostrils. The den of baby red foxes, with their incessant yelping, covered the sound of the crunching grass. Sky's keen senses had picked up Fence's scent the moment Claude dropped him off at the main road. The silver-gray elkhound with her black-tipped tail sat alert, holding her position on the back step without a growl or bark. When Fence reached the inner border, the dog raced to him. Sky flew up into his arms, lavishing him with licks of love and acceptance.

"It's me old friend, old girl, your ally, your buddy. Did you miss me? I missed you pal." He rubbed the dog's furry head with his one free hand. "Good thing you're around. That guard at the gate nearly failed to notice me." Tugging the corner of his pant leg, Sky led Fence home. Fence ruffed the fur on Sky's neck. "Loyalty seems to run in the family," he said with dual definition.

He wanted to surprise them, or maybe he did not want to face them until morning. He entered like a deer moving through a field, unnoticed, so tired, so glad to be home, removing his boots on the porch. He left the lights off, feeling his way like a blind man reading Braille, until he caught a glimpse of Rose's nightlight.

His chest leaned against the railing of her crib. The bed had been lowered. Rose was sound asleep. He kissed his little child thinking she had grown up, disappointed that he had missed two months of her life. An overflowing toy box filled the corner of the room. His childhood treasure bulged out of the trove. An old, brown bear with one eye stared at him.

Making a way to his room, Fence quietly released the load he carried. The trip had been taxing. He didn't want to have to think anymore, just rest from the journey. Assuming Tia would be tucked away in the guestroom, he breathed easier. Getting his life in order had taken its toll.

He ached knowing he had fallen down on the job. What had it done to them? He felt for his wedding ring with his left thumb. It was still on his hand.

He sniffed. An unusual odor filled the dark room, mixed with the smell of leather, the work he had done as a youth. He slipped between the sheets, crossing his arms behind his head to think. *Yes, it's good to be home,* he thought to himself. He rolled to the middle of his big bed and closed his eyelids. He longed for Tia to be next to him, not as Rose's mother, not as an orphan, not as a caretaker for him or Rose, not as a woman needing medical attention, not as his slave, but as his close friend, maybe, someday, as his wife. A second later sleep met him.

Fence's Jaw

FENCE'S clock had spun out of control the moment his head touched the old-faithful pillow. He rubbed his face, knowing he needed to shave. It was too late. Worn out, his body attempted to adjust to the time change, but his mind entered a twilight zone. Instinctively, he rolled to his side. Warmth was near. Immediately Fence faded into a dream.

He and his dad were bow hunting for elk. The partners of the hunt had rubbed raw apple on their arms and faces, in order to deceive the elk's excellent olfactory senses, the superb nose of the wild. The two hunters invaded the woods, dressed like trees. Together they trudged through the fresh mountain snow, ascending the ridge to set up a lookout.

Fence saw the mammoth rack on the elk's head rise high. The bull's thirty-inch windpipe arched upward. The animal breath steamed in the cold; his nostrils enlarged. The bull's bugle whistled through six-year-old ivory teeth, summoning the cows, notifying all males to stay clear, that he was the master. The territorial claim-stake of the elk echoed, sounding a mix of love and power.

The bullfight over the cows, over position, caused a wrangling on the slopes. Impatience brooded in Fence. The fever of the hunt sent chills through him. Not daring to breathe, he raised the heavy-duty bow in front of his shoulder. Cautiously, Fence waited in stillness for the elk to raise its head and look him in the eye.

Then, before Fence could think, he launched the arrow. It hit the mark in the massive beast's lung. The animal lumbered to the earth. The other two males leaped into the air, nearly eight feet high, shooting out like arrows sprung from a bow. Mack's shots followed consecutively, but the herd escaped into the woodland.

Mack chuckled and raised his hunting hat as he stood over the downed elk. "Listen." His ears cocked forward in a hush.

"Grizzly bear sign! They're thrashing through, looking for easy dinner." He winked. *"There will be more elk, son. The bears are hungry. Better the elk than us."*

Fence nodded, holding the ivories up in plain sight. *"I got the whistlers!"* He hung his arm around his dad's shoulder.

Unknowingly, Fence wrapped his arm over Tia.

She slept peacefully under Fence's wing. Daylight peeped through the shades, waking her out of a stupor. Awareness pulled her into reality. The heavy breathing was not hers. *Fence.* His childhood bed, his pillow, his blue-jean patchwork quilt, his smell, his strength, his dreams, his heart. Him! It was too much, too much to be true. Terror gripped her. She did not think he would come back. But he was back and much too close.

Restrained in the mold, an overpowering feeling of suffocation caused Tia to want to run, to find breathing space. Sister Maria Thomas once said, *Life is measured by the moments that take one's breath away.* Tia's breath was being stolen away, right under her nose.

She squirmed, powerless. Finally, she pulled her head under his arc, squeezing out of the clamp. Grasping her things, she tiptoed toward the guestroom. *Why am I so afraid of him? Where did he come from? How did he get into that bed?* Her whole body trembled, quivering in uncertainty.

She traipsed by Rose's room, stopping to admire her soft dark curls. "Rose, I love you." She could not go on. She curled up in the velour recliner with Rose's small white heart blanket. Rocking herself to sleep in the pain of truth, Tia finished the night near her daughter.

It was the smell of her hair that jolted him awake. Tia's hair! No secret code, no ulterior motives, no black market. *Was she on this bed? What a night of dreams! My God, how will I face her? What would Dad do? Probably have me bugle to her.* He laughed inside at the ridiculous idea. *No, that idea is as thick as mud. She once said she wanted a friend, someone to talk to, to talk to her. Guess I need to start from scratch, except for Rose. ROSE!*

He darted out of bed, entering Rose's room in his underwear. "Hey little girl, daddy's home." His doll reached upward.

Tia, lifting her aching neck, tried to get her bearings. Fence had not seen her, but Rose had. "Mama, mama, daddy home."

Speechless, Tia pulled her knees up under the little blanket that barely covered her.

Fence turned around, surprised at her presence. "Good morning, Tia."

She caught the tender words and returned a weak façade of a smile.

Rose's little arms gripped Fence's neck. "Don't go daddy. Stay daddy."

Fence reassured her. "Daddy's home. Home with you." He took a breath. "Home with Papa Mack and Gam Deer. Home where I was once little like you." He glanced toward Tia, before smothering Rose's neck with kisses until she giggled.

Tia's heart beat uncontrollably seeing Rose melt into one with her daddy. The Christmas quilt that she had made for Rose hung around them both, covering Fence's exposure. Her head ached. *Trying to fit a square peg into a round hole only works when the hole is much larger.* She did not fit.

"Come snuggle on daddy's bed," he said, nose to nose with Rose. He peeked around looking at Tia. "Would you come too? It wouldn't seem right without Rose being between us." He smiled again, embracing her heart with his green-gray eyes.

"You're a good mother, Tia," Fence reflected, standing in the doorway. The Jamaican's warning flashed through his thoughts, reinforced by his recent visit with the Englishman Ivan Burns. Now that Fence was home, he did not want Rose or Tia out of his sight. "Rose is talking clearly, making sentences. Her vocabulary has increased. I've been gone too long. I missed too much." He tilted his head back and turned his lips inward with the knowledge, staring at the crib.

Tia's body longed to follow Fence, but her heart was held in a vice grip. She distrusted men. She could not move. *I'm scared, scared of relationship.* For an hour her fear pinned her motionless.

Fence emerged fully dressed to get Rose's play clothes. Neither spoke. The anniversary card still slept crumpled between the sheets. He had found it and left it in place.

Sister Marie Thomas' advice rang into Tia. *Trusting is like a pot of gold at the end of the rainbow. Valuable, but a process gets you there, not short cuts. You must follow the arc.*

Why hasn't she moved? Fence fought with misunderstanding. *Tia looks like she's in a state of shock.* He questioned himself, *Where do I go from here?*

Marie Deer Path spotted her son's boots at the break of dawn, his little signs of trail. Fry bread aroma filled the house. Freshly squeezed orange juice filled the miniature glasses. The smells overtook Fence. He jogged to the country kitchen. Rose hung onto his neck for the ride.

"Welcome home. We've done all you requested and then some." Marie placed a full plate in front of him. She did not ask for answers.

"And more." Fence laughed.

Marie scooped Prairie Rose Flower up into the old-fashioned wooden highchair. "So you've really come home!" She gave Fence a warm look. "Tia waits by the window if we don't have her with us. We've been concerned for her." Marie tied Rose's bib before adding. "The roses. It is good you sent Tia roses."

Fence was sober with contemplation. "Mom, I don't know where to start and when to stop." He gulped the orange juice, dripping honey on the fresh bread. "You're a great cook, do you know that?"

My Name

OUTDOOR sounds broke the inner silence. "Mack!" Tia said out loud. She had forgotten the scheduled morning ride. She kissed the silver locket. "Because of Rose. I must do this because of her." Shoving Fence's return out of her mind, she hurried out the back door to the barn.

Mack held a buckskin horse named Parchment that Tia had never seen before. He hoisted the well-used leather roper saddle. "Think we'll try this guy out," he said, grinning at her. He made no mention of Fence.

Tia wrapped her arms around the new neck, claiming the interesting stallion. "Mack, I'd like to ride him."

"Sure, I'll shorten the stirrups. But, I'll warn you; he can be temperamental. Are you certain you're ready for this?" He paused, smiling at her. "Guess you are. I need to get a canteen of water from the house. Wait here."

Anxious to ride the new horse, Tia hastened up a narrow trail knowing her independence was showing. Checking with high-powered binoculars, she watched buffalo crossing the creek. A lone bull lounged on the ridge. Mack was galloping Gold Dollar, the palomino, faster than usual. He slowed down just behind her. Without looking, she handed the field glasses out to him.

"Thanks!" he said. "How do you like my horse?" Tia did a double take. Fence was the rider, not Mack. Her escape had failed. Blocking Fence out was not working.

"I— I didn't know he was your horse. Do you want to exchange?"

"No, looks like Parch is partial to you. You read him like a book. He doesn't let just anyone ride him." Fence looked off toward the mountains. "Let's ride to the ridge and find out what's going on," he said decisively.

"I think we should go north. Mack wanted to work that section," Tia said, determined to stay in control. Suddenly, her eyes widened.

Fence looked too big for the palomino. She suppressed a burst of upcoming laughter with a huge swallow.

"Okay. Sure." He grinned. "Sounds like you've fallen in love with my father. It's alright, everyone does." He paused. Inside, a twinge of jealousy pinched him. His dad had been there for her. Emptiness had gnawed its way into Fence's life. Regrets, mixed with relief at putting closure to the uncontrollable past, were rapidly setting the stage for the future. Uneasiness rode in his gut. Being next to Tia stimulated desires to be close, to give. Yes, to reach out; or was there a need beyond? His heart raced. He was not ready to personalize the word love or let it have a place in his vocabulary.

Tia adjusted herself in the saddle, biting her tongue. Fence was right about his dad. She twisted toward Fence, speaking in honesty. "Yes. I love your father. He's my friend."

"Did he teach you to ride like that?" Fence watched the natural ease with which she moved in the saddle. "He always wanted a daughter you know," he casually interjected.

"I never had a father. Anyway, not like him." She trotted along.

"No one is like my dad, except maybe my grandfather." Fence caught up with her. She slowed to a walk, ignoring him. He kept trying to break the ice, waiting patiently for her to join the conversation. Each had become accustomed to talking, to reasoning with self. Now the proximity of each other was a breath away, stirrup-to-stirrup. Fence rode closer than he intended. His leg bumped against hers.

Tia's forefinger pointed over him. "See the buffalo with the 'TC' brand? An old black cow stepped on her leg and broke it in two places. Mack and I put a splint on it. Now she runs faster than all the other calves. He told me she's mine cause I wouldn't give up on her. Said that I needed a brand. He even registered it."

"How could I miss? White buffalo are rare. Actually, she's the first one I've ever seen. I suppose Mack told you that tribes consider them miracles. Some Indians worship them." She gave a nod. He noted the capitol "T" with a horseshoe "C," a ringer, pillowed in the bed of the animal's furry hip.

"And do you worship them?" she asked.

"What? I apologize. My mind was somewhere else." Fence's head was in a childhood haze.

"The buffalo? Are white buffalo gods to you?" she asked again.

"No, Tia." He pulled Gold Dollar to a stop, reverting to the identification of the new brand pressed onto the pink flesh. "Mack doesn't usually brand buffalo. I'm surprised he didn't make it 'TLC' with all your tender care and loyalty." He avoided the word love.

Memories of Mack Carpenter, the man who raised him, crowded his thoughts. His father had always taken time for people, time to build relationships, seeing value in the least little thing. How different, how committed, how seasoned, how much Mack gave love to others, starting with Marie, Fence's mother. "Guess I need to take lessons," he said out loud.

Tia's thoughts did not stray away from the calf. She spoke eagerly. "We fed her with a pail. She's an orphan, kind of like me." She pulled up beside the tame buffalo. "I named her Destiny because she was determined to live."

"I believe that." He hesitated, speaking almost under his breath. "You have my name."

Tia looked away. It was too much. Was she a possession, burned with a name? Instantly, she kicked the buckskin in the ribs. The steep climb took her to a big rock, pulling strength out of her. She let the breeze blow the tears off, allowing no more. She would not give pain the right to consume her, no matter what the terms and conditions of the label.

When she finally stopped, Fence was alongside her. The bold sun spotlighted the hidden valley and lit up the surrounding foothills. Fence dismounted, jumping to land. He grabbed Parchment's bit, seeking Tia's attention. "Please, will you listen to me? I'm trying to make a peace treaty with you, but it takes two in agreement. My name does not mean I own you. You didn't lose your identity. You gain identity. Maybe you don't like it or want it, but it's all I have to give you." He struggled, trying to get through to her. "Can we be friends?"

Tia sucked in her breath. "I don't know. I want to, but I don't know if I know how."

"You and me both." Fence's crisp laugh freed her to smile. Her face, modeled before him, revealed more character than he understood. "You know, your eyes glisten when you smile." He helped her take the big step to earth.

Tia ran her hands down Parchment's neck to the saddle. Without a word, she threw the stirrup over the saddle, loosing the cinch a notch. She breathed in the clean air. "It's so peaceful here. The wild is so tame and the birds are so friendly."

"I suspect it's easier to be friends with a bird than me. Better communicators. Most of my talking is thinking out loud." Fence caressed the palomino neck. "Pretty filly—a little jumpy. Dad must have just gotten her."

"He bought her for me," she said, feeling shy. "It's the first animal that's ever been mine."

"I'm not surprised. I mean that he gave her to you," Fence said. "It's easy to get attached to animals. Less threatening than humans."

"Marie says they love without condition." Tia laid her head on Fence's horse and continued. "At the orphanage we had a red macaw named Will. He was quite unusual, singing Christmas carols year round, trying to recite Latin, making us laugh when we were told to be serious," Tia shuffled the words out as she pictured the incident.

Fence chipped bark off a dead trunk with his knife, trying to catch every word. He tooled Tia's brand into the clean wood. "Remember the star you made for the Christmas tree? Contrary to what you may think, I did notice," he said. "You are like the star. I mean, giving direction. I meant to thank you. Tia, what I'm trying to say is this. I've been wandering around and you've helped me get on course."

She followed a pair of cedar waxwings with her eyes. They landed in the lone blue spruce beside them. "Birds seem to always know where they're going, what their purpose is, what road to take."

"You don't miss much, do you?" he commented. As if on cue, concern mounted. *How much does she know? How much don't I know?*

"There's much I don't know and wish I did," she said. "Like who I am."

Once again the Jamaican's admonition surfaced in Fence. A death threat still hung in the air, waiting to steal the destiny of the woman before him. That he knew. Chance Cummings was not the root, only a smokescreen that added to her problems. The newspaper article hidden in the side pocket of his travel bag reopened his concern. Like it or not, the stakes had risen too high to ignore. His main job of bodyguard was more vital than ever. He retraced Tia's brand, molding it to precision, emphasizing the half circle of the C. He had to keep peace with her at all costs.

"I don't think we can handle the full load of each other's past," Tia confessed. She pulled back. The knife was a little too close for comfort.

"You're right about that," Fence added. "It comes layer by layer."

He closed his knife. "So why don't we start from scratch? No questions. Okay? When you're ready; when I'm ready."

He waited for her response. Then Tia's simple words caressed him with the feel of white rabbit fur. "I've never had a true friend," she confided.

Starting to walk, she led Fence's horse. He held loosely to Gold Dollar's reins, taking oversized strides to catch her. "I sold the house. The shippers are sending our things here." Tia stopped, silently taking in every word. Skepticism of his decision made her stomach queasy. After all, why should she be consulted? She pushed the shock and unregistered grief into the background reserved for further understanding. Fence followed up his comment. "It's for the best, at least for a little while. Florida is not a safe place anymore, for you or for Rose," he explained.

"And for you?" she questioned. He did not answer. The meadow, filled with wildflowers, opened before them. A creek flowed out in front. The water talked. Fence got down on his heels and picked a wide blade of rush. Tia marveled at the generational similarities between Fence, his father and the interesting grandfather Reed—the same move of the head, the thickness of hair, the absence of speech. Mannerisms communicated a whole story without the presence of words.

Strength emanated from Fence's limbs. His arm rested on his knee. He seemed to bend into her. Words are jewels only when they say something of worth to the words around them, when they are placed in the right setting. Unexpectedly, they rolled out of Fence's mouth.

"Claude and I made whistles from horsetail when we were kids. It doesn't usually grow this high up." He took the hollow rush between his hands. The shrill, whistling sound vibrated with his breath. He handed it to her. "Try it."

Tia dropped the reins, shedding the leather jacket. Her mouth was dry, but her lungs strong. Her fingers lacked skill. "Like this?" she asked.

"Let me show you." He stood behind her, cupping her hands and arms in his, firmly positioning the reed between her fingers. He held it to her mouth. "Alright, you can do it. Vibrate your lips with a puhhh motion."

Tia whistled the instrument of grass. She burst into laughter. "I did it." She turned to him, covering her mouth in joy.

"You have a nice laugh," Fence said, liking her spontaneity, remembering her hug the night he gave her the jacket. "We made our bows smooth with the horsetail, used it for sandpaper. Feel." She touched the raspy surface.

"Tia?" He put his hand on her back, reinforcing his earlier words. "I want to be your friend." He felt her heart beating like an Irish bodhran in the middle of her spine. An electrical current transmitted to him, making him sweat.

She turned toward him. "I worried about you. The fight?" She shook her head and pursed her lips. The wide scar running the length of his neck was still pink from tenderness. "You had to have stitches. I apologize for all the trouble I caused you. Chance Cummings was an impulsive, unpredictable man."

"I figured as much. His punches hurt more on the inside than out. And, yes, Doc Bridger thoroughly enjoyed sewing me up that day. He likes to needle me." He smiled, looking at her like he was seeing her for the first time. *Had Chance Cummings hit her?* He wanted to ask, but held his tongue.

Covering her insecurity, she toyed with the bridal reins. "I think we should change horses. You look kind of ridiculous on the palomino. She's too small for you."

Fence grinned. "Call her 'Doll' for short. Mack probably wants to have her bred." He lifted the saddle off Parchment in one smooth move.

She took a gulp of air. The horse with the ripe banana-colored skin and vanilla-cream mane had already won her love. "What's wrong?" Tia asked.

"Nothing much. You'll have to ride with me on Parchment." In the process of switching saddles, Fence had discovered a slit on the leather above the O-ring. He turned, facing Tia head on. A frown creased his forehead.

"Fence?"

"Someone is a little knife happy is all. This was meant for me, not you, and, it wasn't done yesterday. Your light weight did not topple the saddle, but mine would have." Fence showed her the cut.

Tia's eyes grew wide. They rolled up toward Fence. "What does this mean?" she asked, somewhat bewildered.

"It means you're not to worry about it," Fence assured her, mounting Parchment. "Come on. Give me your hand." He pulled Tia up behind him.

Hunger pangs reminded her of missed breakfast and the life she had once known with a very different kind of family. Fence seemed to read her mind. "Will you let me take you to dinner tonight? I promise not to give orders. I'll just sit, listen and give you my ear."

"That would be nice. Thank you. You can keep your ear." The remainder of the ride passed without words. She mused on the name Carpenter. Like it or not, she carried it. Her hands gripped the saddle's back, avoiding touching him. Suddenly, she missed the warm humid air and the macaw. She looked over the valley, contemplating. *Is there such a thing as a safe place? I don't think so, not within man's reach anyway. Is Fence's life in danger because of me?*

Mack stood at the split rail fence, chewing on the end of a wild oat straw. He spoke to his Arabian, stroking the old horse's neck. "They're coming home together. That's a relief."

Mack knew a lot more than he let on. He tilted his hat back down before hiking the familiar path toward the house. The dinner bell would sound shortly. *Tia must be starved.*

Exposure

FENCE knocked on the guestroom door. "I need to talk to you." He waited for Tia to answer, hesitant to push.

Tia's eyes roamed the empty cedar closet. *Had Lily slept in this room?* The question surfaced out of nowhere. Tia's scarce wardrobe was absorbed by the woodwork. Clothes had never been a problem before. *What would be appropriate?* Her head circled. Apprehension boxed her in. To be with Fence without Rose in a public place troubled her. Or was it inadequacy? And would it be safe? Reed Carpenter might not be too happy about it. That fact inspired her to be all the more determined. She stared at the simply dressed conifers displaying elegance. Pushing the window up, she smelled the rich fragrance. Almost in front of her a monarch butterfly landed on a silver sage plant with lavender blooms—lambs ear. Fence's voice finally touched her ears.

"Come in. The door's open," she breathed.

He approached her with caution, catching what she saw. "They were a wedding gift to my parents from Doc Bridger."

"What?" Her eyes were fixed on the monarch.

"The lambs ear. The plant? Like you, it's from the south. During the civil war the velour leaves were used to wrap wounds. Doc told me the story when I was young. I never had to use them in emergency medical." He stepped behind her.

"Butterflies teach us what flowers smell like," she said.

"I never learned that lesson very well, only the one about mountain lions demonstrating strength," Fence said, dropping a pair of sandals on the bed.

"I'd like to learn that, strength that is." Tia turned toward him.

Fence grinned. "I think you already have. I've never known anyone like you. By the way, thanks for letting me keep my ear."

"The feeling is mutual," she said, noticing the package under his arm.

"I got this for you in Europe." Fence set the box in her arms.

Embossed roses raised their velour heads from the gift wrapped in silver foil. Tia ran her fingers over the paper, savoring the feeling of elegance. She fumbled with the ribbon. Finally, she looked toward Fence. "Did you have a good afternoon with Rose? She missed you terribly."

"I love that girl. She's incredible. I didn't realize what she meant to me. You've done a good job with her." He pulled out his jackknife. "I'll help. With the package that is." He cut the tape precisely. Out of the corner of his eye he caught her looking at the bronze sandals on the bed. "I'm not too good at sizes. I guessed."

She looked down at her little feet before acknowledging him. "I remember."

"You can wear them tonight if you like," he whispered in her ear.

"Fence?" Her head turned upward. "Thank you." The two words stumbled out as he exited.

The sage green outfit fit perfectly. Tia pulled the silver locket out from beneath its hiding place, putting both hands over the Mother's Day gift. Using the porcupine-tail brush that Marie had given her, she combed her hair with long strokes, more than the length of her arm. Natural oils brought the shine out. Calm wrestled with nervousness.

"Don't be afraid," Fence's mother said. "No reason. An anniversary dinner marks peace. Integrity guides Fence. No harm will come to you." Marie spoke again, this time in riddles. "Little birds move out of safe trees during the day. At night they come home." Marie secured the beaded clip in Tia's hair.

Tenderness beyond the normal had touched the crown of Tia's head, the hand of an industrious and faithful woman. Calluses below each of Marie's fingers on the inside of her hand revealed evidence of years of hard work, and the strength that comes from it.

Tia looked down with a nod—listening—silenced by the rhythm of kind words. *Does she know? Does she know I'm not really Fence's wife?*

Tia reached for Marie's hand, squeezing it firmly. *Marie knew.*

Why do I feel kinship with this woman? Is it because she's a mother, because she doesn't condemn? In that moment an inner knowing answered Tia's question, one so personal, so private. Only one who had experienced the trauma would understand. Somewhere, a time in her past, Marie Deer Path had been raped. Of that, Tia was certain.

She would keep the secret.

Marie whispered, "It's finished. Go with Fence."

The outstretched arms of wilderness met Tia as she entered the massive great room. Mounted elk heads, a black bear and other taxidermied wildlife stuck their noses out. Tia had been in the museum of a room only once. Mack's badger hide, stretched over a dogwood frame, stood in the far corner near the large rock fireplace. Marie Deer Path's jingle dress hung over an old dress frame with its strings of ivory teeth dancing on fringes. An antler chandelier hung over the center of the winter room. The moose chairs, made by the Manitoba Métis—the French Canadian, Chippewa blend—extended generous, oversized comfort. Tia's nerves were on edge. Her golden hair looked out of place next to the dark hides. *I don't belong here,* she reasoned.

A whistle blew out of Fence's mouth. "Whew. I think I'll take you out tonight." His teasing seemed out of place, but his eyes were magnetized to her. "You are stunning," he complimented, wondering why anyone would want to kill such a beautiful woman.

Tia took a deep breath. His cologne reached her nostrils. It was the same draw that she smelled on Rose after Fence held her. He towered above her. *I have to look forever to see his face.*

"Shall we go?" His hand extended to take hers. The diamond on the silver and gold braided band glistened on his ring finger. Tia hesitated, slowly submitting her ringless, right hand.

The Lodge emanated the rugged character of the old west with hand-peeled logs speaking of golden dreams. Tia's sandals sunk into the deep red Arabian rug. The soft wool cushioned her steps, spreading out a welcome mat for her. Glass oil lamps lit the room with majestic light. Fence kept looking at her and it made her nervous. Tia transferred her focus to the pianist touching the ivory keys. The man's fingers danced with skill and passion. The classical notes helped Tia relax.

"Everything okay?" Fence asked, breaking the "no questions" rule.

"It's lovely here." She radiated.

Fence's eyes shined. "Tia, have you ever tried to not ask questions and realized how hard it is?"

She risked a smile. "That's true," she admitted. "Fence? Our relationship is getting more confusing all the time. Is this for show or what?"

"Tia, it's because I owe you." He wanted to say it was a date. But was that true? He took note of the softness of her lips when they moved, before adding, "And, it's our anniversary. I'm sorry. It's been a sham of a marriage." Fence waited for her to look at him. *If she would just trust me.* He spoke the thought out loud. "Guess I haven't proven myself very trustworthy."

At that moment, Ruger Bellows, Fence's old classmate, walked up beside their table. Overhearing Fence, he butted in. "No you can't trust this guy. Now me... that's another story." Ruger's pride spoke with drooling eyes desiring Tia. For years he had carried a chip on his shoulder. He gloated at Fence. "What happened to that Scottish girl you were with? How do you manage to get all the pretty girls?"

"Miss." His scaly hand grabbed Tia's. "Come on for this dance."

"Move on, Ruger," Fence ordered.

"I didn't mean any harm. Aren't you going to introduce me?" he goaded. "The lovely lady needs a man who will stick around."

"That's enough, Ruger." Fence rose to his feet. "Put her hand down. This is my wife. Stop manhandling her."

Tia pulled her hands onto her lap, hiding them from the brash, wiry-looking man. She braced herself, fearing another fight, hoping the dirty man would leave. He continued to dig into Fence.

"Oh that's right, your wife died. Sure you didn't have anything to do with it?" Ruger blabbed harassment. Having cut up Fence's past with his remarks, the little man turned to address Tia. "So, miss, no, you can't trust him. Fence always thought he was better than everyone." His beady eyes stared at her, casting seeds of doubt into Tia. Snarling, Ruger added. "He's just a blond half-breed who finagles his way into an ivy-league school out east!" Boils of jealousy emerged from the crevices in Ruger's forehead.

Fence mustered all his reserve to keep his tongue and temper in check. He had no intention of hitting Ruger unless he had to. The loathsome man's prying dug up old bones. Fence grabbed the smart aleck, holding him against the inn wall with the back of his forearm. "Ruger, you seem to have a habit of stirring up trouble. You're not worth mashing up the Lodge for. Now get lost!"

Fence released Ruger abruptly. The scrawny man tried to swallow, backing away, brushing himself. He realized Fence was a plank that stood up to his word. "Just bein' friendly, that's all, just testing." Ruger's snake eyes squinted at Tia. "Didn't mean nothing by it ma'am." He spat into Fence's empty plate and walked away with a smirk on his face.

Tia wanted to wash her hands and get the touch off. Fence circled the back of the table, sliding Tia's chair out. "Come on. Let's get out of here. Sorry Ruger wrecked our meal." Fence, exposed by all the jabs, put his arm round her, pulling her close. "This wasn't the best idea I've ever had."

"Thanks for protecting me. I didn't want to dance with that man." She recollected another time, another place, when there was no hand of protection, when Chance Cummings laughed at her. She had long regretted that night.

Fence's irritation showed. He mumbled, "Someone should lay Ruger out flat. He has a big mouth. Ever since I was a kid, he wrangled with me, hurling insults, breeding prejudice. He puts down Indians, Jews and anyone else not European white. I have to admit, I had to restrain myself from punching him out."

Tia looked up at him. "Some men have a heart of stone. That doesn't mean they're beyond hope."

Fence hesitated. A bit of trepidation poked at him, remembering other encounters and his native mother. "Like me? I'm not as hard as you think." A sobering smile crossed his face then he added, "Tia, I don't look like my mother either."

She said quietly, leaning into him, "I've got that figured out." They climbed into Mack's pickup. She pulled the seatbelt over her shoulder.

The Cry of Communication

THE uncomfortable scene with Ruger Bellows at the Lodge propelled Fence into an explanation. He owed Tia that much. He ran his fingers through his hair, searching for words. A yearning to make things right possessed him. "I was wrong," he admitted, pulling the vehicle off at a historical landmark. "When Lily died, a part of me died. I can't explain it." Tia would not make eye contact with him. He did not know if he wanted her to. He struggled to come out of the pit and not dig it deeper. "I blamed myself for Lily's death," he confessed.

A sorrowing wind cried through the trees. Fence labored to speak. Loneliness exposed itself on the inside and out. Tia turned her lips inward, pressing them together, unable to express consolation with words. The truth of the peculiar situation was almost more than she could handle. She heard the cry hiding out in Fence's belly, and she identified with it. Chance Cummings would be alive if not for her. Grief for the man who sat beside her began to leak through. Did she feel sorry for Fence, or for herself? She closed her eyes.

Certain times make for big tears, but she would not allow them. She did not want Fence to see her broken. Holding them back, she retraced her inability to understand Fence during the past year. She found herself envisioning Fence's love for Lily. Her lower abdomen shuddered.

Leaning over the steering wheel, Fence furrowed his brow. "How about a look at the view?" he said for lack of better words.

Swinging the door open, she jumped off the running board, walking on her own, uncomfortable with the whole process of communication. His hand capped her shoulder from behind, slowing her to a stop. Warmth flowed through him to her. She did not turn towards him. Fence's voice was mellow. "Beautiful out here isn't it?" From the back he saw her head nod once.

"Tia, I went to Scotland to clear up a mess. Lily's kid brother is in trouble. He blames me for his sister's death. He detests Americans, especially me. He's a user, not just drugs, but people. My gut feel is that he's out to get me. We haven't..." Fence paused during the uneasy interval, contemplating whether he should finish the sentence. "I don't think we have seen the last of him."

"We?" She questioned.

"Yes. We." His right hand raised her jaw. "I want to tell you. Tia, I have to talk to you. I need you for a friend for Rose's sake. Whether you know it or not, you need me." He released her, hoping she would stay tuned to him. She said nothing.

He cleared his throat. "I know this sounds chaotic. I have to get it off my chest, so please hear me out." He stretched himself to be honest and open. "I've tried to lock the doors of my past. They keep reopening, invading the present. You've been getting the brunt of my history. I'm sorry about that."

Tia listened, waiting for more.

Fence felt disjointed. "Add all that to yours, and we make quite a pair." The soft smile that possessed his lips transferred to her, connecting them momentarily.

Recomposing her thoughts, Tia opened her eyes wide to his. "Tell me about her, about Lily." She emanated an earnest desire for him to share more, but retreated. "Guess I'm breaking the rules now. I didn't mean to pry." She cast her face onto the graying gravel under her feet, suddenly reluctant to read the pages of his past.

Almost simultaneously the sun settled. The slivered moon hid in the shadows of wispy clouds with no plans of taking over the night. Cool mountain air touched them. "You're shivering." He nudged her toward Mack's pickup to get her jacket, arching her under his arm. Together they leaned against the passenger door, captured by the mysterious night.

"I never told you. I like it when you sing to Rose." Fence squeezed her closer to him, noticing that she was some place in outer space, looking at the sky this time, giving the stars all her attention. "Rose is enchanted when you read to her." Fence wanted to connect. Bridging the gulf was not progressing like he intended.

She hesitated before giving him an unidentifiable look. Profound thoughts opened Tia's mouth. "Unread pages of men contain all sorts of secrets."

Men. Me? Chance Cummings? Fence looked off into the distance, disliking the truthful insinuation.

"Why did you adopt Rose?" Tia asked abruptly.

Conscious that he was about to say things to Tia that he had never told anyone, he attempted to arrange the words in his head. His arms hung over the tailgate, looking into the empty truck bed as he spoke. "Lily wasn't supposed to have children. She insisted and I was a fool. Our baby, Ann, was stillborn just before the surgery."

He stretched his neck up as if looking for something in the sky before proceeding. "Lily's headaches grew to insurmountable pain levels. The doctors sent us to the Baltimore Medical Hospital, the best in the country." He turned his back to the taillight. "Thirteen hours of surgery. They couldn't get it all. Then, she just went berserk, pulling all the tubes out of her head." Fence scanned the darkness. "She died in my arms." The sigh was almost an audible groan, but not quite.

Tia placed her hand on his arm, seeing the look of lost love come over him. "You must have loved her a lot." Compassion filled her. "Fence, did you know that you called me Lily in the hospital? I don't mind. It's a fearful thing to lose someone you love."

"Guess you know about someone dying in your arms," Fence commented, reading her mind. Chance Cummings had left his tracks on her heart and he knew it.

Tia's chin pointed up. Her big eyes widened and dropped shut. She inhaled and exhaled deeply before speaking. "There's a bridge over the canyon of fear." A slight smile crossed her face. "It's called a rainbow. It reflects off waterfalls of tears."

A tear shot out of his eye, like the tear that broke loose months before, prompted by Tia asking Rose to give him a kiss. He glanced around the area, attempting to move his thoughts elsewhere, away from himself, to the job of bodyguard. "Got a bug in my eye." Fence made the excuse.

Tears appear larger at night, Tia reflected. She lifted her hand to his smooth, clean-shaven cheek, wiping the drop with the inside of her finger. "Liquid love." she said with tenderness. "I had a dream once. I was in heaven just after a rain. Rows and rows of bottles were lined up. God was collecting tears with the gentlest hand."

Fence fought between pushing Tia's hand away or grabbing it and holding it against his chest. He did neither.

She continued to talk. "Tears come from a hidden place in us, a place we hide from others. Pain births tears. Emotions have a way of leaking out of our heart when we least want them." Tia stared Fence square. "God understands the language of tears." She cleared her throat. "I don't like it much, but grief comes to all of us."

"Bearing our cross, right? Using a tool of torture to get a bug out of the eye? You amaze me." He pulled her white linen handkerchief out of his shirt. "This is yours. I had it with me in Europe, sort of my connection to Rose. It helped keep me in line. In fact, it kept me alive." Fence smiled at her. "To be honest, I missed you."

Tia did not respond. Instead she viewed another magnificent aurora borealis display, watching it dance across the sky. "Quite a presentation," she said.

"Mine or God's?" He talked to the air. "I don't think I can compete with your dream or your God."

"I didn't mean that. You've given me more than I've ever conceived." She stared at him with an affectionate longing, remembering the smell of the anniversary roses. *Was that yesterday?*

Fence lifted the locket up from her neck, meeting her eye to eye for the first time, or so it appeared at the moment. Gently he laid it down, deciding to bring closure to the discussion. "Lily and Ann are gone. I can't make them come back. The reality is that you and Rose are here. You're going to have to put up with me until I know you're clear of danger. Do you understand that?"

"You're instructing again." She pulled away. Reconsidering her answer, Tia whispered, "I'll try."

"I don't know how you feel about me." Fence sobered, knowing he had spoken more words to her than he intended, more than he had ever said to her in the course of the whole year. "For that matter I don't know how you feel about Chance Cummings." He stepped into another round of the match by mentioning the birth father of Rose.

Tia searched for a reply that made sense. "I'd be lying if I said I never cared about him. It's the kind of love that covers. Chance was a self-made man, a taker. He made selective choices to better himself at the expense of others." She breathed heavier. The dead man still gripped her jugular vein. "I don't know if I ever loved him. Maybe in a way I did. Can love get mixed up with pity?"

"Anything is possible." Fence looked down at the top of her head. "Like lights from the north."

"They resemble angels' wings don't they?" she said. A panorama of illuminated streamers and arches of northern lights stretched out before them. Tia gazed on the aurora borealis beauty. "Do they return hankies?" she asked with a foxy grin.

Fence could not help but like her. He cracked a smile and hid it.

Instinctively, Tia sensed his openness, allowing herself to move into a more serious tone. "Fence, I understand why Lily felt the tremors that went through her when your baby was not there. I was dying and they held the release papers up to me to sign my baby away, under my face. It's all a fog. The coma kept me from feeling the pain for six weeks."

She wondered if she was sticking her foot in her mouth by telling him more. The truth was that she needed someone, someone who would listen. And Fence was giving her a chance to speak. "I don't know how to tell you this, but this is blatant honesty. I—" She pursed her lips. "I bore the big 'B' for bearer of the bastard child. Hospitals don't want to be associated with domestic problems, or with women of lower nature, even if I was a victim of rape. I hated myself. I was so desperate, so empty. And when I saw my baby that first time, ah, I, ah … when you—" She could not go on.

"You knew," he encouraged.

The words dripped out of Tia. "One year ago. I can't thank you enough."

"Don't thank me too much. I didn't exactly like you. I knew, I hate to admit it, that Rose was yours. Call it connection, or something your lawyer said or something A—" He started to say Abe, but caught himself and made a new sentence. "Guess pride doesn't like to admit the truth." Fence made an inadvertent move toward her. "Are you all right?"

Neither said a word until an arguing older couple walked from the other side of the historical landmark and got into their noisy vehicle, leaving the scene. The interruption threw communicating off course.

"Marriage should get better with age, not worse," Fence commented, looking away from the intruders.

"I like to be with you Fence. I was afraid you would send me away, that you wouldn't come back. I didn't know if I should see Rose, if you would want me to be her mother after all that's happened. If you don't want to be married to me, please tell me so I can free you."

"Free me?" He tossed the idea from his thoughts. "That I can't do. I don't break vows. Besides, I'm still your bodyguard."

Misunderstanding his intention, she said firmly. "I can't be trapped into playing some kind of a game, pretending that we're really married."

"Neither could I. Let's talk about this later. This conversation has gotten a lot heavier than we intended. It's a big meal to digest. For now we have to keep things as they are. Please listen to me. If possible, try to trust me. We're not out of the woods yet. Your life is still in jeopardy." He swallowed hard, remembering the real reason he had adopted the baby and the quick wedding arrangement with Tia. "Let's call it a night and head home."

Seriousness surrounded them. Exposing her to the outer world entailed a necessary game. Unfortunately, it involved risk to both of them. Getting into her good graces had gotten too personal.

Fence turned the radio on, unnerved by the loud silence between them. The warring beat that emerged went against Tia's grain. She looked to the other side at nothing but lights reflecting on the winding road. His life was in danger too. Was it because of her? She did not like to feel obligated to anyone. She closed her eyes again, lifting her treasured hanky to her face. The nightmare was far from over.

Fence punched a new station, something with less noise, something with peace for the moment. The sound track of the new song sunk into them, settling the air, breaking the wind of adversity. The words soothed them. *But, now I know—I know—my yesterdays have not been lost.*

Playing the Game

THE next morning the sound of a diesel engine awakened Tia. Exhaust fumes sucked through the window frame. The smell repulsed her. She turned in the guest bed, knowing she was incapable of sleeping off circumstances. *Why can't I escape?* She dosed in discomfort while distasteful memories of Chance replayed. The nightmare reoccurred, intensifying her breathing. Suddenly she relaxed. *Fence carried her out of tall grass. He was warm. He set her down. Then he left her alone.*

Tia awoke in a cold sweat, hugging the woolen wedding blanket. A mixture of contradictions plagued her. *Why? How? I'm married to a man that I don't really know. I don't know if I like him. We're barely friends. To top it off, he's in love with a dead woman. What am I going to do? So many things to consider.*

Rose bubbled with excitement, fascinated with the big, grumbling truck. Fence lifted her up. She had proved a convenience. He had slept in the chair beside her crib, hoping his folks would not notice he was not with Tia. He probably was not getting away with anything, but he would try. A mixture of feelings accompanied his precarious role of bodyguard, incognito as husband.

Mack and Marie approached him with serious expressions. "You have to have your own home, Fence. That baby is a gem and Tia, well, she's won our hearts. But, you can't stay here," Mack said, looking around the perimeter, inferring the possibility of peril. Fence picked up on the message.

"Where's a secure place? Do you think Gramp would let us use the old mountain home?" Fence questioned.

"Probably, but don't take him for granted. He doesn't like things sprung on him." Mack twisted his head, hearing the oncoming vehicle. "Out of the horse's mouth! Wouldn't you know he would arrive like

171

clockwork?"

Reed Carpenter waved. The gray-haired grandfather pulled alongside the moving van. Immediately, he hopped down from his pickup, speaking like he was hard of hearing to overcome the motor noise. He addressed the man in the lightweight, greenish coveralls. "Better get that truck to the doctor soon as possible. It has a belly ache!"

The orders did not agree with the ready-to-unload man. "Where do I take this stuff? I have a deadline to meet."

"A different state would be just fine," Reed remarked.

"What?" The guy was incredulous. "Is this the Carpenter Ranch or not?"

"What are you doing?" Fence said, walking to his grandfather. He handed Rose to Marie along the way.

"Telling this guy to hit the road," Reed answered.

Fence pulled his grandfather to the side. Crispness filled the air. "Our household goods are inside. Do you think there's a booby trap in there?" Fence's hands were on his hips.

"Well, now that you mention it. Can't be too safe." The crisp reply stung.

Fence's mouth dropped open. "Thanks Gramp, but I already cleared the shipment before I returned. I need to do the talking."

Fence approached the driver. "Sir, I'm sorry. We've had a change of plans. Pull your rig to that big garage and take the load off." The barrel-chested man opened the large back doors of the trailer, anxious to get out of there. The guards at the gate had given him enough trouble. He loosed the dolly to move a stack of boxes.

"Fence, these are for you," his grandfather spoke secretly. "Figured you might need a place to hide out for a while. What's the matter? Cat got your tongue?" Reed grinned, handing over a packet of papers. "A bit of advice now that you own the land." He whispered into Fence's ear, "Never let it own you."

Fence squinted, sorting out the gist of what pertained to what. Was his grandfather subtly placing conditions on him?

Reed popped a friendly grin. "Don't take me so serious."

"Sure Gramp. Thanks. It is just that…" Fence glanced back to the house, seeing Tia standing alone. Reluctance was written all over her. Getting a grip on the conversation, Fence continued, "My mind has been running races lately."

"Well, what are you waiting for? Do your talking and get your wife and child. Been meaning to deed over that place to you. Call it a late wedding present. You could stay lost forever up there."

"I don't plan on staying lost forever. Just safe until I find out the truth." Fence turned toward his parents' house.

Tia's hair reflected the sun. Fence had more to explain. He took long strides to reach her from fifty yards out, gathering Rose from his mother along the way. He started speaking as he neared.

"Tia, good morning. Gramp just gave me a deed. We're moving. I just found out myself." His weak attempt to explain was filled with excuses. "We have work to do." His bluntness showed and he knew it. With a more tender effort he said, "It's concealed and inaccessible, about as secluded as we could get. I haven't been there for years." He stopped for a second. "You'll like it." His attempt to encourage her fell flat.

Tia's stomach lunged within her body. Rose swept down into her arms. "Mama go too."

Fence's left hand extended to the front of her shoulder. "Tia, it will be okay. Please. It's a gift."

Another gift! All the giving seemed manipulative. Something else bothered Tia. Fear gripped her, not so much the new situation but being too close to Fence. At least at the M / M Ranch she had separation. Her thanksgiving was getting lost to the questionable. No rainbow bridged the gap. Purposely turning to the side, she remarked, "This is getting complicated."

"I know. I'm making decisions without you." Words rolled off Fence's lips in appeal. "Tia, would you please come with me and help. I need you."

Need? She vacillated between feeling like a mother, a servant, a friend and a convenience. Mack and Marie watched them. Tia moved closer to him. "Fence, we have to get some things straightened out soon. This charade is getting to be too much. You gloss things over."

"Okay, they're coming this way. Don't be too shocked. I'm going to kiss you." The quick embrace with Rose between them left no time for rejection.

"We'll take care of Rose," Mack volunteered. He appeared overeager to Fence.

The smaller van ate the dust of Mack's horse trailer for twenty miles. Mounting the dirt trail, Tia felt the heartbeat of the wilderness overtake her. They were miles above sea level. The climb was much higher than to the M / M Ranch. Lightheaded, she started to roll the window down, only to turn it up. "I can't breathe."

Fence pulled onto the shoulder of the make-believe ditch. "The dust has settled. Come on. Get out," he ordered.

She felt seasick, only it was mountain sickness. "I think I'm going to faint. I—" She slumped to the ground. Florida seemed to call for her return. The far-away cry echoed in her head.

Fence raised her legs so her head was lower than her body. He slapped cold water on her face, taking his own handkerchief to wipe dust off.

"You seem to make a habit of collapsing on me," he said, hoping to cheer her up. "I'm sorry I shocked you." He bent near her face and whispered the foreign word. "Tia, we're going home. Relax. I'm going to carry you." He lifted her into the van.

"You're making decisions again," she answered, getting her bearings. She was upset with the whole arrangement.

"Yes, I am, but you're worth it," Fence encouraged. "We're almost there."

Surprise Inquiry

WHILE Tia and Fence were in the process of moving to a safer place, an extraordinary meeting occurred in Florida. An interesting visitor made a surprise inquiry at the law office of Mr. Arnold Tuffty. The man asked questions about Tia Bain, the young woman who had searched for her child.

Arnold Tuffty briskly knocked the tobacco out of his pipe, placing the remains inside a covered metal container reserved for such a deed. The smoke was done, but not the day. He started his walk home, replaying the order of events that had occurred since early morning.

Before 8:00 a.m. a swarthy man stood at the door, waiting in the rain with a dark umbrella and a lightweight trench coat, wearing dark glasses. It was a damp and sultry day with no sunshine. Mr. Tuffty's legal secretary, sick from a nosebleed, had not shown up. A vacant chair rested behind her desk.

"Come in," Mr. Tuffty said, opening the law-office door. His arm swung out to the side in a genteel manner.

The visiting man quickly obeyed. He folded his brown umbrella and placed it in the large crock next to the lawyer's. He then opened the belt of his beige trench coat and hung it over his arm, ignoring the coat tree. He looked tall, but he was not over five feet eleven. The visitor carried himself with purpose, conveying the look of a leader.

Slightly taken back by the broad-shouldered, muscular-framed man, Mr. Tuffty inquired, "Sir, your manner of business is?"

"Strictly professional, of course," the man replied, drying his shoes on the entry rug. He removed the dark glasses. His demeanor exhibited authority, but not control. His face had a sad seriousness to it.

"Then we will enter my office. I have no other appointments scheduled." Mr. Tuffty observed the man's quick study of President Theodore Roosevelt, whose picture firmly graced the wall behind his

175

desk. A minute passed before he asked the man to be seated.

Taking his own chair, Mr. Tuffty leaned back and swiveled to a right angle. He packed his pipe, tapping the tobacco into the bowl. He lit it with a wooden match. "Do you smoke?" he asked the visitor as he looked up.

"No sir. I never started the habit," he said.

"Good," Mr. Tuffty exhaled. "Fifty-year-old habits are hard to break."

The visitor's first instincts were to like the old lawyer. The picture of Roosevelt, taking on a lion, intrigued him. But, he was not one to make a quick judgment until he faced facts head on. "Mr. Tuffty, I trust that you will keep this meeting confidential. No one, I repeat, no one must know that I was here or that I contacted you for any reason," he emphasized.

Mr. Arnold Tuffty leaned back even further, looking at the visitor across miles of desk, his pipe perched in the corner of his mouth. He listened, puffing occasionally. "Go on," he encouraged.

"I have reason to believe that you have had contact with a Miss Tia Bain, now Mrs. Fence Carpenter. I realize that clientele names are confidential. However, I have a personal interest in this woman and her daughter." The man combed his fingers through his thick, curly dark hair. "Please notify me at once, if she contacts you." His business card had no name, just an out-of-state telephone number. He placed it on the corner of the massive desk, continuing in his train of thought. "I have Miss Bain's best interests at heart. My stepbrother, per se, may not. He's a manipulator."

Mr. Arnold Tuffty refrained from speaking, keeping his comments in check. The letter he had recently received from Tia Bain, his former client, stood upright in the pigeonhole of the extra desk across from him. He scratched his chin.

"And, who is this so-called manipulator, if I may ask?" Mr. Tuffty inquired.

"His name is William Merdone. Major Merdone. He purposes to ruin your client. He is out of the country now, supposedly TDY. This may not mean much to you, but I have reason to believe that underground forces are at work, involving an international ring, smuggling illegal drugs into the country among other things."

"I see." Mr. Tuffty used his words sparingly.

The visitor was direct. "Mr. Tuffty, this is a matter of life and death.

Help me with this. You will not regret it."

The man's persistence reminded Mr. Tuffty of someone else he knew, a young woman searching for her child. As an attorney at law, he highly favored the quality of diligence in clients.

"I can give you little proof of who I am, but your assistance is vital to the project I'm involved in. It's in your best interest to take my case," the man stated.

Mr. Tuffty's attention was purposely somewhere else. He blew three smoke rings, acting disinterested. Then he addressed the man. "Sir, it is highly unusual that I should take a case with so little information. Conflict of interest has been known to arise in situations like this."

"I trust you will understand the seriousness when you examine this packet," the man reiterated. He moved his knuckles apart to expose the tip of an envelope, clasped strategically between the armrest and the trench coat.

Mr. Tuffty turned to check out Theodore Roosevelt, the picture behind him. Slowly, he shifted back, facing the visitor across from him with a question of his own. He cupped the pipe bowl in the palm of his left hand. With his right hand he reached out. His gaze was fixed on the envelope. "May I?" Mr. Tuffty asked.

"By all means." The man gave him a look of respect.

The front of the envelope gave no indication as to the contents. Mr. Tuffty laid it aside and leaned back in his chair, questioning, voicing his reservations. "And, by what means sir, if I may ask, did you locate me? It seems quite unusual that you would seek me for legal advice, unless, perhaps, you were following someone?"

The healthy-looking man cleared his throat. "No sir. A respectable contact, Sister Maria Thomas, at Christ the King Orphanage suggested I speak to you."

"Oh she did, did she? I must remember to thank her." Mr. Tuffty did not really mean what he had just said about thanking Sister Maria Thomas. The woman he always admired was getting a little too free about giving out his name. *It's high time I speak to her.* His frustration mixed with his affection toward her. He kept his thoughts inside, deliberating.

The observant visitor reached inside his chest's shirt-pocket, extracting an item prior to continuing his explanation. "I have little to give you for the time being, except a silver crown made in England." He balanced the coin with his finger on the mahogany desk. Suddenly the visitor stood and leaned his long body over the lawyer's desk to the desk-pad—the calendar of the month. He placed the crown exactly over the date. "My collateral."

Mr. Tuffty's schedule for the day, recorded on the square of the monthly calendar, held the remarkable coin. Immediately the lawyer moved forward, setting his pipe in its tray. An old eyeglass, one used for magnifying, surfaced from the desk drawer.

"Crown silver," the muscular man stated, watching the lawyer eye the coin. "It's authentic."

Mr. Tuffty examined the mint date. "Ah, 1707. Very fine. Very early. Very impressive." He looked up. "If my reading is accurate, Queen Anne herself would be proud." He gave the interesting visitor a straight-on stare. "I will need time. I'm not a hasty man. However, I assure you, I will consider and study this case thoroughly before I make my decision. You will know within the week."

"Farewell until then." The man reached to shake the lawyer's hand. With a mutual nod, an agreement was made, not in writing, but with the eyes. The unscheduled visitor remembered his umbrella. The sun had come out. His dark glasses were on.

The potential client had a persuasive air about him. It drew the lawyer deep into thought. Using a tweezers, Mr. Tuffty meticulously lifted the coin onto a clean handkerchief. Absorbed in research, he did not look at the time. By noon, he had barely begun.

Loud ringing disturbed him from his study of the crown history. Remembering that his secretary was gone, he moved the books off to the side in order to answer the phone.

"Tuffty Law Firm. Arnold Tuffty speaking."

"Counsel Tuffty, this is Tia Bain, now Tia Carpenter. May I have a minute of your time?" She talked faster than she had before, asking her questions back to back. "Did you get my letter?"

Apprehensive of phone taps, Mr. Tuffty searched the area his guest had occupied, stretching the cord to the maximum. "Yes, ma'am, what is happening?"

"I need to arrange a meeting with you," she spoke quickly.

"Not at my office," he instructed. "There are safer places these days." The words of the visitor lingered in the air.

"Where then?" her voice rushed. "I must hang up now."

"Call Sister Maria Thomas," he squeezed in the words, before Tia hung up.

Mr. Tuffty digested the surprising turn of events, ignoring hunger pains. He decided to reread her letter.

Dear Counsel Tuffty,

I realize our business was completed some time ago, one year to be exact. In an unexpected arrangement, I married the man who adopted my daughter. I've been told that my life, which has gotten a lot more complicated, is in danger. Please be on guard from your end. I will call you soon. Again, I thank you for all your assistance.

Respectfully,
Tia Rose Carpenter

Mr. Arnold Tuffty tucked the letter into the briefcase file pocket. His mind performed a thousand somersaults, which was unlike his usual orderly approach. He let the afternoon vanish into concentration.

For four hours he studied the contents of the packet that the visitor had left, especially the white linen handkerchief with the crown on the corner. His mental faculties lined up the facts. To his amazement, the envelope contained considerably more information than he expected. However, it did not contain the identity of the broad-shouldered, blue-eyed man who made the surprise office call. When Mr. Tuffty lifted the lip of envelope to close it, he discovered the three letters, AMP. Suddenly he took a deeper interest. He exhaled. He had not smoked since morning.

Methodically, the man of law finished his end-of-the-day routine. Heaviness rested on his shoulders. He clenched his pipe between his teeth. The arduous day was nearly over. He fit his key into its chamber. The deadbolt locked into place with a loud knock. Overly cautious, he spun the combination on his briefcase for the third time and puffed out a cherry-flavored cloud of smoke. The recently updated files, along with an old, yellowed map of Jamaica, lay inside, neatly organized. Lawyer Tuffty found himself planted in the middle of an extraordinary situation. He had to keep a lid on it.

Another Woman's Stuff

THE call Tia had secretly made to Mr. Tuffty the night before rang in her ears. The busy phone lines had prohibited her from following his advice and talking to Sister Maria Thomas. She had to admit, Fence was right about one thing. Access to Reed's place proved difficult. There was no phone in the rundown, dusty cabin-like house, and the electricity was empowered by a gas generator. She had lived under worse conditions. But now, there was Rose to think about. Her child was still with Mack and Marie. Tia shrugged off emptiness, staring at the boxes stacked on top of each other.

Fence kicked the door open further, his arms loaded. Turning the corner, he rammed into Tia, giving her a look. Both were in a scrapping mood. He set her aside, making another trip while ignoring her presence. Upset with her stagnant behavior, he sought to make order in the midst of confusion. A mix of loyalty to the past and to the future hampered his productivity.

Tia knelt on the floor with items scattered around her, unnerved by the mess. She hid her hand behind her back, concealing the silver-lined Bible that she had just discovered. *Why can't I come right out and ask him?*

Something had to give. "Let me help you," Fence encouraged, trying to break the ice. Sweat dripped down his face in front of both ears. He crouched onto the floor, picking up a silver platter in the midst of scattered paper. "This was my Grandmother's." He examined the back. "Made in Germany. Mostly sentimental value." Placing the relic in front of Tia, he added, "Being the only grandson on the Carpenter side has some advantages."

"Oh," Tia answered in partial relief. She did not want Fence to know her struggles or see her weakness. His closeness troubled her. She resented his intrusion. Afraid of being caught, Tia had shoved the book under some packing paper.

"Tia?" From the awkward crouched position, Fence pulled her expressionless body to him. He had to break the tension. She remained stiff. "Hey, are we still friends?" She wanted to be alone. His confidence heightened her resolve.

"I never knew we were in the first place, not full-fledged. I'm working on it," she answered.

"We have lots to work on." He looked around the room. Tia did not know if he was talking about friendship or unpacking. Minimizing their conversation, they found places for the loose items.

"The rest goes outside," Fence said, exiting. *If Abe were alive, he would be helping with the move, that and a lot of other things!* He turned around at the door. "There's a playhouse out back for Rose," he remarked.

Tia wiped her face. *A playhouse. Is that what this is?*

Unable to resist the temptation any longer, Tia rummaged through the crumpled papers, retrieving the book. Engraved on the white leather cover was Lily's first name. Tia ran her fingers across its top, guarding preciousness. Carefully she opened the cover.

To: *Lily Mansfield, My Love Forever*
      On our Wedding Day
From: *Fence Carpenter*

Fence's love forever. The power of the words took Tia back. Unable to stand, she sank to the floor amid the clutter. That a man could love a woman with such depth seemed almost holy.

Several minutes passed before Tia noticed the folded note, penned by Lily's hand on her personal stationary. The message, stuck to the pages next to the family tree, was addressed to no one specifically. For some reason, Tia thought it no accident that she had found it. Her hands trembled.

I, Lily Ann Mansfield, am who I am. Other assumptions fall short of reality. I am a Celt, not a lost soul or a pagan. Early in history, St. Patrick reached my family, bringing light into darkness, carrying good news. He brought the message of Christianity and we received it. Therefore, it is honorable that I place him in my family tree, bestowing honor where honor is due.

When you read this book, you will know too, where I am and what I believe.

Lily Ann

The unusual statements revealed a woman who knew who she was and where she was going. Lily did not appear to have needed Fence for stability, security or identity. Tia laid the keepsake on her stomach. No wonder Fence loved her.

Fence found Tia oblivious to his presence or her surroundings. The impregnable woman, who wore a red badge of courage, had found Lily's Bible. With ease, he scooped her off the floor and lifted her to the soft bed. He tucked the woolen Indian blanket around her. Her tough act revealed her vulnerability. He had pushed her enough. Fence put the book into a square, fireproof, strongbox reserved for precious items and files.

Tia slept unaware of distractions until the smell of coffee awakened her. "Where am I?"

"Home, for the time being. Guess I'm going to have to start cooking you breakfast. Keep you from fainting on me. Are you feeling better?" Fence asked, placing a plate of food in front of her. "The water is really good here," he added.

Tia remembered the incident on the road earlier that day, when he poured water on her after she had fainted. She allowed herself the liberty to smile at him. "I'm sure it is. Maybe I won't have to have it slapped across my face."

Matchmaking

ARKNESS covered the mountain when Mack and Marie
Carpenter shut off the pickup. They had followed the road's jagged
line while shining deer eyes stood on the side.

"This is your new home, Rose. Your mommy and daddy wait for
you." The porch light gave warmth to the mountain house.

Ignoring his premonitions, Mack acted like nothing was wrong. Not
all had gone as planned. Sensing the strained relationship between Fence
and Tia, his mouth opened to fill the gap. "Doc is still on the prowl. He's
down south again. Says Chance Cummings was connected to a
professional ring. He's scouting out more information for you," Mack
spouted. "Heard that there have been strangers poking around in town.
Walking Elk won't give out any information. You know what he says
about men whose teeth show, the signs of anger, like ravaging dogs,
ready to attack. He does not trust." Mack forced a smile to demonstrate.
His futile attempt to add humor backfired.

Fence gave his father a shut-up look. Determined to converse, Mack
changed the subject. "Your deer licenses came. Claude got his. Tamsen
isn't going. Her baby is due too soon after. She'll stay with Marie." He
bulged with information. He leaned down and whispered to Tia, "Yours
is here too. I got a scope for your six-millimeter. You won't have too
long to settle in this house."

Tia, embarrassed that her father-in-law would expose her plans,
busied herself with Rose. Mack had not told her that he applied for
Fence too. The new development did not excite her, at least not now.
And, what was this Doc Bridger up to? The man was a little too nosey
for Tia. Her mind mixed with aggravation and misunderstanding.

"Remember, we have a meeting and supper at the M / M tomorrow
night," Mack inserted.

Tension filled the room like fog in a valley. Mack hurried Marie to leave the reunited family alone. "You could've cut the air with a knife," he said, connecting his seatbelt. "One thing is for certain, they're on opposite sides of the fence, in different pastures. I don't know how they'll ever go on this hunt together."

"Mack, they're living in the same house. Quit your matchmaking. They will work it out," Marie reasoned. "They're married. We know that."

"That's about all we know. It's high time for some action," Mack returned.

The Hunt

SLEEPING arrangements returned to the way they had been when Tia first became Rose's caretaker. Loneliness and rejection followed Tia, but determination motivated her. Butting heads with Fence occurred with escalating frequency.

"You can't go hunting, Tia," Fence ordered.

"Yes I can and I will," she retaliated. "I'm not going to faint on you if that's what you're worried about."

"Tia, it's a lot of work, a lot of walking, a lot of effort. I have enough to think about without having you along. What was my father thinking of anyway?"

"Me. He thinks I can do it. He believes in me. Will you give me a chance? I learn fast."

While Fence was overseas, Mack had spent his time with Tia preparing her for a hunting trip. He had started by constructing a list of instructions titled *Endurance Training* with his thick-leaded pencil. He had set her to hiking the mountain daily and weight lifting, strengthening her body and mind. She had eagerly learned the self-defense tactics named *The Strength of the Elbow and the Knee*. Mack had called it his *secret bonus package*. He had said that Fence did not need to know.

"I'm going to sight in the guns," Fence said.

"Not without me." Tia, at his heels, turned her head to address Marie who had been showing her how to make berry pudding. "Please, will you watch Rose?"

Fence looked back at Tia. "You are stubborn headed. But I like you." The rare word stimulated a quick response.

"If you like me, you'll let me go with you. I'm not as dumb as you think," she said.

"I never said you were dumb. You're a woman and not a very big one."

"And you're a man and sometimes you're not very smart. You expect me to trust you. When are you going to trust me? I'm not dangerous, contrary to what you may think," Tia spat out.

Fence gritted his teeth. "Come on. Don't expect any favors. It's difficult enough trying to be your bodyguard. I don't know why you want to put yourself in more danger."

"Maybe you need a bodyguard," she said. "It wouldn't be the first time."

His smile was cockeyed. "I didn't know you cared." He paused. "You don't know how much effort this takes."

Tia set the scope hairs—the cross, preparing the lightweight Remington Mohawk that Mack had given her for a gift. She placed four bullets in the magazine then put noise deadeners over her ears to deafen the sound. One by one she worked the shells into the chamber. Fence set up a new target sheet for her and stepped back. "It's all yours. I gather you don't need my help."

She shot four times. Holes blackened the center.

"You've done this before?" He looked surprised.

"I took riflery my first year in college. I got an 'A' in the course in case you're wondering." She gave him a fake smile.

"Okay. I was wrong." His hand brushed his face. "I thought Chance Cummings taught you."

"That was with a pistol. He didn't trust anyone and there were guys after him," she said.

"I suppose he expected you to save his life, not mine." Fence shook his head. "Remember? I have strict instructions to guard your backside."

"It seems to work both ways. You don't know how much you need me," she teased and added in a more serious tone, "I know about you giving me blood in the emergency room the end of May. Thank you."

"Do you think that gives you the strength to hunt?" Somehow Fence felt he was losing the battle. "All right. I give up. I don't like it. We'll work together. You can go hunting with me as long as you listen to my instructions." He handed her the warm and cold weather gear. "You'll have to wear orange."

"So, deer know colors?" she asked, looking at the oversized clothing.

"You'll have to ask the deer. They see movement. I want to be able to see you, to keep my eyes on you."

"Aren't your eyes supposed to be on the target?" she challenged, feeling a little belligerent toward him.

"You better stay on the good side of me." He handed Tia a hunting vest. "You seem to have a good eye. Can you read the fine print on the tag? I used it as a kid."

She looked closely. "Size small."

Fence nodded. "I thought so. Wear it." He looked at her and shook his head. "Deer have good noses. Walk into the wind." The atmosphere softened in spite of the order. "You'll do, I guess. I've never had a woman hunting-partner. I'm trying to get along with you."

Claude arrived early. They changed rolls several times. One spotted with binoculars and another capped while one waited, hoping a deer would run out. Claude worked the huge ravine. He teased Fence. "Next time, we'll change the rules. We'll hunt closer in, and pack out a lot less miles." He and Fence hung their bucks up in the garage. Tia had not taken a shot yet.

"What are you waiting for?" Fence asked. "I thought you were so all-fired eager to go hunting."

"For you to relax. I have an idea," Tia responded. "It was nice of Marie to help with Rose," she said, changing the subject.

The men skinned and butchered the two deer. Claude spoke, "So, my brother, your Tia kept up with us like Tamsen. She is strong."

"She has a mind of her own," Fence said. "I don't know what to do with her."

"I know one thing. You don't want to die sparring with a woman. Don't fight love. You will lose." Claude spoke with double meaning again, opening the door of his silver pickup. He stuck his arm out the rolled-down window. "Your love is mixed up between living and dead." Claude started the engine. "Thanks for the hunt. I must go now. A woman waits for me. Fence, wise men choose life." He drove homeward, wondering if Tamsen had gone into labor.

Fence found Tia asleep next to the fireplace. He sat by her for a while seeking to get the chill out of his bones. He had barely spoken a word to her all day. He caressed her hair. "Sleep good Tia."

Tia felt him lay his quilt over her tired body, the second time since they had moved to Reed's place. She struggled, not wanting to need him in her life.

Before sunrise, she was on her way down the mountain to a rugged ravine she had scouted out, less than a mile from the house.

The shot pierced Fence out of his dream. *That was too close.* He flew out of bed, awaking Marie in the guestroom, where Tia usually slept. The cold fire held only ashes. Tia was gone. Fence packed his gear and fled in the direction of the shot.

"That girl. If I ever get a hold of her!" Parchment stomped around in the corral, not used to his new surroundings. His ears were back. Fence threw a saddle on him, placing his rifle in the leather saddle holster. "Okay Parch. We have to find Tia. You like her don't you?" Parch moved down the slope sturdily. Fence searched for tracks. "What is she thinking anyway? Independent, unpredictable woman!" he complained.

For over a year she had not gone anywhere, not rebelled, not spoken out. She never said a word. Now her feistiness aggravated him. Maybe she had been around Mack too much. Fence hastened, trotting the horse down the slope. The first tracks he spotted were not Tia's, nor deer. Pressed into the soft ground next to the stream were the paw prints of a large mountain lion. Fence's heart pounded. He had worried about a man killing her, not a wildcat.

He dismounted and led Parchment near the creek bed, scanning the mountainside. The horse was jittery. Tia's deer lay dead before him. She was nowhere to be seen. He cupped his hands to his mouth in megaphone fashion. "Tia!" He turned his body the other direction, combing the woods. No orange. Then he heard her holler.

"Fennnnce! Watch out." The mountain lion flew through the air, landing on Parchment's rump. Tia's shot rang out before Fence could lift his rifle. The cat fell, stricken in the heart. Parchment jumped around, his back bleeding. "Fence, are you all right?" She ran to the scene, staring at the cat.

Fence took a deep breath, looking at her in amazement. He shook his head. "Remind me to give you the expert marksmanship award. How did you ever outsmart that cat? You're making a habit of saving my life. Not just mine. Now it's my horse."

She nodded, but did not come close to him. "Do you think Parch will be alright?" She approached the nervous buckskin, worried.

"He'll be fine. I thought we were hunting deer, not mountain lions." He swallowed. "That lioness showed wild strength. She had nothing up on you," he said in a repentant tone. "Guess I do need you. You're a survivor, Tia. I don't know of many men that would have the courage to do what you did." He stepped toward her. "I'm proud of you," he complimented, wrapping his arm around her back in a brotherly hug.

"I don't plan on teaching lions how to be courageous if that's what you're thinking. I was scared spitless," she admitted. "I'm still shaking. I'm sorry Fence." She cast her eyes to the ground.

"What for? Hey, you've already done a day's work. You're one up on me. Mack will haul in the deer and cat for us."

"I didn't want to kill her. She has two cubs. I saw them earlier," she said.

"That mother instinct is strong in you, Tia. Mack will know how to help them. Come on." Fence walked to her. "How about some pancakes and that June pudding you made? I'm hungry."

He grabbed the rifle and pack from her shoulder with a crooked smile. "Hey sharpshooter? Promise me one thing? Next time you go hunting, would you mind taking me with you?"

A grin spread across her face. Her eyes met his momentarily. She did not have to answer.

It was time to get back to business. Fence was not going to let her out of his sight, despite her fearlessness. Claude had informed him of recent developments in need of attention.

Fix It Quick

FENCE stood outside, eavesdropping and holding his response in check. He had been kinder to Tia since the hunt. The sound of laughter echoed like a faucet running wide open into a hollow sink. Fence peeked around the corner to find Tia and Rose jumping on the old bed. An empty part of Fence craved that freedom, if only for a moment, to be oblivious to danger. He crumpled the note.

Trouble. Meet today after pumpkin pie.

Tia squeezed Rose to her breast, pressing kisses through the child's hair. "I love you."

"Let's go mommy. Jump more. Please?" Rose begged. The brace fell out from under the bed, sending a corner to the floor. Both toppled with hair amiss and pajamas twisted. "Fix it quick, mommy."

Fence heard the crunch. Tia's head was under the bed when Fence entered. "Need help? Sounds like you two are having a quite a time." Plucking the bed up, he put the crippled corner back in place.

"Sorry daddy," Rose said, looking at him with big baby eyes.

Fence grinned. "Guess that bed will never be the same. I don't want you hurt."

"It was my fault." Tia blushed, brushing herself off. Fence burst into laughter. "What's so funny?" she asked, annoyed with him.

"Your hair!" He tried to hold back. "You have dust stuck to you." She wished he had not intruded. Fence sobered, offering his lighthearted comment. "What did they do with you at the convent, I mean orphanage?"

"I didn't get into trouble, if that's what you mean. I saved all my childhood for now!" She released a smile.

"Well, you could have fooled me." He reached to her head and pulled off the ball of dust while she looked at the floor. "We have a couple hours before Thanksgiving dinner. I have a surprise to show you."

Hoisting Rose onto his shoulders, Fence went outside. Tia, determined to keep up with them, followed. "Need a hand?" Fence's smile pressed into her. Holding her hand longer than necessary, he pulled her on top of the monstrous rock. "Welcome to the playhouse." Fence removed the branch covering the door.

"Go inside," Fence said. Rose ran to the red rocker sitting in the middle of the twelve by twelve room. "We only have a few minutes."

"I like it." Tia ran her fingertips along the wall until she came to a large topographical map of Europe. A map of Africa and Australia hung on the other side. *Odd for a playhouse,* she thought. She edged toward the bookcase in the opposite corner. It shelved history and geography books. The bottom shelf was the only one that was filled with books for children.

"I came here as a kid. Only my grandparents and I knew about it. You are the first ones I've ever shown," Fence admitted.

"I love you daddy. Rock me?" Rose asked with warm eyes, resting her head back on the rocker. The near two-year-old was developing a distinct personality and a vocabulary that surprised both Fence and Tia.

"We can't stay." Fence fixed the lock, securing the building. "The clouds are ready to give us a snow."

Tia's hand was on his arm. "Fence?" she said. "Happy Thanksgiving."

He laid his hand on top of hers. "Thanks." Her face was inches from his. She did not back away. Friendship—or maybe trust—repositioned.

Give Me a Crown

B Y noon on Thanksgiving Day a light snow had feathered the ranch. The deciduous trees had already dropped their leaves, but now they hid underneath the fresh white blanket. Corn stocks, tied together in the middle with a braided rope, stood tall near the house—the work of Marie Carpenter. A pile of squash and pumpkins snuggled together on the porch, ready to show off their colors to the guests.

Fence's grandfather, Reed, answered the knock on the front door. Doctor Clem Bridger had arrived. He stomped the snow off his feet.

"Back so soon Clem? Can't get enough of us, can you? Maybe you ought to move west," Reed spoke, shaking Doc Bridger's hand in a swarthy gesture.

"I just know how much medical advice you Carpenters need, and figured that I could be of some sort of assistance," Doc Bridger razzed back.

"You always figure. I think you want Thanksgiving turkey," Reed Carpenter teased and then swallowed. His investigative mind was still dissecting the private conversation he had with Mack that morning. His voice took on a serious tone. "There have been mysterious tracks at the M / M Ranch the past few nights, not just a window peeper. Cameras are in position again."

"I noticed. No guards except Sky?" Doc asked. "By the way how did the intruders get by that watchdog?"

"They shot her with a tranquillizer gun, one like veterinarians use, with a barbed dart on the end. Mack found her and pulled the needle out. He gave her a neutralizing drug to wake her up. She'll be all right. Sky is a tough dog. It takes a lot to put her out of commission. Sort of scary." Reed gave the added information just before the M / M dinner bell rang. "Fence doesn't know yet."

Fence stayed close to Tia, helping her with Rose. His disposition appeared calmer toward her, but his mind was somewhere else. Mack summoned him the minute the pumpkin pie was finished. "Follow me," he told Fence.

Mack entered his den, preceded by Doc Bridger and his father Reed. Heaviness hung in the musty room. The private conference closed the women out. Mack's noble countenance had a look of knowing. He missed nothing, especially the look of worry on Fence's face. "Are you doing okay at the old house?"

"As well as can be expected," Fence answered.

Doc Bridger and Grandfather Reed addressed Fence almost simultaneously. "Seen any trouble lately?"

"If I haven't, I'm certain you have. What is this, some kind of a caucus? What was the note all about?" Fence asked. "I hear Doc has been prowling around down south."

"So I have. So I have," Doc butted in. "Here's the new evidence." Doc laid the brown-papered box wrapped with binder's twine on Mack's large engraved desk for examination.

Reed Carpenter's sun-browned face exhibited a wrinkled smile. "So, sly one, do we have news in a box? Out with it," he chided his old friend.

Doc Bridger began. "Well, here's the scoop. I stopped by the orphanage, first time in years. Sister Maria Thomas gave me a scolding for not honoring the Father, or maybe I just felt guilty in her presence. She gave me this package. Said it came for Tia Bain months ago. They didn't find it until last week, in the narthex of all places. Some ancient medical books, full of mildew, were stacked on top of it."

The Carpenter men waited for Doc to clean his glasses. Whether out of nervous habit or need, he occupied his hands before continuing his lengthy version of the discovery. "Well, the Sister remembered that I was called in for the birth certificate and first examined the orphan girl. She thought the box might have to do with medicine, or wild yams or something. That was her excuse anyway, although she did say it was strange. Her skepticism rubbed off on me immediately. I could almost see her short hair rise under her habit, like she had this sixth sense of caution, and she's not superstitious. She was pretty good lookin' in her day. She's a great protector of the orphans you know."

"Get to the point, Clem." Reed's old investigative bones were anticipative. "What's in it?"

"That's just it. Thought I should be cautious. I always do a checkup first before I do the surgery. Need to find out all the options, or probabilities. You see, it's not perfection that counts, it's progress." He adjusted his glasses and pointed. "You can see by the postmark date that it was delivered more than once."

Fence lifted it carefully. "Jamaica! This was sent two years ago!"

Mack's eyes lit up. "Chance Cummings perhaps?"

"Dad, I don't think this has anything to do with Chance Cummings."

"You diagnosed that one right," Doc said, reaching into the bulging bag and pulling out some papers. "Thought I'd run it through an x-ray machine when no one was looking. You guys call it a scan." Doc shoved his glasses back on. "There's steel in there all right. No gun or bomb. Since you eagle-eyed investigators are on top of things, specialists that is, maybe we'll get to the heart of the matter."

Intrigued by unsolved mysteries, the Carpenter men fastened themselves together in their various roles. "Go ahead. You can open it up. I'll be first assist." Doc smiled, pushing his glasses up his educated nose.

"Well Fence, what do you think?" Reed quizzed his grown grandson. "She's your wife. Shouldn't she be in on this? Seems to me she holds her own."

"I don't think so," Fence said.

Mack wrinkled his brow and shook his head. "I agree." The ride with his new daughter-in-law the day Tia put a splint on the ailing buffalo calf's leg sealed that. "Son, we better intercept this one. We have to do everything we can to protect that girl. This is one time we intervene, call it covert action if you like. Guess I might call it love." He winked.

Fence rolled his eyes. "Okay, Dad. Call it what you want." Fence pointed his chin toward to box. "I'm going to find out what's inside."

Reed hovered over him. "The Island of Springs," he commented.

"What?" Fence said, concentrating on cutting the string. "Gramp, what are you getting at?"

"Arawak Indians call Jamaica the Island of Springs," Reed repeated.

The string snapped. "Shoebox. Made in England."

The men wasted no time getting a synopsis, examining the box and its contents under their investigating microscopes. It was what was inside that shocked them. A Caucasian doll, stuck full of hundreds of pins, was wrapped in a dirty linen rag. The doll's eyes were poked out.

"Voodoo." Reed pointed out. "It's a death curse. See where all the pins are placed, one in her heart and many in her head, like a crown of thorns—involves some kind of African ancestor worship, witchcraft that is." Reed looked at his friend Clem. "Good thing you intercepted this."

Fence picked up the rag. "Smells like opium."

"Time for our spy glasses to get dusted off." Mack rounded the old oak coffee table.

Doc, off in his own train of thought, interjected, talking to himself, "I wonder what ever happened to that handkerchief, the one that was under Tia's head when she first arrived at the orphanage? And the basket she was in?"

"What basket?" Fence's insides were churning with how much he should reveal and how much he did not know.

Mack returned the eye roll to his son. "Fence, where's the hanky—the one you showed me?"

"She has it. I gave it back and I don't think she'll part with it." He cleared his throat. "I had it with me in Europe."

"You what? What is it with you, son?" Mack scratched his chin and looked past him toward the doll. "One thing is certain, you never do the ordinary. One minute you're with us. The next, you're across the sea. You could give prior notice. What are you holding back?" His hand reached for the shoebox. "You and Tia are married, right?"

"Yes, of a sort."

"Of a sort? What are you, just her bodyguard? What about Tia's family? Do you know anything about her?"

"We're it, family that is." Fence lifted his eyebrows to see his father's reaction. "Doc just told you more than I know. She was raised in an orphanage. She never knew her parents."

"Why are you so secretive? How can we get to the bottom of things if we don't know the truth."

Fence answered, "I know Dad. I should have come clean with you from the start. But then you would have had trouble acting innocent." Fence looked at the English shoebox, thinking of Ivan Burn's words, *progress naturally.*

"Fence?" Mack looked out the window at Sky. "I need to tell you what happened last night."

The serious mood in the room concerned Reed. Doc's hands were fidgety. He had cleaned his glasses three times already. Reed pulled Doc to the side, ready to break tension with a game of checkers. "Nothing like a board game to help us think," he said to Doc. They eavesdropped as they made their moves.

"Give me a king!" Doc ordered.

His competitive friend snapped back with a chuckle, "I'll crown you all right!"

"That's the key!" shouted Fence, overhearing the two older gentlemen. "The Crown! There's a Crown on the corner of Tia's handkerchief. And her name isn't Tia. It's Tiara." The men all looked at Fence.

"Well Doc, you're the one that told me that. Isn't a tiara a crown— a princess crown with jewels?"

Once again Reed's knowledge of history surfaced. "Awe, Jamaica, a jewel in England's crown."

"Out of many, one people," Doc added. "It's a mix of people. The gold coast. The Spanish used it for a supply base."

Reed crowned another king. "England issued gold crowns in the 1500's."

Fence stared at them, waiting to speak. "All I know is that the crown is key to unlocking the mystery of her life, one move closer to discovering why and who hates her enough to want to kill her." Fence drew up a chair. "I think it's time I lay everything out on the table." The men were all ears. "A year ago today I encountered a Jamaican, not in any usual manner." Cautiously, Fence relayed the strange meeting.

Doc removed his glasses, his thinking mode in gear. "We're onto something now. Maybe we all need to put our heads together and play a game of Clue!"

The men covered seriousness with short-lived laughter. Entering a new stage of the game, they mulled over the next move. Concern for Tia weighed heavily on them all, especially Fence.

Pounding Alarm

A pounding alarm turned the men's heads, upsetting the checkerboard. "Fence! FENCE!" Tia beat on the oversized den door. The urgency of her voice overtook him. She shoved the door open. "It's Rose! She's having a convulsion. Her temperature is 105. She's—what's that?"

She ran to the voodoo doll and started pulling the pins out as fast as she could. "There will be no curse on my child!" she shouted. "What are you all doing in here?" She charged out.

"You got it wrong! Where's Rose?" Fence pursued, nearly stepping on her.

Tia answered rapidly, throwing off a feeling of betrayal and bewilderment. "Marie is dabbing her with vinegar. She has to be okay." Tia tried to collect her thoughts, twisting her hands.

Minutes later, Doc Bridger hovered over Rose, who lay in Marie's arms, limp and weak. Medical knowledge swarmed around them. The hasty examination revealed pneumonia.

"Let's get her to the hospital!" Fence rushed them. He grabbed Rose up with Tia running behind.

Mack hollered, "You forgot the keys."

Tia climbed into Mack's pickup. Fence reached from the driver's side to hand her Rose. Spinning out of the driveway, the dust flew. Tia rolled the open window up.

Fence breathed hard. Only that morning he had watched the two of them playfully jump on the bed. Noticing Tia's forlorn face, he pondered, *Someday, I'm going to see her laugh again.*

Rose had a way of bringing them together, of bringing the truth out. She quit thrashing and lay in Tia's arms, looking miserable. The little rose kept her good disposition, giving them a sad smile. Medical staff put her on a respirator and started an I.V. Rose had no strength to resist the jostling. Parental love blanketed the little girl despite the tension. The pneumonia strain was bacterial, not viral.

Sweat dripped off Fence's face. He pulled the wide chairs up by Rose's caged bed. The staff asked them all to wear masks. Fence communicated with his eyes. He lifted them to get Tia's attention, like the day they got the silver wedding rings from Claude. She could not read them. Exasperated, he grabbed her hand and pulled her to the hallway, pulling his mask off. "Tia, there's a chapel on the east side. Will you go with me?"

She did not answer, but followed a step behind in a brisk walk. Fence stopped at the door. Tia brushed past him, heading straight to the altar, kneeling down. Fence moved in next to her, touching her shoulder with the side of his arm. He spoke out loud. "I don't know how to pray." He held his head, fighting anger with himself. "He can't take Rose too."

Even a non-praying man prays when he's desperate. Sister Maria Thomas's words came alive to Tia. *In the face of death, man thinks twice. Human hands have little control.*

Fence started suddenly. "God, if you want to punish someone, punish me. I love her so much. Please let her live. Don't let it be meningitis. Help me ... trust you."

Tia reached to his hand and squeezed his fingers, giving Fence a look of hope. "She will be all right," she whispered. Something passed between them that neither could explain.

In the sterile room, Tia stroked Rose's forehead, reaching over the cribbed bed. She hummed softly. Exhausted, she hung her head on Fence's arm. Drowsiness overcame her. Half-sitting up, she slept.

Two people, Tia and Fence Carpenter, locked together in difficult circumstances, with different views, different perspectives, did not realize how much they needed one another. Each pulled a ton of weight. Had they teamed up, their strength would have multiplied. Unable to look at each other, they waited, alone.

Improvement came slowly, accompanied by parental relief. Seeing their daughter suffer made them long for Thanksgiving morning, when Rose had asked to be rocked with a sparkle in her eye. At dawn the fever broke. Rose budded back to life.

"Yes Marie." The phone rested on Tia's shoulder. "We're coming to your home."

Marie spread out the feast, the homecoming dinner, on the supper table in the rearranged room. She always prepared more than enough. They ate family style and tried to beg off eating more. Papa Mack, in charge of the conversation, ushered the family and guests into the library.

Reed and Doc Bridger wasted no time, heading straight to the game table in Mack's den. "I have a riddle for you, Doc. What makes this sentence unique?" Reed asked. "A quick brown fox jumps over the lazy dog?" He started to sort puzzle pieces, waiting for a reply.

Doc scratched his face. "You're the expert at putting puzzles together. I take them apart."

The voodoo doll was gone. Tia scanned the room, shaking her head. "I have the answer." She cleared her throat. "It contains all the letters of the alphabet, a to z."

"How did you know that?" Reed piped up, grinning at Doc. "The girl is smarter than we thought."

Tia hated when they talked like she was not present.

"Of course she is," inserted goodhearted Mack. "Tia? Fence? Come over by me for a minute."

"Speaking of puzzles, here, I have a present for you. Catch!" From six feet away, he threw a yellow envelope into Fence's chest. A cheesy cat grin spread across Mack's face. Fence remembered the ill tasting Cheshire cheese that Lily's father had used in Scotland, luring the mouse into the trap.

As if making an excuse, Mack added, "Ahhhh, it's really an anniversary gift. Think we missed it. Paper isn't it, the first one that is, or is it a clock?"

Fence blew the five-by-seven open and pulled out the contents. "Two airline tickets to Jamaica?" His curiosity sparked, but he kept quiet.

"You two need a vacation. Rose will be fine with us." Mack emitted another Grand Canyon smile, closing it with his famous wink.

"All right, what are you guys up too?" Fence's resolve heightened. "Something's going on and you'd better let us in on it."

Three gray heads popped up at the same time, each holding a puzzle piece, acting innocent. They could not give away the whole plan. Tia's naïveté played too important a role.

Apprehension filled the air. Tia and Fence had no intention of leaving Rose, although she was well and off in her little world of play. Tia gave Fence a puzzled look. He whispered in her ear, "This is as much a shock to me as you. Like it or not, I think we better hear them out."

Reluctantly she conceded.

The men with the big plans mapped out the mission, briefing them on their assignment. The first item of business included a shopping trip to buy Tia some clothes and get her a passport. "It begins tomorrow." Mack added. Tia shook her head in disbelief.

The Woven Basket

A *haircut?* "Fence! When are you going to stop telling me what to do?" Tia snapped.

"It wasn't my idea. Your father-in-law came up with this one, lock, stock and barrel!"

Tia walked out of the salon with a below-the-shoulder-blunt-cut and an attitude. Her blond hair, now golden brown, had a bouncy look to it. Fence complimented her. "I like it. You look natural. I like the fight in you too," he commented.

"You mean I didn't look natural before," she spurted.

Fence bent to her ear. "I didn't say that. Drop it. You look great."

"Remember Tia, keep your eyes open. Watch out for snags. We won't be far off," Mack reassured her.

Tia looked at Fence. "Now, what does that mean? 'Won't be far off.' What is he thinking of anyway?" Tia asked, not expecting an answer.

"You," Fence said.

She stuck her lips out. "Guess I asked for that, didn't I?"

Tia boarded the passenger jet with Fence scurrying her here and there. She gritted her teeth, whether out of anger or fear, she was not sure. Her pulse raced. The night added to the tension.

"Tia, you're shaking." Fence's concern wrapped around her. "What's wrong?"

"I don't know if I want to tell you. It's this whole affair, leaving Rose, not knowing what's going on, this plane."

"What about the plane? Is there something wrong with it?"

"Yes," she blurted. "I don't like planes. Chance rented a plane once to take me flying. He hoped I would miscarry." Tia gripped the armrest, looking out the window at nothing. "He stalled the plane and did aileron rolls until my—" She grabbed herself tightly and closed her eyes. The plane's rapid climb filled her empty stomach with knots. Shivers

201

covered her.

Fence grimaced. *I wish Chance Cummings hadn't died so I could kill him now.* The inner anger rose up. Suddenly repentant, he chose to let go of the memory of the dead man and focus on the needs of the living. He pulled the motion sickness bag out from the seat pocket in front of him. Holding it in front of Tia, he encouraged, "Angels fly high. They come down to earth too." Fence lifted his elbow and arm over her, "Will my wing do for a start?"

His massive hold settled her down. Somewhat reassured by his strength, she relaxed and dozed. Peace removed the memory for the moment. The smooth flight continued to comfort her. She breathed a sigh of relief when the plane touched down. "Take courage Tia. Where's all that feistiness?" She stared at her hands. He reached for them. "Hey, look up will you? We have to be on alert constantly."

His admonitions shook her out of complacency. She lifted her chin. "You're right. I don't want to admit it. I'll get out of myself. Will that satisfy you?" She managed a smile. Fence felt relieved. At the International Shop he bought her a bottle of perfume.

Humidity's heavy breath fogged around them as they walked out of the Florida terminal. Tia took quick steps, struggling to keep up with his long stride. Fence grasped her hand, half pulling her along, while he hailed a cab with the other. "The Sacred Heart Cemetery please."

They approached Christ's Child Orphanage from the backside, passing the aboveground tombs. Sister Maria Thomas lifted the bar that rested in the heavy wooden arms over the door, welcoming Tia with open arms. Incense filled the room. The exuberant hug took Tia back to her childhood and the home of safety. Fence's observation broadened. The adhesion between Tia and the grandmother figure was unlikely to evolve in any other setting. Undaunted love flowed from the elderly woman. *What other keys does the wise old monarch have cocooned within her?*

Council Mr. Arnold Tuffty sat in the spotless receiving room without his pipe. The sight of Tia sent him to a stand and honorable bow, like she was the Queen of Sheba. "So we meet again Miss Bain, I mean, Mrs. Carpenter, with my greatest respect and honor." He lifted his lawful body simultaneously with Tia's hand, kissing the top of it. *The girl is no longer blond!*

Mr. Tuffty stretched his hand to shake Fence's for a meeting of minds. "And to you Mr. Carpenter. We meet under unusual circumstances once again." Fence ignored the edge in the lawyer's voice. The two men had one thing in common, the welfare of Tia. Neither took his protective eyes off her.

The floral smells of the courtyard overtook the odor of the lawyer's pipe tobacco mixed with Tia's fragrance. "Come, my family." Sister Maria Thomas spoke with an affectionate authority, raising her hand to adjust her habit. "Do not doubt, my daughter Tia. You are crowned with life." The old woman walked as she talked, imparting the events that took place when Tia first arrived.

They sat next to the fountain on low stone benches. Fence asked only one question. He did that in a very cold and platonic manner. "What about the basket that Tia was left in? Do you still have it?"

The elderly woman gave a gentle nod in cautious response. "It's in the bell tower, if you wish to climb up to retrieve it. There's an ancient travel trunk once used on old ships. It's inside."

Mr. Tuffty used this opportunity to insert his commanding statement. "It would be wise for you both to be on the same page. This is a dangerous business with lots of legalities." The musing lawyer advised. "At the last meeting you were both at odds, if I recall. Miss Bain then, now Mrs. Carpenter, entrusted me as counsel to search for her child. I'm not quite certain how the two of you became attached, but it is strange indeed. I have my questions and reservations regarding your plan of action." He shifted toward Tia. "Ma'am, I trust you are not brainwashed by the man beside you."

Tia perked up. "No sir. I am not."

Sister Maria Thomas intercepted, giving her answers. "And so that's as much as the honorable Mr. Tuffty and I have discovered." She gazed at Tia. "You must be very careful. Royalty runs in your bloodline. Your Father in Heaven knows."

Tia fell down to her knees, linking her arms around Sister Maria Thomas' cloak, laying her head on the woman's stomach like a little girl. The Sister ran her knotty hand through Tia's thick hair, giving her a motherly blessing. She kissed the top of Tia's head. "You are Tiara. God's face shines on you."

Arnold shifted in his chair, rekindled by the memories of his youth and the woman he had lost to another love, greater than his. But, it was honorable to let Sister Maria Thomas go. He could see now that others needed her mercy more than he ever did. He would look on and love her from a distance, as a sister, as much as he loved who she was and what she stood for. They would always be bound together as comrades, as friends.

He marveled, watching the strong Fence Carpenter climb the rungs of the creaky wooden ladder to the top tower without fear. The youthful man had love at his fingertips, and a mission before him. A slight bit of envy crept into his legal thinking. The honorable Mr. Tuffty, with the almond blossom hair, knew he had lost the case years ago, along with the woman he would always love.

Sister Maria Thomas skirted a path to the tower, leaving Tia alone with Mr. Tuffty. He spoke first. "Mrs. Carpenter, may I have a word with you?"

Tia nodded.

"I'm sure you are aware of the danger you're placing yourself in by going to Jamaica. I can't stress enough the need for you not to trust everyone, even Fence Carpenter."

"You're right, Counsel Tuffty. My biggest concern is leaving my daughter, Rose. She's so far away."

"Well, ma'am, I want you to know I received questionable information just prior to your quick call. Do you, by chance, know a Major Merdone?" he asked.

"At one time, I knew of him, but that was over two years ago. I don't particularly like the man." Tia did not want to think about the past. She questioned, "How do you know him?"

"I don't. I'm just asking." He stood and walked away, following the trail toward the tower. Sister Maria needed his assistance.

When Fence took his last step down, Mr. Tuffty stood waiting. "You'll need this," he told Fence, handing him the yellowed map. "Keep it quiet."

Meanwhile, Tia retraced her childhood, visualizing herself, crying on the orphanage steps. She missed Rose, longing to hold her.

Did my mother ever miss me? Tia's heart ached. *Who was she? Who am I?*

Handle in hand, Fence carried the unusual woven basket, pondering the fact that Tia, Rose's mother, had once been in it. He imagined what transpired twenty-odd years prior. The two Carpenters, Fence and Tia, left together with a different vision, no less difficult to think about. Jamaica held its breath.

The Sea

FENCE and Tia agreed to end all conversation under past names, assuming the role of two newlyweds. False identification for a Tucker and Vanessa Johnson pulsated on the interior of Fence's lightweight jacket, thanks to Gramp Reed's ingenuity. Doc Bridger had their new medical records in order, amazingly. Carrying on the awkward act confused their relationship even more.

"I don't know why those two aren't retired. You should see Doc's desk," Fence said while they waited for their baggage to be cleared. "He's secretary-less. Of course, maybe he couldn't find one who keeps secrets." Fence leaned over Tia's head. "He thinks he's a spring chicken. When he and Gramp get together, they're like two boys with a match and a powder keg."

Tia, still resolving her aggravation, pictured the two old men as cartoon characters. "How come they think they're so good at problem solving?"

"They've had experience being the problem. They know how mischief thinks." Fence twisted his head to check behind them.

"Well, I hope this isn't a wild goose chase," Tia said, irritated with all the conniving.

"If it is, the goose doesn't have a chance. We're going to find some answers." He reached for her hand. "I'm here for you."

She breathed in and shrugged her shoulders, visualizing the voodoo doll stuck full of pins. "This is not going to be easy." She gave him an I'd-rather-be-anywhere-but-with-you look.

Smells of the sea met Fence and Tia, alias the Johnsons. Jamaica, where the feet of Christopher Columbus had once walked, beckoned tourists and businessmen to come and enjoy. A fine mist of young lovers with dreams of basking in the luxury of Caribbean sun strolled haphazardly, oblivious to any cares of the world. Fence and Tia attempted to fit into the vacation portrait.

Blue-green ocean water gently lapped the land. Tia's feet waited to sink into the white sand and liberate her toes between its grains. Salt particles flavored the air and kissed her lips. She tasted the white coating, adjusting her sunglasses and floppy white hat. The new, loose clothing had given her freedom from heat's bondage. Instantly Tia connected with the island; the kinship impregnated her with life.

Fence clasped her hand, his fingers between hers. They walked with their arms touching. In the midst of a dozen people, he stopped short and pulled her close to him. Spontaneously, Fence lifted her shades, leaned down and kissed her on the lips, hiding their faces from exposure and any spy-natured viewers. The façade took her aback. Her face turned red. She whispered, "What did you do that for?"

"I'm just playing the part. Don't get so shook up." The drama, performed in public, irritated Tia. Fence acted oblivious to the world around them. But not so, every move he made was calculated. "They're like rose petals with beads of dewdrops Mrs. Johnson."

"What are you talking about? And, quit calling me that." She looked bewildered, wanting to draw the line and set the boundary. Caution told her to be yoked to Fence, but there was little comfort in it. The flustered heat index spiraled.

"Your lips, Vanessa. It's a code for mutual love. Remember Rose, rose petals?" His eyes danced. She nodded and looked at the sandy ground. Adjustment locked them together.

Walking the seashell streets, Fence's visual circled the perimeter. His investigative instinct heightened, alert to sights and sounds of danger, attentive to homemade doll shops and basket weavers. The wooden faces of storefront vendors gave nothing away with expression. Behind the masks hid unseen powers of voodoo, interwoven in the cultural fabric. Ordinary tourists either ignored it or accepted it as commonplace in the Islands. Fence kept Tia close. They moved as one, discreetly observing the pattern of the people. He guided her into an artist's small, street-side shop.

"Bet Mr. T. would like this place." She mouthed the code for Mr. Tuffty, attempting to appear fascinated with the drawings.

"I, for one, am glad we left him behind. Hey, look at this." Fence lifted the old frame out from the back. He whistled. "This is one beautiful bird."

The shop owner answered him. "Yes, an old resident of the island.

His name is Amos. He came from the Ivory Coast. My grandfather was a young boy at the time."

Tia listened with her back turned. The attractive bronze woman undoubtedly impressed Fence. Tia's gut felt uneasy with the beautiful woman's advances.

"The artist is my grandfather. He will draw you, if you like?" The woman shifted her feet, leaning toward Fence.

"Thanks. I would like to meet him." He smiled at her. "I'll buy this." Fence lifted the African Gray. "So, where does the bird live?" he asked.

"He has no master now. He vanished into the Blue Mountains long ago. Will you come back tomorrow?" She rubbed against Fence's arm, seducing with more than words. He did not move away, nor did he introduce himself. He gave her cash. "I'll be back." Fence walked outside the door to wait for Tia.

Tia took her time, finishing her search before slipping out. Giving Fence a disgusted look, she said. "Did you forget we're together? Aren't we supposed to be newlyweds? That woman totally ignored me. She took quite an interest in you."

"So, we were having a fight. That wouldn't be so unusual would it? I didn't see you being exactly friendly to her. You don't know me very well do you? I'm your friend, not your enemy." He answered, swallowing hard. "Are you jealous?"

"No. I thought we were on a mission. It's just that she had other motives, like charming you. She manipulates with her body."

Fence pretended to ignore Tia. Her intuition was right. It was not her imagination. She was perceptive. Tia's straightforward approach reminded him of Abe. *If only he were here to help solve this mess.*

A different movement filled the night than the day. Australian, European, American and Asian guests flavored the air with superiority. The tourists shelled out coins from nations abroad with a clattering sound, bolstering the Jamaican economy. Most visitors overlooked the poverty-stricken, motivated or blinded by pleasure and all the glitz. However, hidden in the middle of the outward show, undercover drug deals thrived and political power played.

Fence and Tia sauntered amidst the international dialogue. She hooked his arm. On purpose, he turned her toward the sea. "Listen," he whispered.

Within earshot stood a skinny man immersed in intense conversation.

"Poachers leave bodies of rhino and elephant stripped of ivory, fermenting and full of flies, wasting away. To safari they say, but… we of Africa know better."

The towering African dignitary spoke up. "They disgrace the landscape to line their pockets."

"It's a shame, if I must say. The ignominy of such invasion is frightful." A heavyset man grunted, faking his agreement.

"Gold bellies are never satisfied," the graying Kenyan said, resenting the grunting man, but agreeing with his point. He stepped to the forefront. "Z countries have suffered much. Zimbabwe, Zaire, Zambia, even Tanzania … stripped by deplorable greed. Ravenous, spineless men cannot control their lust." He spoke English slowly. He made his point, and then gave room for the Australian to speak.

"Bloody thirsty varmints they are," the ordinary, fun-loving Australian said in a sober tone. "Poachers, eh? Low on the totem pole, in the gutters in my book."

The extraneous discussion continued as Fence and Tia moved toward their dinner table. Servants graciously waited on them, proud of the hospitality that flowed through their native Euro-African veins. Creativity covered the open-air tables. Giant displays of food arrayed in fans and flowers, made into animals, gave fruits and vegetables new dimension. Rooster tails of reds, yellows and oranges demonstrated Jamaica's extensive flair for decorating with food. Smells of breads and elegant desserts went far beyond the ordinary. And fish—the net was full.

"I'll have the red snapper, Tucker, and you can have the stuffed crab," Tia told Fence, feeling resistant.

"Oh I can, can I? I didn't know you liked fish so much. In fact, I don't know much about you," he said, winking like Mack, his father.

"I'm amazed at that. It seems my life has been an open book to you. You'll have to learn fast," she answered. "It's been a long trip. The more I'm around you, the less I like you."

"I'm gathering that. I'm still married to you. Just try and play the part. I'm not the one you need to be afraid of," he replied.

"I'm not so sure. I don't know if I can trust you. How did I get into this anyway?" she said, mostly to herself.

"Remember, you found me." He gave her a full-toothed grin.

"I found my daughter," she whispered.

"Well, tables turn and you need me, my blood that is. You are walking around with part of me inside you, like it or not." As he spoke, two little black boys, twins, ran up to Tia and grabbed hold of her legs while Fence talked. Standing edgewise he added. "That fact does not make me understand you. One minute you're grateful and the next you're off in another world."

She knelt to meet the ebony children face to face, pulling them into her arms. They had come from a hut made of boards. They smelled so good, so clean, yet they lived with so little. "And what are you two doing tonight?" she quizzed, loving the colorful children. They smiled and jabbered in a local dialect, not altogether foreign to Tia. "Tucker, we must give them gifts, the soap on the dresser in the resort room?"

Fence had trusted no one but himself for months. Even with Tia, he resisted. For certain, he was not naïve enough to trust children showing warmth to her. He connected to the island in a different way than Tia. His native blood identified with Arawak canoes, tobacco and fishing. For some reason Ruger came to his mind. He looked over Tia's head, observing the crowd.

Reggae music steadily filled the air. The traditional melodic patterns and modes of African drumbeats pressed out calypso rhythm. "I'm glad you're enjoying this, but keep your head clear." Changing the subject, he pulled her to the side. "We're going snorkeling tomorrow."

"I'd like that. There's something about this place, like I've been here before, like a part of me is here." She watched the drummers. "I'm not afraid."

It was evident that Tia delighted in simple things. Casually, Fence wrapped his arm around her back, more for her protection than comfort. Leaning his head toward hers, he said, "The next move is mine."

Fence left her in the seaside suite with the picture of the African Gray. Tia could only imagine why he cut the evening short. He vanished for hours. The memory of lying on the van floor at the ransacked cabin returned. *Someday we're going to be free.* She paced, and then took a quick shower.

Apprehensive, Tia spread the birth handkerchief on the bed and then spoke to the painting of the bird. "Amos, if you're alive, I could use some company right now."

Beware

FENCE navigated the streets looking for signs, wary of tentacles of sleek and shrewd men, monsters of the deep that invade land with corruption. He whisked in and out, sensitive to those with shadowy pasts who make a habit of sucking blood from the future.

His thoughts bounced back and forth to Tia. *She better not do anything dumb. She seems to have a belligerent streak.* He wrestled with trusting her. Leaving a guard outside the room was not his idea, but he felt a twinge of relief. *She might take off and hunt mountain lions on her own.*

An unusual message, sealed with a silver star, awaited him at the front desk exactly on time: midnight.

Beware, killer sharks.

Claude Walking Elk did not sign his name.

Fence knocked the arranged signal, swallowing hard. Spying through the peephole, Tia unbolted the door, thankful that he was back. She had waited for him. "Where were you?"

"Out with another woman," he half teased, catching sight of the hanky spread out on the bed like a map. Tia had been lost in the study of it.

Fence spoke immediately. "Let's walk the beach and search for treasure."

"What?" she asked incredulously.

"Yes, before the crowd comes onto the shore. The wind changed and blew in lots of shells." He grabbed the woven basket bag half filled with towels. She put the hanky inside her shirt pocket.

The empty beaches were lonely and enchanted. From one end to the other their sandals submerged into sand. Soft humid spray moistened their skin. A cool breeze sent a chill over them. Tia wrapped up her arms with her hands, protecting herself. Fence reached around her back, imparting a slight squeeze and release. "The moon is tipped over. Natives believe it indicates rain or a tropical storm coming."

"This whole trip is tipped over," Tia lashed. A conch shell's open pink ear lay listening at her feet. She bent forward and picked up the shell. "Did you know that a sound in perfect pitch could travel indefinitely?" Lifting it to her mouth, she blew the island horn.

"Why did you do that?" Fence discharged. "You're waking up everything in the sea and everyone else around here!" His aggravated look revealed anger.

"Fish are waiting to dance out there. The voice of the conch calms the ocean roar. Did you not learn that?" She gulped giving the excuse.

Tia dispensed the shell to Fence's waiting hand. Rapidly, he removed the instrument from sight, tucking it in the newly found but old woven basket. "Your find is safe," he blurted.

"You're angry I did that, aren't you?" She would not let it rest. The intense need to communicate with him hovered over her tongue.

"I'd rather you didn't draw attention to us," he admonished.

"We're walking the night away, Tucker." Tia said the name, remembering their first meeting over a year before, the first time she had said his real name, Fence. If nothing else, they still had commitment. Side by side, they wandered further down the shoreline for a couple of miles. "The sea welcomes the sunrise with a song." She started the new subject, appealing to him. "Today is a new page."

"More like a new chapter. Vanessa Johnson, isn't it?" Fence looked into her wide-open eyes. "I lied. I wasn't out with another woman." He wanted to kiss her. It was not an act. "Sit on the sand with me please."

Tia did not argue.

The quietness filled with the softening of the sea. Together they took in the beauty of things they could not buy, things that last past death, letting the moments pass without words. Finally Fence spoke. "I wonder how deep those footings go to get those tall buildings to stand. Kind of like forming a friendship—takes quite a foundation when you're next to an ocean." Fence's architectural training surfaced.

"Building a friendship takes time. One must set a firm basis, one without lies," Tia answered, weighing the essence of real relationship.

Grabbing her hand, Fence pulled her up with him. Tia's insides shook, swirling with the sea's undercurrent. "You're pint size, but you have gallon character," he said.

She stared at him. Without hesitation, he drew her to him, touching his lips to hers, pressing her close.

Tia, unwilling to respond, trembled. She put her hands on her stomach, remaining cautious. "I'm not in the mood to be manipulated." He had stepped over friendship to the beyond, just when they had started to communicate.

"That wasn't my intention. I'm sorry, but I'm not sorry. Guess I crossed the line," Fence admitted, looking over his back. "That could get into my blood," he confessed.

Her face, with friendly lines, caught his eye in wry humor. "What? The acting, the sea or the sunrise?" She smiled at him.

Tia's method of getting his mind off the kiss, off the closeness between each other and onto what she could accept at the moment, did not hurt his feelings. On the contrary, her play on words appealed to him. The waves started to do their morning lap. Fence's romantic notions slipped away. The seriousness of the mission roared with the tide. He was her bulletproof vest, vital to her protection. He hung close to her, protecting her with vigilance. She could not repel him in that.

"Race you back." Tia grabbed a handful of damp sand and threw it at him.

Catching her with one hand, he twisted her body around. "Hey, you don't have baggage to carry." The weighted-down basket lay in the sand.

"I wouldn't be so certain about that." She pushed him away.

"You can't get rid of me that easy," he said, muffing her hair.

The wind gave them a soft push in the footrace. Imprinted into the shore were the outlines of steps of two, running side by side, separate but connected. Neither would or could admit it. What she did not know was that they were being watched. Maybe she did not want to know. She had never felt this free, ever.

Unlocking the door, they stepped softly inside the crisp room, breathing hard. Weapons rested on the bed. "Connections," Fence said with expression. "We have connections." He leaned down and whispered in her ear. "No chances. No breakfasts in bed." He inserted a smile. "We live in a fast time, a fast age. Islanders don't live by it. No clock, just an inner knowing it is right," Fence double-talked.

She tried to read through the lines. The man of plans was forever changing plans. "Life is not a chance-ridden thing," she said. "Don't you know that one decision changes the outcome of a whole future? I think we should stay put."

"If we stay here, we may not have a tomorrow," he whispered louder than he intended. "I and F, two letters spell a big word for you, don't they?"

"Yes they do," she answered. "And 'if only' spells two bigger words. If only we had stayed put," Tia said, clearing her throat of sea taste. "Each can involve regret."

"Or reward." Fence inserted the positive.

Moments later they checked out without rest.

The Star

RICH black hair, braided intricately with colored beads, graced the heads of beautiful Jamaican women and children. Tia reached out to hold the diapered baby. "Hold like this," the charcoal woman instructed. "Pat with fingertips, not the flat hand. Keeps baby cooler."

Warm compassion oozed out of Tia. "History can't hold you when you're cold. Science can't give love," she said, returning the baby to the mother.

"What are you implying?" Fence asked. "Are you a philosopher too?"

"No Fence, I'm a mother. Women encompass a broad circle. I learned that from yours."

"I believe that," Fence answered, thinking of his Indian blood. "Decades ago Arawak Indians sheltered African slaves in the hills, like American Indians did."

Tia's free hand reached across for Fence's arm. She held it tightly while they walked the black slave gardens. Rich beauty made years of sweat and toil go unnoticed by most, but not by Tia. "Can a man really own another man?" she asked.

He stopped. "The need to be free never stops. The need to be important, to be valued for who you are and not what you do or have."

A multi-colored windsock hung limply on the spindly pole near the gazebo in the historic park, displaying rich color without tatters or fading. Stately palm trees leaned backwards in the background. Tia read the tourist guidebook out loud. "Since the 1830's slave release, the island has thrived."

The tall Jamaican rambled through the path of Fence's mind. What would it take to find tracks that were long since washed away—long since covered over? Who would find whom? Was the man connected to the Maroons? Fence discarded no possibility.

214

"Do you think my ancestors owned slaves?" Tia asked.

"If they did, they were like you. I mean kind."

"So much unwritten," Tia inserted, stopping by the hummingbirds sucking nectar from fruit blossoms.

"Rastafarian influence permeates this place." Fence commented. "Covers the whole island religiously."

The old car Fence rented left little to be desired. The cloth seats, that were once brown, had faded to gray. A bamboo-like foldable seat insert, positioned to help keep the driver cool, sat cockeyed. Fence straightened it out and sunk down on it. Tia, sinking into the opposite side, felt lost beneath the dash. Scooters sped by them.

"This is as good a place as any," Fence said, handing Tia snorkeling gear. "We weren't followed."

The buoyancy of the warm ocean water lifted them. Brilliant fish, all kinds, electrified the water. Iridescent, hyacinth and zebra colors moved at varying speeds, sometimes fast as lightning. A different time, a different place than they had known, momentarily relaxed them in the surreal experience.

The ocean salt weighted her hair. Tia longed for a shower and sleep. Yet, she did not want to miss anything, especially any discoveries. She looked at Fence. "Is our assignment to go day and night? I'd like to just vanish into the jungle for a while, someplace with shade." The heat index had swelled upward.

"Looks like it, doesn't it? Some notion of a vacation! I have an idea. Might take the heat off. I think we're both ready for a rest. We have one more thing to do first." He pulled out a detailed map, yellowed and crackling with age. Mr. Tuffty had relinquished it to him at the last minute.

"I thought he was my lawyer, not yours." Tia took hold of it.

"Be careful. The thing is fragile," he said, pointing to a spot in the jungle. "A lot has changed since this was made. It will be a challenge to follow. He mentioned something about a bird."

"You don't seem to be in the habit of letting me know what's going on. I'm not stupid, you know. Why can't you confide in me?" Tia's frustration showed. His constant planning unnerved her, that and his warrior instinct. "What happened to this friendship bit? Or are you still investigating me?"

He gave her no answer. The truth hit too close to home. Fence plunged into the mixed lines of the map, avoiding her. "Shh," he said.

Tia wanted the dreadful game to end.

Fence finally spoke. "You were born near here."

"How do you know that?" Tia desired the truth of who she was and where she had come from. Fence focused on protection and solution, on putting an end to the destructive force, the power of death that followed them. The newspaper clipping hid in his pocket, burning through to his skin.

He pulled up beside an old seventeenth century mission. "Was I born at a mission? You're really grabbing at straws. We're a mess, all full of salt." Loose clothes covered their swimwear. She questioned him with her eyes.

"We're going in. Understand? It will be cool inside. Doc told me about it. It's part of the plan." Fence opened her door.

"Like the picture of the bird?" she asked.

Again, he avoided her eyes.

Inside, an elderly priest, whose head was covered, communed. Lit candles dripped wax on the entry table. Fence stood at the back, staring at the ancient tiles underfoot. The building had survived more than one hurricane. The Patron Saint of Wildlife, St. Francis of Assisi, stood near him. Fence touched the bird on the statue's outstretched arm. "At least the birds in this place are friendly," he said to himself. The first line on the bronze inscription blazed out at him.

Lord, make me an instrument of peace.

Tia knelt in reverence in a pew near the front, thinking of Rose and the confusion of her life while impatience pressed at Fence. He slid in beside her. "Come on. Let's get going."

"You were the one that wanted to come in. You're going to have to wait," she whispered.

Out of nowhere appeared the elderly priest wearing a heavy gold cross on his chest. Father Juniper bowed to them in greeting, beckoning them to the front altar rail. Tia arose immediately in obedience, nudging Fence into the aisle. She wrapped her hands around his arm and moved forward. Fence assented, questioning the safety of kneeling. The man of God laid his hands on their heads, blessing them like little children. "You will receive communion together to renew your vows."

Strange, Fence thought.

Although Tia responded to Father Juniper without hesitation, she too had not expected to find herself participating in communion.

Reverently, Father Juniper addressed the Heavenly Father, holding the holy sacrament—the bread and the wine—high for blessing. Both Tia and Fence kept their heads bowed while he broke the unleavened wafer to serve them the Host, Christ. The supernatural moment of partaking went deeper than the physical, a union more than words, more than flesh, more than circumstance. Tia and Fence's eyes met.

Then, the priest lifted the communal napkin, extending the cup of wine to Fence's mouth. Fence's eyes grew big. The chalice napkin appeared to be identical to Tia's handkerchief.

Father Juniper wiped the rim before lifting the Eucharistic cup to Tia. She glanced at Fence out of the corner of her eye, desiring some dimension of understanding to come between them. Glad for his willingness, she did not wish for more.

"Gifts for you." The priest took the folded napkin, placing it into Tia's folded hands. "Your hands? Sir? Place them over hers," he addressed Fence.

Like an umbrella, Fence sheltered Tia's small hands inside his, locking the napkin in the middle. His eyes fixed on Tia in a moment of truth. For a second she returned the look, drawn away by the item they held between them. They lingered while the blessing tied them together, waiting for the release.

Fence ushered her to the car. He lifted her chin. She quaked inside. "I didn't plan that," he said. "I'm as bewildered as you are."

"Maybe you did and maybe you didn't. He's watching us." The priest stood at the doorway.

"Okay. I need you to kiss me back and don't complain." He wrapped his arms around her. She had no choice in the matter. Driving away, he said, "Thanks. There's something about those guys, like the saints of hopeless cases. They desire to be effective."

With a tinge of sarcasm she commented. "Sure. Somehow I don't think this was by accident." She thrust the chalice napkin open on her lap next to her own. "Look, I want to know everything you do." She studied the two cloths.

Fence pulled the car to the side of the road. He examined the white linen cloth. "See the six arrow marks, points facing out? The new cloth doesn't have arrows. Connect them. See what happens," he said, placing it back on her lap.

She drew with her finger straight across, much differently than

Fence would have done. "A triangle. Two triangles, one on top of the other in opposite directions." She scrutinized. "Looks like the Star of David. What do you think it means?"

"I don't know for sure. You're the expert on stars. Maybe you're Jewish. Abe Pearl was." Fence restarted the car.

"Who is Abe Pearl? What do you mean, 'he was?' Is he dead?" She ran her fingertips over the corner crown.

"Yes, Tia. It's possible he's connected to you in some strange way. He's the main reason I adopted Rose, at least at first. I didn't know I would get a package deal with you."

"What makes you say that? It doesn't make sense. If I'm Jewish, what am I doing being baptized and raised in a Catholic orphanage? How did this guy know about me?" she asked.

His anxiousness showed. "You ask more questions than anyone I've ever known. I'm not sure how he knew about you, or if he knew. Something Barbados said." Fence's smile lines, caked with salt, cracked as he talked. "Authorities said Abe committed suicide. I don't think so. He's buried near Lily. I intend to find out who murdered him. Right now I'm more concerned about you."

"Sometimes I don't like you very much," Tia said.

"Why? I know I'm not the greatest communicator. But, I have some good qualities. Try to be a little agreeable." Fence attempted eye contact. "That priest acted liked he was expecting us. He seemed to recognize you. What do you think?"

"Okay, what else can you cook up? Maybe I look like my mother?"

"Or your father, on a smaller scale that is," he emitted.

"What else have you picked up from the wash of the sea?" Tia snapped. However, she sensed what he said was truth. Relenting she asked, "Where do we go from here?"

He teased. "Someplace together, alone, romantic and beautiful, some isolated bungalow, some deserted beach. Some place cool."

Not enjoying his sense of humor, Tia bit back. "We've been to the beach and we're alone. You make me feel like an item. Are you certain this is not someplace Abe Pearl or Mack recommended?"

"I don't think so. More like Arnold Tuffty." He leaned toward her, whispering, as though the outside listened in. "I think we missed the turn." Fence turned the car around.

Amos

FENCE plunged deeper into island jungle, past the coconut trees and through thick undergrowth. Birds of paradise hid in the green amidst other wildflowers. Peacocks and various birds, both tame and wild, showed their colors. The ambience of the place soothed Tia.

"If you want the outermost bungalow, you'll have to put up with an old bird, Amos. We're still repairing the other units from the hurricane last year. Not much shakes that old one," the elderly black caretaker explained. "You'll be closer to the falls."

"I like things with history. We'll take it," Fence said, paying in advance.

The man's round wife deposited a pile of sheets, two pillows and a stack of towels into a large, clear garbage bag. "There's no daily maid. Lots of privacy here." She gave a rough smile.

The man rambled about his problems in running the place while studying the scribbled signature. "Smith? You say?"

Fence detected a sound of disappointment in the caretaker's voice. "Well, my wife and I will be no trouble." He placed a generous tip on the table in front of the old Hispanic woman, noting the closeness of the mixed-race couple.

"Gracias. No problem." Her teeth neatly formed the words.

Exhausted from the incredible heat and long chapters of the day, Fence and Tia entered the secluded cottage. It was rundown and overgrown with tropical growth, unused for some time. Tia, having slept in much worse places, brushed the dust off the table. It certainly was not what ordinary tourists would consider luxurious, or for that matter a honeymoon suite.

"Looks okay. There's only the bird to worry about and that shouldn't be a problem, seeing how you know something about these birds. The caretaker said he's been around for years and won't leave this place."

Fence set the dried fruit and nuts on the table. "Guess he likes almonds."

"Maybe he's the one in the painting. He looks pretty docile to me," Tia said.

"I talk," spouted the African Gray with the red tail.

Tia approached the free-roaming bird. "You're a pretty bird."

"Careful. I bite. Not shy."

Tia jumped back.

Amos did not move his mouth, but laughed like a man. "Pretty girl," the bird squawked.

The waterfall behind the quaint hideout rubbed against pure limestone rock. Tia washed her hair in the clear water, bathing herself of the white, sandy salt residue. She hurried, unable to relax. Amos followed her, flipping his feathers in the edge of the falls. "I see I have a companion. Well, close your eyes." She already liked the bird.

The African Gray sat nearby. Tia dried her hair in the sunlight. Speaking in a childlike voice, the bird said, "Peek-a-boo. Pretty girl safe." Spooked, Amos flew off into the wild.

Fence scouted a wide circle around the area, waiting his turn to get the salt off. He rubbed his tanned face. Three days had become one. Rest could not come soon enough. Too many interruptions had invaded his life. Being unsettled had kept him alert. "Someday I'll settle down," he said out loud.

"Pretty girl safe." Amos appeared out of nowhere, spiraling around Fence's head. The bird's incessant jabber annoyed him. "Why can't you be quiet like your picture?" Fence grabbed a handful of unshelled sunflower seeds out of his pants pocket. "Not almonds, but these should shut you up."

The African Gray pecked the seeds out of his hand, cracking them with fervor. The words dropped out of his mouth like shells. "Crack nuts. Crack cases. Not crackpot."

"For not being a large bird, you sure have a big mouth. What do you say for yourself or do you only echo words?" Fence quizzed, sounding sarcastic.

Amos puffed up his head feathers.

Tia approached Fence from behind, observing the interaction. "You'll never make friends that way, let alone learn island secrets."

"I gathered as much." Fence faced her.

"Birds are sensitive creatures." Tia spoke to Fence with deeper definition.

His body turned sideways. "So, my friend, Amos, you are very smart."

The bird sprung into the air. Fence's attempt to make up to Amos with flattery fell far short. The African Gray held his tongue in. The bird was not in the mood to be patronized.

Fence raised his eyebrows. "Guess I blew that," he said, referring to the bird.

I Hate You

TIA settled into sleep before Fence returned from the falls. The neatly fixed bed was barely made before she plopped on top, hugging the pillow.

The door squeaked although Fence opened it slowly. Tia did not hear him. Fence tried to rest in the worn wicker chair. Crossing his arms, he leaned his head neck against the three-inch wide space. His heels, propped on the edge of the footboard, adjusted. *Finally peace and quiet.* He covered the escaping yawn.

Discomfort aggravated his body. His back ached as did his neck, right where Chance Cummings had put his knee. He had no plans to tell Tia that. He shifted, finally standing. Quietly, he repositioned his pillow against the back of the bed frame near Tia. Seconds later he slept, half sitting up. His body jerked, waking them both. She immediately jumped up and started pacing.

"Didn't mean to wake you."

"I'm so tired I can't sleep," she answered. She started to pace back and forth.

Fence patted the bed. "There's room for you. I didn't mean to chase you off," he invited.

"It wouldn't seem right without Rose in the middle." She reiterated his words in an off-the-cuff manner. Finally, she dropped beside him, curling up.

He stroked her head like a kitten until she fell asleep. "Hey, everything's going to be all right." His voice had a soft touch.

Had her incision healed? An intense passion rose within him, making it difficult to sit motionless beside her. He started to stand up. Her hand reached out, appealing to him. "Please, will you hold me? I don't want to be alone."

The pistol, holstered next to his heart, encumbered him. He unbelted, laying it nearby. The gun had protected him in more than one way. He made certain the doors were latched. Fence knew what loyalty was, what keeping one's word meant. After all, broken words lead to broken hearts. He would keep his. Force wins nothing. Placing strict restrictions on himself, he chose not do as Chance Cummings, not to let her fall into the hands of rape. Trying to constrain himself, he put a straight jacket on his mind and body. His eyes glossed over. He cared. He really cared for her. He had a decision to make. He reached for Tia and held her. Then, silently, the release came. The load lifted off his heart. Tia needed him.

She had no intention of submitting to him. He had tried to be her friend, to help her, to protect her. Smelling his strength, she fell weak into the security. He held her breathtakingly close. "Fence, I need you. Please don't let me go," she said.

"I have no intention of letting you go." He held her tighter, controlling his passion.

She touched the scar on his neck. She could hear his heart next to hers. "I, I, I," she stuttered. "I like to be close to you. I missed you when you were in Europe."

Fence pulled the hair off her forehead, holding her face. "The feeling is mutual." Then he released her, holding back the desire to kiss her. He rolled off his side to his back. Instinctively, she leaned over and hugged him, wrapping her arms around his stomach, kissing his chest.

"All right, how can I resist you now, my friend?" he said. "You're teasing me."

She bounced up quickly, kissing his face, his cheeks, his chin, his eyes. He grabbed her and said. "You are asking for it? You want to kiss me? Then you're getting kissed back." There was no escape. She melted into his embrace. Former ties snapped. Old grips released, setting them free for the moment. Her tender stomach rested against him. Then he knew. He knew he loved her. He had loved her for a long time, since the first time he had looked at her. She was beautiful, captivating. "I love you Tia," he said. "I love you." Tia could not control the tears. She wept until sleep overtook her.

Morning dawned on them both in a bittersweet moment. The pain inside was great. Tia stood across the room looking out the open shutters. Alarm, written all over her face, revealed a frightened young woman. She looked at him, half in anger, half in fear. "What if I'm pregnant? The doctor told me I might not live through it." She turned her back toward him.

Fence took a giant step toward her, placing his hand gently on her shoulder. "You will, Tia. You will live. We're in this together. I'm not going to let anything bad happen to you." He thought better than to mention that they were married.

"But what about Lily?" Tia reasoned, trying to keep her composure. "I don't know where I fit."

"With me. I know that now." He paused. "Lily would want me happy. She'd never begrudge me that." He looked at Tia with eyes of compassion. His insides had come alive again. Lily, no longer an interloper, had taken flight. "I've let her go. I'm done holding on to her," he reasoned with honest confession.

"You can't just move me into position and expect me to take her place. I don't even know who I am."

"Well, memories can't keep a person warm at night. Like you said, neither can history or science. Time moves ahead, not backward. Tia, no roads lead to yesterday. Those days are gone. I'll never get them back. I don't want to get them back." He continued with his speech. "Yes, I'll always love my first love. No argument there. But Tia, I love you twice, three times as much. Don't you see? We were meant to be together, for this time, for this day. Do you hear me?"

She pulled away from him. Even in death, Chance Cummings kept trying to come alive, to reattach. Irritability surfaced. It would take her time to adjust, to break out of being alone—alone and possibly pregnant. The last time she found herself in such a situation she was bruised and broken. And now, of her own free will, she had let herself be loved.

She was Mrs. Fence Carpenter, but what was her real name? *Who is my mother?* Suddenly the need to know grew larger than life. *Was I conceived in love? What kind of a man was my father?* It haunted her all the more. Tia stepped further away, reluctant to feel too much for the man who now was her husband. More important matters loomed over her.

Stay at a distance; remain aloof. Indulging in passion carried guilt, even if they were married. Tia would not allow herself the delicacy of love. Yes, she needed him. Once again she felt trapped. Protective walls went up; pain resurfaced. She felt like a butterfly struggling to break out of darkness. She hurled at Fence, erupting like a volcano. "You have roots! You have parents! You have a past!" Accusations flew out of her mouth.

"You have me. My blood." He pointed to the bend in his arm.

"I want to know *my* bloodline, and you are not in it!" She reached for her sandal. "So, I was born near here? Where and how do you know that?"

Tentacles of hatred wrapped around her fair neck, cutting off her breath. Hidden anger that had lain low in her heart, the rejection and abandonment, the rape, the confusion, it all blew out like vomit at Fence. The molten fire that poured out had brewed since birth, like anyone who does not know how to be loved, but desperately craves it. She hated Chance Cummings, spending months trying to tell herself she loved him; that she had to love him. And now, Fence Carpenter, the man she married because of Rose, hovered over her. She could not let herself like him or perhaps, tell herself she loved him.

Delving into her own judgment, she refilled with anger, with disappointment in herself. She wanted to slap the man next to her and hurt him. Any monastic manner about her submitted to retaliation, to fear, to shame. If only she could push out, push away from—

Abruptly she turned toward Fence with jabbing words shooting forth from her lips. "I hate you; I— I— hate you. Leave me alone. Stay away from me. Don't you see? I don't want you near me," she lashed out at him. "Oh why, why did I let you get close to me?"

Confusion clouded Fence's thinking. Reasoning with her would accomplish little. He backed off, unable to fight her, the victim of her misplaced anger. Bitterness had once clung to him. Tia had swallowed its poison. Accepting Lily's death had helped him understand the difficulty of not knowing, not understanding, of self-blame. Yet, he did not really understand.

"I take my hands off. You can spit fire all you want, but we're in this together, like it or not." He unlatched the door, grabbed his weapon and walked to cool off. When he returned, she was gone.

He regretted his haste. Overcoming fear to love resulted in fear to lose. Just what he did not want, emotion interfering with duty. No guard was stationed nearby.

Poisoned

DAGGERS hang in the same closet with hurt. Tia had thrown them with her tongue at the man who was trying to be kind to her, at the man who said he loved her. She sat by the noisy falls hating herself more than anyone dead or alive, inwardly knowing that hatred never achieves peace and always proves unproductive. *What if he gives up on me?* She needed him, but survival by independence was the only life Tia knew. She had always been alone, except for God, and He never wastes anything, even pain. To depend on man was not yet a reality. She did not know whether that was good or bad.

Fence had closed the gap but not enough to cause her to trust him. She wanted to. Oh, how she wanted to. Sister Maria Thomas's words tore at her. *Anger is in the business of dismantling peace, of tearing down bridges. It can't wait to get an opportunity to destroy.* Tia reached to a flower, desiring to catch a wandering butterfly with her hands. It flitted off. Forgiveness eluded her.

Thoughts of her birth parents mysteriously pulled her into the unknown. Curiosity—the longing to know—engaged her in the unseen battle with the past. Finally, her insides settled. Sheer determination pulled her to her feet. Amos, the African Gray, was with her. He said, "Pretty girl, I love you."

From a distance Fence saw her walking toward him like he was not there. He held out his hand, lifting his eyebrows. "Peace?"

She nodded and looked down, unable to apologize. A tender, sheepish mellowing covered her.

Amos rode on the back of Tia's shoulder.

"I didn't know I had all that in me. I don't want to be pregnant," she admitted.

Fence stroked her tearing cheek. "Maybe you aren't. I was wrong. I took advantage of you."

"Oh Fence, I'm a wreck. You didn't take advantage of me. I don't know who I am, or what my real name is. If it wasn't for you, I wouldn't be alive. You gave me Rose and a home. I owe you so much."

"I don't want just your gratitude, Tia. You've given me that. I don't want you to be my slave or Rose's caretaker. I want to be more than your bodyguard. Call it equal footing, not me towering over you. Men have desires and you are very desirable. I don't trust myself with you."

"You mean you don't trust me," she said.

He looked far off wanting to punch the air and divorce himself from the whole situation, but they were stuck together. His compassion won out. He touched her shoulder while his logical mind hunted for the right words. He gave her what he could, his strength and support. "I'm with you no matter what happens. I want to learn to trust you. I still want to be your friend." He wanted to say husband.

"I don't have much to give. I feel so empty. I'll never be Lily," she said.

"No. No one could be Lily. No one could be you. None of us know if we have a tomorrow. We have no choice but to live in the today, and not abuse it." He held out his hand to shake hers. "Friends?" The subject of pregnancy dropped. Although close in proximity, they were still disconnected. Tia braced herself against him with splintered affection.

"Well, lady, come on. I have something to show you. I won't touch you, okay?" Once again, Fence reached for Tia's hand. She let him take it. He dropped it. "I've changed my mind. I'm carrying you back." He lifted her before she could say no. "I know what it is to be angry," he said, setting her down in front of the doorway. "We have to talk. I have to talk. Someone has to talk besides the bird!"

Fence reached into his pocket, producing the news clip. He laid it on the round wicker table and pulled up the two white chairs. Tia stood motionless over him, watching his eager hands flatten out the paper. The date caught Tia off guard, the same day she first met him, the day he yelled at her, the day she had her hopes so high. It was the day she fought despair.

"Before going to Scotland," Fence explained, "I stopped at the house and in the box of recycled papers, I noticed this article. I decided to keep it when I saw the date on top. I stuffed it into the side of my travel bag. Anyway, it's a long story. While I was over there, I read it and got to thinking. I know it sounds crazy. Could they possibly be your parents?" Fence looked up, questioning. If only he could read the map in her mind.

He followed her with his eyes.

Jamaican Baby Vanishes, Still a Mystery.

The headline captured Tia's full attention. She leaned down, reading the small print. Horror registered. Her hands flew to her mouth. The chair caught her as she sank into its flowery cushion. She knew. No one had to tell her, or explain.

"Poisoned?" she barely uttered, desperate for knowledge, for strength, for truth. All the sap seemed to run out of her. She shook her head in unbelief. "It can't be. It can't be, but I know it is. It's them. It's my parents." She picked the paper up and pulled it to her heart. "Why did I hope against hope that they were still alive?" Silent drops fell from her face. She shielded the words with her arm, not wanting to saturate them. Agonizing grief dripped over her. Fence gently touched her pink cheek with his handkerchief. Words were not enough. He said nothing.

Looking again, attempting to process the new information, she uttered, "Fence, the picture?" Her hidden thoughts spoke out loud. "Could this be a wedding picture?"

"It's possible. This man looks like you," Fence said. Diverting to the present, he added, "We never had a wedding picture taken of us, did we?"

Absorbed in her own history, Tia did not answer.

He spoke again, tugging her out of the trance. "This secluded place is perfect to work out of. Is that okay with you?"

Instantly she sparked, playing havoc with him again. "You never asked me before what I thought. Now you think it matters?" Her sarcastic answer threw him off.

"Yes, you matter, what you think matters." He tried to keep his calm by heeding his grandfather's wisdom. *A man's true nature appears in a crisis.*

Fence had to get Tia back on track, back to the assignment, without her tying his hands. The hurt in her eyes disturbed him. Covering up compassion, Fence let firmness dominate. "Okay, let's get one thing straight. If nothing else, we're here to find out the truth. You are under my protection. I can't have you bucking me or disappearing on me. This is still a matter of life and death, like it or not. We've got to get to the bottom of this or we'll be looking over our shoulders forever."

Fire burned inside her at blazing speed so soon after her submission.

"Okay, you're the boss, you and the rest of the Carpenter clan," Tia spurned. "I'm not happy about it."

He felt the spitfire spewing at him. He was glad for it. She'd be more on guard. "Hey, take some time to look it over." He put his hands behind his head, trying to tilt the big chair back on its heels. It did not help. Fence shot up and walked impatiently around the room. "I do my best thinking walking."

"I do my best walking thinking," she countered. "Besides, I'd like to make my own trail for once."

"You've already done that," he said. "Will you come with me to a library to do some research? Would that meet with your approval? And maybe back to that mission?"

She nodded, submitting to his leadership. The idea of a productive discovery lifted her spirits. Why was she fighting him so much? She did not want to. It was not like her. Her emotions were out of control. They mixed with the turmoil of her lost identity and the loss of her parents.

Knowing her mood swings needed to stabilize, Tia looked into Fence's gray green eyes and apologized. "I'm sorry, I don't know what's wrong with me. I think I miss Rose. I don't know. My life is such a mess! Please, I know I need help."

Caressing her soft cheek with his knuckle, he smiled and said, "Me too."

She returned his smile with a knowing and a question at the same time. "You're sorry, you don't know what's wrong with you, you miss Rose or you need help? Which is it?"

Amused, Fence rolled his eyes. "Yes, all of the above. You're a hard one to keep up with." He cared for her a lot more than he understood. He checked his gun. "Tia, the truth is close."

Tia shook her head. "Fence, do you think that whoever poisoned my parents, poisoned you?"

"It could be. Jamaica has a history of poisoning masters. They call it open rebellion. I'm not sure how I fit into the picture. Yes, I'm your bodyguard, but there's more to it than that."

Amos flew to the drawing of himself. "Amos bodyguard. Love Pretty Girl."

Fence rested his hand over her arm, giving Tia a brotherly squeeze. "Take courage, my friend. Looks like we have the bird on our side."

Missing Page

TIA sidestepped, steeped in thought, instead of focusing on the building in front of her. The library, banked with elderly books, smelled musty. Its marble floor reflected prestige and dignity. Fence checked the files before ascending the steps two at a time. Tia hurried with him to search the dark halls of the past.

The ink, still quite legible, was not smeared. Picking up Tia's hand, he pointed to the page number. "Vanessa," he whispered softly, concealing her real name, "A page is missing. It's been removed. We can't extrapolate information from what's missing. Or can we?"

"Quit using such big words. I have enough to sort out," Tia snapped. He aggravated her. Yet, she noted his care. She ignored him, eager to delve into time's yellowed pages. So many questions plagued her. Deep inside she hoped that the woman who bore her died without pain. Her azure eyes clouded over in a glossy blur. *Was my mother like me?* She scanned the dark aisles of sleeping books. If they all could speak, they could not fill her emotional void, fulfill her dreams or bring her parents back to life. So many questions swarmed in her head.

Fence whispered, "All evidence of your birth? Someone doesn't want any proof left that you ever existed."

"You're saying I don't exist? Well, they didn't count on newspaper articles abroad, did they?" Tia desperately wanted to fit. She did not want to relinquish her heritage.

"I'm saying you have to face the facts. There's no headline news at this library, at least in written form," he said. "No one comes alive in books."

Defiance overcame her. "I don't know about that." Tia rose up. Fence pulled her back to her chair.

"Look at this," he said, opening an old copy of the Jamaican newspaper.

Plantation Profit Credited to Slaves.

The article with its 1834 roots captured their attention. *Were her parents plantation owners? Had Barbados worked for them?*

"This library echoes with emptiness," Tia said, fighting off an anxiety attack.

Fence pointed. "You're right. Time to go. I found a cemetery map. Spike up your courage."

Who Lies Here?

Eternal Peace Spoken Here. The gate's gold inscription hung over the entrance. The mission adjoining it was built to keep out hostile barbarians, enclosing the age-old tombs.

Who lies here? Is this where my parents were laid to rest? Tia's spine tingled. *Is this the burial place of martyred saints?*

Fence pulled her next to his ribcage. "This is it, their burial site."

Tia swallowed hard. To be part of a family, the childhood dream of orphans, stood still within her. She did not want to view death or what could have or should have been. Superstitions wanted to mount on the wall of her heart. She dispelled them. "Oh mama, papa, if I had only known you." She bowed her head reverently, remembering her childhood vision, repressing tears.

Secretly, Tia had clung to hope, the miraculous possibility that her parents were alive. She could not move on until she understood the complexity of her past, nor could peace settle in her heart.

"You are their miracle," Fence murmured to Tia.

He let it soak in for a minute. A rustling noise caught his ear. He turned in place, tugging her to go. "It's not safe here," he mouthed.

She did not want to leave or let them go. Kneeling in place, Tia remained in thought. *So much destiny ... unfulfilled.* She traced over the engraving, the name only her fingers could touch. Then, she rose purposefully. "I'm ready."

Approaching the outskirts of the burial grounds, a huge callused hand stretched toward them, the white of the palm upward. A younger version of Barbados, the Jamaican Fence had met in New York, spoke in a basement voice. His massive hands disappeared. "You are in the right place. My father will meet you when the night is being crowned." His coconut white teeth exposed themselves in a short smile and brief nod. His eyes spoke much more in coded expression. Then he walked past them, passing the aboveground tombs, leaving them alone again.

Tia reeled with anticipation in the miserable heat, leaning into Fence. He led her outside the gate, holding her up. "I'm feeling sick," she confided. Her head swam with urgent desires.

"Cemeteries have a way of doing that," Fence answered.

"It's more than that," she stated.

He looked at her squarely. "What is it?"

"It's the voodoo doll. Fear keeps trying to crumble me. Did you look inside it?" she asked.

"Gramp took its head off. I didn't want to upset you."

"Well, what was in it? I'm tired of secrets," Tia said, pulling herself together.

"Cocaine." Tia read his lips. "Mack thought it was laced with cyanide. Doc checked it out and it was."

"I never envisioned my life to be so full of confusion, much less poison." She shook her head.

"There seems to be a lot of symbolism. I can't put my finger on it," Fence said.

"I think I need a cold drink of water. Maybe some food, if you don't mind? I am among the living and I don't intend to have my name on any tombstone," Tia whispered.

"On that we agree. Let's let the dead rest and get back to the land of the living, at least until midnight." Fence glanced at his watch. "That's one appointment neither of us wants to miss."

Pirate's Wharf

WEDGED into a Jamaican inlet, the Pirate's Wharf in every way resembled an ancient mariner's haven. The dinner special, displayed on an easel blackboard with copper-colored chalk, read: Catch of the day—Swordfish. Miniature anchors served as door handles. They contrasted severely with the massive anchor arched next to the wharf.

Inside, an array of nautical charts hung on the weatherworn walls. A mariner's compass with its magnetic needle gave the look of direction. Over the doorway a large marlin poked out its long, sharp snout; the relative of the spearfish was mounted on two large hooks. The smell of fish was strong.

The nervous Jamaican waitress seated the bulky man in a back corner along with his wasted-looking companion with dyed red hair. She fidgeted trying to get the order straight. Distraught by the man's rudeness, she apologized twice to the customer. Across the room her boss watched with a disapproving eye, prompting her with hand motions. The evening rush was about to begin.

"I was stupid," the woman said as soon as the waitress had left them alone at the corner table. "I didn't realize who she was or I'd have pulled the plug, but then you would be clueless how to get access to the banks in Zurich. That is, if she knows. She pulled through when others wouldn't have. Who was to suspect her anyway?" The cantankerous woman downed the brandy set before her, lighting another cigarette. AryAnn knew no other way. Her body had lost its vitality, degenerated from chain smoking and abuse. Her squinting eyes pierced the man across from her. She snarled. "The bitch. She doesn't even look like a Jew."

"We'd have found a way. Don't lament over spilled beans." The bulky man schemed, imagining a pyramidal cockpit of limestone with a pointed stake centrally fixed in a deep depression. Near the bottom lurked a sea monster, tangled in black roots, awaiting a victim. The cagey idea gave Skully great pleasure.

"And how do you propose to set this troupe-de-loup? Count me out. You catch the fly in your own web," she snapped.

The cross man gritted his teeth. "I hate the wretch," he said, not knowing what woman or man he spoke of. He despised them all, even the hag in front of him. Childish rogues were more subservient than she was. He smirked. "How quickly a potion of cyanide saps life out. Have you forgotten?" Gust Skully dropped the poisonous bag on the table, glaring at her balding head.

AryAnn gulped, having swallowed too much to turn back. "You're a hard man to please," she said, trying to smooth out resistance. She disdained the slouch of a man she served. Eight years as his pawn reinforced antagonism in her.

He would not be foiled by her vomit. *Everyone needs to be taught a lesson.* The words of his barbarous grandfather came upon him. The sting of the whip that had wrapped around his neck when he was a child still coiled like a snake—still burned prejudice into him.

Saliva built up in his mouth. He had killed at the old man's orders. Who would conceive that he, a once innocent child, would carry a poisonous bottle into the home of so-called royalty? He fumed inside, recalling the event. He would spit in his grandfather's eye if he had the chance. *Ignorant and prideful men are blind to little runts who carry booby traps and live grenades, sightless to brats who will poison their own mothers to get what they want.* Skully, cruel to the core, conspired.

"Woman!" he ordered with his machete tongue, pulling on the corner of her thin red hair. "She will die by your hand yet," he snapped, letting her go. "Make it look like a voodoo ritual."

AryAnn spat at him, pushing away from the table, leaving the vulgar man alone. Skully finished his meal, stirring up evil thoughts.

He had let himself go. Sluggish weight had come on him that he did not have the energy to shed. Who would have guessed that he would slip in and out of countries under the disguise of loyalty and honor, smuggling various drugs—cocaine, opium, heroin? A variety of private airports in third world nations had served as cover for the illegal activities. He had flown the secret missions without interference. For several years he had played the game, occupying positions to his best advantage, covering defeats with his connections to foreign dignitaries.

"It's good they all think I'm dead," he scoffed. "No one will recognize me." He belched. His gluttonous shape and overfilled, unshaven face took any sense of dignity away from him. He did not care. He was on the edge of becoming a rich man and no one had a chance if they stood in his way, at least according to his thinking. Only a few grains of patience remained within him. He squeezed the bag of poison. He could not keep his fingers off it.

His second appointment was thirty minutes late, but ready with an excuse. "Better late than never," the Scottish kid said. "Lucky I got past the door. I showed my false ID. Picked it off an American. Aye? Altered the year of birth. Got into the country by the skin of my teeth."

Skully smirked. "You chose the right man to come to. Jamaica is beautiful, is it not? Did you bring the goods?" he asked, referring to the opium.

"Aye, sir, I did—the best you can get. I want cash," the kid said.

The opium smelled rotten. Skully wondered where the poppies were grown. Besides, any excuse not to give the full value suited Skully.

"A deal is a deal." The lanky kid wanted to rush.

Skully took his time. Slowly he removed the American money, reluctant to exchange it for the opium sack. He stuck the two bags into his oversized shirt as soon as Edin Mansfield slipped out of the Pirate's Wharf. *The kid had better be on the up and up. Certainly Major Merdone knew what he was doing by getting the new runner.*

Humoring himself, Skully laughed out loud. *I'll double my money by morning. Jamaicans are so superstitious they will pay a fortune to break a curse—easy as taking candy from a baby. Naïve wretches! What would I do without them?* He bragged to himself, patting his belly.

Skully's Lust

FENCE and Tia Carpenter, incognito as Tucker and Vanessa Johnson, neared the coastline. From the moment they had set foot on the island, they had watched the gold and gifts of tourists disappear into the day, into the night. Jamaican play and gaiety hid a history book of poverty and violence. Only did the free sea seem to hold a treasure trove that provided life sustenance. "No one owns the sea except in dreams," Tia said out of the blue.

"Treasure hunter greed. People consumed by lust and vengeance thrive on it," Fence said. "Dad calls them greedaholics. Says a man is without because his inside is empty, not the outside." Fence looked at Tia head on, desiring to give her his heart. "Generosity doesn't carry regrets. All my life I've watched my father give. He's richer than anyone I know and not lonely."

"That sounds like him. Generational secrets passed down to you?" Tia looked up at him. "He's right you know. Mack is rich because he gives."

"He's rich because he loves," Fence said. "Money never lasts long. It can't buy health. It can't buy acceptance."

"It bought slaves," she answered.

"Slaves still own their hearts. No amount of money could make them love their master." He smiled at her. "I think my father would give you anything."

A calm filled the car. "Why do people think that money can buy love?" Tia asked.

"Well, the need for love can drive a man to do some pretty dumb things," he said with a smile in his eyes. "I'm sorry that I've made you feel like a possession. That was the least of my intentions. I married you for Rose, to care for her. I couldn't make you love her. You did that naturally. To be honest, I didn't know you'd be my assignment until later. I didn't know I'd fall in love with you. That wasn't in the plan."

"Oh yes, the plan. Plans without flexibility remind me of a tree that doesn't bend with the wind. It cracks off at the first storm."

"At least I'm not indecisive," he said, feeling defensive.

Tia turned over their situation in her mind, chalking up his words before speaking again. "Rose stole my heart. I could have said no. I accepted your offer, not for money or a home and certainly not for love," she said, trying to make a point. "Must be the fighter in me." She stared at him. "So, this was all planned. How did you know I would say yes?" she asked.

"I didn't." Fence parked the little car in a village where the smell of fish prevailed. He reached for her. "Are you ready to go in?"

She nodded. They entered the Pirate's Wharf famished after the day's search. "Fence, thank you. I mean for the conversation. Sometimes I feel like we've had to jump one hurdle after another. Is there any such thing as a normal life?"

"I think not. Neither of us understands the race. It's a guessing game. We don't know if we're chasing the lion or if he's chasing us," he commented, leading her by the hand into the seaside establishment.

"I won't order for you this time," she said, liking his smile.

They ate eagerly, both hungry to be loved and accepted. A numb knowing filled their insides. "I'll be right back," Fence said. He left her alone momentarily in search of a restroom.

The minute Tia Carpenter had entered the Pirate's Wharf, Gust Skully's eyes had pointed toward her. The habit of eyeing women took over as it often did. *Nice, very nice,* he thought, lusting after the attractive woman's body.

The woman sat at a side angle. The tall tree of a man beside her blocked a total view. However, Skully saw enough. His illicit appetite intensified. "Maybe I should have gotten those glasses," he grumbled to himself. His eyes seemed to be going bad. The fact ate at him. Twenty-twenty vision was required to fly aircraft. Since he was ousted from his duties in the United States, his flying was put on hold. *Awe! Those were the days.*

Teaching at flight schools had served him well. It was Major Merdone who pulled the strings for Skully to train pilots. As a civilian instructor Skully put forward his best side. He managed to maneuver test results, even give expert flight advice. Whether or not the men were his Cessna beginners or had moved on to jets, it did not matter. No one questioned the severity of his check rides. He lived up to his reputation of being tough, often putting undue pressure on trainees. Some students flunked out, never making Red Carpet Day, never graduating from basic beginners. Those instances happened naturally. He was not responsible for them, but there were others—recipients of his displeasure. The system worked. Skully twisted it in his favor.

Skully's lust for women and diversion into pornographic materials blindsided him. He began threatening, blackmailing women. Some succumbed to his seductive wishes, worried that a husband or boyfriend would wash out of the program, never to become a pilot, never to have wings pinned on a uniform. Skully wallowed in the power he had over their lives. *The fearful creatures are putty in my hands,* he had said. *But Bain, she's a different story.*

Bain had reported him to the base commander for blackmail. She had bypassed Major Merdone, going straight to the top.

Skully smoldered, perverting the facts. It had been three years. *I took the hit! Who does she think she is? Where does she get the nerve, bucking me?* He rattled through the past and the present, stewing. A woman had been responsible for his dismissal. That was beyond acceptance.

The ocean water lapped quietly. The shady man shifted to get his scheming into perspective. Suddenly he realized who Tia was. *Oh, for the luck of heaven! I think it is Bain. She walked right in the door. Her hair is different. Yes, but the face. I would know that face anywhere.* Skully raised his corpulent body, not able to help himself. After all, she was sitting alone. He brushed by her table.

"Excuse me," he feigned. "Don't I know you?"

Something about him looked familiar. She would not let the beastly man have the satisfaction of knowing. "I don't think so," she said quickly, not liking the smell of him. *Fence, where are you?* A silent call for help was evident in her eyes.

"Maybe you would like to come with me. I think so," the crude man said, having no intention of giving himself away. He gloated in confidence. The desire to plunder her was overwhelming. Too bad he was alone. He had no one to set her up but himself. He reached down to tug her up, pinching her arm in his trapping clutch. Tia grimaced and tried to pull away. The touch triggered ugly memories of Chance and his abuse.

"Take your hands off me! I don't know you nor do I want to. Here comes my husband."

Fence squeezed through the crowd at the door, making his way toward her. Someone was making a hit on her and he did not like it. "Vanessa!" he called out ahead. She looked scared.

The big-faced man dropped the grip. "Sorry, thought you were someone else."

Tia sprung into Fence's arms. "You okay girl?" he asked. She nodded into his chest. When he looked up, the man was gone. Fence ushered her through the crowded bar area, squeezing between happy hour lovers and trays of oysters on the half shell. Haste pursued them. Together they slipped into the night, leaving the pirate behind. She was still breathing hard. "Tia, you're with me now. I'm in this with you. Please don't close me out."

"I'm not," she whispered. "I need to think." Her arm was turning black and blue. She disliked the bulky man, not like Chance Cummings or even Ruger Bellows. In fact, she detested him, but why? She walked haphazardly.

Without notice, Fence's arm flew in front of her. "Wait! There's a man by the car we rented."

As he spoke, a limousine zoomed into the space immediately outside the wharf, dropping off a rich tourist. The unloading transpired rapidly. Fence nudged Tia toward the limo driver, offering the man a hundred-dollar bill to take them to the bay.

"Why not? I have until morning to kill time anyway," the driver grinned.

Fence hastily shoved Tia's head down, pushing her inside. She snapped at him. "Do you mind not being so rough?"

The driver adjusted the rearview mirror. Fence reached over Tia and buckled her seatbelt. They were still in earshot when the rental car exploded behind them. Tia looked back and gulped.

"Sorry," Fence said. "I didn't want to alarm you." He kissed the side of her head.

The Dark Silhouette

GLOOM hung over the Eternal Peace Cemetery. A foreboding smell filled the air. The dark, sultry night mixed with eagerness to bring closure to uncertainty. Tia shifted her feet back and forth as she stood in place. It was half past midnight. She breathed to Fence, "I don't like it."

"He'll be here." Fence pressed against her back. His eyes searched the blackness. An hour and fifteen minutes escaped into ominous unknowing. Fence lifted his chin to the side. "Start walking." He nudged Tia forward, his voice barely audible in the stillness.

One step and a deep voice spoke in a gentle low tone. "Tiara Kenworthy? It is you?" The elder black man stationed himself in the midst of the lean, tall trees, invisible to them.

Her face quivered. She searched the white in the man's plausible eyes. "You came! I am Tia," she answered unwaveringly.

"I've been here waiting, watching. You are one and the same, the one I rescued? You were alone on the floor. Come with me."

He held out his huge hand and she took it. Fence grabbed a hold of her other one. They followed "Barbados" through the invisible grounds. He knew where and how to go. The path, ancient and familiar to him, twisted and turned in mazelike formation amid monkey-like trees with arms and limbs coming from all directions. The dark silhouette led them. Finally, he stopped by an aged tree. A bench encircled it. Across from it rested an arced seat, the head marker of a multitude of flowers and fruit-bearing trees. The man in the dark motioned for them to sit.

Fence squeezed Tia's hand. "We've been searching," Fence addressed the inconceivable man, taking his place next to Tia. "Who are you?" he immediately asked.

The midnight man towered over them. He spoke carefully. "I am not a stranger. There is no need to know my name. It is enough that we

241

meet." The man crouched down to meet them, presence-to-presence, alongside the marbled birdbath and stoned arc, kneeling with one knee on the ground. His hands rested one on top of the other. His back stood straight up. His ivory teeth, along with the whites of his honest eyes, glowed under his snowcapped hair, making a direct line to Tia.

Tia leaned forward, returning the Jamaican's stare, desiring to know more. She did not want to miss a word. "My father? Did you know my father?"

The man answered, "I knew him from birth, a man of his own mind, even as a child. He had blond hair. He was a determined one. For over a hundred years his family employed mine. They hid us in times of trouble. We served them willingly."

"Why did you wait so long to tell me all these things?" Tia addressed the man head on.

Fence listened to the sound of her voice as her words pierced the darkness. A pride rose up in him for her. She was deep, much deeper than he had wanted to admit. As long as he had left her in shallowness, he did not have to deal with how much he loved her. But now he knew.

The man tilted his head. "You are much like your father, Miss Tiara, asking questions, seeking answers, digging in the rubble of the past. For his sake I will tell you." A moment of silence passed between them. The man continued. "My roots trace to Ethiopia. I am a Jew. Yes, you say 'but you are black.' For centuries we worshipped Jehovah God and blew the antelope ram horn. Our blood will prove it."

"Well, how? How did you come to Jamaica?" she asked.

"Slaves of another land, stolen from our homes, from our fields, transported in rat-infested boats to West Indies Islands. We know work and agriculture. We know devotion. We know how to run with the wind. Your father's family bought us. We were free with them. We had purpose. We served them honorably."

"And my mother? Tell me about my mother," Tia urged.

"Yes, Miss Tiara, your mother. It is a story long hidden. She was born in Europe in 1939 to a young Jewish woman. A British soldier rescued the child, sneaking her out of Poland, sparing the infant from the SS. You see, when Hitler invaded, babies were thrown against walls and Jewish men were hung from trees. There are rumors that the honorable soldier had loved the courageous, beautiful young mother who begged him to take her baby. The soldier left in the confusion, escaping out the north border. He raised the baby as his own, or perhaps she was his own. I do not know. He never married. A Jamaican nanny, one of my family, cared for your mother. She grew up an English citizen, but she was much more. I speak of internals not externals," he said.

"So, my mother was Jewish." She tried to sort out the confusion of history.

"Of the tribe of the Lion, Judah, from Jacob and Leah," he responded.

"Sir, my father?" she asked.

"A noble man robbed of destiny. Robbed I say." The tall man hesitated before speaking again. "Your father met your mother, Abigail, when she traveled to Jamaica with her British father on a business trip of sorts." His speech was firm. "Your father was warned not to marry your mother." The Jamaican shifted his focus momentarily to Fence. "Jews rarely marry Gentiles." He turned his head to address Tia again. "At times love supersedes wisdom. You see, love listens to no critics. Abigail was dark, beautiful, very innocent. Your father went off with her. There was great love between them. They were married at the mountain mission you visited yesterday. It was a private wedding. He knew she was Jewish."

"Why were they—?" Tia cleared her throat, wondering how the man knew where she and Fence had been. "But why? Why were my parents killed?" she blurted.

"Jewish sympathizers were looked upon poorly, just as those who loved the slaves. Like his ancestors, your father loved us. He treated us like his family. Haters despised him for his strong stand. He would not waver." The man stood up, too tall to see. His words continued. "Anti-Semitic Hamans still exist. They have tried to exterminate us through the centuries." He leaned toward Tia's face. "Miss Tiara, do you hear me? Your mother was a brave woman."

"Why is there no record of my birth?" Anger wanted to rise up in Tia. "Is this story true?"

The Jamaican's head now touched the branch above him. Fence and Tia rose in unison, feeling dwarfed by the historic man.

"Miss Tiara, you must be guarded at all times. Your parents no longer live. The basket cradles your history. On your twenty-fourth birthday much will be revealed."

"I don't even know when my birthday is, or how much I weighed or why I have to live this lie. My hands are empty," she said.

The man shook his head. "Riches can't be poured into full hands. Empty hands, ready to receive, hold great opportunity. You will know answers soon enough, possibly before the week is out. There is always hope." His white teeth peeked through. "Your parents live on through you Miss Tiara, through your children."

"Sir, my parents live in heaven. I saw them swimming in a clear river with a king. They were happy. I do not let go of hope," she admitted.

The Jamaican felt the kinship. "I am Simone, your servant." He bowed his head in honor. "You speak of the River. It is of the Messiah. When He comes I will know. It is enough that you live."

"Sir, this means so much to me. Please, are my grandparents still alive?" She reached out to touch him but he was further than her arm's length.

"Recently departed. The estate is tied up in legalities, precipitating the search for heirs. If none are determined by year's end, the inheritance will be unclaimed," he answered.

Tia sought his face. "There is no one to prove who I am, except you. And, it seems, no one knows you exist."

"The time will come. Now follow me. I will lead you out." For a moment Fence glanced behind them. When he looked ahead, Barbados—now Simone—had vanished.

Armed

FENCE ordered, "Stand still. Let me get this adjusted. Women don't usually wear shoulder harnesses. But you, you're different." He hooked the belt. "Now. Put on this loose shirt and tie it at the bottom. There. It doesn't show." Fence looked her over, feeling apprehensive. "The gun is loaded. Please be careful," Fence instructed.

"I plan to be." Tia gave him one of her determined looks.

"Give me your word I can trust you," Fence said, thinking of the deer hunt. The truth had not made anything simpler, just truer. *What if she takes off again?* Fence cocked his head to the side.

Tia's hand extended to him with a tender shake. "My word." Her grin showed pleasant satisfaction. "Your mother gave me the idea."

"Not my father?" Fence replied.

Tia took a deep breath. "There's more than one way to be armed, more than one way to fight a battle." Tia lifted her head to him. "For years I've longed to know my own mother. Now I know that I will never know her except through Simone."

Holding back his concern, Fence gave her a nod of approval.

Popping up near Tia, Amos said in a tenor voice, "Amos go too. Amos armed."

"You're a brave bird," Tia complimented. She set her hand out for a bird perch. "Amos, I think you know a lot more than you let on. You can be my partner. Fence told me you're on our side."

Fence's eyes enlarged in reluctant consent. "I said he's neurotic. He can't provide a fig of defense. All I need is a bird blowing our cover. He's liable to shoot off his mouth at the wrong time." Fence flattened Mr. Tuffty's map, pretending to be wrapped up in it.

Tia directed her conversation toward the bird. "Amos, help me get to the bottom of this mysterious basket." She stretched it wide open. Only a little baby would fit inside. Her fingertips caressed the linen fabric lining the interior.

"This is very unusual cloth," Tia said, examining the intricate quilt-like stitches. Curiosity peaked inside her. *The basket cradles my history. What did Simone mean?* She ran her fingers down wired lines. "Strange. This lining appears to have been placed inside in an odd manner."

"Looks like a woman's corset," Fence interjected with a side-glance. Amos poked his bill under her hand.

"Amos! This is not a nut!" Tia exclaimed. The bird bit off the end of a stay, cutting a quarter inch opening at the top.

"Hey, let me see that." Fence moved in without invitation.

Tia struggled to stay in control. Her hands pulled the lining away from the basket's wall. Awkwardly she pushed up the stiff stay. Fence wrapped his hand around hers to offer assistance. The action hindered more than it helped. "Thank you, I can manage," she admonished.

"Must be late nineteenth century or older. The stays are wood, not wire," Fence inserted. "European woodworkers use strands of limber wood like we use for bows, probably softened in water, rounded and dried into position." Fence moved around her in slow motion. "What woman would want that around her?"

"What man would use a girdle inside a basket?" she rebutted.

"Love me, love me," Amos sang.

"Shut up. Eat this." Fence grabbed a Brazil nut and underhanded it to him. "Give that bird one key and he doesn't shut up." Fence disliked the bird's continual interruptions.

"One key, one key." Amos pushed the nut to the floor and tugged at another stay. Biting into the end, he jarred the basket to the floor, tipping it sideways.

Tia's face turned red. A row of cut diamonds poured out of the stiff straw. Tia dropped to her knees. "No wonder the basket was so heavy." She swallowed, picking up the polished, multi-faceted gems, one by one.

Fence whistled. "Looks like we're carrying a diamond mine." He towered over her as he reached for his knife.

Tia's mouth dropped. "No! There has to be an easier way." She ordered, "I don't want you to cut up my history. This was my mother's. Maybe she was rescued in this basket, just like I was."

"All right. How do you propose to find out?" Fence quizzed.

Tia eyed the bird. "Amos would probably bite them all off if we let him."

"It's your basket. I'm just here for protection. Seems like you don't need me for much." He turned away. Tia's fussing over the bird annoyed him.

"What is a diamond next to life?" Tia whispered. Her fingers ran the length of the seam. The tedious job of working the discolored girdle free took Tia longer than Fence had patience for. Finally, he heard her take a deep breath. A lambskin lined the basket beneath. Hebrew letters raised their heads to touch her.

SHALOM ALEIKHEM

Tia pointed to the miniature writing and translated. "It means 'peace be upon you.'"

Fence kept his tongue inside. *Peace to me? She'd probably get the bird to bite me if she could.* Fence and Tia had already bitten each other with too many cutting remarks. He felt a bit injured, left out of her world.

Absorbed in the material, Tia spoke without thinking, "We have something to go on now."

"We?" Fence asked.

Tears welled in the corners of her eyes. She did not need a war with Fence on top of the emptiness of knowing little about herself. "I feel really weak." She pressed the lambskin to her breast. "God help me. I have no strength in me."

Fence folded the map, eyeing the family tree embedded on the document. "You're a lot stronger than you think. You're more real than anyone I know. Life is not a performance, not a game for you. You make humility and honesty your companions, your friends." Fence wondered if he would ever reach that status. "You're strong because you know how weak you really are."

Tia's mind flipped to the discussion on the beach. "Secrets hold too much power."

He ran his thumb up the middle of her forehead, letting his fingertips run through the hair on the top of her head. "We have come a long way since I made the marriage proposal."

Tia approached the doorway. "I'm ready. Let's get our picture taken."

"Not so fast. There's one more item." He pulled the red strands out of his tropical shirt pocket. "I found this on your shirtsleeve last night.

Do you have any idea where it came from?"

Tia studied the wad of hair in the clear plastic bag. "No, not unless … unless?"

"Unless what? Finish your sentence," Fence probed.

"Not unless it came off the man that grabbed my arm at the Pirate's Wharf. His hair was salt and pepper though. It could have come off anyone who rubbed against me." The odd sample reeked. Tia spoke her thoughts. "She's a smoker!"

"A woman? How do you know that?" he asked.

"Men don't dye their hair that color." Squatting to the ground, Tia brushed the sand off her sandals. "She's a technician of some kind, maybe works in a medical or chemical lab and uses some sort of drugs." Tia stood abruptly, calculating a plan. "Why can't we beat them at their own game? Set up our own trap?" Tia's courage mounted. "Let's make him the victim."

"I thought you said we're looking for a woman. Anyone ever tell you to be an investigator? You're reminding me of Abe again, my old partner."

"I'm your new partner, remember? And I intend to find out who murdered my parents."

She talked his language now, propelling herself forward. He liked it. "I'm with you. But, there will be no hunting pirates, red haired women, or mountain lions without me." Fence let himself smile. "Maybe we'll make a team yet."

Tia jumped up, quickly kissing him on the cheek. "Thanks." Fence let his stomach readjust. The impetuous move caught him off guard.

Instinctively, Fence snatched her off the floor and cradled her. She squirmed. He nuzzled his chin into her hair, inhaling the purity of innocence, expressing his kindness. "I know your parents loved you. I'm sorry that I've been so hard on you. You're worth a whole lot more than a bag of diamonds." His admission calmed her.

He backed to the bed and sat with her on his lap. There was no laughter, no mention of the intimacy two nights before. It was too close for her to consider. Pretence suddenly lost its place of prominence. Her body relaxed.

Sensing soberness in the room, Amos waited on the doorknob.

"Maybe Amos should be our partner," Tia said softly.

Fence eyed the bird. "A silent partner." He stood Tia on her feet. He had learned one thing in the past year; when Tia set her mind to accomplish a task, she followed through. He would not hinder her. Something told him they were done butting heads for a while. He had to trust her. "It's time to write a new page," he said, holding the door open. "Only twenty-four days until Christmas. Guess I know what you want."

She stopped in the doorway to ask, "Why do I get so angry at you?"

Fence bent over. "Because you hate me, or, maybe..." He hesitated. "Maybe you love me?"

Help!

THE phone rang with persistence. Reed Carpenter dropped his razor on the table. "Can't even let a fellow get up," he said.

Fence spoke hastily to his grandfather. "Gramp, you're right. Trouble breeds trouble. I hope we haven't bitten off more than we can chew—drugs, poison, a car explosion, murder."

Reed rubbed the gray stubble of a beard. "Yup, birds of a feather flock together. That's one thing you can count on. Sometimes it's hard to tell who the culprit is, but they leave a mess of evidence behind someplace, some little tail feather." He took a breath. "Twists, turns, bumps, that's the way of life. Makes it interesting. You always said you liked adventure. Gets pretty dull if the road gets too straight."

"Well, the bumps have been keeping me awake. I could use a little smoothness for a while."

"Yup, well, not yet. Fall asleep at the wheel and you'll miss seeing the varmint. Stay on your toes. One always gets the sleepiest before daybreak. Remember Abe's request to help a lineage live on."

Fence turned his head to make certain Tia was safe in the car before speaking again. "I'll say this for you Gramp, you always could detect the false. Guess you can see better than I can, but I'm learning."

"Sometimes it takes the unusual to accomplish the impossible, the most unlikely. How are you two getting along?" The coy tone gave Reed away.

"This has been no honeymoon if that's what you're asking. She's not who I thought she was, that's for sure." The admission held some regrets. "We've uncovered a couple of clues, some red hair. Need you in Florida to do some detective work. Doc can help you."

Fence waited for his grandfather to clear his throat. "Count on us." Reed Carpenter whistled, anxious to get his feet wet in the precarious situation. "It feels good to get my teeth into the nitty gritty. Oh, by the way, tell that little wife of yours that she's a genuine Carpenter." He squeezed in the comment before setting the receiver down.

Reed looked in the mirror at his half-finished whiskers, speaking to himself. "Guess I'm still good for something." He laughed heartily, resuming the draw of the razor blade.

Fence hung up the pay phone and turned to Tia. "I'm supposed to tell you that you're a Carpenter. Don't ask me what he means, but I think it's a compliment." His unexpected, broad smile infected her. She nodded in agreement.

Meanwhile, Reed placed a call to Dr. Clem Bridger. "Time for a game of Chinese checkers. I'm coming in. It's a little tough to squeeze in between all the Florida football fans, but I managed to get a flight out in the morning. I even got fifty-yard-line tickets, twelfth row, down close. How's that for finagling?" Reed waited for Clem to write down the flight number.

Doc coached. "Get here in plenty of time, before the kickoff. We have a lot to go over. I don't want to miss anything."

"You won't. It's time for us to get in the huddle. See you then," Reed concluded.

The Sketch

THE old man sketched skillfully. The large frame absorbed the small frame of the artist, making the passers-by stop to see life inside the picture. His arthritic left hand, locked in the painting position, rarely opened, incapable of stretching out flat. Breaking out of the crimp to cleanse the creases took more effort than the artist was willing to give. Age lines on his hands, filled with artist's chalk, leads and colors of reds and blacks, appeared almost white from intentness. He lifted the palate with his assisting right hand to form the tender line aside the eye of the side profile. The subject matter sat motionless like a cadaver. The portrait, more filled with life, gave a frightful response to onlookers.

Fence stood outside the Little Artist Shop observing the strokes of the owner nested under a canvas awning. Strangely, he admired the artist who seemed to capture more history on canvas than in most books. *A deep man with a big picture.* Fence's concentration strayed to the sunset paintings leaning on each other, directly inside the shop. The pictures appeared out of line with the late morning.

"I will return later," Fence spoke to the air. He wished to avoid the caresses of the man's granddaughter. It was too late.

"You're alone?" she questioned, with fretful desire for the tall, handsome man. "This way." She hooked his bent arm, pulling him into the small shop. "I must reach out and grab life or it will slip away," she said.

Her long, heavy mane was banded at the base of the neck and hung to her hips, reminding Fence of South Pacific women. The natural, rusty red tint glamorized the ebony underneath. Her almond-shaped eyes, surreal in formation, showed a severity. It was directly opposite of her skin, which was much softer and lighter than her weathered grandfather.

She brushed her face against his shoulder sending a chill through his bones. Fence pulled to the side, bumping into customers. "Is this an original? I'm certain we've seen this picture before." the wealthy man and woman questioned. Innocently, the two broke the granddaughter's seduction with a magnifying glass.

Fence retreated to the outdoors, leaving the brush stroke examination to the experts and the seller. He stopped in the shallow doorframe, mummified by the old man with the patient hands. The subject was gone. "My son," he spoke to Fence in clear English. "Be seated. I will sketch you now."

Wary of intruding ears, Fence stayed standing, wondering what to do with his hands. He slipped them into his pant's pockets, jingling the coins at the bottom seam. "Will you sketch by the ocean, away from the shop? The vacant pier, the one with the broken braces and barnacles?" Fence suggested cautiously. "I pay well."

"Certainly," the meticulous man answered, cleaning his hands. "And when shall this be?"

"Sunset," Fence said calmly. Noting the artist's crimped posture, he added, "Master, I will bring the studio chair for you."

"No my lad. My heart is at the sea. I live and die by it. The weathered pier of which you speak has withstood many storms." The artist wiped his palms, leaving color in the lifeline. "It is all that remains of my arrival as a servant boy from the Ivory Coast." The old man stretched his neck upward. "Are you alone?"

Fence let his hand rest on the old man's shoulder. A wealth of knowledge hid in the mines of the artist's past, in the lifetime canvas of his heart. "Not quite. There is the African Gray," Fence replied, staring into the pronounced crevices of the artistic ear. Leaning toward him, he breathed a whisper. "And, there is my wife."

"I see. You're the one that bought the painting then, the one of Amos," the artist said. He examined Fence's eyes with a blink. "Until then, son."

Inside the Cover

TIA shifted nervously at the appointed meeting place, the front of the library. She ran her fingers through her hair. The thickness dropped to her forehead in heavy waves. An afterglow of Fence's caress on her forehead warmed her. He had treated her like she belonged. He was right, about some things—as much as she did not want to admit it.

A deep breath of ocean air calmed her while she contemplated her next step. Other thoughts raced through her brain. *Some Jamaicans will steal you blind,* Lawyer Tuffty had said before they left Florida. *Call it the survival instinct of the impoverished.*

Sister Maria Thomas had rebutted, *A person's worth lies inside the cover, not on the jacket.*

Those with nothing grow desperate, Mr. Tuffty returned. *A cover gives clues to the interior.*

Maybe it was the way Mr. Tuffty had looked at Sister Maria Thomas that triggered Tia to suspect. Now, as Tia stood alone at the library portico, comprehension registered. Mr. Tuffty loved Sister Maria. His body language leaked the truth. He loved a woman he could never have, one who had given her heart to a higher calling, one who became intimate with God, one who took the vow of poverty. As a result, Mr. Tuffty had married his occupation. The law became his wife. The honorable Mr. Tuffty absorbed his loneliness in court cases and discussions with old lawyers. His wealth never won a heart. Suddenly, the message of two that once had strong feelings for each other took on deeper meaning. Tia softly cleared her throat.

If I had stayed on to teach the orphans, if I had never left, I never would have known what it is to be a mother, to carry a child. I never would have met Fence Carpenter, or found Rose. I never would have known the depth of motherhood or the arms of love.

Tia tried to hide the thoughts. Instinctively she spoke, "Since when did I become an expert on love that I can read what's inside a man's heart?" She looked off into space. "Where is he?" Her insides imploded. A wrong move might result in an explosion of the plan. Fence was late.

Tia pushed her mind back on track, summoning courage to match the unknown. Killing time, she faced the outside wall. Cautiously she adjusted the holster tucked above her waist. She did not want to use the gun. Anxiety wanted to strangle patience, but she chose to stop it. Carefully, she forsook the library pillar, entering the building that held an arsenal of information.

Across the street, the balding red-haired woman wallowed in shallow thinking, scratching the eczema between her fingers and in the side bends of her arms. AryAnn held no trust in the man whose powers gripped her throat. Her life had taken a nosedive since her first encounter with the wretched, conniving thief. She no longer lived for herself. Skully had a ring in her nose controlling her very breath, her very actions, her next step. Her pulse had beat for years to satisfy the repulsive man. However, after the revolting meeting at the wharf, AryAnn burned. She would follow through, but she would choose her own way.

Sadistic ideas had begun long before Gust Skully hooked her, but he stripped off the remainder of dignity. She never called him by his name, which she knew was phony, nor would she risk sudden death by doing so. However, the bottom recesses of her soul still possessed rebellion. "Man cannot have everything." Her female independence had a brisk way of locking horns with dependence on males. It brought the fight out in her. *Not all my brain cells are hypnotized by Skully's hedonistic plans,* AryAnn snarled.

Freedom to do as she wished doubly cursed her into false pride. She touched the bald spot, regretting that she was forced to wear a blond wig in the hot climate. Already sweat droplets beaded her forehead, not from the temperature. She rehearsed the proposed crime, detailing the order, the time, the expulsion. Skully was right about that. Premeditation keeps one in charge. It plans for errors, for discrepancies, for a multitude of circumstances. *Preparation is the key to follow through.* AryAnn distorted truth in order to let hatred rule.

She ran her itching finger across the blade, checking its sharpness. The stone had done its job. Sticking a knife in the belly of the Jewish girl was not as discreet as lacing her food with cyanide to let her die a slow death, but it was faster. The itch was getting to her. Beneath her fingernails, dry skin and blood caked—her own of course. The stench of dead blood had become so much a part of her that she could not smell it.

AryAnn connived, running the scheme through the simulator of her mind, pushing out the possibility of backlash. Just get the job done. Money was not the issue. Power was. Of course, power always occupies the upper room in mind control. She ignored the negative idea of failure and now eagerness fueled her passion to kill, not because Skully compelled her to, but because it was in her blood too.

AryAnn concealed the weapon. Her emaciated body, orange from smoke, hoisted the rust colored tote over her wiry shoulder. "Bain, your day has come." AryAnn held back a snicker of anticipated accomplishment. *All the victim has to do is step my way.*

Fence appeared magically, startling Tia from behind an aisle of science books, not at all where they had planned. He passed her the note. "All is set. Bait is taken."

"You didn't show at the right place," Tia whispered.

"But I'm here now." He moved closer.

"Someone's been watching me."

"I know. Stay by the table. I'll be right back." Fence retreated into the shelves, looking for the records he had placed there previously. The task took him longer than he had intended. He brushed the dust off his fingers and turned the corner. A hair's breath away stood the artist's granddaughter. Her approach was direct.

"You rushed off," she confronted.

"And, you followed," Fence stated.

"Sir?" she said. "My name is Rae, Del Rae Zane." She bowed her head with a submissive demeanor. Holding her cupped right hand out to him, she turned it face down and lifted it toward Fence's lips. Fence did not kiss it.

"You do not trust me?" she said. Her eyebrows rose in question.

"Trust? That remains to be seen," Fence answered.

Del Rae opened her left hand. "Take. You will need," the granddaughter emphasized.

Fence hesitated. His eyes traveled to the object in the center of her palm. He had no intention of touching her. He waited.

"It is not from me," she explained, still in her glamour mode. "Open your hand." She dropped the warmed metal in—an odd shaped key. "Use to unlock an artistic door."

Fence scanned the aisle. Del Rae picked up on the distraction. "You look for her, the woman who came to the shop with you? I have much more to offer." The beautiful woman's white cotton dress looked even whiter than before.

"I can believe that," he said, skirting by her.

The five-minute encounter frustrated Fence. He stuck the key in his pocket. *Didn't the bird mention a key?* A new avenue of thought opened as he moved through the books. Tia had vanished. *How can one woman give me so many problems?*

The librarian had her nose in a world atlas, oblivious to the internal activity in the bowels of the building. Other students sat like statues. *Tia, where did you go?*

Close Quarters

TIA turned abruptly, catching her shirt on the corner of the library table. Fence lingered away from her longer than expected. Instinctively, she pulled into the shadows of marble, exiting down the back steps to the main lobby.

She slipped her small frame through ten inches, shoving the weight of the ladies' room door open with minimal noise. The unreachable window, inched open near the top of the ten-foot ceiling, let in dull light—itself longing for more. The heavy, overcast smell made Tia wish to be anywhere else. She stood in the corner of the dark room waiting, holding her breath. *Fence, don't leave the building. I'm still here.* She scolded herself. *Why didn't I tell him about the detour?*

Expect the unexpected, Fence had cautioned. Perhaps that would be enough to carry them both, although she doubted it. Hopefully, the loud thumps of her heart would not give her away. Looking up, she studied the hand-painted, mint green ivy trail that wound around the women's restroom, forming a wagon train of leaves on the bumpy ivory brown.

The drumming on her chest quickened. Two kinds of fear wrestled within, the destructive punched the healthy, much like the fight between Fence and Chance. *Too much time to think about death.* Tia steadied her hand. *I'm not ready to die, God. I have too much to live for, for Rose, for Fence. Yes, for him, but it's more than that. My destiny, I know there's more.* She felt sick.

Tia searched the stream of light. *When you walk through the valley of the shadow of death, do not fear evil.* Sister Maria Thomas had drilled the psalm into all the children, the faith-for-fear approach.

The massive, antique door opened sluggishly. A catlike woman pushed with her shoulder, avoiding the touch of anything. The mother-of-pearl knife handle stuck out of a leather tote pocket, such beauty for such grave intentions. The ancient abalone engraving material, taken from oysters of the Persian Gulf beds centuries before, carried with it the prestige of a prince. The weapon had been passed down through a fraternal order to her father. AryAnn had stolen it and saved it for such a time as this.

The watch ticked a stringent, grating vigil. AryAnn had just enough time to get set up. The side room would serve the purpose. She had tracked T.R. Bain, alias V. Johnson, with Skully's tips. Her entrance echoed with megaphone intensity. Inconceivable thoughts and purposes would pass over most heads, but not hers. A woman-to-woman meeting hung in the wings. AryAnn was anxious.

Instantly, the back of a small arm rammed AryAnn against the wall, the other jammed under her esophagus. "Your mission's ended whoever you are," Tia blurted out.

AryAnn had not counted on Tia's arm strength or agility, or her presence. No time existed to scrutinize or search out a plan. The close quarters of the women's room hindered freedom of movement.

"Why do you want to kill me, or is it the demon in you?" Tia probed, pushing away the woman.

"You cheated us out of what is rightfully ours. Now you will die for it." AryAnn's vile breath exhaled into the air. In a land of no law, she might get away with murder. Even in Jamaica, the possibility existed. She thrived on the idea. In most fights, anything goes. Instantly AryAnn maneuvered under and around, grabbing the sharp weapon out of her backpack. The knife slit down the side of Tia's clothing, slashing into hidden holster leather. The vicious instrument dulled into slow motion.

"You'll never kill what I have," Tia said, regretting losing the upper hand. Her stomach jumped. She must maintain her wits. Her mind must stay on top of the situation—smarter, more precise. Tia spoke fearlessly. "I was born to live. I've been spared from death many times."

"You do not remember me? If that military doctor hadn't gotten in the way, you'd be dead." The woman reeled forward.

A flurry of twists and turns with tangled arms teeter-tottered them against the sinks and stall doors. AryAnn's wig, snatched off by the lower stucco wall, exposed her balding red head, immediately casting shame on the woman. The effect rendered her powerless until anger charged out. She grasped for her knife in a stooped position.

As if out of nowhere, Tia swung her body, circling away from the crazy woman. Her tight fist thrust forward, moving in a straight line toward the possessed opponent. The knife burst forth, airborne into aimlessness. The sharp sound of metal struck the floor.

Tia's tenacity, like a new rubber band, snapped with adrenaline. The conditioning Mack had given her made her bones strong, her body thick. Tia moved her center of balance forward with her foot, taking a gigantic breath. "HAA!" The loud yell blew out of her. Simultaneously, all 110 pounds of her body weight went into action. Tia drove her heel forward, instantly connecting with the small of the killer's back. The blast, out of nowhere, shattered the wretched woman's kidney.

AryAnn did a double take, shocked by the weaponless defense the little Jew exhibited. Excruciating pain devastated her power. She called forth a futile curse. The last thing she had expected was a karate kick. No one had warned her. *Whatever possessed the runt?* Unwilling to accept defeat, AryAnn ran headlong toward her victim, but Tia had made an arm shield of her own, lifting her knee to crunch into the woman's stomach. The blow jammed upward into the flattened chest cavity. The rigid, cruel floor left no room for mercy.

Gasping, the redheaded woman struggled to get air. Her collapsed lungs sunk into her back. She fell face forward. The toll of tobacco facilitated her defeat. She could not move.

Holding the door open with his foot, Fence stood letting light in. Tia, perched over the woman, carefully rolled AryAnn onto her back. "What happened?" he said louder than he intended. Slippery tile under foot caught him by surprise. He caught the door to keep his balance. "I heard a yell."

"We need a doctor." Tia caught her breath. She twisted to the side and threw up.

"For you or her?" Fence said in a sarcastic tone, getting his bearings.

Tia nodded toward the woman, indicating what Fence already knew. He felt for the woman's wrist, laying his head on the woman's heart. The strongest muscle in her body, her heart, had quit beating. "She's dead. What did you do to her? Only a shell of humanness left."

"I just ..." She threw up again. Fence pulled out a brown paper towel. Tia cleaned the floor, trying not to gag. Fence, ready to pick up the knife, had put on a glove. Tia's arm slammed in front of him. "How are we going to destroy a knife filled with hatred?" she asked.

Fence snatched it up. "I could drop it into the tank of the old toilet. Maybe if it gets washed enough, it will come out clean," he said in half-humor.

"Don't be smart!" Tia lifted herself to a stand.

Fence faced her head on. "I asked you not to do things alone. What happened in here?" Realizing someone might have heard the noise, he murmured, "Come on. We'll talk later." He grasped her. "Let's get out of here. Do you hear me?"

Together, they passed by the librarian, who slept slouched over a pile of cards. She had had a hard day and was unaware that it was about to get harder.

Do Curses Lie Here?

FENCE hid the new rental, an open-air jeep, in the overbearing vines. Passing through the crowd of mind-boggled tourists had gone without interference. He desired to quiz Tia, but thought better of it. *If she knows martial arts, why hadn't she protected herself from rape? What was wearing the gun all about if she had something else in mind?*

"What are you doing?" Tia asked, not volunteering any information.

"Following a hunch," he said, noticing she looked a little pale. "Are you sick?"

"I just need a break. The sight of death disturbs me. I didn't think she would die."

"What did you think?" he asked. "You hit her with some kind of blow."

Tia did not want to tell Fence that his father taught her offensive-defensive moves. She said, "Following instincts, I guess."

"Some instincts!" Fence's pace hastened. He stopped to trace another trail on Mr. Tuffty's map. "Go in front of me," he instructed, sounding domineering. Irritation had built up around him, mainly because he disliked knowing partial truths.

The further they hiked, the more overcome with jungle they became. Tia stopped suddenly. Fence scarcely avoided a collision with her. "What is it?" He pressed his head over hers.

Deep blue and pearl-white tiles looked lost in a sea of palm leaves. Off to the side, wild mushrooms poked out fuzzy heads. Tia shivered. The altar, quite common in Jamaica, brought uneasiness.

Fence picked up the pale green weed growing next to a broken tile. "It resembles marijuana. Natives smoke it in the islands. Smell."

Tia took a whiff then backed away, her head swimming. "I feel intoxicated without even touching the weed."

"They use them in magic rituals." Fence visualized the voodoo doll as Doc popped off the head. Instinctively, he threw the weed to the ground.

"Along with a few other drugs," Tia added. She tilted toward Fence, hesitating, holding back her instant thought. *Why had Mr. Tuffty given Fence the map? Too many coincidences to add up.*

"What is it?"

"Nothing," Tia denied. "Just an idea."

Fence gave her a weird look. "Right! I can't figure that. You're not a very good liar."

Her flesh crawled. "The insects are annoying me. Jamaican mosquitoes fester the whole island." She slapped at one.

"You're hiding something." He dug deeper.

"This place is eerie, like it comes out of the underworld," she admitted, feeling like she had to throw up again. Kneeling to the ground, she picked up a handful of dirt, holding it out to Fence. "Do you think there are curses here?"

Fence looked into her hand. Tia was much different than Del Rae Zane, the artist's granddaughter. Perhaps Tia held a different kind of key, but he would not give her the satisfaction of telling her that. "Well, there's one thing I'm not, and that's superstitious. Yes, there are curses. Doesn't denial of a curse break its power?" His eyes seemed to touch hers. "Didn't we have a blessing by the priest, Father Juniper or whatever his name is?" Fence reminded her. "This is more than superstition, more than some spirit worship."

She whirled and started to walk away. Maybe he was right. Immediately she stumbled. A lopsided tile caught her toes, tipping her forward. Fence's arm flew around her. "Wait a minute. Be careful. You're racing. Please, listen to me." The orders came out naturally.

Tia spoke quietly. "This place is odd. Are you certain this is the right way to reach the mission church?" She cast her eyes to the ground. "Look. Even this tile is strange."

Fence hunkered to the ground to have a closer look. "Appears to be wedged under an old vine. Probably been here for centuries." His face turned upward for a brief moment. "Sorry, but I need to use that redheaded woman's knife." He swiftly pulled it out of its sheath. The tool became a shovel. Digging around the border, Fence maneuvered the tile out of the resting-place. He flipped the block on its back in the process.

By this time, Tia was crouched beside him. Using a palm leaf, she whisked the millipedes and grubs off, leaning carefully over the top of his arms. What they saw next was totally out of place. A gold crown was embedded in the center of the block. "Looks like the crown on your handkerchief." Fence dug around the coin and flipped it out. He wiped it clean with a handkerchief he usually kept folded squarely under his billfold. The luster returned, revealing a sixteenth century date.

"Look," Tia said. There are six triangle points on the tile." Sudden silence dropped on them. Even the birds were in a hush. "Where are we going now?" she whispered.

Fence jolted up and gave her a rude look, moving away from her. "Someplace where evil isn't in charge." He pushed her ahead of him. He did not intentionally want to sound antagonistic, but knew that he did. His insistence had turned to control. When a man rejects his feelings, some type of emotion wins out. His was anger and maybe a bit of bitterness, the inner irritation at himself for risking Tia's life.

The abrupt shunning shook Tia's perspective. What had broken their connection? "What are you afraid of?" she asked. "I thought that the Covenant, the Blood, the blessing nullifies the curse." Tia questioned, "I don't know where you stand."

The anger lines on Fence's forehead moved. "I want you to be quiet. Don't question me."

The Clink of the Coin

FINALLY Tia and Fence reached the aged church and entered through the back door. The walk had been long and hot. Tia's head swam. "I need to sit down."

"All you need is a little prayer. Good for the soul, you know," Fence said with a sarcastic tone.

Father Juniper lay prostrate before the crucifix stationed above a simple altar. Peace filled the sanctuary. "Looks like we've come at a bad time," Tia whispered, not wanting to interrupt the man absorbed in worship.

"You disturb us not," the base voice of the tall Jamaican uttered from behind. It was Simone. "We waited for you," he said. He had overheard the needling barbs between them. "It is unwise to abuse with anger in a house of kindness." The Jamaican backed away from them.

Conviction slapped Fence in the face. His mouth lowered to Tia's ear. "I think he's talking about me," he spoke softly. "Guess I should apologize," Fence said, stepping ahead.

Tia's head hung down, making it difficult to make eye contact.

Fence spoke to the top of her head. "Can you find it in your heart to forgive me? I mean for everything, from the beginning?"

Tia started to speak, edging closer to Fence's warmth. Her circling head leaned into his chest to brace herself. "I ... I ... I think I'm going to faint."

Without hesitation, Fence caught her dropping body. The flat, wooden bench was barely long enough for her. He looked for mercy from Simone, but the tall man had stationed himself behind the statue of St. Francis of Assisi, like a sentry. *He's a strange man,* Fence thought.

The priest, now awake, had heard the apology. The arm of his brown gown hung over Tia. "For her head," Father Juniper said, placing a small, blue velvet pillow into Fence's hand. "She is with child?" he asked automatically.

"I don't think so," Fence answered, startled with the possibility. "I, well, we ah... Too much heat."

"Yes," the priest said. "You have new vows. All is well." He bowed his head in a belated greeting. Fence swallowed, tucking the pillow under Tia's head.

Hearing the conversation echo into the foyer, Simone approached. The memory of the baby he had carried to safety twenty-four years before moved into the present. An ancient ache in his heart consumed him. He looked up. Age had crept up on him.

Father Juniper perceived the distress, the labored look, on the black man's face. He wiped his brow. Compassion was almost too much to bear. He too, remembered a child in his arms, quickly baptized, quickly sealed, escorted away in the night. He addressed Simone with an honored bow.

"My friend, we have the same roots." Father Juniper spoke kindly to the tall black man. "Roots that connect us to Abraham, Isaac and Jacob." He untied the knot on the rope of his priestly brown garb. Meticulously, he removed a linen prayer-cloth, folded against his undergarment over his chest. JERUSALEM, embroidered white on white, rose across the end of the rectangular shawl. Over the middle rested the outline of a blue star. Father Juniper displayed the cloth, but never moved his eyes from Simone.

"Come, my friend." The priest raised the shawl higher to drape over the black man's bent head. The move stirred lost emotions, below the crust of the present. A silent tear dropped from beneath the covering.

Fence thought it looked like the crowning of a king. Humility hung on the men in front of him. He could not quite grasp what was happening, but he knew it was significant, a Christian and a Jew? Fence was becoming part of something beyond him, something that Tia already knew or at least sensed, something deeper than flesh.

"It is the dewdrop. Heaven is weeping." Fence looked over his shoulder to see who spoke, but no one was there.

Flat on her back, Tia focused. No face accompanied the words she heard. *A dewdrop?* An unearthly feeling of mercy overwhelmed her. *Where am I?* The scene above her had to be a dream, all in her head.

The cloaking lasted only a moment. Simone let the shawl fall to his expanding shoulders, as if he and the priest had switched roles. Both stood side by side in silence.

Tia, coming alive, wished she had a camera. Instead, she recorded the picture with her heart. The sacred moment possessed a seed of timelessness. Fence pulled her to a sitting position. Her body remained stiff and motionless, her mind photographing.

With a miniature move of his pointer finger, Simone signaled for Fence to sit next to her. The arrangement had a charismatic effect, drawing them together. He began to speak. "Miss Tiara, there is one piece of information I have not given. It is time for you to know." Simone's right hand clasped the strings hanging from the Jewish prayer shawl. Tia looked up to give attention to the Jamaican. He stood staunch.

"Miss Tiara." The tall man's eyes drilled into her as he continued, "You have a brother who has gone before you, adopted in America. His name..." He stopped to speak delicately. "His name is Abraham Maxwell Pearl."

"What?" Tia and Fence said in unison.

"History of the present generation is not recorded on your lambskin. My regards." Simone bowed and backed out.

Fence followed the man with his gray-green eyes while details of the past eighteen months replayed. *She's Abe's sister! He set me up.* His stare locked in the shock. He focused on the new knowledge. Attempting to connect it to understanding, he looked at her up and down.

Meanwhile, Tia sat spellbound, drinking in the new revelation. Fence snapped his finger in front of her face. "Come out of it. Wake up!"

Tia blinked, shaking her head out of the trance. "I have a brother."

"Apparently. Wait here a minute please. I have something to do." Fence reached into his pocket, bringing forth the crown found in the tile. With soft but sure steps, he advanced to the Table of Remembrance below the cross. His hand was sweaty. The offering plate lay exposed next to a weathered Bible. A gold marker blocked a portion of the text. Fence tossed the crown into the crucible. "For the orphans," he stammered, looking up. The clink of the heavy coin, gold against gold, filled the cavity of the sanctuary.

The act of honor touched Tia. Fence's unprecedented move reminded her of Mack Carpenter, the father who treated her like his own daughter. Most men would try to extract the ancient value of the coin. They would be unwilling to break greed's heart, to halt the pumping for power and pleasure. There was a deeper level to Fence, one that drilled beyond the face of surface.

Tia rested her chin in her hand, staring into space. She felt a lot better. Fence had thrown off a desire to hoard treasure. This recognition made it harder to act like she did not like Fence. She cared for this man, this friend of the brother that she never knew. She—a woman of courage—feared to tell him. *Did he know all along? Was this his way of saying he was sorry?*

Fence returned straight to Tia with moccasin silence. Her arm stretched to him. Compassion rolled out of her, but he did not see. He helped her to a standing position and whispered, "We have an appointment with an artist." He hooked his hand into her arm. Then, without hesitation, he lifted her face, pecking a quick kiss on her lips, nodding at her. "Interesting life you lead." He moved her forward.

Tia raised the palms of her fingers to her closed lips, hushed by the wooing of the moment.

Chin Up

THE artist instructed, "Arch your back, young woman. Lean your back to your husband." The man left his easel to adjust the subjects over the captain's wheel of the rotting boat. "It is good you came early, so I have sun." He placed Tia's thumb under Fence's left palm, wrapping her four fingers over his with enough room to expose his wedding ring. "Relax. Do not be so uneasy. I will not keep you long."

"Sir?" she said. "This boat is dangerous."

"Shh. You must not talk," he said, settling the matter. "Chin up."

The work seemed to take hours. Neither had patience. Fence was beginning to think the whole thing was a bad idea. The creaking boat, half sunk, was apparently good for nothing but character. Both minds were at work, neither guessing the other's intention. The canvas backing left little visual appeal to the two married strangers.

"Please, no movement of eyes," the austere man said.

Earlier that afternoon the African Gray had joined Fence and Tia at the old bungalow. Tia had insisted they take the bird along.

Amos landed on the stern, saying repeatedly, "Paint Pretty Bird." He had recognized the old artist. He obnoxiously flew around the old man's head, longing to be the center of attention. "Remember me. Remember me."

"Amos, my friend, I do not forget you. You have come to watch, not be in the picture. You are old, like me," the man with the brush said subtly. "We both have seen better days."

"Paint me," Amos begged in a whiney voice.

"All right, find your perch." It was obvious that Amos had the man wrapped around his talon, his little finger that is. Amos, accustomed to obeying the artist, landed swiftly on Fence's forearm.

Hindrance to movement was all that Fence could think about. First, the bird talked too much, and now he ruled the roost. Fence's inner arm squeezed the hidden gun.

Where and when she had come on board, Fence did not know. The man's granddaughter was standing below them on the starboard side with a lightweight, misty flowing gown, looking like a ghost before dusk. Her hair dipped over the railing in a seductive manner. The artist finished the last touches, neither bothered nor concerned with his granddaughter's presence.

Tia pulled away from the circular frame, the spoked contrivance, no longer capable of giving direction, no longer a controlling force of motion. Vacating the captain's wheel, Tia edged closer toward the artist. Her head moved in front of Fence. She spotted the beautiful woman looking toward the sun setting on the sea. Tia's heart tripped. She was jealous, not of the woman herself, but of the way the artist's granddaughter attracted Fence.

Disembarking was about as dangerous as remaining on the rickety ship. The pier had half-fallen into the sea. Amos flew to the man of art and flipped his beret to the deck.

"He remembers me well." The artist turned the picture away from Tia. "It will be ready tomorrow at the party. The finishing touches need to be made. You must come Madame."

Tia retained a steadfast gaze on the old man. "What time?" she asked with poise.

"Same as today, no earlier, no later." The smooth, artistic answer was relaxed.

"And may we inquire where this will be?" Fence asked a bit abrasively, disturbed with Tia. Or was it the painter? Perhaps it was himself. He surveyed the other woman, the artist's granddaughter Del Rae Zane.

"The first place shall be your last," the old artist answered, walking away. Swiftly, the granddaughter was by the man's side, giving assistance in departure.

As soon as they were out of earshot, Tia looked at Fence. "Do you know what this is all about?"

He threw his hands up in the air. "Don't ask me. I know less and less all the time."

Tia, with both hands, fully grabbed Fence's arm muscle and pinched her fingers into it. "Well, there's a kingpin out here somewhere and we have to knock him out."

Fence ripped himself away. "You seem to know more than I do."

Underneath, a besetting aggravation with Abe Pearl grew. He started to steam with anger at his best friend, who was not even alive. *Why did Abe trap me? Why didn't he tell me the truth? Why couldn't he confide in me? Surely he knew. But, she doesn't look like him at all. Maybe he didn't know.*

Fence's brain sorted facts. He wondered what had come down both sides of Tia's bloodlines, father and mother. Irritated, he spurted, "Evil forces seem to be coming out of the woodwork. Let's get back into the light. A few more people around us. We aren't doing too well alone."

Angel Food Cake

THE day before had been almost too big to swallow. Tia's stomach churned thinking about it. Fence had been none too gentle. In fact, he had been downright obnoxious. Sandwiched between the paradoxes Fence showed, lay a thin spread of tenderness. Nothing made sense anymore. She stared out the east door while the dusk turned to daylight.

Fence started to stretch. He had endured the night in the same small room, crimped in the chair. Out of one eye he watched Tia sneak around. "Morning," he mumbled. "Are you watching the sun paint the morning?"

"Yes," she spurted. "At least the sun is real." She turned away, reflecting on the evening before. *The painter—the artist?* Tia could not put her finger on how the artist fit into the picture of her past, let alone her future. His granddaughter was another story—swirling around on the half-sunken ship.

Fence finished drying his face. He threw the towel onto the table in anger. He spouted, "Goals and acquisitions of murderers stretch beyond the norm of ordinary thinkers." He stopped to consider. "They seem to like the limelight though. They puff up their feathers in pride and greed and see what they can get away with."

"Isn't that what we're counting on—their lust working to our advantage?" She latched the second sandal, waiting for him. "Are you ready?"

Fence opened the new rental car door for Tia. Amos perched on her forearm, resting his head under his wing. Tia carefully eased into the passenger seat.

"Remember that madness rules at the final point of action. Be cautious Tia." Fence swung the door shut. The words expressed the danger of attending the party.

The insight grieved Tia. Her lifegiving instincts could not imagine what wrapped around the mind of the demonic. She fidgeted. "I can't comprehend what controls such compulsions. Fence, what causes men to stoop to murder, to kill innocent people? Does reasoning cease to exist?"

Fence fought the fury rising in him, the desire to take up the cause, to extinguish the killer's flame, to exterminate the exterminator. He zealously longed to bring justice and dispose of the killers. "Hatred consumes men," Fence said. Was he speaking of himself?

Tia wanted to scream. She argued instead. "To lose one to bring life to another, is that justifiable? To take freedom from one so another might be liberated? Is that what war is all about? Doesn't a higher authority exist to settle the injustices of mankind?"

Her questions rose and fell with the waves. If Fence was listening, he kept it secret. Neither knew what to expect. She cast her eyes to the sea, wondering how many men had died trying to conquer it. *Please God, show me. Why am I here?* Her silent prayer seemed to hit deaf ears.

The seaside resort had reserved a first class suite under the names Vanessa and Tucker Johnson. Tucked inside the basket with a new interior hid an unusually compliant Amos. He made no remarks as they registered.

The bungalow of simplicity in the jungle where they had hidden did not compare to the luxurious resort. The French bidet, too prestigious to figure out, annoyed Tia. She made the necessary adjustments. Her queasy stomach resisted settling down. She vomited for the third time. The pulsating shower opened gracious arms, never more welcoming. She let the water rain over her and took her time getting ready for the party.

A moment later Fence caught himself grinning. Tia looked revived and quite attractive in the sleeveless, crimson red and white floral cotton dress. A matching triangular shawl covered her shoulders. She had tied the shawl in a square knot above her waist. "Lady, I have to admit. You're fit to kill." Fence complimented her.

"That's not funny. My life is on the line." She latched the double string of ivory pearls in place, adjusting them on the soft skin of her neck. The basket hung over her arm resembling an oversized purse, reassembled for the night. Amos sat on a miniature feather pillow inside, gently muffled with a clamp around his bill for the time being.

Stepping onto the patio, a whirlwind of color and aroma greeted them. "Jamaicans sure know how to party." Fence surveyed the heart-shaped patio. A menagerie of ribbons and flowers, intertwined and curled together, intermingled into the outdoor scene. Meticulously manicured plants, old and young, good and evil, formed a zoo outside the heart. Two giraffes stood tall with necks crossed over each other. Two different greens made up the zebra stripes. A sea green fence encircled the outside wall of the heart. Ivy monkeys, hanging by their limbs and tails, dangled from the hidden wires. A plush carpet of grass warmed the earth beneath.

"It almost looks too inviting," Tia replied. The gun, strapped to her inner leg, felt cumbersome.

Above them, pearl-shaped Chinese lanterns dangled in neat rows resembling human hearts—pearl drops. The oriental gems radiated romance amid the flair of Jamaican charms. Salsa music penetrated the night. A fever filled the air, electrifying the place. Fence positioned himself next to Tia.

In the far-left corner, the bottom of the heart, the aged artist stood next to the veiled picture. His granddaughter gloated close by, apparently waiting for Fence. The crescendo of anticipation swelled.

Tia checked the veranda mirror near the superior vena cava, the main entrance at the upper-right corner. A living garland of green graced the mirror's oval head. Underneath, an earthenware crock embraced a heavy-laden jade plant. Slow movement inched into place.

Tia missed Mack Carpenter, the father who imparted strength, confidence and worth to her. She straightened her back and held her head higher, running the steps through her brain. *Carry the jewels inside the basket along with the handkerchief and the African Gray. Mingle amongst the guests. Notice any unusual characters. Release Amos when Fence gives the signal.* No one had to tell Tia that in order to get solid evidence and expose the murderers, someone or something must cause them to act. She was that someone.

"It's risky business to become too confident," Fence said over her shoulder. His remarks did not sit well with Tia.

"Too little confidence can ruin the plan." Suddenly the hair on the back of her arms arose. *The calm before the storm,* Mack had called it.

As if on cue, a bright spotlight boldly flickered. It reflected off the looking glass, photographing the mirror and Tia. Her arm flew up, shielding her face. It was too late.

"Happy Birthday!" the *maître d'* announced. The shout caught Tia by surprise. "For the occasion Mrs. Johnson. Welcome to Jamaica." The starched towel over the Chinese man's forearm hung down. The headwaiter bowed with formality. "Our custom to honor such a day."

Off to the upper left, Simone's son entered, disguised as a butler. He carried an angelic-looking cake, lavished with whipped frosting and crowned with twenty-four rosebud candles. The centerpiece, placed on a roundtable, glowed. Without turning her head, Tia's eyes rolled upward. The idea of being the center of attention, if only for the moment, disgusted her. Was this really her birthday?

A few nearby guests stared. An odd dignitary bowed, engrossed by Tia's obvious exquisiteness. She swallowed the saliva forming in the back of her throat. A gutsy spit at him was out of the question. Adding to her frustration, Fence breathed down her neck, giving her the shivers. "I'm fine. Please give me some space."

Fence circled the perimeter, leaving her for the moment. His eyes spun toward the dark artist. The man's elegant granddaughter flipped her hair to the other side of her head, flirting conspicuously with Fence. Her dazzle did not go unnoticed.

"So it is your wife, you say, it's her birthday?" she asked. "Twenty-four years?" Del Rae Zane edged closer to his arm, seeking to rest her chin. "She is merely a child."

Wheels turned within Fence while he answered. "Quite enchanting, isn't she? But certainly lacking your keys to maturity." He soothed the woman by playing along. He ruled out no one.

Fence's eyes followed Tia as she moved across the veranda. What Tia possessed, few possessed. Irrevocable keys to bravery made their home in her pocket. Perhaps Del Rae Zane had them, but he doubted it.

Off in the distance the beach's beautiful shoulder mirrored light from other seaside resorts. Stars saying goodbye to the sun seemed to vie for evening attention, while an invisible undercurrent moved amidst them. There was more to fear than the sea's destructive force or a surging storm whirling wind and death about. The crumpled message Claude left Fence the first night weighed on him, reminding Fence that a dangerous shark loomed near. Fence felt certain there was more than one.

Across the room Simone's son stood with his chin straight out and eyes fixed in his butler costume. "Do not eat the food," he warned Tia. His lips barely moved.

Tia blinked a nod of response. She stood beneath the gold diagonal cross of the Jamaican flag. "I have no plans to." Fence had given her orders not to trust anyone or eat anything—not that she was hungry. Food had not agreed with her for several days.

The patio started to fill with people. At first, the skin color of black dominated the party, not just those serving, but prestigious guests. Gradually, a progressing number of Caucasians mixed in. Fence anticipated that the possibility of the so-called pirates resisting the public eye to be unlikely, especially if there was something in it for them.

Undoubtedly, evil would be disguised. There had to be a lure—a Lazy Ike or a daredevil to cause a confrontation. The tide seemed to flex its muscles in anticipation. The assembling of key players to nab the so-called pirates and the evil ship had begun.

Inconspicuously, Claude Walking Elk passed Tia's birthday present to Fence. He had been able to get the large diamond and several smaller ones set into a lavish dinner ring. "Amazing!" Fence said. "It will serve the purpose."

The Pot Simmers

DARK clouds progressively moved across the island, hastening the storm. Unaware of AryAnn's failure to follow through, of her sudden demise, Skully grumbled. *When has she ever shown up on time?* Her rebellious nature and lack of responsibility caused him discomfort. *Women can't be trusted to do a man's job.* His most incompetent flunkey gave more leads to stage a kill than she had. The small assistance of the black twins also proved a plus. "Children pull off more in mischievous innocence than adults admit," he muttered.

Skully groomed himself to the best of his ability, flattered that he still had a bit of the movie star "look." That and knowing the bitter dark chocolate cake was scheduled to arrive with the party food. The added touch of maraschino cherries, his idea, gave the devil's food the look of glamour. He pulled in his stomach and examined himself in the mirror. He did not look so bad. He rubbed his newly-shaven face. *It will be a grand birthday party, if I ever get there.*

His self-glamorizing did not last long. He wondered if T.R. Bain had ever received the voodoo doll. Planting seeds of fear was his specialty. He rubbed his hands together, more anxious than usual. The bulky Skully, rotten to the core, plunged into his dark and twisted thoughts.

Skully kicked his feet up on the coffee table in the lobby, holding an issue of *News Today* in front of his face. He did not want to miss anything, especially the possibility of seeing T.R. Bain, or whoever she was portraying herself to be. She would show up, somewhere, even if AryAnn did not. His informants were on top of things—so he thought. He rubbed his bothered eyes, attempting to clarify the picture. A blur blocked out the newspaper's words. *My eyes are going to pot.*

Ironically, Skully was not aware that T.R. Bain had secretly become Tia Rose Carpenter. Merdone had left out that detail. He still did not know. All he knew was that T.R. Bain had foiled his plans more than once—living through the accident, slipping by AryAnn in the hospital, vanishing from sight.

Skully had lost track of her, that is, until the word came down from Merdone. Recent implications pointed to T.R. Bain belonging to a wealthy Jamaican family, the very one his grandfather had attempted to annihilate. *Now, isn't that a coincidence?*

His eyes peeked over the top just enough to glimpse the coming and going of the so-called elite. He loathed the power they possessed. He loathed women for taking power from men. Indignant, he scowled.

His sleek-looking boss rounded the corner, entering at a brisk pace. The so-called dignified man did not give Skully so much as a glance. *Better than giving me the evil eye.* However, Skully knew that his boss had eyes on the back of his head, and in the corners. He had learned that early on. Merdone purposely ignored his existence until he wanted a job done. Since Skully had faked his death and changed his name, Merdone used extreme means to communicate instructions.

Skully lowered the newspaper to think. He dissected his connection to the sleek Merdone. His animosity started to build. Skully grunted in crocodile rebellion, raising the paper curtain to cover his nose. *Well, everyone serves someone, even him.*

While Skully was skulking with his nose behind old news, Merdone passed by with a persistent foot, holding his head high. Every hair was in place, his shoes were spit-shined and his clothes had no wrinkles. He had operated in elite circles and looked good among the professionals. He considered himself wiser and much more skilled in communication than the filth of the earth, as he referred to Skully and his stool pigeon, the so-called AryAnn. They were too brazen, too brisk, too impetuous, too reckless and much too degenerate for him. He had stooped to hire the man as a civilian flight instructor at the insistence of a Colombian official, but that was short-lived.

Merdone had spent the first sixteen years of his life in the Rocky Mountains. His mother had a different name, never marrying his father. Then she married Avery Pearl, a Jew. On top of that, she adopted the kosher kid, giving him what he never had. It still ate at Merdone. His mother forgot him, left him lost of her attention. She had lavished her new son, Abe, with affection.

Merdone's decision to leave home two years later and join the military—not just enlist but go to officer training school—had been an easy option. He cut the apron strings, the ties to his disappointing mother.

He decided to transform himself into a man of prestige and power. And now, Abe had been dead a year and a half. Enough time had elapsed. The path cleared for Merdone to return to claim the inheritance. But there was a glitch. Abe had done an ancestral search before he died. There was another heir, T.R. Bain.

Merdone had decided to make a personal inquest, lowering himself to return to the deteriorating old courthouse near the mountains. In a twist of irony, he discovered that Tia Bain, after her affair with Chance Cummings, had married Fence Carpenter. It all hooked together too bizarrely. But, that was not on his mind right now.

As Merdone paced through the lobby, he concentrated on the recent invitation. It was neatly tucked inside his dressy white jacket. He felt lucky—proud that the Jamaican ambassador planned to honor him at the elite party. He wanted to look as polished as possible, having risen to the precipice of success. He intended to attend the celebration and then discreetly move out of the picture. And so, William Merdone walked past Skully with pride pinned on his heart. The garden patio was a step away.

The Lure

THE evening progressed at a slow pace for Tia. Establishing a foundation for existence tugged at her heartstrings. Across the patio Fence carried on a conversation with someone who looked familiar—Claude Walking Elk.

"Little ... little," Tia signaled, getting his attention.

Fence gave a nod of understanding, recognizing the Jamaican language pattern—repetition of words. Her demonstration of "little by little" encouraged him—that, and the fact that she seemed to be waiting for him.

Colorful couples arrived from various nations—Germany, Ireland, Argentina, Austria, England, South Africa, Australia—a mixed bag of people, speaking their own vernacular mixed with English. The party grew. Stately men with trimmed beards, dressed loosely in vacation white, appeared slightly relaxed without the trappings of coat and tie. The whole cast necessary to bring forth the jewels of truth, honesty and justice moved into place.

Another birthday was recognized which made Tia leery of the validity of the day. All sorts of scrambled ideas filled her head. Fence had moved further from her, not by yards, but by the wall of people forming. Her heart ached. She turned. Claude Walking Elk stood in front of her. Fence had sent him.

"You have a son then?" Tia addressed Fence's friend, tensed by his presence.

"All is well." Claude Walking Elk spoke gently.

"And you are here? Forgive me, but understanding is not registering. Does she not need you?" Tia said. "You abandon her?"

"Her wish is for me to be here. Marie Deer Path attends her. You share a birthday with the newborn, Whistle."

Tia tensed. "You cut your hair?" she questioned.

"For my brother Fence. And you cut yours?" Claude remarked.

"For my father," she answered with acuteness, assuming Claude would know Mack Carpenter was behind the move.

Whistle—the infant's name, whether real or imaginary—fit the Walking Elk family. Of the people present, few used valid names. The guests remained prudent and unknown, a mass of no names. *Today, will I know?* She questioned herself. *Will I know who I really am?*

"This seat is spoken for." A snide woman with overdone, pasted-on makeup curled her nose at Tia. The harsh word steered Tia away. The glamorous, but phony women had separated themselves from the males, involved in their own repetitive discussion of latest clothing trends and movie star gossip. The snotty clique chattered aimlessly, occupying time with snipping and fruitlessness, obviously oblivious to what was really going on. Tia, drawn to the masculine side, wrenched them off her back, unable to deny that she preferred Fence's company.

A tall, striking, sleek man in his early forties gravitated toward her. "Madame, best wishes on your birthday." He laid a long-stemmed, South American red rose into her small arms.

Graciousness caused her to nod a thank you; discernment prevented her from speaking. The man's aggressive posture tightened her up. She felt sick again, vaguely remembering. It had been three years since she'd seen the man that Chance Cummings knew, the one who had asked her to dance, the one she disdained—Major Merdone. Her stomach churned. She squeezed around him, brushing the reed basket against his arm. *Did he recognize me?* No one came to her rescue— not that she needed anyone, but perhaps. She took a deep breath. Fence was out of sight, not out of mind.

Fence approached Tia from behind, wrapping his arms around her. "Lost?" he asked. He held her against him.

"No," she said abruptly. She covered her mouth and spoke up to Fence, as if telling him a secret. "That man over there ... I don't like him. He just gave me a rose for my birthday. His name is Merdone. Before we left Florida Mr. Tuffty asked if I knew him."

"Do you?" Fence asked. His arm strapped her waist.

"Only of him. I saw him once before, three years ago. He has tricks hidden under all his medals."

"I know," Fence whispered. "I've been watching him. We have to get proof. He runs too clean a ship. There must be someone here who does his dirty work—who connects him to the underground."

She tugged on his sleeve. "Do you think he suspects us?"

Fence kept his comment to himself. "Stay with me." He leaned his chin on the crown of her head. "Don't look now, but I think we have uninvited guests."

"Unwelcome you mean." She cleared her throat.

"Both," he added, releasing her and stepping to her side. "Stay here," he instructed. He passed in front of her, disappearing into the crowd.

The patio plan was not shaping up like Tia hoped it would. Once again, her eyes searched for Fence. Instead, she spotted the familiar array of characters from Fence's life. Reed Carpenter and Doc Bridger were waiting on the periphery. She was too far away to hear what they were up to. All she knew was that they must know that she was the lure to entice the killers into the trap.

Fence's grandfather Reed and his old friend Doc Bridger blended in with the integrated mix of men. "Don't want to strain your brain," Doc said in a hushed tone. "But, look toward the left ventricle—the lower chamber of the patio heart." Doc spoke in medical terms.

Reed's eyes shifted in reply. "Arnold Tuffty isn't it? Who's he with?"

"Hard to say, but I don't like him. You know about becoming who you associate with, about receiving blood and forcing it out."

Reed responded. "Lawyers have to walk in precarious circles. Maybe the left hand doesn't know what the right hand is doing."

"Reminds me of a badger … always digging around." Doc Bridger's handkerchief hung down while he cleaned his glasses.

"Well, the bait is out. Fence's wife looks quite charming. He has good taste. Too bad we have to use her." Reed turned his head canvassing the central point, watching Fence sneak up on her.

A small conversation brewed near the front entrance. Gently, Fence maneuvered Tia into the mainstream, near the fountain at the heart-center. They slipped behind the green-zebra specimen. Communication pulsated around them. They listened.

"No different from Indian tragedies," Claude Walking Elk spoke to the South African. "Someone will always take the law into his hand."

"Why are you sulking in pain?" The lanky lad from Scotland jumped into the discussion determined to intervene into the category of deep thinkers. "Why do you stand around and talk about it? I say do something!"

"Keep your tongue in, young man. You'll learn the hard way." An old native with a deep chest injected his wisdom, bowing his head and avoiding a collision of eyes.

The squatty man with the stern, overland jaw spoke abruptly. "Force and violence ruins men."

"Renegade Robin Hoods," expelled the man with the white goatee. Fence Carpenter's European friend, Ivan Burns, stirred the pot. He ignored the long-jawed man and the Scottish lad.

Then the Irishman's pent-up emotion stirred. "I wouldn't exactly put them all into the same category. Motivation makes a difference you know?" He wiped sweat from his Irish forehead. "Who of us has died with a red badge of courage plastered across our chest, worn to cover the fear that lies beneath? Nay, none. A badge bolsters hearts to do the impossible, the improbable."

"You mean, mow the enemy down without feeling, without running away, don't you?" snapped the lanky lad with the Scottish accent who was eager to get into the battle. He spoke without thinking.

"Anger pays nothing," Claude said. "Not silver, not wisdom. Clenched teeth are not a sign of peace."

The Scottish lad backed up. A war raged inside Edin Mansfield— hatred versus love. Sweat formed on his brow. The stolen words of the journal regurgitated.

Some things need to die, like anger that burns in the heart . . .

Right away the young Scottish man, Edin Mansfield, felt sick to his stomach—worse than any drug he had ever taken. His hatred and hunger for the American dollar had cursed him. He had brazenly connected with Merdone, who actually found him through an unorthodox channel. Like a chain reaction, Merdone had hooked him up to Skully. It appeared that no good thing ruled his life. Suddenly, Edin Mansfield, Lily's younger brother, was not so sure of himself. He fidgeted, mulling over the situation.

Fence Carpenter did not appear to recognize him, but Edin was using his name and his identification. *What if someone asks? What if Merdone is setting me up? What if the words in the journal are truth? What if the words are my—? Edin gulped. My sister's? Lily's? There was no signature, no name, bu—? Why did Fence Carpenter have it with him in Scotland? What if Fence Carpenter came here to give it to—me? What if he did care?* The thought thrust through his heart. Within a second it seemed to kill anger. Distorted reasoning lost its stronghold. In his contemplation, he counted the pearl-shaped lanterns in his head, in Celt.

The other men debated the valor of taking the law into their own hands. Claude Walking Elk separated himself from the group, delving into a discussion on silver work with a sheik from Shiraz. The Arab chief, covered in garb, spoke methodically. The old-world presence of Muslim power and romance caused a stir among a clique of young women nearby. Cognizant of the attention, the Iranian purposely cast his eyes on the artist's granddaughter, Miss Zane.

Fence and Tia passed by the cockpit of men who snapped back and forth like roosters, ready to grab each other's neck. "Tia," Fence whispered squeezing her, "Arnold Tuffty is here."

The elderly distinguished lawyer had arrived smoking a horrid horned pipe filled with a familiar tobacco scent. Killing time, he tapped out the old and stuffed it anew.

Like chessmen on a heart-shaped board, the pieces were set in place—the pawns with little power—along with the bishops, the knights, the rooks, the kings who avoid capture—and, the powerful queen.

Discreet people, presented incognito as vacationers, stood as mummified Egyptian statues on the edge, observing with a third eye. An unseen hand seemed to move them. Other players hid in the wings of the right and left ventricles, the bottom-half of the heart. A steady increasing rhythm palpitated in the inner chamber … thump … thump … thump. The stage was set for drama.

Fence leaned into Tia. She whispered, admonishing him, "I can't hide behind someone else, with a real or phony name. This is my battle. I intend to see it through to the end. To win I must risk everything."

He spoke into her hair. "You are one independent woman. Don't do anything dumb." In a gentler tone he added, "I'll be around just in case." His chin lifted. "See the Scottish kid? He looks very familiar. Think I'll try to find out who he is."

While Fence was gone, the twin boys, who Tia had met on her first day in Jamaica, entered with platters of fresh pineapple and ruby red strawberries. Then they recycled the angel food cake platter. They put the chocolate cake into place. Mr. Tuffty noticed the strange scene, as did Tia. He edged his way to Tia's side. "Children break ranks when mischief becomes more than a game." He looked straight ahead as he passed her.

"I don't like chocolate. Never have," Tia quipped over Mr. Tuffty's back. Thinking of her parents' death and of Fence's poisoning, she would not disregard any possibility.

The basket bag sat undisturbed beside her. Opening it, she freed the blindfolded, muzzled Amos. She held him in her hand. Carefully, she scanned the room. The old artist had maneuvered the covered manuscript behind the landscaped giraffe, waiting to unveil it. Tia's body swung a full circle, resulting in a head-on collision with Mack Carpenter. Fence's father's appearance was as unexpected as Claude's. She should have known.

"Let the bird go," Mack quietly instructed." He will draw attention away from us."

"Mack? Where did...?" Tia blurted, wondering where he came from.

"Shush daughter. I'm here. I keep my word." Mack's eyes of promise were swallowing the room. "Remember, eagles fly higher than any other bird. They love the storm." He quickly departed to the opposite side, not letting Tia give a rebuttal. *Amos is no eagle.*

The whole Carpenter clan of men had emerged on the scene, infiltrating the heart. Fence had deliberately left out details. Mr. Tuffty was apparently up to something of his own making. Tia burned at them, all except Mack. She bit her tongue, embittered that her idea was pirated away by men. They had butted into her business. To admit that she needed them, all of them, was humbling. The pressing crowd, building up around her, made her uneasy. To top it off, a dogfight of disagreeing men might blow her cover. She looked at her feet. Wearing the sandals Fence had given her gave her a strange sense of comfort.

Amos was the only one present in the room who seemed out of control. The bird zoomed swiftly out in front on the terrace, sweeping the air in confusion. Guests gaped and wondered how to catch him to halt the distraction. His bird tongue licked the fruit. The pedestal platter of mixed nuts served as a greater temptation. He landed on the spoon handle, popping nuts all over the table.

The kitchen staff plotted to kill the bird. One volunteered a pellet gun but did not have it with him.

The *maitre d'* made a quick declaration. "Someone get that bird under control."

Fence, standing in line of the order, gave the Chinese man an uncanny look, disregarding the disturbance. "Who knows when a wild bird will be tamed?" Fence volunteered, shrugging his shoulders.

"Crack nuts. Crack cases. Not crackpot." Silenced by a megaphone voice, the bird landed in the open basket. Amos stuck his head under his wing and feigned sleep.

"Calling everyone to attention!" The island governor spoke crisply. The crowd hushed. "I have the distinct honor of recognizing a distinguished guest tonight. He has invested in the country and assisted in stimulating the Jamaican economy." The island official reached forth his hand. "Major William Merdone, I hold here a small token of our gratitude—a medal-of-honor." The dignitary fixed the medal with the colored ribbons to Merdone's jacket.

Immediately following the little ceremony of recognition, the elite party was interrupted. The narrator spoke out with alarm.

"A notification has just come to me that several million dollars in diamonds and a double strand of natural pearls are missing on the premises. All entrances and exits will be blocked while a search is conducted. No hasty movements will be allowed." A murmuring buzz filled the patio heart. Suspicious eyes of distrust scoped one another out, viewing from top to bottom, like a man surveys a woman, his intentions usually less than honorable, but not always.

Together the small black twins ran to the man of authority with a scrap of paper. "Attention: A second message has been retrieved from the floor. Not to alarm you, do not panic." He swallowed. "We now have a bomb threat. Please remain calm. The evacuation process will proceed with caution." He consulted a man in uniform before continuing. "A quick search will be done upon ex—it."

Even as he spoke, total darkness quenched the Chinese lanterns. The ocean's reflection brightened after eyes adjusted. Storms, not uncommon for Jamaica, brewed in two realms, the natural and the supernatural. Tia and Fence Carpenter were in the eye.

Fence grabbed Tia's waist from behind. The quick impulse startled her. "It's just me, Fence," he whispered. "Are you all right?" Her head nodded against his chest. "You can hide with me if you don't want to hide behind me."

"What's the business about the bomb?" she asked.

"Not our idea. The fish are biting, taking the bait." Fence pulled her closer, lifting her hand in the dark. "Your birthday gift." He slipped the ring on her right ring finger.

"Will it work?' she asked. She talked of the plan.

"It will," he encouraged.

"Then thank you." She kissed his cheek.

The Lure

"I love you," Fence quietly mouthed.

The Linen Room

CONFUSED party guests were escorted to the exit door in the dark. "This way," the man in white said quietly. Other guests lingered behind.

The man who had organized the exit approached Fence and Tia. He spoke to them privately. "A lawyer smoking a pipe says there's someone you must see. It is all set."

Tia and Fence cautiously followed the linen form into the darkness, perplexed by the change in plans. "Don't be alarmed. He's your friend, is he not?" the man spoke of Mr. Tuffty as he held out a small flashlight. Fence took it, but waited to turn it on. The man in white continued. "The appointment has been arranged in the last few minutes following the ceremony. The meeting will take place in the linen closet—at the end of the building. I laid the handkerchief on the empty table at the lawyer's instruction." The man in white left to attend to a cluster of frightened women who would, undoubtedly, have new gossip material after they calmed down.

It seemed peculiar that Mr. Tuffty would arrange such a meeting, but he was strange anyway, according to Fence. The unexpected bomb scare had thrown the night off course, and then the blackout. Tia wondered how Mr. Tuffty knew about the handkerchief.

Tia ambled slightly ahead of Fence, wary of danger. She did not want to disturb any unforeseen object along the way. The miniature flashlight Fence had given her helped slightly. Did she dare whisper? She waited until they reached the door. "Looks like a bomb shelter, not a linen closet." In the shadow she watched Fence nod his head in confirmation.

The room was no ordinary linen room, but much more—large—cool—a place of intrigue. Ten-inch concrete walls and a thick concrete floor enclosed the rectangular space that ran the length of the building with entry doors on each end. Originally, it was designed to be a storm shelter, capable of holding fifty people. It doubled as a storage room, which soon became its primary function.

All-purpose utility tables lined the middle of the room, like a giant flaxen reed. Most were stacked high with motel items in need of repair, spare televisions, broken bed stands and extra blankets covered with clear plastic. Dressers were stacked atop each other on one side.

Two large moveable carts on rollers occupied the front-end space, one full of cleaning supplies. The other housed necessities, extra towels, bed linens, and miniature bars of soap. Numerous other items lined the side shelves. The leftover pieces gave the room a crowded look. In fact, the so-called linen room seemed much smaller than it actually was, making movement cumbersome, the reason the staff dubbed it the "linen closet."

Cockroaches slipped into the corners at the first sign of Tia's flashlight. A high intensity flashlight hung from a lone wire, spotlighting the linen handkerchief. "Anyone here?" Fence asked. No one answered.

Tia charged straight ahead toward the item on the table. She could not get her own handkerchief out of the basket fast enough. The two handkerchiefs were identical. Both had arrows that pointed outward in six directions. She held back a gasp. "It's the same." Her insides wanted to explode with excitement.

Fence ordered in a whisper. "Get back Tia. Move out of the light." He could come at any time. He gently shoved Tia behind him, moving the colt pistol to his hand.

Tia, out of the lone stream of light, stood in the blackness of a corner. A vertical opening between the shelves, where a door should have been, hid her. She lowered her back against a brief space of bare wall, seeking the weapon of defense. Her gun, haltered to the inside of her thigh beneath her dress, proved more difficult to get her hands on than expected. Fence's back hugged a shelf nearby. A minute of silence passed.

Suddenly the man entered the linen room. A muffled cough escaped his mouth and then he murmured, "Hello. Hello— Mr. Tuffty, are you here? I have a message from the Jamaican ambassador that there is a basket for me in here—certain evidence that confirms my inheritance?" The uncanny man spoke into the gray light. He spied the hankies from a distance, and made his way toward them. He picked them up tediously. He was wearing white clothing, like most everyone else, and he had white gloves on.

Tia and Fence saw no one at first. A dark, mystical mood hovered. The linen closet held the foreboding presence. Fence breathed into the darkness. "Who is it?"

"Abraham Pearl," he said. "Mr. Arnold Tuffty, is that you?"

The man's outline shadowed a few feet away from Fence. The voice sounded strange, but the accent sounded familiar. The heavy door closed.

Fence answered. "No, it's Fence Carpenter. Aren't you supposed to be dead?"

"Yes and no," the man answered.

Fence tried to maintain the dialogue. He kept his voice calm.

"You aren't the Abe I know," Fence interjected. He signaled to Tia in sign language, hoping she saw the shadow of his fingers telling her to shift to the outside of the room. Her form was scarcely visible. Her perfume was near.

"Imposters have all kinds of ways of maneuvering, all kinds of contacts. I have connections in high places." The man flinched, looking over his back. A mouse scampered across an empty shelf to its nest. "I've been tracking you for years. Now you married T.R. Bain? She will regret snubbing a major."

Snubbing a major? Fence had no idea what the eerie man was talking about. Fence wondered about Tia's past. Distorted truth surrounded them.

"Power then, is that what you want; or is it your brother's inheritance?" Fence kept digging, searching for a question to throw the man off.

"It's not what I want! It's what I already have," he declared. "It's what I possess. It possesses me. It is what I am and who I am." Tia knocked the small shelf off the bigger one with the basket as she stood up.

"Stay where you are." The man ordered, stopping them in their tracks. "This is an automatic," he hollered, cocking the gun. "And, I am quite skilled at using it."

The clock ticked in Fence's brain. He spoke with caution. "I don't know you."

"You never did and never will," he answered emphatically. "But she does!" He pointed the gun toward Tia. He had seen her. "She's merely a dog, knocked up by Chance Cummings. I have no time for dirty Jews or their lovers."

The sleek-looking man moved to the side corner of the room. "Your end has come. You were supposed to have blown up in the car. Now you will both disappear. I'll have to wrap you both in white sheets," he mocked. "Now, hand over that bag. My patience has run out."

Fence yelled, "HIT THE FLOOR!" Shots blasted out, bouncing off the linen walls. The noise, muffled by the soundproof room, exploded in Tia's ears.

Tia threw herself to the floor, losing the gun. The bag flew several feet forward. Fence held the back of her heel and anklebone, his face at her feet. She hindered Fence from shooting again. Heavy breathing filled the darkness. A crack of light exposed the man seizing the basket and slipping out. The imposter hunched forward, walking backwards through the servant's hidden exit. Tia held in a gasp. She recognized him. Merdone, the prestigious, former major, had gone off the deep end.

"Stop!" Fence hollered. He surged up and over Tia, compelled to push after the man who ran the jagged line. His shot went wild. He squeezed through the small, servant's door, weaving his way back to the patio in the darkness. His father, Mack Carpenter, met him.

"It's Abe's stepbrother." Mack gave the quick information to Fence. "I was trying to figure out all night why he looked so familiar."

"I know Dad. I figured it out a long time ago. Something Abe said once—that his mother cried for her first son. He entered the military and never returned. Dad, help Tia will you? She's back in the linen room." Fence started to walk off, and turned. "And, she hates mice."

Fence made his way in the dark to the pair of giraffes with the crossed-over necks. He stumbled over something.

The body wrapped in a white sheet had been hastily left behind. Quickly Fence bent to the ground and pulled the sheet off, shaking his head. He drew out his pencil flashlight to examine the corpse. A spear had pierced the old man's heart. The kind artist with the creative eyes who had called Fence "son" would draw no more.

"Grandfather? Where are you?" Del Rae Zane groped in the dark.

"He's here. I'm sorry. He's dead." Fence spoke softly

"No! No!" She sobbed. "I betrayed him. I listened to that dark major." She bent over her grandfather, kneeling, moving her body back and forth in distress. "Grandfather, I am sorry. I am so sorry."

Laying his hand on her bare shoulder, Fence helped her stand, offering a moment of comfort.

The grief-absorbed young woman flung her arms around him, vice-gripped his waist and rested her head on his chest. Her insides moaned. It was not an act. Her remorseful tears wet his shirt. He attempted to disconnect from her. "I didn't tell the man about the key." She tried to redeem herself.

"The key?" he asked.

She whispered, "Open the metal container behind the painting of you and your wife—behind you. Grandfather was the one who gave the key to you, not me. He wanted you to have it." She begged him, "Open it. See inside." She was still uncontrollable, rocking into Fence.

Pushing Del Rae Zane away, Fence dropped his hand into his pocket. Being sidetracked irritated him. He wanted to get Merdone. Hastily, he removed the large artist-cloth. The back of the canvas faced him. Not bothering to look, Fence leaned the picture against the giraffe. His large hands fumbled. He tried fitting the key into the top lock of the large, metal box. It fit. Hastily, Fence removed the cover. His flashlight shined on the multitude of sketches, seventy years worth from the old-world to the new.

"Evidence, all the evidence you need to convict an underworld of crime," Del Rae Zane said. "It's all there—good and evil, light and darkness, truth and deception. From childhood to old age, Grandfather recorded history with his eyes first and then on paper. For you." Del Rae Zane's hand reached to his arm, pleading—wanting her repentance to make a difference.

Fence could not get his thoughts off his wife, the one he loved. *Tia, play it safe.* It was half-thought, half-prayer.

The Grand Finale

TIA stumbled out of the white room, heading in a new direction. *What makes a man go mad? What spear pierces the heart so deep that it kills love and wipes out mercy? Is it a man given to cruelty, born with an eye for evil, without a father to love him?*

Outside, Mack scratched his chin, looking into the darkness. He had every intention of following Fence's instructions, but a large form moved on the grass nearby—like a snake. Mack's eagle eye zeroed in on the pirate, Skully. Immediately, he sensed the man's connection to Abe's stepbrother, Merdone. He was not going to lose the pirate down a hole.

Just then Mack felt a tug on his sleeve. It was Tia. She had found him with her small flashlight. He tipped his head toward the bulky boa, alerting her.

Tia used hand motions to explain her idea to Mack. It would require a team effort to drop the fishnet that hung over the main area. Mack was game for it. He immediately signaled Doc Bridger and his father Reed Carpenter to action.

Oblivious to what was happening around him, Skully wormed his way beneath the Chinese lanterns using a yellow flashlight. Skully had found a gold coin. There had to be more. *Never come between a man and money,* he said to himself.

The sleazy pirate, Skully, crawled on his insecure knees seeking the lost diamonds. Skully, too eager, too bent on the kill, floured his path with greed. A grunt gave his location away.

Mack pulled out his new jackknife and zipped a cut through his side. Tia snatched the cake knife while Gramp Reed and Doc Bridger used medical scissors to snip the far corners to release the huge square.

Skully's hands were full of zircons, fake diamonds, when the sky fell above him, apprehending him in little squares. *Where is Major*

Merdone? The bomb! Tangled in the web, anger rose and revenge boiled over him.

Tia stepped on the big man's hand. She had removed and opened her shawl. Quickly, she wrapped it over Skully's eyes on top of the mesh. "Sir," Tia said, "Your greed has captured you."

The man caught in the fishnet's custody squirmed, crying out, "Merdone!"

Outside the patio heart, Merdone grimaced. *The greedy jerk loses his head when it comes to jewels. Forgets I'm in charge.* He placed his hand over his stomach.

When Merdone realized all exits were still blocked, he took stock of the situation. His original escape route, barricaded by Walking Elk, was not an alternative. Controlling himself, Merdone entered the patio, holding his gun with one hand. He clutched the basket bag and his stomach with his other. In a cool manner, he briskly walked across the center of the heart. It seemed empty of people. Distant resort lights reflected off the water giving the only light. *Where is the Scottish kid? He's all talk, too interested in the dollar and drug deals. He never wants to take orders.*

Hearing commotion nearby, Major Merdone slipped under the devil food cake table and out into the shrubs, pulling himself to his feet. His mind replayed what had happened in the linen room. The double shots had taken him off guard, coming from two directions. He had not counted on Tia having a gun. When Fence pushed her away, he was certain she was subservient. But it was her shot that hit him in the stomach. He missed. She had not.

He had purposely drawn in the racist Skully after researching his background—the perfect fall guy with no scruples, able to maneuver a network of crime and cover the dirty work. It kept Major Merdone clean-cut, if things went as planned, which they had not.

Under a table or trapped in bushes is no place for a man of dignity. Merdone fidgeted with his cigarette lighter. Nothing worked. His magic trick with flint failed. His matches were wet with blood. *If only the Scottish kid had done his job.* The major conjured another plan. The trickery Tia used to trap Skully fascinated him.

It's a shame someone so beautiful will have to die. Merdone, thirty-nine and holding for two years, felt a bit shrill. He had no plans to be true to anyone. The model young woman who intrigued him had lured him in for five years. Perhaps he harbored a secret desire for her to live. He thought not. *So cunning, her netting Skully.* He spit. *Her downfall is that she's probably Abe's sister and a Jew at that.*

Irritable, he ripped open the basket, searching for something to light the fuse. The surprise blew out of the bag like a bat, narrowly missing Merdone's head. Amos, the African Gray, more than ready for action, dive-bombed him, attempting to bite his ear.

Fence's Australian friend guarded the gate leading to the garden. No males had left in the last five minutes. Other secured valves held inside anyone who remained. Claude—commissioned to search the exterior with Ivan Burns, the Englishman—nodded confirmation to Fence.

Somewhere in the heart were dangerous, polluted men. Rapidly searching the supply room, Fence returned with a battery-operated spotlight. He emerged with it shining.

Instinctively the tall Merdone seized Tia. She turned, unexpectedly, into his arms. Thrusting her to the floor, he set his foot on the middle of her back and cuffed her hands behind her. Out of impulse, he took two shots at Amos before pointing his gun at Tia's head. "She dies now!" he said loudly.

"NO!" exclaimed Mack Carpenter, progressing toward him. "Listen to reason. Take me."

"Never. You will all die with me," Merdone declared. His stomach had quit bleeding. The fuse was lit. Ready to pull the trigger, he pressed down on Tia's mid-back.

Mack swerved Merdone's hand upward, fighting the man's gruesome strength. Two bullets left the chamber. The second raced after the first. Both caught Fence's father in the chest.

Fence, in a full run, crossed the large veranda, lunging on Merdone and Mack from the side. Tia, bound beneath, tried to catch her breath. Mack's legs gave way, toppling him on top of her.

Furious, Fence rammed his fist into the injured man's stomach, over and over again. No supreme power came to Merdone's rescue. No twinge of agony crossed Merdone's face, only a grimace of hatred. Finally, the man doubled over, eyes bulging, knocked out cold. Fence spewed out, "Too bad you must die to learn how to live. I have no sympathy for you."

The lanky lad had reared back in, eager to be involved. His lips burned. "What happened?" Edin Mansfield eyed the jewels. No one recognized him, he thought.

The Australian stood behind the young Scottish man, speaking to

Fence. "Ya knocked the bloody buckshot out of him, I say Fence." Slapping the lad's shoulder twice, the Australian added, "Right-O-Chap?"

Edin gave an "Uh-huh."

Already, Claude Walking Elk had Merdone in custody for the Jamaican authorities to extradite to the United States. Escape was out of the question. The ex-major, strapped to a gurney, had no power to move, much less speak. All the medals in the world could not free him.

Tia lifted her head off the ground, her hands still locked behind her. She called out, "Amos, where are you?"

"Crack case!" The bird's pecking exposed his whereabouts. The bomb lay in a dozen pieces, useless and unrecognizable, in the shrubbery. Amos shook his head. "Bad bird." He perched on the corner of the painting of Fence and Tia, and, of course, himself. If birds smile, the African Gray had one.

No one had eaten the devil's food. Amos had placed four bare drummie bones to form the "X" crossbones on its top. An empty walnut shell, resembling a skull, stuck out just above the little bones. Whether or not the bird knew what he was doing, he had given the deadly poison warning. "Smart bird," he squeaked, flitting to the lantern line to perch.

Reed elevated Mack Carpenter's head, the elder man embracing the middle-aged, the father embracing the son. "Mack, why?" He opened Mack's shirt.

Still on her stomach, unable to move, Tia groaned, "Fence. Please. Help me."

He loosed her from the entrapment. His mind was on his father.

Tia got to her knees and leaned over to Mack. "Don't die Mack. Please don't die. You're the only dad I ever had. I need you."

Mack managed a weak wink. He gave Tia his last smile with his Irish eyes, "Daughter, you have my son. I have peace and promise. My soul is well," he uttered. His eyes rested. The Chinese lanterns returned to duty, spreading out dull light.

"Mack, I love you," Tia whispered, leaning her head on his chest.

"Tia, he's gone," Doc Bridger said. "He gave his all and what more can anyone do? He thought the world of you."

"He was willing to die for me, for Fence, for justice."

"Uhm. Uhhmmm." Council Tuffty cleared his throat, swallowing the tobacco taste. He stood over Tia with a colleague and a nice-looking man with dark, thick hair and blue eyes. "Mrs. Carpenter, I have someone here for you to meet, someone who did a search to find you, someone who simulated his death and went undercover, someone who Mack called 'son.'"

Tia attempted to focus through the blur of tears. She and Fence looked up simultaneously. Mr. Arnold Tuffty spoke loud and clear. "Meet your brother, Abraham Maxwell Pearl."

Dead or Alive?

THE cruel question stared Fence in the eye. Was she dead or alive? He braced himself for the fretful moment, pacing. His heart, pricked to the depth of him, squeezed in and out. He arched his back, lifting his jaw. His peace rocked back and forth. Hope banged heads with hopelessness. His mind struggled to stay on course. His body said otherwise. Sweat rained out of his face, passing between his day-old whiskers. His pores wept.

He had run a long line. As if losing his father, Mack Carpenter, had not been enough. Seven and a half months of added grief and indifference stood between him and Tia. And then there was awkwardness between him and Abe who had set him up. "What really happened?" Fence asked him. Abe just gave him a big smile and said, "Someday I'll tell the whole story."

At the sight of the doctor, Fence charged forward, expecting him to hold answers.

"Hold it. You're not in charge," spoke the neatly groomed man inside the greens. His mask hung below his chin, used up and wanting removal. His shirtsleeves were rolled to the elbow in rows.

The lump in Fence's throat lodged, neither swallowed nor rejected, impairing his speech.

"Mr. Carpenter, I'm afraid I have both kinds of news, good and bad, almost too close a call to make. We nearly lost them all."

"All?" Fence's eyes saucered into space.

"Sir. Your wife will bear no more children." The weary doctor spoke with finality, shoving back the surgical cap concealing his meticulous black hair. "Sit down, please. He pulled an armchair in front of Fence, backing him to the vacant seat behind. Fence sank in discomfort, bouncing the dread of not knowing and knowing.

"This day will live long in all your lives, so mark it well." The doctor's head swung, noting the other waiting room occupants longing to know. "Life and death is not in my hands, or yours."

Preparation for the worst lay on the platter served Fence. He feared getting to the heart of the matter. Impatience crowded him. "Doc?"

The physician cut him short. "Hold your peace, sir. I'll get there. Learning to listen is a lesson long lived." A mysterious grin took over the doctor's early morning face.

"Your wife has a will to live like no one I've ever seen. Like a mountain lioness with cubs I wouldn't want to tangle with. She's full of fight."

"Spitfire you mean." Fence stuck the words in automatically. The corners of his mouth started to turn upward. "You are saying?"

"Yes, I'm saying she's one lucky cookie, or should I say one blessed mother."

"What do you mean?" Fence tugged for information.

"I mean you get a bonus with her, more than you bargained for." Doctor Tello held back the laugh ready to explode.

Fence's ire was getting infected with the joy imparted by the doctor's strangeness. "What's this all about? Why are you laughing?"

"Apart from the fact that Mrs. Carpenter has her tubes tied and appendix out in the exploratory surgery, she gave you a double present."

"What are you trying to tell me?" Fence struggled to get the picture.

"Yes sir. Twins. Healthy little fighters. Mr. Carpenter, you are the proud father of a newborn son and daughter."

Fence gulped. "And my wife?"

"She'll live to tell about it to your grandkids." Doctor Tello shoved his chair out by the arms, looking taller than his five feet, nine inches, relieved that the emergency C-section was completed successfully. The cut, alongside the prior eight-inch vertical exploratory incision, had seemed endless. He stitched the straight seam, next to the crooked scar of the woman's past. Tia, under anesthesia, stayed motionless, unaware that a burden had been lifted from her.

The intelligent doctor glanced at Fence's mother and the younger stranger, before returning his eyes to a rising Fence, "Mr. Carpenter, we need a day or two to make certain she's totally out of the woods. Do not jeopardize her life again. Guard her body with your life, no matter how strong she acts. This is the end of her childbearing. Do I make myself clear?" Doctor Tello waited for his admonition to sink into the woman's husband. "One more thing. Your wife is one remarkable woman. Give her lots of love." His lifegiving hand stretched out to Fence. "Congratulations Mr. Carpenter. You can go in now."

Fence swallowed. "Thanks, Doc. Call me Fence." The doctor acknowledged him with a smile and vanished to remove his scrubs.

"Tia?" Fence entered the sterile recovery room. "Hey courageous one, your bodyguard has come to visit." His finger nudged her cheek.

"Fence?" She whispered, awakening out of the deep sleep. "I'm still here," her hoarse voice uttered. Fence watched the large tear sneak out of her eye duct.

"They collect those in heaven you know," he said.

"I know."

"Should I get a bottle?' he asked.

A sacred smile swept across Tia's face. "Not for me," she said. "Don't make me laugh. It hurts."

He rubbed the top of her hand with his finger. "Thought you might need a friend."

Her eyes were on his. "You probably think I need a lot more than that."

"A bodyguard?" He winked at her, cupping her shoulder in the palm of his hand. "Hey, you did great. Why didn't you tell me you had two?"

"I haven't told you a lot of things." She looked the other way. Clearing her throat, she spoke. "Fence, will you forgive me?"

"For what?" he asked.

"For not trusting you, for not telling you the truth, for…" She hesitated, pushing pride down. "For hating you, for hurting you on purpose."

"Guess I didn't want to admit I was hurt. All that tough guy stuff keeps a man from being real." He let go of her. Turning anger in had wrapped them both in pain. "Yeah, I've been a bit bitter. I've been pretty rotten to you too." He stepped to the other side of the bed. "I forgive better when I look you in the eye."

"Why? To see if I'm truly sorry?"

"No. To see if you forgive me," he said.

"Fence, I need you. I mean I need a husband." Her lids slid down over her exhausted eyes.

Fence's lips glazed hers. The RN pulled him away. "Let her rest."

Why didn't Tia confide in me? Why didn't she tell me about carrying twins? Does she want me or a does she just need a husband? The desperate seriousness of what had just taken place tangled with renewed thoughts of fatherhood. Taking stock of the past hour, Fence sought out Rose.

Rose ran her little girl fingers through her grandmother's dark hair, putting her cheek against Marie's. Her daddy's voice sent her running to him to catch his words. "Love you Dad-dee."

"Rose. Rose! We have a baby! We have two babies!" The little girl squealed in delight. He careened her in circles. "Your mama is wonderful!"

"Daddy, can I see? Please?" Fence carried her to the nursery and pointed to the miniature Carpenter slips, blue and pink.

Marie Deer Path stood looking through the glass at the incubators. "Shush! You two will wake whole mountainside."

Fence grinned. "Do you hear the sound? It's like Papa Mack, bugling from the mountain top."

"Yes. I hear his whistle. It is good." Marie walked softly away with an inner glow, the kind that grandparents have a tendency to have. Wearing a humble look of love, both new and old, the visionary woman saw beyond her pain to a fuller horizon.

Reed stood outside, holding his heart in joy, his nearly eighty years fulfilled. He felt young again. Somehow he liked the idea of being a great grandfather. "They all have the Carpenter brand," he said, remembering his son. Doc Bridger nodded his head.

The florist handed Fence the interesting arrangement of baby breath, the peace rose and an olive branch set in the middle of an ivy plant. One word rested under it *"Peace."* Pinheads of misty rain fell on him. He hurried down the street and up to her hospital room. He laid the gift on the bed stand beside his sleeping wife.

Fence raised the wool Indian blanket over her. Slowly, he placed a hand of hope on hers and raised it to his lips. The presentation was not elaborate. Fence slipped the ring, full of diamonds, back onto Tia's right hand. Without a word, he said a million words. He swallowed hard.

Trying to slip out unnoticed, he heard her whisper, "Fence? Will you stay?"

Fence stopped in the doorway and turned. "Sure, it would be my honor. Doubt if you could drive me away." He pinched her toe. "So, you need me?" Tia's eyes blinked a confirmation.

"I need to tell you something," she said. She wanted him to come closer, but he held her ankle. "Fence Carpenter. I love you." It burst out of her mouth.

A grin spun Fence's face up, not ready to take her seriously. "Hey, you must be better."

Her arm was in the air with the I.V. dangling from it. Her fingers beckoned him. He responded, watching her eyes. "Fence, please. Listen to me." She said it again with emphasis, talking to his heart, releasing herself of pain with the confession. "I love you."

He pushed the hair off her forehead. "I know, courageous one. You doubly love me. You are one amazing woman." His arm slid under her neck, pulling her face in front of his. "I love you too." No words could say more.

The Afterglow

THE treasure arrived just in time for the twins first birthday. *How you live reflects what you treasure.* Sister Maria Thomas's words came to life.

What would Tia do with gold crowns, with silver coins, with a fortune of riches, with treasures of immeasurable worth, with the crowns of kings, while orphans lay two and three deep with no milk, no love, no hope, no peace? It would be like she never had it in the first place. The wind would only catch it and who knows which direction that would come from? Could it give a day longer of life? Perhaps for some. Could it give her health or peace or love? Two orphans, Tia and Abe, could not keep what could help someone, someone who may be like them.

Marie Deer Path Carpenter stood at the entry door welcoming all the special guests—Abraham Maxwell Pearl, Claude and Tamsen Walking Elk with their one-and-a-half-year-old son, Whistle—Doctor Clem Bridger—and of course, Attorney Arnold Tuffty who toted a special delivery letter.

Marie placed the twin marble cakes with white whipped frosting on the dining room oak table. A large candle towered above the names of the honored children on each of the layered creations. The highchairs, scooted close, were yet unoccupied. Rose sat joyfully on Uncle Abe's knee, her arm around his neck, watching Gam Marie.

Abe marveled at how his friend's mother, Marie Deer Path, embraced the new. Her year of tribute to Mack had passed with purposeful remembrance to the man she would always love. "It is the Indian way," Marie said. The white eagle feather headdress the Shoshone chief had given her in honor of her husband, hung nobly in the arch above the bow window. Abe squeezed his sister's child, Rose, the dual connection with Fence and Tia. The family had taken him in as if he had always belonged.

Abby Reed squirmed in Fence's arms, crushing the paper in her hands. Tia held Mackabee Clay while he ripped the ballooned wrapping paper off the gift from the orphanage. The presents had stiff, tough pages. *First Birthday Book for A Boy* nestled next to the *First Birthday Book for A Girl*. The universal language of love engulfed them all.

"Fence, the letter?" Tia asked, "Please, will you read it?"

Dear Ones,

The faces of the children lit up like candles when they received your most generous gifts. Your heart of love will not go unnoticed by your heavenly Father. Our most gracious appreciation for your generosity.

Yours Truly,
Sister Maria L. Thomas

Rising up, Claude Walking Elk stood below the white eagle feather headdress. He lifted Fence's flute with the cedar bird on the end from the horseshoe holder. He brought the instrument to his lips, playing the sound of love.

Fence placed his hand on top of Tia's. Once again he leaned into the future, but this time with unencumbered vision, with clear eyesight. The excuse of bodyguard no longer holstered his chest.

Tia and Fence had something in common, not just children or space or parenthood. More than a child connected them. Tia, free to dance like the eagle, had found her place. Not just in the physical or emotional, but in the Spirit where peace soars in freedom and a song is created.

And Rose, sitting on her Uncle Abe's lap, did her most special thing. She sang her favorite song, *Peace.*

Tia's eyes filled—with another treasure. Fence lifted his napkin to catch the tear rolling down her cheek. Her eyes closed, envisioning vase-like bottles being filled with teardrops. The strong and kind hand moved with gentle strength, catching the ageless tears. None were wasted. The hand, wearing a size fourteen elk tooth ring, looked a lot like Mack Carpenter's. Tia tilted her head back in the warmth. She was finally home.